The Light of the Rising Sun

Frank McEwen

The Light of the Rising Sun

BY

FRANK METHVEN

DORRANCE PUBLISHING CO., INC.
PITTSBURGH, PENNSYLVANIA 15222

ISBN: 978-0-8059-7743-1
Library of Congress Control Number: 2008922236

Printed in the United States of America

First Printing

For more information or to order additional books, please contact:
Dorrance Publishing Co., Inc.
701 Smithfield Street
Third Floor
Pittsburgh, Pennsylvania 15222
U.S.A.
1-800-788-7654
www.dorrancebookstore.com

To the memory of
Jeannie,
with my love

Author's Note

Back in the mid-1930's, during the greatest depression in the history of our country, my cousin, Wallace Lee, and I, in our mid-teens, took a trip on one of the stern-wheel Ohio River coal boats belonging to our great uncle, James Tobias Hatfield of Kentucky. The stern-wheeler was the Henry C. Yeiser. We were en-route up the Ohio River to the Kanawha River and the Hatfield coal mines in Reed, West Virginia. The crew told many stories that summer. I have never forgotten the story told by one of the crew members concerning a stern-wheeler on which he had worked.

—F. M.

Other books by Frank Methven:

A Call To Arms

The Sound Of Hills

"Through the night of starlit skies, From which love's miracle doth come, The glory of the true heart shines, In the light of the rising sun."

—F.M.

Chapter One

Dawn broke slowly on the river that morning as copilot Brant Mitchell rose to go on watch, and saw the mist rising pearl-like from the water. The dawn was as pale as the sun on a wintry sky. The last of the stars had disappeared. On the shadowy shore images began to shape. The winter hills had thawed and softened, and were now green with spring crop. A cleft in the hills revealed the sun peeping through. Then, as he dressed, he watched the sun come over the eastern hills, reflecting a soft, red-gold over the mist of the Ohio River, ever-changing, always beautiful. Sunlight danced on the bubbles of the boat's wake. The valley was brilliant, with billows of clouds rimming the sun. It was a warm morning that would soon be hot. On deck, he inhaled a big lungful of the morning air and stretched as he watched a piece of driftwood float by with a bird on it taking a free ride. Far off, there was the cry of an eagle. The distant hills were crowned by the golden sunrise in the summer calm of a dozing river. The banks had been undercut by the floods and the trees undermined. The trees mirrored their own shapes in the shadows. Brant listened to the familiar rhythmic splash of the water behind the paddle wheel as it churned the soft, amber current. Smoke streamed from the twin stacks like floating clouds. Occasionally, sparks flew upward and vanished. The engines, throbbing like a mechanical heart, caused his mind to throb with the fear that his father, the captain, was becoming aware of his son's attraction to the young chambermaid on board the boat. It could end his career. Ashore, the migratory swallows were restless to nest. In the distance he heard the cry of water birds. The river caught the first flash of morning sun. Summer seemed to *have come overnight. In the distance the honking of wild geese.*

Around a bend the river widened into a large bite of tan water and, as Brant stepped out on deck, he watched a string of ducks that were winging down the river. They were flying with the wind, which lessened their effort. He heard the distant whir of their flashing wings in the sun, and heard the scream of a hawk circling, and saw the shadow of its wings on the water. The sounds came clearly across the coffee-colored river. He glanced at the opalescent sky for signs of weather. It predicted a clear day. Dark billows of smoke poured from the tall twin stacks as the paddle wheel responded and the sternwheeler struggled against the current. A heavy thrumming vibration telegraphed throughout the entire boat. Was it a warning? The sun was shimmering over the water as the Storm Bird moved on. The far bank was dense with growth, the distant fields were golden with grain.

Brant turned his head. If he stared too long into the glare on the water it made his head swim. It was a golden morning and the river hills climbed right up from the amber water. The river was lower in the summer; more of the bank was showing. "I need a cup of coffee," he muttered. From the galley he heard the cook's little radio playing, "When The Moon Comes Over the Mountain." Kate Smith was singing. Flies buzzed at the screen door to get to the aroma of food. The humid heat was stifling.

It was Sunday. From habit Sunday was a special day for Cole Hamilton, even as cabin-maid on the boat. Sunday had always been precious to her. It was a day of going into town, to church, visiting, and doing things with other families—getting off the farm. A soft, warm wind was ruffling her lovely hair.

The sun and a light breeze had driven the mist from the river, and as Cole walked along the deck toward the galley her dark hair was lighted by the gold of the sun. Brant was eagerly moving toward her. She watched him striding with fresh, eager enthusiasm—a magnetic core that made him attractive to everyone. A glow came onto her face. Her joy was as warm as the day. She marveled that one so young could be so composed, seemingly so unafraid of the wrath of his father. She wished that she could be that self-confident about the outcome of his attention. To her, he was a superior person, so irresistible. Her heart ached because he was so handsome, so sought-after, so fun-loving, so devil-may-care, so far above her.

Cole's spirits had lifted at the sight of Brant, her face brightening like the sun. Her movements toward him were light and quick. She saw him walking jauntily down the deck and stopped, waiting for him. He was a young man in love with the world. The sun created his shadow on the bulkhead. Brant Mitchell. She loved the ringing sound of his name. Just the sight of him striding down the deck gave her a feeling she had never experienced before. People were drawn to him, Oh, how she would love to take pictures of him in the wheelhouse navigating the boat, but it would be too obvious to all.

Cole wore plain dresses, not form-fitting. They were feminine, and her long legs and youthful body made her appealing in the simplest of attire. Occasionally, she wore a skirt and blouse. Brant walked into her gentle, childlike smile—a beautiful smile intimate with joy and hope. Each time he looked into her soft eyes her stomach flipped. He had the gift to captivate and her heart was pounding.

His face reddened, knowing that his father was watching from the pilothouse. He nodded, gave a one-sided twist to his mouth and walked on, avoiding her eyes. He was gone before he could be touched by her warmth. He just removed himself, bright and cheerful, away from her. The brightness left her face. She was not aware the captain had been watching. A blackbird flew over, its shaggy wing tips ruffled by the wind. An omen? There *were things yet to learn along this river of work, adventure, and achievement.*

Cole watched Brant go, speechless. He had not spoken, and she was too bashful to be forward. He merely nodded. That hurt most of all. She flushed at the slight. The coldness in his attitude made her hopes sink. The other night, in the shadow of the lifeboat, he had kissed her, but now she feared that the jaunty walk and carefree whistling covered a deeper trouble. It caused a shadow to cross her mind. Each time he had talks with his father, the captain, she became alarmed, thinking the captain had sensed her hopes and dreams, yet she knew that Brant must have these work-a-day talks with his father. Her mouth hovered between trembling and weeping. She was too hurt to speak.

Cole turned as if she had been stung, tears started to her eyes. *He could have at least said, "Good morning," or "See you later," or something,* she thought. And she could not go to him. *Am I being childish?* she wondered. What was the meaning of it? Her eyes went dark as she stared after him in wild dismay. *Is he unaware of my tenderness and hurt?* she wondered. The cold hand of dread had touched a warm heart of hoping, and her small hand gripped the deck rail as a little child would cling to the hand of its parent. She was afraid, yet was not certain of what she feared. She bent her head and tears ran slowly down her cheeks. Her fears bordered on the neurotic, having come from deep within. She subconsciously compared this to her childhood days of heartache and loss. Getting a job aboard the *Storm Bird* had opened up a whole new world for her.

Cole doubted herself primarily. Her lack of self-confidence was the deepest mistrust she had of herself. It had developed through a lifetime of tragedy and want. She was afraid he would lose interest in her. That, as a mere cabin-maid, she did not have what he wanted. That his family had much higher hopes for him. She felt deficient, the painful helplessness of uncertainty. Then she straightened, wiped her eyes quickly, and moved on toward the galley where she heard the cook, Bess, bantering with the off-duty crew. She needed Bess. She needed a strong person. Through the galley doorway Bess had seen the brief encounter. Bess referred to the galley as "my kitchen."

One of the deckhands walked past Cole and she gave him a tremulous, "Good morning." He nodded, almost smiling, watching her closely, his narrowed eyes steeled against the glare of the sun on water. He had known and observed the captain's son since he was a boy, and there was a strange intensity on his face. Cole felt comfortable in the presence of this tall, quiet Scot who went by the name of Chain.

The men worked a schedule of eight hours on-duty and eight hours off, and at the end of each eight-hour shift they came to the galley for a meal. In addition to regular meal hours, coffee and pastries were available at all times. The coffee was strong enough to tattoo their tongue and hot as blue-blazes.

"I'm always cooking or cleaning up," Bess argued, pointing a wooden ladle at a deckhand. She was flushed and bustling as usual. There was so much food the men were careless of it. On their time off the crew had an amazing capacity for doing nothing but eating, Bess' kitchen was their inspiration.

They had just departed their southern-most port of call at Shawneetown, Illinois, and were steaming up river toward Rising Sun, Indiana. Cole came into the kitchen, blinking. It took a moment for eyes, which were blinded by the sun on water, to accustom to the duller light of the boat's kitchen. It was an excuse for her tears, but Bess looked at her with a discerning glance. Cole bumped into the deckhand, Chain, as she entered and softly said, "Excuse me." The warmth of his smile helped to lift her spirits. His smile at Bess was even warmer.

The stove-warmed kitchen made the windows steam and it was like having curtains on them. The crew could not see in or out at times. The galley had the fascinating scent of a variety of herbs and spices and their results in the pot. Bess believed that a good-smelling kitchen is a happy kitchen. She enjoyed being busy.

Bess Thatcher liked especially to make fine sauces, flavorful gravies, and gourmet soups, and the dining salon, as she called it with dramatics, was an odor of magnetism for the crew. The Storm bird had a reputation for good food and a respected skipper, and this drew a good crew.

There was a decided aimlessness about a few of the crew members on some of the less-demanding riverboats, like a seed planted and nourished by a bird. They had served on a number of "rust buckets" around the country and, to them, their boat was the only home they had. They came from parts of the country other than the Ohio Valley. There were those who would not live permanently in a town as long as they could continue moving. They had lived most of their lives along river frontiers of hard work and hard play. Some did not care on what boat they worked, what river they sailed, or whether they made job progress. Theirs was a hunger for different places, different faces; their lives as restless as the waves upon the river shore, always searching for the golden hills beyond the rainbow. There was about their lives a temporary feeling, a search for adventure. They had an itch to be moving. And it was also said that a few of the riverboat crews were made up of bits and pieces left over, the wanderers of a nation's navigation system, their lives as bent and dog-legged as the rivers upon which they sailed. Brant had heard a snobbish academic refer to them as the "sub-set," and it angered him. The captain and Brant respected their crew. They faced danger and sometimes death in delivering their cargo. Only by working together could they make the voyage safe as well as successful, their good qualities far outweighing a few lesser traits.

Cole seldom entered into conversation with the crew unless it concerned her work and the boat. She was too new to the boat for familiarity, and too shy and retiring by nature.

"I'm just not accustomed to their joking," she confessed to Bess, admitting that she was only uneasy in the presence of one of the deckhands. She lived within her own world, and had not taken on the free and easy way of the crew. She had not become a part of the coteries and alliances, and not adroit at maneuvering among them. She had the feeling of being alone among many. Captain Mitchell had given strict orders about the men fraternizing with the women. Filthy language was forbidden. The captain's orders were law and they accepted it.

"The first one to disobey those orders will be put ashore!" he had said. The crew was respectful and friendly toward Cole, even protective. Except one: deVoss. He's got hot blood, *Captain Mitchell thought,* and he better cool off before he gets into deep water.

Cole only felt uneasy around the deckhand Durand deVoss. Though without experience, instinct warned her to be careful. As she served the table she glanced at his cadaverous face and thin, wispy hair. He was a stoop-shouldered man and his mouth drooped at the corners. He stared back at her with eyes that spoke, but he did not speak to her. A change in tone had come over the boat with the arrival of Cole. She was new there, a stranger causing a momentary separation. Yet, it had not become an uncomfortable situation. Bess knew from experience that the attitude would soon change, that at the moment Cole was too unworldly, too unknowing for their realism, seemingly a child.

Cole glanced at deVoss and found him watching her. She sensed that he was always watching her and the unspoken desire was obvious. She wished that Captain Mitchell and his son were there, but as officers they did not eat with the crew.

Cole noticed that Bess was flushed with working at the scarred wooden mess table that was always clean and polished; her constant scrubbing kept the kitchen walls whiter than old bones. She was making corn bread as she policed the behavior of the crew. They liked Bess and treated her with respect. *Thank goodness for Bess,* Cole thought. She had never been on her own before and needed reassurance. Bess, sleeves rolled up, was busy at the breadboard.

Cole unfolded the tablecloth and spread it, smoothed it, and prepared to set the huge table for the rest of the crew coming off watch. She could have used oilcloth, as most boats did, but she liked a cloth table covering, though it added to her heavy wash load. Bess insisted upon a well-ordered kitchen.

"I like corn bread because it's gritty and the coarse texture has more flavor and sucks up more butter and honey," Bess told Cole, fanning herself with the fancy apron she wore and watching deVoss out of the corner of her eye. Her decorative apron was a rare gift to herself.

Bess was filled with honest indignation and laughter, but had the ability of self-preservation among a crew of typical men. She enjoyed their better traits and, unlike Cole, could handle the other. She realized that Cole was too young and naive to cope with them.

"Time to hang on the feed bag!" Bess said, looking at the waiting crew. "The best sauce for a meal is hunger," and she laughed heartily, her laugh warm and sincere. The crew enjoyed her humor.

Glemp pointed to Shark saying, "Better get food on the table fast or he'll eat the tablecloth! He's hungry as a bear." His humor was entertaining. Hearty laughter was a daily part of their diet. Except for deVoss, Bess had a genuine liking and respect for the crew.

Spoon in air, deVoss decided to risk reciting his favorite poem. "Beans, beans, the musical fruit, the more you eat the more you toot, so eat beans every meal!" he shouted.

Bess waved a huge ladle in front of his slanting forehead with the warning, "Mind your manners, deVoss, or I'll bean you!" The crew howled with delight. None of the crew argued with Bess, well knowing the wise old saying, "Don't bite the hand that feeds you."

"You'd better shut your mug and start chewing your cud, deVoss," Glemp shouted with his mouth full, a wide grin on his stuffed face.

Cole started serving the hunched backs eating along the table. Some of them ate with their elbows on the table, making noises and long arm stretches as if it were a lesson in survival. The coffee was so strong a spoon could stand up in it.

Bess nodded gravely at Cole and pointed a thumb at deVoss. "He should eat with a shovel," she said. "And he's got the nerve to complain about constipation." Bess had a stern voice, but a soft heart and the crew knew it. They shouted their approval and agreement, everyone laughing and talking at once.

"You got that right!" Glemp agreed, pointing. "Look at him! He tears into that grub like a starving dog."

"Who wants this job of mine? With this?" And she pointed at the engineer. "They can have it, depression or no depression." She was speaking to Cole, but for the benefit of the men. She watched Cole with affectionate pride, for in a few short weeks Cole had become like a daughter. She warmed inwardly, and stirred the pot on the stove with a work-roughened hand, watching the girl under her eyelashes, well aware that she needed protection. The heat had sapped Cole's energy. There was a glint of mischief in Bess' eyes.

"Just in time!" Bess exclaimed. "Here come the rest of them. Time to slop the hogs!" She enjoyed her crude joke, and so did the crew, but Cole was afraid to smile. She was afraid of several things. Mostly of trouble between Durand deVoss and Brant Mitchell. If trouble developed between them, and she was the cause of it, she felt certain deVoss would use it as an excuse to go to the captain with an exaggerated story of a relationship with his son. DeVoss had furtively made enough advances toward her to cause her to believe that he would trump up proof if he had to, using this to get at her.

Bess referred to breakfast as "Morning Prayer," and supper as "The Evening Service." A half-dozen men crowded into the room and sat at the table, hungry for food. They gorged themselves as though they had not eaten for a week, or that it was their last meal. Delicate manners were of scant importance.

"Off with the hat!" Bess demanded of the engineer. From morning till night he wore an old engineer's cap that looked like a rag. She had to fight him to get him to take it off at the table and then fight to get him away from the table.

Cole placed before them a fresh-baked ham in a ring of apples, careful to avoid any physical contact with deVoss. She moved a bowl of sweet butter to make room for the ham.

"Keep that Shark away from them taters!" Glemp shouted, reaching for the ham. "He eats like it's his last meal on earth!" Shark grinned, elbowing Glemp. A huge mouthful of bacon, eggs, and toast prevented him from answering. He ate like a winter-hungry bear at his first spring meal. His well-earned nickname among the crew was Pot Roast. deVoss stared at them in contempt. He had no sense of humor and did not have a friend in the world that they knew of, yet he strutted around as if he owned the boat. The men served themselves and started eating ravenously. Silence at a river-boat kitchen table was out of the question. It was a noisy table with jibes and occasional swear words. Bess insisted on a minimum of swearing in the kitchen, no filth. The crew tried to control their language in the presence of Cole and Bess, but sometimes failed. Bess did not like it for herself, and especially not for Cole, whom she observed was shy among boisterous men. She knew little of Cole's childhood, and wondered what could have developed in her such a need of affection.

Cole was remembering the little prayer her mother always said before a meal.

"Up and down this whole dad-blamed river there ain't no better grub than what Bess puts on the table," Glemp said to young Hank. "We're eatin' high on the hog, boy. Chow down!" he shouted, smacking his lips. He had eaten enough to explode.

Cole shook her head in wonder at the almost daily routine of which the men never tired. She felt more comfortable in the presence of Captain Mitchell. deVoss always finished eating first, wolfing his food, then sat staring at the others, licking his chops as he used a broom straw for a toothpick. All he spoke of and praised was the French quarter of New Orleans, that he missed the subtle and delicate balance of French food—a barb at Bess. He said, "New Orleans is the only civilized town in the United States," and bragged of the riverboats on which he had served as an officer, that he had seen the famous Mississippi Caves and they had not, and of the aristocratic women he had escorted. He was the typical flamboyant riverboat gambler, bragging that he was a regular attendant at the world-renowned Théatre d' Orléans. He often used the French word "insouciance." Nobody asked him what it meant. He made it a point not to mention the number of towns in which he had hit the bars, card-rooms and brothels. It was said by the ladies of the establishments that his attempt at this fandango was hilarious. For him there were no freebies. Bess described him as having had a constant change of menu. Cole shuddered, looking the other way as Bess continued to watch him closely with narrowed eyes, knowing that he liked to put on false airs along with his pretended degree in navigation. His crude bragging of his conquests during The Roaring Twenties angered her. "For generations my family has lived in Vieux Carré, the most aristocratic section of New Orleans," he bragged in his effusive spray of words, his lip curled in contempt. He referred to his associates as the "crème de la crème" of New Orleans. "Back home, I was famous for my breeding of top-quality hunting dogs, and hunted with aristocrats," he boasted. He considered himself a person of importance, and thought this crew to be incapable of cultivated thought—merely a dry-mouthed, hungry gang after a demanding shift.

Turning to Glemp, deVoss bragged, "The first European to explore this Ohio River valley was Robert Cavalier, sieur de La Salle back in 1669. That was a century before the Marquis de Lafayette."

"How would you know?" Glemp challenged. "You weren't there."

"It's history," deVoss retorted. "Proven. It's in the encyclopedia. And the first permanent settlement on this Ohio River was a few years after the Revolutionary War."

"Them highfalutin' airs you put on, deVoss, are phony as a three-dollar bill," Glemp snorted, his cheek bulging with food. "La Fayette helped us win the war thank God, but you're a long shot from him. As different as night is from day. I think you're a descendant of the old Mississippi River pirates, or them bayou smugglers down that away. You like to think you're at home down in New Orleans, but you're nothin' but a fish out of water."

"He thinks that thick head of his knows everything," Shark agreed, "and struts around like he's cock of the walk, big time!"

Bess frowned at deVoss as he devoured Cole with his green, fishlike eyes. He had been watching her movements closely as she served the men at the table, and he started to reach for her. The galley was small, and he could smell her fresh, sweet scent as she passed. He quickly withdrew his hand. It made him breathe more rapidly. He stared at her surreptitiously, following her every movement with a thirsting look. His stomach felt tight watching her. Looking at her movements made him sweat under the armpits. He considered her an extremely alluring interlude and a cold smile of planning came over his face. Each conquest called for another.

Cole, sensing his desire; turned and saw him watching her, saw him draw back his hand. His eyes moved slowly, hooded like a turtle. She turned away and sat down, nervously tucking her skirt in around her knees, shivering. Though not expensively dressed, she had a natural quality of poise and grace. deVoss rolled his eyes toward the sky, kissed the tips of his fingers, and leered at her suggestively, saying nothing, but bringing embarrassed laughter from one of the men. His open lips showed long upper-front teeth. He would have given a week's wages for a smile from her, and had set his plans to get more than a smile; a coup de gráce. He loved the French term.

What happened as Cole finished serving the meal irritated Bess. It more than irritated her, it infuriated her.

Cole remained conscious of deVoss watching her and had seen the movement of his hand toward her body. Knowing that he wanted more than to touch her, she opened the door to the deck and stood there, waiting. Her blood was pulsing with fear. DeVoss stood, looking at her for a long time with his eyes half-closed, thinking, planning. He wanted to touch her hair, put his cheek against her skin, to feel his breath on her neck. Wanting her had become an obsession, heightened by her fear of him. It excited him. She was beautiful, even in work clothes.

Sitting next to deVoss, Glemp nudged him and whispered, "You'd better forget about her, deVoss. You're a day late and a dollar short," and he wiped his mouth with the back of his hand.

Cole was afraid of deVoss, sensing that he was dangerous. One time he had slipped a note under her cabin door telling her to keep her door unlocked that night, that it would be well worth her while. She had been terrified. That night, when she heard the handle turn on her locked door, she thought she was going to have a heart attack. Afraid to tell Brant, she had told Bess. Bess was determined to go to the captain at the first opportunity. "That man's deadly as a snake," Bess said. Cole busied herself removing dishes from the table.

The fact that he terrified Cole meant nothing to deVoss. He had enjoyed hurting other women. Because of his past history he was constantly on the move.

As the crew filed out of the kitchen Cole said to Bess, "I have to go to my cabin for something." The only time she was not uneasy was when deVoss was off the boat.

"I understand," the cook answered, tightening her lips, planning to have an understanding with deVoss. *There's nothing that will ever bring that man into the fold,* she was thinking.

As she left the kitchen, Cole glanced at deVoss with loathing. She could not control this feeling, and it showed. He was the only person she had ever met that she dreaded and feared. His intent was so obvious it terrified her. She was certain that he would try to harm her. She said nothing in answer to his suggestive nod. He reminded her of an insect as he looked at her and the fantasy crawled into his mind. His eyes never left her beautiful figure.

DeVoss was aware of the resentment and disgust she had for him. More than resentment and disgust, he sensed the fear that women had for him, a neurosis that would always be a part of his saturnine character. He had never seen a woman he had craved whose face did not have the look of nausea and rejection in it. And when he could not have them he hated them and wanted to destroy them. He was a man sick with loneliness. It was an eating away from within. He would always be a loner. He was a cold man, craving warmth. His was a combination of deep inner weaknesses: the fear that he would never be the man he wanted to be, along with a hatred for those who were what he sought to be. Much of the dislike of deVoss was due to his cutting tongue and lack of humor.

Each time deVoss passed a group of women and heard their laughter, he imagined he was the butt of their humor. He fancied that they were laughing at his clothes, that he was not as tall as they desired, that his shoulders were too narrow, his chest too thin, his behind too big, his nose too long and pointed, that he was too skinny with bandy legs, or a hundred other imaginings that caused this humiliation. It ate away at him like waves on the muddy shore. He had become ingrown with bitterness and hate, and this hatred and vengeance were nourished by his shame. As a result he was a man imprisoned in his own contempt and, in a choleric reaction, he fantasized their scathing remarks.

"He isn't the type of man to attract any woman!" or "How would you like to be married to that?"

An intense man, he would howl with hurt and fury inside himself at their imagined rebuffs, and vow to get even with them as he walked cringing under their supposed scorning ridicule. He would have rather been considered a thief or a murderer than this. It was a punishment that ate at his innards like rust. It was destroying him, and had poisoned his life and thinking. Something had died within him. He had spent a lifetime forgotten. The only woman who had given him a few moments of happiness, affection, and release was a lady of the streets, and his shipmates guffawed that he had to have the cash to buy what he wanted. For him there had been no freebies.

DeVoss believed that unless you had money and women there was no purpose in life. He was a man who worshiped money and adoration. It was his God, and he had more than he needed due to his cleverness at cards. He believed that money was the only friend he had. He was a man who knew the price of everything and the value of nothing. He spent a large portion of his money on dress clothes, hoping it would make an impression and give him class. His clothes were expensive; he loved the feeling of fine cloth. He would have liked to have been considered the Beau Brummel of the river. He would never admit it, but once he had taken a correspondence course to improve his grammar. He had a twisted pride in his assumed superiority; arrogance and conceit were his stock in trade.

DeVoss held back, loitering in the kitchen. He whistled softly as Cole left the room, his eyes following her. She went directly to her cabin to hole up like a sick animal, and it was a long time before she came out. Bess and deVoss looked at each other warily. Even with the doors and windows open the galley was stifling.

He puffed on his slender Cuban cigar in silence, thinking, then turned to Bess. "She doesn't look at the Captain's son that way and you know it." He attempted to smile. It brought to Bess' mind a warning from her mother: "Whenever a man smiles at you when you know he hates you, be very careful."

DeVoss was making a direct point of letting Bess know that he was well-aware of what was going on, under what he considered Bess' sanction. *Women spend all their time feeling sorry for themselves,* he was thinking. He brushed a hand over large elfin ears that long sideburns did not cover, and sat hunkered down in his chair. His constant slurs were stirring her emotions. "I've traveled these rivers from New Orleans to Pittsburgh on the finest palace boats afloat," he bragged, attempting to impress Bess, giving his hollow laugh.

"No smoking in the galley, deVoss. You know that!" was her curt reply as she wiped her brow with a towel.

"Says who?" deVoss snorted. "That's a sorry rule. A bunch of hogwash." His voice was cold. The fact that he was unpopular with the crew did not phase him. His self-centered craving to control was, ironically, causing self destruction. He believed he did not have to worry about these lower-level people, and his blasé attitude infuriated her.

Bess clenched her teeth. "The only thing I'm sorry about is having you on this boat," she answered, eyeing him closely. She was never hesitant in speaking her mind. Bess had become an expert in reading the hidden inclinations of a man. She was studying him as he stared down at his plate as if examining the design. *If it's possible for the evil inside a person to affect their outward appearance this can be said of Durand deVoss,* she was thinking. She had a gut feeling that this man was capable of murder.

DeVoss looked up slowly, sharp eyes darting out of a hard-angled face, then lowered his eyes. Never in all his life had a woman looked at him the way he had seen Cole look at Brant the night he spied on them on deck. No woman had ever loved him, not even his wife. She had married him when she became pregnant with a child that was not his. She had left him to protect the child, and had reported him as a psychotic beast. It had been years since he had heard of his wife and his daughter. He wanted to believe it was his daughter.

Bess continued to glare at him. "Better mind your manners," she said sharply, continuing to stare at him suspiciously, her eyes glittering in anger. It was a warning. She detested his repugnant attitude, and was barely able to control her temper.

DeVoss looked ready to spit. A dark look crept over his tightly drawn face, and he narrowed his eyes until the lashes almost touched. He knew that Bess was aware of his intentions toward Cole and his hands moved nervously, rubbing his eagle-beak as he spoke, his eyes shifting, his thoughts obvious.

"It could work yet between me and Cole if you would help by staying out of the way," he pointed out. He spoke hurriedly, feeling very clever. "I have my ways of making it work." His laugh was an unpleasant sound because it was mirthless. His voice had a strange quality—heavy and wheezy like a distant boat whistle—and his eyelid, the one that drooped, quivered into a nervous wink that Bess hated. To her, he had the ways of a cunning animal, and was drawn to women like bees to a flower. She was measuring him with keen eyes that were slit with annoyance, knowing that he was a man that would have to be dealt with. He was getting under her skin and her back stiffened at his remark.

"She's an orphan who the captain put under my care and I intend to watch out over her," Bess stated emphatically. At a tender age Cole had become forced to leave the small farm home where simplicity, love, and joy had predominated. "I don't like to go to the captain unless I have to," she continued, "but if you force me to I will." There was a pronounced sting in her voice.

He was taken by surprise and looked startled. "You know better than to do that," he muttered slowly, his lip curled. His eyes were ugly and always shifting. Bess shook her head.

"She's an especially fine girl," Bess responded, turning away from his expression. "Why don't you go after a woman in town and leave the child alone." Her tone of voice had hardened.

DeVoss did not answer, but he crossed and re-crossed his legs restlessly as he sat, his face wooden, slumped in his chair.

"DeVoss spends money lavishly on himself and his women," the engineer had told Bess. "The ones he buys, that is, but he won't send money home to help support his aged parents. He's so tight he won't give you yesterday's newspaper."

"You may think you have your ways, Durand," Bess continued, "but you'd better not let the old man learn of your plans for Cole. I saw where you put your hand on her, and..." she let it hang.

DeVoss listened with cold indifference, grunted, and continued to watch the doorway through which Cole had left, as if he could still see her and feel her—hoping she would return, knowing she would not. He remembered her the night on deck when Brant took her into his arms. Her beauty caused an old, aching desire within him. The perspiration on his face gleamed, his lips moved, his mind thinking much. His thoughts and plans were more obvious than words.

"You touch that girl and you're looking at doom's day!" Bess stated coldly. The hard words were clipped, her teeth clenched.

DeVoss' face tightened. "Try to stop me," he said, snidely.

"No wonder the good folks of New Orleans ran you out of town," Bess continued, giving him a hard look, her expression demanding.

For a long minute deVoss hesitated, then repeated, "Try and stop me!" He dared her, his voice rough, his belligerent mood evident. He liked remarks that struck like a snake.

With instinctive mistrust Bess continued to study him intently, staring at him, pressing her lips tightly together. She then straightened her back, saying, "Let me put it to you flat out, deVoss. I'm sick of your intentions! The captain won't have to do anything to you if you touch her again. I'll do it! I can't stop you from looking and I can't stop you from thinking, but if you so much as touch that girl I'll call the sheriff when we tie up in the next port!" Her voice was hard. DeVoss licked his lips. He was well-aware that she would. He could not understand her love for Cole. His mouth opened, but the intended sneer did not form. In hostile silence they glared at each other. There had been others like deVoss through the years. She could not remember all the forgotten faces and all the wasted years. Her keen intuition was warning her of trouble.

As deVoss stiffened and his face took on an expression of hate, his mind became ruthless. He knew and understood. He could see the determination in her stance. Then, he gave a fake, high-pitched laugh that sounded artificial, but was natural for him. His eyes were scornful with contempt and he shrugged his shoulders. There was the usual guarded look on his face.

"Why, Bessie, I wouldn't do anything against the boat rules, you know that," he temporized again, giving his dry laugh.

Bess raised her eyebrows and let out a burst of false laughter to equal his. "This old kitchen's heard many a lie," she snorted, "and that's the classic." She had learned not to believe a word he said.

DeVoss thought quickly. "Maybe I can make it worth your while to change your mind. You're the only one that could influence her. At least you could turn your head." He believed this. "I have far more money than I need and I'm very generous to women who do me favors," he said with obvious intent, drawing his sleeve across his mouth. Cole was well worth the try.

He had an alert, fox-like face and an ingratiating smile. It was his crude attempt at guile. "Well, how about it, Bessie? Can we make a deal?" His voice had become soft and oily. He attempted polish and a silver tongue when it was to his advantage. Bess looked up from the stove, a look of loathing. He was not difficult to read.

"No deal, deVoss! You'll never understand. I can't throw you out of my kitchen or go to the captain because you haven't done anything...yet. If you had, I would, and I'm waiting for you to make a mistake so I can." Her tone was glacial. "So, I'm telling you to leave the kitchen. Cole's coming back to help me

clean up and prepare the next meal, and I don't want her in here alone with you!" DeVoss opened his mouth, then shut it. He pretended not to hear. "Talking to you is like whistling in the wind," she stated.

He remained silent, scheming and considering various plans, squinting his eyes against the glare of the lightbulb, then shrugged and turned away, unable to hide the look of one who was lying.

"If you don't like it, you know what you can do!" the cook added emphatically, pointing down the river, hoping that he would. DeVoss gave her a look of contempt, his dark eyes narrowed.

"Yeah, I know what I can do, and I may just do it unless you play ball with me." His mouth stretched in a nasty grin.

"Just try it!" Bess dared, her face hard, eyes narrowed.

"No need to act mean, Bessie. There are things we could talk about. Things that I could do for you. There are a lot of expensive things you would like to have," he said, giving her a slanting glance. He did not want trouble floating his way. Not from Bess.

Bess lifted her chin a little. "I have nothing to talk to you about," she said crisply, realizing the extent of his superiority complex. She had made her own way through the years.

DeVoss snorted, pushing his hat back on his head. "Maybe you do, Bessie," he said with relish. She hated to be called Bessie. His eyes were slowly studying her from head to toe and back.

"There isn't anything you won't do to get what you want, is there." Bess stated. It was an accusation and not a question. *The big frog in the little pond,* she thought as she studied him.

They both lapsed into a determined silence. DeVoss was enjoying his moment. He did not intend to hurry. He was watching the flies that were circling the unshaded light bulb. Then he followed the progress of a fly across the table. He glanced at the fly-blown overhead, and cleared his throat, his snigger infuriating.

"These damned flies seem to breed all year 'round in here," he griped. He glanced at Bess, knowing she realized the inference. "You ought to do something about that" Sunlight through the window glared on his pinched face. Flaunting had turned him ugly. *Bess paused. She knew this man far better than he knew himself. Then she broke her silence. "Yes, I intend to do something about it and make sure it's only the flies doing the breeding." Her face was flushed, her anger rising. There was a sharp edge to her voice.*

"I have a right to be interested in whom ever I want!" he boasted.

"You have no right to do what you have in mind!" Bess retorted.

"Well, Bessie, I'm not the one to talk to about that and you know what I mean. Hell, Bessie, you and me should be friends. It's to your advantage. Why fight? She's just another little riverfront girl in which we have the same interest. I have the money to treat her good." He spoke so softly of Cole he made excited, almost psychogenic gestures. Bess rolled her eyes in frustration. *Another man who only gives in order to get,* she thought.

Bess made an effort to hold her temper, but failed. She moved directly up to him. A rolling pin lay on the table. Her features were hard and set, and she spoke in a cold fury. "I told you, deVoss, you touch that girl and I'll bonk you on the head with this!" She placed her hand on the rolling pin. "You'll rue the day!" She could smell his terrible breath. They stared at each other in hate.

Then he shrugged and scratched himself, holding his temper. "What's she to you?" There was no answer. "Maybe you'll have to change your mind about Cole and me," he went on. "She's dirt poor and I got money." It was true that he seldom lost at cards and often had huge sums of money.

"It's not Creole luck," he bragged. "I'm a master at faro and poker." It was true. No one could beat him at cards.

"Creole baloney," Bess sneered. "Even the Cajuns wouldn't own you. You're nothing but a flatboat picaroon!" DeVoss stared at her in hate. Then Bess nodded as if beginning to understand his plan. "Exactly what do you have in mind, deVoss?" she asked in disgust, looking at him sharply. *What one human schemes for another is inconceivable,* she was thinking.

"Exactly? Well, it means exactly this, Bessie," he said threateningly. "You try to set Cole against me and I'll go straight to the captain and tell him of the secret of Cole scheming for his son, and you helping them. You know where Cole will go, and you in the other direction, and I have the money to follow Cole. Then where's your precious little friend that you seem to be saving for yourself? Word could get around the boat that you love her." He spat out the words. He was a man of a restless, wandering nature, poisoned by envy and hate; sullen of feature.

Bess turned her cold eyes back to him. "Yes, I love her," she said, "but not in the way you plan on smearing it around, so keep your filthy mouth shut!" She didn't have to say another word. He made no reply, but quickly got to his feet.

With these parting remarks and a glance at Bess deVoss turned his back on her and slithered out of the galley, mumbling to himself. Had he remained Bess would have hit him with a rolling pin, and he knew it. He was no fool.

"That man is not only sick with desire," Bess mumbled with anger and fear, "he's as evil as Hell. I'll bet he can't look at himself in the mirror when he shaves," she added with vehemence.

DeVoss was new on their boat and on the Ohio River. The severe depression had forced him to travel in search of work. Riverboat jobs were scarce and he was well-qualified with an excellent work record. Though deVoss had chosen his qualification references shrewdly, Captain Mitchell had his misgivings and was watching him carefully. He had the uneasy feeling that the man was mentally deranged and planned to replace him the next time they were in home port. He also noticed that deVoss did not have to pinch pennies like the rest of the crew and wondered about it.

Bess was thinking of Cole. She had become like a daughter, the child that Bess had never had and always wanted. A child... so wonderful, so precious. She was remembering Old Rip's words when he described deVoss, "He talks like a man with two mouths." Bess had nodded in agreement, well-endowed with the wisdom of experience among men, her mind filled with all sorts of worries.

Who is this man? Bess wondered. *Why is he on this particular boat? His chance of getting Cole is like a snowball in hell!* She paused in thought. *Am I getting myself into something that is none of my business?* Her lips tightened. *I don't think so!* And there was always the disturbing question in her mind: *Why is he all the way up here from New Orleans? There are plenty of boats down that way.* She felt certain that this man could become dangerous, that he was the combination of a desire-hate syndrome.

Chapter Two

The next day, as the stern-wheel towboat entered the main channel of the Ohio River and headed up stream, Brant Mitchell came out of the wheelhouse and down to the main deck. The morning had dawned radiant and clear, the sky bright and pink. It was an incredibly beautiful morning with the sun now blazing. From the boat he had a sweeping view of the Queen City, gateway to the south. The Suspension Bridge joining Cincinnati, Ohio and Covington, Kentucky was silhouetted against the sky. Cincinnati was one of the principal ports of call on the Ohio River. The shore seemed to be a long wall of buildings. The boat was heading up stream toward the Kanawha River and West Virginia, behind the huge stern wheel there was a sea of white foam. A wedge of geese was moving north and the river air rang with their joy of life in a valley steeped in sunshine. "A lot of water has flowed under that bridge," Captain Mitchell mumbled to himself as he watched his son.

Brant Mitchell was tall and slender with an athletic build, wavy blond hair that was cut short, and a dimple just off center in his chin. The style of his recent haircut was typical of the young. He was inclined to amiability, generally, giving him a boyish, open face. He walked the deck with his head at a rakish angle, glancing at the riverbank, golden in the sun. He noticed that in the big cities the girls were wearing their skirts quite a bit shorter. His smile had more purpose than warmth.

As a rule, on many stern-wheel riverboats, the officers were not required to wear dress uniforms. It was more a personal choice and Brant's father, Captain Mitchell, preferred to wear a uniform.

"If you are going to be an officer you have to look like one," the captain had said. "It's a matter of respect.

Brant looked up and down the deck, and, being certain that no one saw him, opened a cabin door, stepped inside, closed the door behind him, and stood looking at Cole Hamilton. He had not seen deVoss watching.

"You shouldn't come in here," Cole said breathlessly, startled, but her eyes were shinning, forgetting his slight earlier that morning, and she was blushing deeply. She stood looking at him, her heart in her eyes.

"I just wanted to have a chance to talk to you, that's all."

"If you get caught in here you know what will happen," she answered in warning, though her face was girlish and bright. "I'll be put off the boat! That's what will happen." Cole could hide nothing. Her thoughts and emotions were that honest. All of her feelings were in her eyes and in her voice. She knew nothing of sham and artifice. When she saw Brant her heart beat furiously, his nearness was a stimulant, the feeling was as natural as a river flowing its course. Her eyes looked straight into his with joy and excitement.

"That's why I walked past you this morning," Brant said, feeling in charge of the situation. "You're right, I admit; if my father gets wind of this, one or the other of us will go down the river. He's watching. I'll only visit with you a few minutes."

"I've been hoping all day to talk to you," Cole admitted in honesty, momentarily forgetting her fears, "but I don't like this secrecy. I wish we could be more honest and out in the open," she added. Her tone was serious, her chin lifted in pride, and her innocence shone like the eyes of a child.

"Not yet," Brant said hurriedly. "The time isn't right." It was said evasively. "I'll know when we can talk to my father. I just wanted to see you and have a little private talk with you."

"We shouldn't be alone," she emphasized uneasily. She had been raised to believe certain things without question, causing a series of conflicting emotions, yet she was thrilled that he had taken an interest in her and by the way he looked at her. His presence in her cabin was electrifying. It radiated a message.

His reaction to her beauty and tenderness was one of possessiveness. She was too appealing for him to resist. He looked down at her rounded, young breasts and she blushed and turned away.

"Who would watch me in your cabin?" He was watching her deep blue eyes. "My father doesn't sneak around. Anyway, this is the first time I've ever been in your cabin."

"It's deVoss I'm worried about. He terrifies me. He moves like a cat, night and day. I don't think he ever sleeps. I feel him around all the time." A deep, natural instinct warned her. To her deVoss seemed as shadowy in the day as in the night. She had the feeling that it was just a matter of time until he did something terrible.

"Don't worry about deVoss," he said importantly, "I can handle him." He was more concerned with Chain's guardianship of Cole, suggested by Bess, and moved closer to her.

"I don't know," she said uneasily. "He's the only one on board mean enough and sly enough to go to the captain. We should be the ones to go to your father." Brant stopped her words with a kiss, his pulse pounding. Cole was both shocked and thrilled.

It had been a summer of intense joy, a summer Cole thought nothing could corrupt. She was overpowered by a sense of exultation, an awakened force of life ,over which she had no control. He was just too desirable, and she had never felt this way before. It swept her feelings along like a storm, engulfing her in blinding flashes. It was more than she dreamed could happen; an impellent beyond reason. The first burst of ecstasy in her existence was overwhelming, an admission into a state of forbidden dreams.

Brant was dazzled by the radiance of her face, his pride in her reaction to him, and was unaware of the depth of feeling and meaning. It would be impossible for his vanity not to be flattered. It gave him a high feeling, a sense of achievement. Brant was accustomed to girls in the river towns fawning over him, but Cole's depth of feeling was new. Yet, it thrilled him as the excitement that is only stirred by the hope of a new conquest. It was the a surge of infatuation.

Cole's face was innocent and beautiful. "It's not a big boat," she said uneasily, "and I'm afraid that deVoss saw you come in here. He seems to be everywhere at once." Brant could not understand her constant fears of deVoss.

Cole's cabin, though the same in size, was so different from those of the men. It was freshly painted. She had painted it, using pastel colors. From as far back as she could remember she had liked light, bright colors to offset her dark moods. Many of her books were there. She spent her off-duty time curled upon her bunk, reading. The book she was currently reading was John Fox Jr.'s Trail of the Lonesome Pine. *She considered Mr. Fox one of her favorite writers, and lived to the fullest the tragedy and happiness of each book. Her impressions of life were made upon these books, stirring something deep within her.*

"You read a lot, don't you?" Brant asked, glancing at the books.

"Yes," she said, shyly. She read so that she did not feel lonely.

Brant was quite surprised and pleased at Cole's cabin. It was fresh and clean with no stale or heavy odors. Her cabin did not smell of men's socks, tobacco, and sweat. It was cozy, actually, and inviting; feminine on a coarse, masculine boat. The room had become hers. It excited him. For her, it was a cabin that, until now, had been the site of more pleasure than pain. In it she felt safe and secure. She thought of how much more appealing she would look in her new dress.

Cole wanted Brant to think of her as mature. Each night she examined herself in the mirror, hoping she was fully a woman. She had never had the opportunity to be vain, and was not aware of her sensuality and had no understanding of it. Her only thought was that perhaps those women that spent an hour every morning making themselves beautiful were the smart ones.

"I'd love to have your picture," she said, in a half-childish way, "but I wouldn't dare put it up in here." She had never had a picture of a boy. The only thing she had of Brant's was a handkerchief that he had dropped on the deck one night, which was now scented from her lilac sachet. She had laundered it and kept it in her dresser drawer.

He opened a dresser drawer and looked at her personal belongings, a freedom which should have annoyed her, but did not. In the drawer was the Bible her mother had left her. Her real mother. He shut the drawer on the Bible. There were fresh flowers on her dresser. It was lilac time, her favorite time of the year. The cabin was heavy with the scent of lilac.

"Flowers?" He raised his eyebrows. "On this boat?"

"I got them in Oneonta on our return down river when Bess and I were shopping for supplies." She would have bought him flowers, but she knew that he could not keep them unnoticed in his cabin.

"Aren't the colors rich?" she asked after a pause. She touched, with gentleness, a bloom with the tips of her fingers. She loved the touch of flowers, and looked at them as if gathering something from their beauty and scent. She was excited and elated that he had noticed. The delicate blue vase that held the flowers was one of the few treasures from her mother.

"They're yours, really, only I have to keep them here."

Cole always threw flowers away before they wilted. She did not like dead flowers near her. She did not like to watch anything die, not even an insect. There had been too much death in her young life. All of these things made the gentleness of her room surprising to him.

A loud noise on deck so startled her that she jumped back. "Oh!" she exclaimed, then grinned with embarrassment and relief. "I thought someone was coming in."

"That's just a loose davit swinging against a stanchion. Don't be so jumpy!" He wanted her to be relaxed and loving.

"I can't help it. I don't want anything to go wrong. Your father's a good man, but he's a stern man—strict about regulations."

A huge leather-bound scrapbook was on the dresser. Cole had been keeping a scrapbook of personal memorabilia since she entered high school. The newspaper article about Brant Mitchell being the youngest licensed pilot on the river was the latest entry. Brant was much impressed with that. The association with each picture, article, or program brought her close to those she loved and needed: a picture of her dog, Jack, squinting in the sun; half forgotten moments brought to life. She was sensitive about things like a photo album and the lift it gave her spirits.

Cole frowned, moving to him. "Aren't you afraid of your father?" Her voice was low and soft. She was a person who did not challenge authority and she needed Brant's optimism.

"Let me worry about him." Brant grinned disarmingly as he held out his arms, wanting to kiss her again, as he had the other night on deck. He had heard the expression, "Sweet sixteen and never been kissed." It was true. His lips were the first to have touched hers. She had trembled with a totally new feeling. It was like coming out of darkness into light. The closeness of her sweet flesh excited him. "Come here!" he pretended to command.

"You don't talk a whole lot for a girl, do you?" he asked. To Cole, their embrace became more wonderful each time. She did not wear perfume, but a scented soap gave her fresh, clean youth the cologne of a spring flower garden, and her breath was always so pure and sweet. She had a delicate scent that was her own.

Brant looked down at her gravely, but his eyes were bright. He felt the vibrant, true heartbeat of a girl's first love—a love that had been growing through the weeks. He noticed a soft colored blush on her cheeks. He was the first boy she had ever kissed. She flushed with pleasure, a look of shy delight. The natural force of her love had become irresistible since the first night on deck filled with ecstasy and fear, making it impossible for her to comprehend the illusions and fears of her new life. She was experiencing a feeling beyond her reasoning—a natural gift.

The splendor of this summer had been a new world for Cole, a break in the continuum of her tragic life. Something strangely wonderful had happened to her for the first time. Never before had she felt like this, opened up her heart like this. *If she told him again how happy she was she'd break down and cry from the eternal longing for someone to have and to hold. She could not think of anything else and the magic of that summer night came sweeping back, leaving her breathless, quivering with anticipation. To ache so with life was a new experience. Her entire being was afire with love. She looked at him tenderly.*

"Oh, how I wish I could go dancing with you," she said in her lovely soft voice, laughing. Her laughter was light, almost musical. He did not answer. "Maybe someday," she answered for him and buried her face in his shoulder. "Have you ever done the Lindy Hop?" she asked, looking up. He grinned, shaking his head yes, but not going into detail.

"Glad I came?" His tone was boyish, his manner winning. Without waiting for an answer he pulled her to him.

"Yes. Oh, yes." Her eyes and face betrayed her emotions. All of her passion went into the few words with him. Life for her was rich with love and her eyes, with such truth, were blazing bright. Red crept up her neck and blushed her cheeks as he pulled her to him. Her words were as soft as her expression, the euphoria of her beautiful dream. To become aware, suddenly, of a rapture such as this was overpowering. All the emotions within her had been released. There was no hiding from it.

"Oh, yes," she breathed again, softly, becoming more hopeful of their future together, forgetting her stepmother's warning that fairy tales do not always come true.

Her touch was shy as she considered him with a strangely different tenderness, a woman's half-fearful reaching. Her complete lack of sophistication gave her a childlike earnestness, and she nestled closer to him as he held her tightly.

"Brant?" she asked, breaking the silence, leaning back. He was amazed to notice how long her dark eyelashes were.

"What?" he said, not caring for talk, only wanting to kiss her. There was a bloom, a radiance; in her he had never seen before.

"You always say we have to wait to talk to your father about us, but you never say why. Why do we have to wait? I believe that our secret meetings are wrong."

"It's too long and complicated to talk about it now," Brant answered. "It has to do with boat regulations and other things he worries about. My dad's only concern at present is the examination for my master's license. Right now just isn't the time and place to talk to him about us," and he pulled her to him again. "Anyway, what we're doing isn't wrong. It's natural," he added. Cole looked away uneasily.

Cole's was an unsophisticated passion that touched her life at the root. She did not know how to be flirtatious nor coy. She looked up into his face with the look that only a woman in love, and believed loved, can have. The thought kept her full of joy, along with the hope that these moments would last forever.

"And your father?" Cole asked again, gently, with uneasy persistence. Seeing he was not going to answer, she continued. "I'm worried about your father. I was raised to believe that secret meetings aren't right unless we are going to be married. We shouldn't become too close until we have his blessing. You should have a talk with him. He trusts us. He brought me on board through the recommendation of a friend of his when I had no place else to go." The simple way she held her hand to her breast when alarmed amused him.

"Let sleeping dogs lie." He liked adages. "The old man's busy up in the wheelhouse. He has enough worries. Navigation. When I'm down here he has to be up there. We're safe." His only thought was for this moment.

"Maybe," she cautioned, giving an uncertain nod. "Chain might be in the pilothouse." Her voice had a touch of shyness. She was a modest girl by nature, and did not like to cross him.

"Nope!" he exclaimed smugly, not liking the mention of Chain and the thought of her confidence in him. "Chain would only be up there in an emergency, and I would hear the bells." She knew this was not necessarily so.

"It worries me," she repeated with gentle reproof, in fear that she might destroy his career as well as their love. Her hand slipped over his, exerting a tender pressure. She had never had polish on her nails. "Don't you think...."

"Forget it!" he interrupted. "Let me handle everything. Let me do the worrying about my father," he added, his attitude postulant. "You just keep your mind on us."

"I will. I'm sorry." She spoke trustfully, afraid of offending him. "All I think of is our future together." She sensed that his bravado was covering a reluctance to have a showdown with his father concerning them and she was not certain why. He would not speak of it. She hoped she could change his mind about that.

Cole regarded him hopefully. "My stepmother said, 'It's a strange thing about love. You don't need to have it returned to love somebody.' She said that loving was enough. I wonder if that's true?" She was frowning slightly, needing reassurance, worried about what could happen to them. She ached to have him love her, to say he loved her, thinking there was no one in the world to love her. Her eyes were searching his, searching for realization.

"If your mother told you that it has to be true," was all he said in answer, hoping for a change in conversation.

Brant was proud of having her and wished that he could show her off in the river towns. He would have loved to drive around with her in his Model B Ford convertible that he stored in Cincinnati. It rankled him that he could not. The reality of her existence and his hope for a conquest came to him with an overwhelming force. His emotions came more like the beat of a drum than the softness of a violin.

He watched her in silence. There was a quality beyond his knowing: his unawareness that betrayal creates destruction and ruin. He had not reached an age to have acquired enough character to realize the lack of it.

"Do you feel the way I do?" she asked again, timidly. Like a child, she wanted assurance and had a need to be wanted.

He shook his head a little. He did not answer her question. Instead, he said, "I just want to hold you and make love to you." She felt her face flush.

Cole could not decipher his makeup. She did not try. She was not prompted to make the search. Perhaps, subconsciously, she was afraid to delve too deeply. She hoped, in the simplicity of her being, that he was sincere. All of her heart and body and soul were now involved with one person. He was able to weave a spell that could enchant her from reality into the web of dreams. She was both happy and scared. Life was no longer hopeless, yet it was edged with dread. Never had she anticipated such a yearning.

Flushing with pleasure, Cole turned back to him and tossed her head. "I don't care. I can't help it. I want things to work out well, for us to stay together." She did not belong only to herself. She believed that love was greater than all other things. She loved him so much, so completely, so hopelessly. She was only seventeen and had never been in love before. He had built a romantic image of himself that he believed was the truth; his life was intensely alive with the fun of living.

Yet, in all, Cole had an underlying feeling of urgency about themselves, an uneasiness that the summer was passing without determination. She felt that she must have an understanding with Brant, a settlement, an admission of his intentions. She had been raised to believe this was of the utmost importance. She planned to do that at their meeting tonight.

Is he teasing me? *She wondered, but that was all. For the moment she did not stop to settle it in her mind. She dared not. She could not determine his feelings through his eyes and voice. She thought his hesitation was the adoration and flame of tenderness of a shy boy's early groping. Sheltered, her imagery was often unrealistic, mystical. Every summer he had lived among men since he was twelve years old.*

Cole wetted her lips with her tongue; a motion that set him on fire. "I shouldn't sound so brazen, telling you how much I care," she said, coloring. Her simple grace was not a pretense. Her heart was in her eyes.

"Cole," he said in reflection, changing the subject. "An unusual name. Cole Hamilton." He tilted his head. "Where did it come from?"

Her expression had the open joy of a child. He was interested in her. He wanted to know about her.

"I don't know how different it is." She was embarrassed. "I was told my people were English. Cole is a family name. Maybe it would have sounded better on a boy, but I was all they had, or could have."

"I don't think so. It sounds beautiful on you, Cole Hamilton." She was not certain whether he was joking or not.

"That was a nice thing to say." Her voice was warm and young, and it had a ring of innocence. He liked the way she puckered her mouth when she spoke thoughtfully, and the touch of her hand on his back shook him. It made him feel mature, a conqueror. The vanity of his acquisitive personality was stimulated. He felt real confidence.

Brant pulled Cole tighter to him. "Are you going to let me see you after my shift tonight?" He was hoping she would. Hoping for the first time alone at night in her cabin. Cole stood silent, afraid, guessing his thoughts as he looked around at her cabin room.

"Here?" Cole finally whispered. "In my cabin?"

"Yes," Brant answered without hesitation.

In Cole's exaltation her first thought was: *He loves me!* Her innocence and inexperience were obvious. With each meeting she had hoped for the wondrous question: "Will you marry me?" He had not mentioned marriage, nor spoken of their future. Not yet, but she was certain that he would. Brant accepted her silence as acquiescence.

Brant's smile was one of the triumph of a man who has had his way, and he smiled down into her face. He was proud of his masculine powers, yet wondered what the odds were of getting into her cabin twice in one day without being caught.

Cole glanced up, looking directly into Brant's eyes. "Brant, we both know what the boat regulations are. If we're caught, it's the end. The end for me, anyway. We're gambling our lives and I wonder if we have that right." Her tone was gentle.

Cole saw their reflection in the mirror, as though looking at a movie. She watched Brant in the mirror, studying him and herself. It was as if she were certain of this summer's happiness, but that the girl in the mirror was not. The girl in the mirror was frightened, knowing that it was impossible for her to resist him.

Brant shook his head.

"We haven't been doing anything wrong," were the words he used in answer.

Brant had been popular with the riverfront small town girls and this pleased him. Power had privilege, and even the young second officer of an Ohio River stern-wheel steamboat carried this advantage. He had grown to like this mini-power. The river towns were filled with rewarding pleasures.

Young Brant Mitchell had all the assurance that was based on imagination. He knew also that though he was but the son of a captain of a riverboat, to her the difference in their status in life was that of pauper and king. He turned away from the look in her eyes. The look was not an act of deference, it was an act of love, and her intensity made him uneasy.

Cole was only a girl—seventeen, soft and hoping—yet her love had grown from a tiny point of feeling, a few weeks ago, to a huge flame of fire, and an incredulous peace that she did not understand. She sensed things she did not think about: she was so vulnerable in childish bewilderment at the ways of life.

Out of the silence she whispered, "Tonight?" and shied from the sound of her voice, feeling uneasy in her mind.

"I'll be here tonight." Holding her closely, he watched himself in the mirror. He was unaware of the extent of his vanity. Their stolen hour was almost like a game: he was playing with passion, she was playing with love, her life: each hour had recorded a memory intertwined with hopes, enmeshed in dreams.

Her look deepened. "You took me by surprise this afternoon. I'll have on my new dress tonight!" She spoke with the eager simplicity of a simple joy, a constant passion. Not even Bess knew that she had bought this new dress to wear for him. She thought it was so sophisticated. She trusted Bess, yet she had not confided in her. It had hurt her that she could not dress more elegantly for him. She had read of elegant ladies and the word elegant had become synonymous with desirable. She knew that he was impressed with refined girls: pretty girls wearing beautiful clothes. She tried so hard to act up to what she thought his vision of her could be: beautiful and well-dressed: elegant.

"We must be very thoughtful concerning tonight." The soft voice was hesitant. She did not want to plan what might happen. Let it happen. "I know your father likes me," she went on, "but I wonder if he would tolerate his son marrying a chambermaid." Again the fear of losing something loved, the need to be reassured. "We could go to another boat," she suggested. Hers was an unnatural fear of losing him that tightened her heart. "I know your father would put me off the boat." Though nervous, her voice was a gentle rebuke.

Cole looked forward to their next meeting with more hurting than hope: the fear as well as the wonder of what could happen and the belief that she would say, "No," without a proposal. She planned to do that.

"Oh, don't worry about my father! You make too big an issue of it. I can handle him," he said awkwardly. He believed himself. "Just think about tonight and the meaning of it," and he brushed his cheek against hers. He did not like her talk of marriage and going to another boat.

Cole wanted to believe him. When she smiled in agreement, one dimple formed. Then she looked away, out across the river, her face still had a childlike quality. She felt the sweet, warm breeze of summer, and the air was still and clean with a deep warmth. It was as if she had been born this very summer and had become mature with this very feeling. Her touching love stood naked in her eyes. He saw sunlight falling on her hair. If only he could have but scented the meaning of the breath of love that breathed through the sunbeams on her face. The entire world seemed to stand still.

Cole experienced a happiness so intense it was as if she were in pain. She was ashamed of the tears streaming down her cheeks and felt certain that tonight he would ask her to become his wife. That was all she wanted. His wife, *she repeated to herself, carried away by imagination.*

"Before you go, I have something for you. A very special gift." She suffered the pangs of a shy person: sensitive and embarrassed, afraid of being hurt.

"What?" Brant asked, daring her.

"Close your eyes and open your hand...."

"What's going on?" he interrupted, but did as she requested. From out of her dresser drawer Cole lifted a small, beautifully hand-carved wooden jewel box. It had belonged to her natural mother. From the jewel box Cole took an object and placed it in Brant's hand, believing that this would bind them together forever as assuredly as an engagement ring. To Cole, it was a gift to her husband-to-be.

Brant opened his eyes and looked into his hand. On his palm lay a beautiful watch of soft, etched gold.

"Wow!" he exclaimed, louder than he should have. Cole became frightened and put her finger over his lips, then looked at him, again shy, but spoke with pride.

"I want this to be yours," she said. "From me with love. For you to have always. With it, each day in the future you will remember this night tonight."

Brant raised his eyebrows and whistled softly as he looked at the elegant, thin, gold watch in the palm of his hand.

"It was my father's watch," Cole said softly. "I have treasured it above everything I own."

Brant stood looking at the watch in awe. Cole enclosed his hand gently in both of hers and drew his hand to her heart, hoping that his heart was melting. He was unaware of the meaning of the ceremony. To her it was as if they were being married, the most sacred of life's involvements.

Cole was happiest when her heart was thrilled at doing something for him, such as the childlike pleasure of giving surprise. Her face, had he noticed, was a study in love. His face was studying the watch, counting the hours until tonight.

He stared at the watch in silence. Had he bothered to look into her eyes he would have seen himself and a time she could never forget.

"Brant..." she hesitated "...do you love me?" She spoke simply, from her heart, unable to help herself. She thought this would lead to a proposal. Proposals had come this way in the novels she had read. Her hands clutched his like the hands of a lonely child, her blue eyes soft, questioning, her thin face looking up at him. She misunderstood his silence, mistaking it for an awed feeling. They misunderstood each other. Her parted lips showed the quiver of hope. He did not know how it hurt her to have asked that question. She wanted desperately to hear it. She had never heard him say it, though she believed he expressed it. She needed someone who needed her, who loved her; someone who would be only hers. Her expectations caused her to believe that love was the key to paradise, that this memory would last forever.

As she waited for his words he flushed, hoping he had not been wrong in accepting the watch; that it would not complicate their relationship. He just could not say no to such a gift. Her eyes had a look of eagerness, expectancy.

"I'll be here tonight, won't I? Doesn't that tell you the answer?" Again he had answered her sincere yearning with a question. "Just leave your door unlocked tonight." He spoke hurriedly, not wanting more questions. "This will give you the answer," and he held her tightly and kissed her.

Her face lit up at his words and the kiss. She loved him, and because she loved him she trusted him and believed him. He believed himself. "I'll be waiting," she said simply, not wanting to part, always hoping for his proposal.

Cole was extremely sensual. It was so strong it came out of the unfathomable distances of fecund people's past. He had not the slightest inkling of the meaning of that small, warm body he held in his arms.

He turned, opened the cabin door a few inches, and looked along the deck, then added quickly, "See you tonight, honey." He slid out of the door and slipped along the bright deck.

When he had gone she stood where he had left her. It was as if she were seeing the world for the first time. All her life had meaning now, there was nothing more for her to ask. He would propose. She was certain of it. She had to believe that. Then she spoke a very soft, inward "Goodbye," and closed the door quietly behind him. She stood as if in a trance.

Cole hesitated a few minutes, opened the door wide, and stepped out onto the deck. She walked toward the kitchen, not seeing the deckhand, deVoss. Step by step he was executing a plan. Excitement was in her eyes, making them as bright as a button. The sun, glancing from the river, brightened her features. The summer sun had given her fair skin a rich tan. It was a glorious day. Yet, even the bright sun could not match the brightness of her eyes. Her heart was flying with the birds overhead, she felt buoyantly full of life. She could not remember when she had seen a more beautiful day, and she could not help but be effected by the splendor of the morning. The world was so rewarding she wanted to laugh and cry at the same time. She walked as if the deck were clouds, as though she were on the streets of heaven. She could not feel her feet on the deck. She wanted to sing and dance. She wanted to smile and she wanted to shout, certain that their love filled the entire earth. Had it been a rainy day the sun would have been shining; she had the youthful belief of eternity, unaware of the cloud that can darken a life. She had no idea of what life held in store for the future. She laughed aloud with joy, swelling like a rose on a warm spring day. Never had the sky been so blue, the air so fresh.

"Love to some young men is like a bed of flowers to a honey bee," Bess had said to her in warning and she had not understood.

Cole moved down the deck naturally, the artless grace of not knowing her beauty. She did not need the assurance of those who know they are beautiful in their bodies, she was thinking only of the coming night, Brant, his proposal, and their marriage. And so was deVoss. His plan was simple: conquer or destroy. Cole's need was bigger than her. She forced herself to let each day stand by itself, as if each day was a forever. Something powerful enveloped her, but each tomorrow was not the same, with the moment gone. The next day Brant was occupied, but not so with her; the fire never burned down. It was a strong, strange, and wild feeling that breathed in the darkness of the night, and Heaven was forgotten in her paradise. She wanted this moment to last forever. She walked down the deck in a haze. Her entire world was today. She was filled with the promise of high expectation, joy, and her future—beyond doubt. Never had she felt so happily secure and needed. She looked at her reflection in the cabin window and smiled. The sun was the exact color of her new blouse.

Later, during the moonlit night of hopes and dreams, the soft summer moon cast a shadow, silhouetting deVoss as he prowled the deck near Cole's cabin. He was slinking around like a hungry wolf. He knew every nook and cranny where he could eavesdrop unseen. A cunning smile of planning slowly creased his evil face.

Chapter Three

The next morning the light of the rising sun made mirrors of the windows of the town buildings along the riverbank. They blazed like coals in a forge. The air was hot and still. It was spring, and the high mountain snow melt was freshening the river. Cole entered the kitchen shortly after deVoss returned to his berth. She was wondering if anything could equal the glory of a river sunrise.

"I waited until I saw him leave," she said to Bess, respect and affection bright in her eyes. The fresh coffee smelled strong.

"Figured you would," the cook answered, pursing her lips.

"I can force myself to tolerate rough, crude men," Cole continued, "but that man is evil. I'm afraid of him." She shuddered, thankful to have Bess. "He's so obvious." She paused. "Do you think he's insane? He acts crazy," she said simply.

"Yes," Bess admitted, "not only mentally sick, but mean, ornery, and rotten. That type can be dangerous, so be careful!"

Cole remained silent, thinking. She was horrified.

"He's about as slimy as a fish," Bess continued. "He's the type of man who could beat a child or woman to death." *What is it about some men that makes them capable of killing,* she wondered. Then, looking closely at Cole she said, "You look tired. Not sleeping well?" she asked, wiping her hands on her apron.

Cole hesitated, nervous. It was as if Bess was looking straight through her and could read her very soul. "Did he say anything about Brant and me?" She spoke softly, with a warm coloring, living in the whirl of confused emotions.

Bess watched her carefully, reading the message. "You don't have to explain, honey. I can tell when you talk about Brant." Bess had correctly read

Cole's startled look, the eyes opening wide. She turned and went back to making bread. *The age of innocence,* she was thinking.

Cole blushed. She felt as if she had shouted a nameless secret aloud to the world and feared for Brant. "You know?" She looked at Bess with such alarm that the cook was startled. "Already?" She should not have to feel ashamed, secretive.

Bess maintained the appearance of someone who is unknowing, but in reality knew all that was happening on the boat. "You're new to the riverboat life, Cole, and it's important to know that what occurs on a riverboat is known by everyone on the boat as soon as it happens. Rumors on a boat are a dime a dozen, but when the real McCoy comes along they go wild. They'd rather eat gossip than my cooking. Idleness creates gossip, and there's plenty of idleness and gossip on this boat. Believe me it's just as deadly as family gossip." *Poor child,* she thought. *So lost in the real world.*

Cole stared in shocked silence. She sat down slowly. She had opened herself up to risk. She had endangered Brant. "I thought..." her words trailed off, her face crimson.

"They don't have to see him and you together to know what's happening," Bess said. Cole covered her face with her hands in shame. "I've never been in the Captain's cabin," Bess continued, "yet I know that when he dresses he puts his left shoe on first, always, and his left leg into his pants first, always, yet he puts his right arm first into his shirt. There's no secrets among people who work this close together." Bess spoke grimly, knowing the girl was sensitive in the extreme—to the point of a complex—and lived in a world of daydreams.

Cole uncovered her face and raised frightened eyes. Bess was looking at her with sharp intensity. "You think with your heart instead of your head," she said, then paused. "The captain doesn't know yet, I can tell you that much, but he will...and soon. Then his wife will know, and that will be the end of it. Brant is her baby, and always will be, and she never lets him forget it. I'll bet the captain is already suspicious." She put the bread pan in the oven. She often referred to Brant as a playboy.

Bess did not want to sound holier than thou, or like a crab, but wanted to protect her. Her concern was tender and sincere. She knew that Cole had never deliberately wronged or harmed anyone and that goodness was the substance of her being. Cole had no experience with evil planning. She had no knowledge or experience in playing a game for what she wanted. Her feelings were a natural and unavoidable truth. She had a gentleness and a sweetness that was difficult to blend with the boat life. Cole was experiencing a deep, vital change of living, so different from that with which she was accustomed. Bess was aware that the innocent, with pure feelings, are often guilty before they realize it. She glanced down and resumed kneading the luncheon biscuits. "I don't suppose it will do any good to tell you that you're too young and swimming in dangerous waters, will it?" she asked, touched by a childlike nature without hidden calculation. Bess knew that nothing ever remains the same, that such enchanting moments often fade as a beautiful sunset, and the regret that each has to live with their own mistakes. Cole had no idea which way the wind was blowing and was unable to succumb to logic. Bess saw that she could easily be hurt and was vulnerable to the extreme. *Too often the heart responds before the brain, she thought.*

Cole listened in silence. She truly believed that she had a place in Brant's life. To pretend she did not love him would be living a lie.

"No," Cole admitted simply, "I only know the way I feel." Her eyes were shining, a flush on her cheeks. Her love had lifted her to the mysterious dimension of realization beyond explanation. She was animated as she spoke with a newly awakened joy, unaware that love can also open one to pain. Love and loyalty came naturally to her. Her expression was so deep and true that it did something to Bess as she watched. She could sense the reality in the emotion. Bess was realizing that a fire burned within Cole, that she was unfamiliar with such happiness, and that she was reaching into the unknown and all the dangers in that age of sudden love. It was the simple impulse of an undisciplined heart. It seemed but a dream. Bess' practical outlook on the future was that Cole had a rendezvous with destiny. *So easily made are the plans of the hopeful,* she was thinking, *but who can control youth's dream of Utopia?*

"He's a smart kid with a good career ahead of him," Bess said carefully, "but he's not old enough as yet to have wisdom. He runs as wild and free as a dog loose from his chain. Yet, I do have the feeling that some day he will be the man his father is." There was hope in her voice, a wanting to be a protagonist in uniting this young couple. "Be careful," she added. "Only time, experience, and knowledge will make him the man you believe him to be," *and I want him to be,* she thought. She did not give much credence to some of the normal, boyish things he said and did, but sensed that beneath the surface was an inherent depth. She hoped that sooner or later he would come to a realization. *His Ma should have boxed his ears,* she was thinking, yet believed that he would change for the better with time...*it's in the bloodline.*

"I love him, Bess," Cole exclaimed, her eyes bright with hope, and no longer trying to hide her emotions from her only friend. Her face glowed when she said, "I love him more than my own life. It's something I can't help or control. I would give my life for him." Brant was her dream. She was caught in an entirely new web of emotions, a feeling so strong she could not resist it. She believed Brant to be the answer to a prayer and adored him with all her heart. All other thoughts were cast aside.

Bess was genuinely impressed by her sincerity. "There, there now," she said soothingly, as though she were talking to a child. She was hearing the innocent words of believing, of not knowing the impossibility of pure and perfect joy or that often the difference between dreams and reality can be as opposite as night and day. *Such a beautiful girl,* she thought. Cole's smile was so gentle that it turned her heart, yet she was uneasy about the depth of Cole's moods, and her inability to understand or control her emotional surges. She was witnessing the purity, sincerity, and rarity of unconditional love. She felt that Cole was destined to love tenderly, deeply, even to the extreme of devastation unless that love was returned in equal depth. That, young and inexperienced, she loved to the degree of what could become tragic because she loved so completely. She refrained from saying the things that were uppermost in her mind and her expression was one of desire to help. She was looking at a child on the verge of womanhood. *We get a lot of lumps and bruises when we enter the real world,* she was thinking, well knowing how love blindly overlooks faults. Turning to Cole she said, "Don't push too hard, honey. Take it one step at a time:" She had learned much in her forty years of life. *Poor child,* she was thinking, *she's letting emotion govern her logic.*

Bess placed a gentle hand on Cole's shoulder, realizing that her entire life centered on one person. She sure doesn't need this after all she's been through, *Bess thought. "It's a beautiful emotion, honey, but if you don't hope for too much you won't be that disappointed," she said gently as she shook her head, not hearing the small kitchen radio playing a love song. She was trying to lessen the intensity of Cole's moods and feelings. "A riverboat can be a romantic setting, so be careful," she warned, knowing that many that smile today, cry tomorrow—that love often develops into a storm of one kind or another. A sweet sadness touched her as she looked at Cole.* She's as hopeful as a child waiting for apple pie, *she thought. Bess had learned that the heart can be an unreliable counselor and that Cole was a born romantic. Young love is the most giving, and Cole was too engrossed* with dreams to consider reality. Cole's need moved something deep within her.

Bess understood. Being away from home, school, friends, and church, Cole had a deep need for companionship, to be close to someone, and since becoming an orphan she had longed for kindness in a cold, hard world in depression. It was stirred by a deep hungering for affection and the timeless cry of a lonely heart. These were powerful forces in her life and Bess was aware of Cole's eagerness for a friend. It was a hungering that she could well understand. Only with her did Cole feel a sincere tie. They had bonded as though knowing each other for a lifetime.

Bess was discovering that Cole loved in an almost pathological way, that her instinct was not strong enough to overpower her yearning. Her loneliness was deafening her to the knowledge and experience of others and she knew no way of combating loneliness. Cole had the feeling of being solitary in the face of the world. There was no home or family to which she could return. Bess poured another cup of coffee for the two of them and in her look was the thought; *You don't have the slightest idea what you're in for. Nothing is as simple as it seems.*

Cole took a sip of coffee from her private cup that was decorated with flowers in an arabesque fashion. She was proud of the fancy cup. A salesman had given it to her as a premium when Bess purchased his brand of coffee. He had been affected by Cole's withdrawn manner and had told Bess that he hoped the pretty cup would cheer her. It was a cup from which she sometimes drank happiness and sometimes grief. Bess knew the hurt of a lonely feeling deep down inside. A fleeting pain touched her face. It was the memorized pain of a cheating heart, of years of loneliness and uncertainty. She had been trapped in a terribly mistaken marriage.

This is what she could not forget as she stood withdrawn into memories; not only on her mind, but in her heart. Old pains were reawakened.

She would never forget the few written words of farewell; "I have hurt you deeply, and have destroyed myself." She shook her head slowly. Never to be forgotten were the years of heartache in the sorrow of regret. She remembered it as clearly as if it had just happened. Her depth of love had been great and she was now a victim of a deep hurt. A picture was destroyed, a memory crushed. She suffered from the love-hurt syndrome that culminates in the sorrow and regret of farewell. She had the realization that love can be the most illusive of all hopes and dreams; The one thing that cannot be compelled and mingled with the hurt was sadness. His farewell letter was a cry for forgiveness. She had learned that one may forgive, but that one can never forget, that it isn't merely one more moment in time, and that words can be more crippling than the physical. What a fool she had been. Or, would the correct words be, what an innocent she had been. Even the most sincere apology can not erase the memories, the loss and the hurt, or the pain of exclusion from being cast aside with no one to turn to in the ruination of a dream. It was a pain like no other. She stood for a moment in thought, the memories flooding back, crippling the beauty, purity, and trust of her life and marriage. She had learned that memory can be Heaven and memory can be Hell. She had not had a normal childhood in a single-parent home, and unfortunately had not had a normal marriage. He had been an ideal husband in every way except faithfulness. He was a man blind to the gift of blessing in a true and pure marriage. Though she had the strength to bear it, nothing could erase what had happened. If only this river could flow backward and flood out the past, *she thought. Her gray eyes softened in thought of what could have been. There had been nothing to fill the empty place inside, nothing to erase a loneliness so deep she thought she would die from it. He had gone like a will-o'-the-wisp, a man whose love had changed like sunshine to rain. If only the memories could be different, not the torture of retrospect.*

"Do you love her more than you love me?" she had asked.

"Oh, so much more," he had said in honesty. Those four simple words said it all. There was nothing more to be said.

Like a riverboat, Bess had learned to cross a bridge when she went under it. She was a survivor—too strong a person to be destroyed by grief and agony.

In afterthought she was thankful that she wasn't one of the many married couples in an impossible marriage who were stuck with each other for life. What is it? *she wondered. Is it destiny? What is the right word? Some called it fate. That she was the victim of the love-hate syndrome and the tears of memory, well knowing the unhappiness of loneliness. She sat in silence, gazing at the warm stove in thought of a lost face from the past, knowing the heartache and sorrow of having her man stolen by another woman, which only a woman who had experienced the pain could understand. She would have preferred to look back on something beautiful, but there wasn't anything beautiful. The poetry of her life had turned to prose.*

"We often use our senses instead of our brain," she said to Cole, pushing aside old memories and trying to smile. "I know, honey, I've been there." *Who knows all there is to know?* she wondered. *Who can see beyond the years? It's all in the cards.* Her eyes were soft with memory and the number of regrets in each life. So many lives are interchangeable. They had never really gotten to know each other. How difficult it was to forget the unwanted things in memories. The wound heals, but the scar remains forever. She had the feeling of guilt that she had failed in vital ways.

When Bess had mentioned Brant's mother, it troubled Cole. Now there were two formidable barriers to overcome. She had not met the captain's wife, but could hear the concern in Bess' voice.

Bess saw that beyond Cole's soft, smoky eyes, in a beautiful face, there was a sensing of trouble, and she could not help but wonder if Cole was running from loneliness blindly into pain. Was this an extension of healing?' Could it be a normal, simple step in searching for a way through life, or an obscure doom?" She well remembered that certainty in her own life that had fallen apart. She looked down at her hands, work-worn from daily labor. The smell of coffee, pastries, and food that Bess was cooking filled the cabin air. Bess kept her hair tied back when working over the stove.

Cole had been gazing out over the river with a sense of promise of what lay ahead and suddenly said, "Just think of having a life that is comfortable and safe and secure and with love." Her voice was soft and dreamy. "What's life without someone to have and to hold and to love? Just think of that. That's all there is in the world that means anything. What could be more precious? Brant and I will have such a love." Her natural feeling had built the poetical illusion of the perfect love. She could not imagine anything otherwise.

Her stepmother had often said to her, "Hold fast to your dreams," and in her mind and feelings there was no doubting, no denial—only an overpowering realization. A dozen beautiful images flowed through her mind. She became more excited with hope as she went on. Her face was flushed with excitement as she stood aglow in the warmth and beauty of that vision. She was swept by a current stronger than she had ever dreamed. Everything in her future seemed resolved. Just the thought of it being otherwise made her feel aching and empty. It was the natural yearning of a needy heart, and it seemed so little for which to hope. This belief was everything in life to her. It was the hope that gave her the courage to go on alone in the world. She was pouring out her feelings to Bess, as she had to no other, and was brightened with the relief and joy of unburdening. She refused to believe that things could be different than her need and longing, and she dreamed of the time, place, and circumstances that would fulfill her hopes and prayers. In so doing she casually dismissed the thought of Brant's mother, not realizing that often reality does not quite measure up to dreams. She had been accustomed to love and tenderness.

Hard knocks had taught Bess to be practical. She was realizing that she had better have a serious meeting of the minds with Cole before the situation got out of hand. "You make it all seem so easy," she said with a smile, thinking no one could be as perfect as her visions. Her voice was calming.

Childishly and sentimentally, Cole imagined herself with these things. She imagined herself as a bride, beautiful in white, and Brant handsome beyond description. She tried to visualize what their married life would be like in his world. Bess was realizing that longing had overpowered Cole's reasoning, that her hunger for a home and love dominated her thinking. She had not thought of marriage failure. She had been raised to believe that marriage was an idyllic state, that this was the majesty of love and life, and, above all, she did not realize the strength of family influence: Brant's family. Cole had no knowledge of the imperfections in love. Her hopes were built on wishing and dreaming.

An overflowing heart conquered her mind. She did not use the words, but she believed that truth, purity, and beauty went with love. It was the answer to her dream of womanhood. Her teacher had spoken of poetry as the gift of love from one to another. If only she was to receive this precious gift. Bess was realizing that Cole was a romantic, almost mystical—that to her all the important things in life were simple, an escape into a dream world. She chuckled and raised her eyes Heavenward at youth's translucent vision of the perfect, loving heart. "You've got your head in the stars and you're blinded by the light," Bess said with a touch of humor. Then she saw Cole withdraw and was sorry she had made the ill-chosen comment. To refute her, someone would have to prove to her that there are no intangibles such as the magic of love, the soul, and the spirit. What is the force that moves the heart? *she wondered. To say that it is chemistry would have no meaning to her. Bess chuckled silently.* With her it's not in the blood, but in the soul.

Noticing Cole's change of expression Bess altered her delivery. "There's a simple old saying that's true," she continued with a soft smile. "'You have to know someone longer to understand them better.' Hard words, maybe," Bess admitted, "but words that have to be looked at." She was aware of the hard, cold fact of the captain's attitude because of his wife, and how this affected Brant in his relationship with Cole.

"You just don't understand," Cole said. There was a sudden hurt in her voice. She did not know how to convince Bess that she was not concerned, that everything was fine; those tender, private thoughts of what might be. She didn't want sympathy, she wanted love.

"Oh, I understand real well, honey," she answered calmly. "I know what it is to go through a living hell and have no one there to turn to." She was thinking of years past and gone, of being the victim of a wild emotion devoid of reality. She was well aware of the long and lonely years of waiting for the right one. But what youth ever thinks about tomorrow, and tomorrow, and tomorrow. She was well aware that no one has ever known of all the incomplete lives, and that only a rare few would care. Something inside her had been broken with the vanishing of a dream, and she wished that she could absorb some of Cole's pain. She did not mean to argue about it, as Cole had become a meaningful part of her life, and she could not help but think that Brant was a very lucky young man.

Has Cole's love become an addiction? Bess wondered. *An illusion that love is immortal? She fails to sense the meaning of proportion. There is a danger of her losing herself in such a love, a relationship between unequal partners. One person was doing all the giving, and the other person doing all the taking, and she has so much to offer. Her heart's as soft as this bread dough.*

"I just know how I feel," Cole said stubbornly, unable to hide a heart in turmoil. "It has to be love. It just has to be when it hurts so much inside." Her eyes sparkled. What more could she say. To her, it was a feeling too meaningful to express in words.

"Yes, your heart," Bess admitted, "but what about his?" she questioned, emphasizing the frailty and complexity of human behavior. Never would she admit how anxious and subtly protective she had become because of Cole. In her heart she was worried. She had taken Cole into her life and was becoming more aware of Cole's inability to cope with the thought of losing Brant. Hers was an unnatural reaction bordering on terror. *Every dream has a price,* Bess was thinking as she waited for Cole to continue. She could see the need and longing in her eyes.

Cole dreamed that all young men of good family hoped for honor, justice, love, truth, and decency. She clung to the importance of these thoughts that had become vistas of her future, to a love that grew stronger and stronger, because it could not be controlled. No other thought occupied her mind. She felt safe and secure under the illusion, unable to center her mind on anything other than the thought of Brant. Growing *up as an only child on a remote farm with no brothers or cousins had given her little knowledge of men. She was unaware of the complexities surrounding her. "I've dreamed of wearing a beautiful white wedding gown and kissing Brant over a multi-tiered wedding cake," she exclaimed. Brant would be the most magnificent wedding gift she could ever hope for. It was a beautiful dream. She turned to Bess. "If that isn't love, what is it?" she asked, her face aglow. "Someone to care that I am alive."*

"You're in love with someone you think you know," Bess cautioned. "There are all kinds of men along this river. A woman's lucky if she finds a man who's even half as good as she believes him to be." Bess had learned that happiness is often accompanied by grief and that Cole was possessed by love.

"I know that he comes from a fine Christian. family," Cole answered loyally, wishing Bess had not said such things. She disliked the interference and imagined that Bess did not understand. She was not interested in logic in regard to her feelings, believing that in longing and yearning she had found the sweetest mystery of life, unaware of the fatal things that come and go. "His people are highly respected in their community," Cole remarked. Bess saw the exaggerated respect for those Cole considered of genteel family. Cincinnati was the only major city in which Cole had been. She had never dined in a luxurious restaurant, shopped in an elegant boutique, or ridden in a limousine. She had told Bess that she dreamed of seeing Tallula Bankhead and John Barrymore on the stage, and Bess was secretly making plans for Cole's eighteenth birthday. She was going to buy her a new dress. Blue. Her favorite color. Bess glanced at her own dress, which was plain and of neutral color.

"You didn't have a chance from the start," Bess said gently. "Brant's too perfect for you to resist. Any man that perfect on the outside can't possibly be that perfect on the inside. No one who has ever lived is all they think they are, or would like to be." Her voice was quiet and kindly.

Cole smiled in spite of herself and said, "Oh, I'll admit there are some things I don't understand about him." Many things puzzled her very much—the confusion of dreams confronting reality, of how odd life can be with its strange turns and twists. "But, my stepmother told me that the deepest human need is for sincere love, and..." Want and need had made her voice lift.

"Honey," Bess interrupted in a stubborn disapproval, "Brant doesn't even understand himself, or what's formed his own thinking. It's a constant brainwashing from home that starts when they're children and it's the women that command these forces. Good or bad, most men are the product of a woman's mould from the womb; a remark here, a comment there, a hint, a command, a subtle suggestion, and undercurrent of innuendo, a bribe, a threat, or tears. Some men never get weaned. Brant's thinking has been preplanned and he doesn't think about it. In growing up, Brant was deprived of the daily influence of a caring father." Bess raised her eyebrows again. "Has he said anything about his mother? Most women will excuse conduct in their sons that they would never tolerate in their husband and Mrs. Mitchell commands the captain in family matters," she added, feeling uncomfortable discussing the Mitchell family. She occupied herself by watering the bright colored potted plants in the kitchen window. *She refuses to believe that something so precious is beyond her reach, her expectations,* Bess was thinking as she watched Cole intently.

Cole looked at her questioningly, wondering if she was teasing. "No. Brant's never once mentioned her, but I'm hoping the captain will be a fair man." She became thoughtful.

"There's more to people than what's fair," Bess answered simply. She laughed, and her laughter was sincere and honest. "I met her one time and we'd better change the subject! I don't want to get involved in the captain's family affairs. She came only one time that I know of to the boat, because something that is offensive to her is the commonplace, the unrefined, of lesser degree, although she tries not to show it, and you are of the dirty, the sweaty, and the poor. I recall a portion of the conversation I overheard when she visited the boat. It was when Brant first came aboard the boat to work and she was reminding the captain of a girl in which Brant had shown interest, a girl with an unknown family and background. She was concerned with the genetic factors in such a family tree. Those are matters of vital importance to Brant's mother and her people. They dwell on them. It's in their breeding and it's in Brant's, whether he knows it or not, and it could effect his decision toward you. The door was shut against that girl. Don't ever forget one very important thing: Brant was raised by his mother. His first name is her maiden name." To Bess, the milieu in which Cole was raised was as different from Brant's as the river is to the ocean.

Cole's impatience deepened, but she remained silent. She would never have confessed to Bess how uneasy she was about her plans for the future with Brant, because all of her plans and dreams through childhood had terminated in grief. It was as if her life had been a study in pain.

"Be careful," Bess warned. "They love you for a while, but many men are not honored by a secret as precious as yours." She saw Cole's face change from positive to defensive. The words hurt and Cole pushed them aside. She did not want to hide her feelings, she wanted to be honest.

"It's no secret," she said serenely. "Brant knows how I feel. Sometimes to think of the captain's son being serious enough about me to marry me is frightening." She had become more aware of her own self, her own personality. She was sensitive about her limitations. Always there was the sense of inadequacy, the feeling of the ephemeral, yet her voice had all the hopefulness of a heart yearning for love. It was the youthful enchantment of visions.

"He asked you to marry him?" Bess asked with suspicion. It was the intuitive spontaneity of her reasoning. Cole's head was down. She remained staring at the kitchen table, not wanting to meet Bess' eyes, her face clouded. It was less painful that way.

"Well, no," Cole said, hesitating. "Not exactly. Not yet, that is, but I know he loves me. He has proven that."

"How?" Bess shot back. It seemed unbelievable to her that Cole did not know he was simply thoughtless. She lacked the instinctive knowledge more reliable than reasoning. "In what way does he love you?" she asked as she peeled potatoes, thinking, *There's a big difference between desire and true-heart love.*

Cole did not answer. To her it was simple and natural. She thought of it as providentially intended. She was so proud because she thought he loved her and shy because of her pride. Why should that love not last? Since he was her life, it was natural he would marry her. The thought that he loved her gave her strength and conviction. She must believe they could win the captain's blessing, blanking out his mother. She was sure of it.

The two women were silent, listening to the music. A soprano voice was singing, "I'm always chasing rainbows...." *She's prime for the dreams and folly of youth,* Bess was thinking, hoping that it would turn out otherwise.

Bess did not have to change the station on the radio, the stations changed themselves. A newscaster was announcing the prospect of war. As the boat passed each town it seemed that each had their own radio station that drowned out that of the previous town. On the little Atwater-Kent battery radio were the songs that were the constant reminder of thoughts wistful with the longing of other nights.

"What would there be without love?" Cole asked, listening to the music and staring into the face of the cook, battling her emotions and doubts. She so much wanted the blessing of Bess. "The most important thing in the world is having somebody to be close to, to love," Cole said. It was necessary that she believe Brant was hers. "He's so wonderful in every way," Cole added. There was a stirring thrill that accompanied her words. It was her image of Heaven on earth.

Bess was silent for a long time, busy at the stove. "Did he tell you he loved you?" she asked. Again there was no answer, only a glance. Her concern for Cole returned. "Down here on the river they call it lust. A man takes, a woman gives. You should know if he loves you. You shouldn't have to wonder, and I can tell you're wondering." Bess hated herself for questioning Cole's dream, but was more in dread of what another heartbreak would do to her. Cole had become the daughter she had always wanted. She was sincere in her concern.

Cole listened to the words, but her mind was numb to reason. She had closed her mind because she was afraid to take the words seriously. She dared not. She did not know the fear of loving too much. All she had ever known was losing. This time she must not lose, she must make her own way in life.

"Oh, he loves me," Cole exclaimed, her head up with pride. "I know he loves me. It's not my imagination. I know how he feels," she added, subconsciously believing the heart to be stronger than reason. So many things were going through her mind.

Yet, her mind was uneasy, not certain that it was her heart that wanted him to love her as deeply as she loved him. She did not realize that no two people are equal in their capacity to love. She did not know that they also vary in inner strength. She had not acquired a depth of perception, and was delighted with everything she saw and experienced.

"I'll tell you what. I'll bet he hasn't asked you to marry him. I'll even bet that he doesn't tell you that he loves you," Bess said, shaking her head in doubt. Cole looked away.

I've seen them look at each other, Bess recalled. *To him, love is a toy. To her, loving him is her life. She's like a child with a tear in her eyes, wondering, kissing a dream. She may just as well reach out there and try to grab a handful of that river fog.* Her heart ached for this child.

"I don't believe that," Cole said, shaking her head, defiant with loyalty. She could only follow her heart.

Her stepmother had told her, "The most sustaining thing in life is the glory of a dream."

The cook looked intently at a seventeen-year-old girl whose brief insight was too unprofound for the subject of marriage in view of the obstacles. She would never forget hearing her cry in her sleep. *Another dream beyond the hope of reality,* Bess thought.

"It's different with Brant," Cole said ungraciously. "He wants me. He truly does. He told me so." Anxiety had made her cross.

"Sure he does," Bess answered, stirring a pot on the stove.

"It's going to be different with Brant and me," Cole reasoned, saying words that had the beat of hope in them.

"Sure," Bess nodded, her face flushed from cooking. "Opposites attract. The captain's handsome son and the beautiful chambermaid winning over the witch of a mother. It's an old fairy tale, honey." There's a human story in everyone you talk to, she was thinking. Bess knew that the very soul of this child was as innocent as the dawn of a new day, never doubting the purity of her heart. *He's her entire world,* Bess was thinking.

Cole felt the blood rush to her face. "I believe we're only opposites at present," she said, frowning, misunderstanding. "Tell me this, then. What is more wonderful than a home and a family? We'll have a house of our own on the river where we can just sit and talk during the evenings," she said, trying to visualize the life she hoped to live. "To have somebody to care whether you live or die. Just think of that, Bess. To have a home of your very own," she emphasized, blind with love and wonder; she had the innocence and trust of a sheltered life. She craved the joy of belonging. She could half close her eyes and see their home. She had forgotten her yearning to be a teacher. "If that's not to be for me then where do I belong?" Bess was moved by the simplicity of her words, her need and hunger for love, knowing that it came from no other source than the purity of her heart.

"I'll merely say this," Bess answered. "You deserve the very best to share it with, and Brant Mitchell has a lot of growing up to do to become that man, though he is out of good stock." Cole shook her head again in disagreement, but remained thoughtful.

"Few women can be completely sure of a man's love," Bess said, breaking a silence, thinking back on all the forgotten roads she had traveled, of all the human mistakes, and the most poignant of all memories: the regret of what might have been. She knew that regret constitutes a major degree in the College Of Hard Knocks. Experience had taught her that memory is a powerful mixture of sweetness, sadness, good times, and bad times, and hard knocks bring the realization that even true love can be a gamble because no one completely knows another in the swirl of emotions.

Cole shook her head again. "I'll believe that when he tells me that he doesn't love me, or that his mother comes first." Concerning Brant there had been more than a hint of mistrust in Bess' voice.

"I'm sure about our love," Cole said stiffly. "I know!"

Bess nodded. "Good. But I say be careful. There's too much involved." *Her dreams are those of a child,* she thought. *She is on the eternal search for nonexistent perfection.*

"There's no way you can know that," Cole replied. Then she gave a half smile back. She knew that she had a friend. Bess' friendship and love had been her only warmth and help. Her words were as comforting as her apple pie. She was deeply appreciative, and looked at Bess with gratitude and affection.

"I'm sorry, Bess," Cole said gratefully, and laid her small hand on the hardened hand of the cook. She was so thankful to have Bess. "I know you mean well. You've been more than kind to me. You've been the only friend I have, and I appreciate your help, but you just don't seem to understand.

"No? Well, maybe not. We'll see." Cole had touched her heart with what she said. The years had left their mark on Bess, and deepened her patience and understanding.

They stood in friendly silence with separate thoughts, the smell of fresh coffee heavy in the air. Bess mashed the potatoes with an unnecessary vigor, and the French wire whip fluffed the potatoes into a froth. She was making something for the captain. It interested her that the captain placed the least importance on food of anyone on the boat. The thin sound of the small radio was playing a mountain ballad.

"The captain's a good man," Bess finally said. "Tell Brant to talk to his father about you two. Maybe, just maybe, he'll bend, fight the home forces." Cole looked away. "Be careful, Cole, no matter who they are, or what they promise."

Cole flushed, breathing in deeply. "Oh, no!" she exclaimed in gentle rebuke. "It isn't like that. He isn't that way. He isn't that selfish." Brant was her first and only love, and she saw nothing but good in him.

Bess turned to her gravely and looked straight into her eyes. "Well, has he or hasn't he?" she asked with gentleness, knowing. Cole lowered her eyes, her face scarlet, but did not answer. She could not lie to Bess. She and Bess had a kind of affinity. It was a deep comfort to have another woman on board, *and it was not in her nature to deliberately hurt anyone she liked. Her simple honesty and truth were the richness of her. She shook her head, no.*

"He may try to get as far as your cabin," Bess said softly, "but I'll bet he hasn't gotten as far as the suggestion of marriage. Again, I say, be careful."

Cole remained silent, looking through the window at the river. The window glass was old and had flaws in it, causing imperfections in the scene.

"Young men are interested in one thing," Bess said.

"That sounds so crude." Cole's voice had a strain in it. She had invested all her life and being in this love, and during this summer she moved as if she were in a spell. There was no past, only this summer. Awake or asleep, her dreams were of their marriage.

"I'm telling the cold truth," Bess said simply, not going into details. "The truth is often unpleasant and unwanted. When I was young it seemed that everyone thought they had the best advice in the world. I can only tell you what I've learned the hard way." *One brief summer, she thought, and Cole's life will never be the same. A golden vision is upon the girl.*

"One way or the other, Brant will be in my dreams forever," Cole said in a whisper, looking directly into Bess' eyes. "I love him enough for both of us," she added simply. She was proud of it and made shy by it. Bess was appalled by the poetry.

"Men don't want to think about the things they do that tear at your heart," Bess said testily.

"He's different." Cole pressed her lips together.

"If you believe that, honey, you believe in miracles." The cook grimaced at the dramatics of Cole and made a scoffing sound, realizing that it was impossible for Cole to rise above her dreams. *She's just another plaything in the hands of an excited boy,* she thought.

The heat in the low ceiling kitchen, under the deck, was almost intolerable. The kitchen was almost as hot as the engine room. There seemed to be no breeze at all. The day was nearly done, with only a rim of light over the hills and ridges. The feeling of night was already in the air. The ridges poked up to where they met the night. A hot, hazy dusk had fallen. The crew would soon be in for supper.

The cheap sounding radio played many of the bitter songs of want, longing, love, and hope that could have come from the daily life of these people. They were songs of feeling, and of the soul: the simple music of the heart.

"Trouble goes with people," Bess said to Cole, "and people go with the songs of trouble." The songs were so true and lonely it was as if they had lived a thousand years. Bess continued to hum as she worked.

The sun went behind the ridges and the summer gloaming fell over the quiet valley. A blanket of silvery mist was creeping over the river. The mist lay thin among the canyons as the shadows lengthened and deepened, and the evening air changed suddenly, cooling, bringing a sweeter scent. The pulse of the summer was on the river.

"If Brant isn't the right one, you'll find another soon enough," Bess warned Cole, thinking of the steadiness of young Hank and his looks at Cole. He had told Bess that Cole's face looked as soft as the fuzz on a peach. "You'll have a family and..."

"No!" Cole gave an involuntary cry. "And only pretend to love? How can I put someone out of my life who is unforgettable in every way?" Just the thought of having a son that would not look like Brant was deadening. Her childlike sincerity effected Bess.

"You're young," Bess warned, realizing that she was not yet of age. "You have time to give Brant more thought. Or, more time," she added. "He's a fine young man who hasn't fully matured." Another short silence followed. *No one knows all that is in another's heart,* she mused, believing that no one in the world knows for certain, in all respects, who they are marrying. There was no guarantee.

"There will always be only one man for me," Cole said after a pause in thought. "You're wasting your breath. I want Brant and I'll fight in every way I know how to get him. If I can't have him, what's the use of going on?" She did not believe Bess concerning Brant, yet she stared out at the brown river with a cold fear. It was as if she had two minds, but only one of them wanted to believe Bess.

An anger was burning within Bess as she looked at Cole. "Nothing can ever be explained." She was doubtful of young Brant Mitchell, but only to a degree. "We all have to learn the hard way," she said tartly. She pushed her glasses up on the top of her head. "I learned that early and it isn't easy. I've been down that road." In regard to some matters it was best not to go back in time to a composite of pain, sorrow, and regret. In Cole she saw a past part of herself.

Cole's eyes were dark with hurt. She said, "I already know. When I was growing up on the farm my stepmother told me, 'Love is like the full warmth of the sun,' and she knew."

"Love is a matter of chance," Bess said flatly, knowing it was a waste of words. "Had you met a different man, at a different time, under different circumstances, you would be telling me a different story. Time and location change lives." Bess was looking at a girl who knew so little of the people on a busy river in a beautiful valley. "At present, Brant Mitchell is too young and too self-centered to be tamed by a seventeen-year-old girl," she continued. "Listen to what the crew says about him."

Cole's face flushed with resentment but she bowed her head and did not answer. She was fond of Bess and did not want to argue with her, but she did not believe her. She would never discuss Brant with the crew. She was crying. These were not the tears of joy of a day before.

Bess looked down at Cole's brooding eyes and realized she had a burden she had not expected. She had not planned to be the victim of an affectionate heart. She was certain that Cole was looking into a future, unknowingly, that was of sorrow and grief, and a wave of affection and tenderness went over her. Experience had made her capable of feeling the pain of another. "Well, maybe you're right, honey. I sure hope so."

What little night breeze there was only carried the heat into the kitchen. Bess put her arm around Cole's shoulders and drew her head to her breast. "Don't ever be ashamed to cry, honey. It opens the heart. A thousand years from now this river will be here, but what's important to you now is what happens to you this summer."

"I wish I were home," Cole sobbed. How often she thought of home.

"You're new with us," Bess said, "and I've learned not to pry, but I feel that we have become very close." Her curiosity was natural, but not idle. "Do you have family to talk to?" she asked, wanting her to speak. She knew she had to, and wanted to be of help. *I wonder who this girl really is?* she was thinking.

For the first time Cole spoke quietly to Bess of the bittersweet memory of yearning, of her childhood with her parents, and then foster parents. She thought of the home in which she had lived—warm, real, and untouched. She had been raised in the insular security of a devout farm family, and believed that without love there was only loss and darkness. It was a relief to unburden on Bess. Not all memories are happy ones. So much had changed. She had loved her small town life. It took her back again to memories dear that seemed so very long ago.

Some memories were painful and some memories were bliss.

"I stopped grieving for my natural parents when I realized how loving and wonderful my foster parents were. My stepmother's heart was as sweet as her garden." She was sincerely grateful for her foster parents. As an orphaned child she had rocked to and fro in her bed calling, "Mother, mother!" She had a loneliness and longing for affection.

It was a child's cry for love and her stepmother had tenderly called in turn, "I am here, child, I am here." And every day that she went to school her stepmother stood in the doorway of their farm home and waved until she was out of sight. Yet, she often lovingly said, "Never forget the woman who bore you. There is no greater love than that of a mother for her child." Those loving childhood days lingered in Cole's mind as cherished memories, pushing aside the tragic days with fantasy, depending upon the strength of illusion. Now there was no one to feel sad because of her pain; no one to hug her, calm her, or love her. Bess understood the lost feeling of not having a single blood kin to turn to, causing the unrealized fear of living beyond the moment. She knew that the breaking of old ties is not easy. Cole's need turned her heart.

Bess looked at Cole carefully. "Who were your people?" she spoke softly, sensing that Cole Hamilton was not a tatterdemalion of the river shanties, the lower level. *Interesting,* she thought, *curious.*

"I don't know a great deal about them," Cole answered. "They died before I really got to know them. They were from Scotland and were killed in an automobile accident here. I was young and don't remember much except the brutal shock of not having them all of a sudden. They're buried at Forest Lawn. I don't get to go often to see my real folks, but once in a while I just feel that I have to go. It is some sort of urge I get. I take flowers. My mother loved flowers. She loved all living things." Cole would keep these memories always, that portion of a young life spent in dreams. When she thought of her parents a feeling of warmth came to her—the warmth of a mother's love. She spoke of her parents with a look Bess would never forget. Cole's memories came in short sentences. "I'm so thankful for the photographs I have." She could only live those days again in memory and was filled with a bittersweet nostalgia. She paused in thought, somehow knowing that a parent's love lasts for all eternity, and that part of her heart was buried at Forest Lawn. "Gone." A pause. It was said more to herself. "You know what that means? Gone?" Another pause. "Never to be seen again, never to be heard again, never to be held again. Gone." Her stepmother had told her that her parents were not only kind. Good, and loving, but of quality and refinement. Bess well understood the traumatic effect of a child's loss and what it meant for their loved ones to be gone.

"I've heard of mean step-folks," Cole continued, "but I loved my stepparents because they loved me and I knew it. I grew up with love. I had never been far off the farm except to church, school, or a Grange dance. I had no kin to visit." She had never been away from home, and was so thrilled when her step-folks took her to visit Abraham Lincoln's birth place, south of Louisville, and then to the beautiful bluegrass meadowland and the race horse plantations near Lexington. "My step-folks' people pioneered Kentucky long before it became a commonwealth and then they moved from the Mammoth Cave area of the Highland Rim up to the Ohio Valley, where I was raised.

Bess said nothing, hoping this conversation would help Cole forget Brant. "My stepparents are both dead now," Cole added. "They died within one summer of each other. My Daddy went first and we lost the farm. My stepfather didn't even have a fine suit to be buried in. A neighboring farmer gave us one. I'll never forget the sound of my stepmother's voice crying at his grave. It broke her heart. Yet, through it all she had maintained a natural dignity.

Cole needed to talk and hurried on with her story as Bess sat listening, understanding. "I graduated from high school this past spring. I skipped a grade." She said this with bashful pride, remembering her school days of laughter and joking with all of her friends, with never a serious care in the world. "Our valley was so beautiful," she said, pausing in memory. Her life had been made up of simple things that were lovingly given. She had lost all the safety, security, and comfort of a loving home and was shocked into the hard and realistic outside world, her school days gone forever. *Only a recipient can realize the depth of such pain,* Bess thought, knowing.

She had left those precious school days behind, and would never see them again. Since the loss of her parents, stepparents, home, and friends she felt lost, yet had always gained strength and courage to go on when she heard her stepmother singing, "In the sweet by and by we will meet on that beautiful shore."

"My folks had their heart set on me going to college and I wanted to go, too," she continued. "Daddy had been working himself to death on the farm to make it possible." Their tobacco crop enjoyed the rich soil of a bottomland farm. "I was going to attend the University of Kentucky," she was proud to say. "I was going to major in history and English literature. Maybe teach, I hoped, or be a librarian." The county library had been her refuge. "I'll never forget the words of my English teacher, Miss Goode. She said, 'There are only twenty seven letters in the alphabet and all of us have access to them, yet few of us use them to the best of our ability.'" Cole loved school. She had spent most of her lunch money on books.

Cole had been an excellent student, passing the college entrance exams easily. She had wanted to go on to college, believing that learning would place her on a level with those in the books she had read and so admired. She wanted to learn and do and be. She had grown up realizing the difference between her farm life and that of the banker's daughter, having been treated to her condescension for the partially educated—her arrogance and distain.

"When my folks died, I had no one and had nothing." When her stepmother became ill Cole was the nurse, the cook, the housekeeper, and school girl all in one. She worked the garden, milked the cow, and took care of the chickens. "In the winter I did everything I could to keep their feet warm so they'd keep on laying eggs for my mother," she said. When Cole moved among the farm animals they considered her as one of them, the old cow following her around like a puppy dog. She was fifteen years old and alone, with no one else to help her or care. "We had no telephone and I had to walk a half mile every day down Turkey Foot Road to pick up the mail at our rural route box," she added. She did this for a year, then her stepmother died. During her childhood she had experienced one deep loss after another. Then she experienced the shocking realization of being alone in the world during the bitter days of depression in the '30s.

"I don't know what I would have done without the help of Father Chuck's wonderful wife," Cole continued. "She was a Godsend. She took things into her hands. Then the County Welfare Bureau helped me. A man from the Welfare Bureau is a friend of Mr. Whitfield and he got me this job." Bess well knew what it was to be alone.

"I'll talk to old T.J. Whitfield himself," the Welfare Director said to Cole, "and see what can be done. That boat job could be a passage to your future." The director of the Bureau told Mr. Whitfield that, if possible, they would try to locate Cole's relatives in Scotland through the Anglican Church.

Thomas John Whitfield owned the Whitfield Reliant Coal Co. He had grown up in a poverty-stricken family and went only to the fourth grade in school. The church donated a pushcart to him as a boy and he trudged the streets of Covington, Kentucky, pushing the cart and selling kindling and coal. In time he created an industrial empire. He owned the coal mines in Reed, West Virginia, he owned the fleet of riverboats that transported the coal from the mines to the industrial centers along the Ohio and Kenawha River, and he owned the fleet of trucks to carry the coal from the distribution yards to the great industries. Yet, though he ruled an empire, he had never forgotten his boyhood poverty and want.

"I was lucky to get work of any kind," Cole said, looking into the understanding face of Bess. "Lots of families are homeless and hungry. Lots of men are jobless and walking the streets." The Great Depression was causing human depression. Newspapers told of men committing suicide because they could not support their families. The instinct of self-preservation kept others going.

"And a lot of women are walking the streets," Bess said grimly. At first Cole did not understand, then she reddened. "I'd rather die than do that," she said with a shudder. "I would kill myself before I would do that."

"More than one woman has said that." Bess spoke flatly. "There are girls your age on the streets who are older than I am."

"But I love this valley," Cole continued, dismissing the horror of such a subject from her mind. Her heart forever turned toward the valley of the Ohio when in need; her refuge. "I can't help it." The only roots she had ever known were in this earth, along this river. She had never been away from home, so she loved everything about this river: the hills, the valleys, the little towns, the bright days, meeting new people, the soft nights. Now that she had been able to see the seven states that bound Kentucky she was happy and ready to settle down. "I love this valley," she repeated. There was almost a song in her voice. To her the river was poetic and mysterious. Yet, she loved Brant even more. "My mother always said, 'Love is where the heart is,' and she would know."

Cole had wanted to see and experience life, color, and motion in the world beyond the hills of their farm, but now she was afraid of the world she was seeing. All the world she had known before was from the top of the hill rising behind their farm, from one horizon to the other where the hills met the sky. Her imagination was wrapped up in the wonder of what lay beyond those hills, and had stirred her to dream of other places, other people, and other experiences; a place to find herself. Now she felt certain that she had found herself in the love she believed Brant had for her—that her need had been fulfilled. Brant was the final part of her valley.

This valley and this river were the other part of Cole's being. She considered everything in the valley her own, including Brant, and the very special glory of loving, forgetting all else. Her mind had searched for the utmost boundaries of the earth with a fierce inward hunger. Now, because of Brant, she felt a friendly warmth in the valley and the hills. Yet, when she looked at the endless expanse of the sky she felt a troubling loneliness, and her eyes would invariably return to the hills. A dome that covered the entire world had become too vast for her peace of mind. "And to think someone said the hills and valleys were monotonous," Cole said to Bess.

"Only a rare few women can stay home and enjoy it," Bess answered. "I like this knocking around." It was the urge to get away from something, which showed in her voice, and the urge to be someplace else, which showed in her eyes; a wanderlust. She had learned that the happiest days are the first to flee. Bess had a wide, full mouth, and was attractive when she smiled. She smiled at Cole.

"The hills of home," Cole sighed, thinking. *Treasured memories.*

"You won't last long among these riverboat people," Bess said sadly, "and I'm sorry. You're too poetic and dramatic." As Bess looked deeply into the sensitive face she realized the depth of Cole's fear of being alone. Cole tried to laugh it off.

"Maybe I do dream more than I should, but my mother said that dreams do come true, so why shouldn't mine concerning Brant?" Cole's daydreams outnumbered those in sleep. Bess considered Cole on the verge of another life, in the frightening stage of no longer being a child and not yet a grown-up. There was no going back. Bess shook her head in resignation, then smiled fondly at Cole, well knowing the full depth of emotion in a first love, and thinking: *She grasps at hope like a child reaching. for candy with both hands; the confusion of need overwhelming pride.*

Looking at the clock on the bulkhead Bess rose in a hurry.

"Come on, honey," she said, "we've got all this mess to clean up. The men will be here soon." She was in fear that sooner or later Cole might discover a lesser Brant Mitchell and the thought saddened her. In her was a natural bond of warmth and sympathy. *Even some older men often find it difficult to understand women,* she thought, *so how can she expect understanding from a carefree boy?* Her only hope was that Brant would outgrow his boyish ways. She could not help but like the young man.

In looking at Cole, Bess softened, saying, "But, you're right, honey. It's good that dreams are larger than reality. That's the fuel that keeps the love boat going. They help achieve the improbable." She was aware that Cole was enchanted with the magic of the moment. *Blind young love reaches immeasurable heights,* Bess was thinking, and a boy Brant's age, footloose and fancy-free, has *a lot of growing up to do. Cole's depth of love is blinding her to other possibilities.* Bess' personal experience had taught her that between the simplicities of youth and the complexities of adulthood is that delicate period of awakening, often precarious; remembering well the young love that had turned her life to ashes. It caused pain that time can never heal, of darkness from which there is no escape. The memory of those years of hurt had not been easy to push aside, causing her to become a very private person.

Bess put her arm around Cole. "But, to be honest, honey, I'll have to admit that the hardest to get are worth the most." She nudged Cole and grinned. "That is, if you get them," she added, and moved back to the stove.

Cole did not answer. Her feelings were deeper than words, a natural feeling deeper than her understanding. She had a deep feeling of the need to be wanted, to be loved, to belong, to have a home of her own where she could create memories. She did not want to look back, she only wanted to look forward.

Then Cole spoke quietly, as if to herself. "I have nothing." The expression in her eyes, the look on her face, and the sound of her simple words devastated Bess.

Bess stood at the galley stove in thought; the thought that many think of a riverboat as a romantic life of adventure and excitement, little realizing the hardship, work, and despair that come with it. She had much more of her thoughts to tell Cole, but she held back.

Cole had been studying Bess intently. "Thank you kindly for your friendship, Bess," she said softly. There was no doubting the depth of sincerity and need. There had been too many lonely days and empty nights for both of them. They were listening to a song on the old Atwater-Kent battery radio, the beautiful old song, "Remember Me When I Am Far Away," that could not help but stir the memory. Bess' soft smile said more than words. She was thinking that in each of us is the eternal search for a perfection that is so wanted and needed, and stood in wonder *at the poetic beauty of this river valley to so effect the heart and soul.* Down this river of human stories many lives have penned *the theme, hoping for a happy ending,* she realized.

Chain walked past the galley window, and Bess' smile deepened with meaning.

Chapter Four

Steaming along the Ohio River the next day the Storm Bird passed the most fascinating of all riverboats. The boat that had a special meaning for Cole as well as many river-town people. The owner of this boat said, "My boat takes the minor keys in people's lives and changes them to major keys." The boat was Billy Bryant's Showboat, a medicine show afloat, heading down the river for their performances at Cincinnati. From river town to river town it went, bringing entertainment. Overhead the blue sky was fluffed with white clouds and the ripples of the river were shining in the beauty of the morning sun over the river breaks.

Cole watched the Showboat approach. The sun was glinting on her dark hair, bright in the early sunshine. She was standing on deck in front of the kitchen door. Down the river the *Showboat* floated, dreamlike, trailing its smoke in the summer sound of merriment and joy as the sun blazed down upon the river. There was no mistaking which boat was passing when Billy Bryant's *Showboat* steamed by. The river mist had cleared and it became a beautiful golden day with the sun shining in her eyes. The wind was warm and moderate, and carried the unmatched sound of the full-throated whistle of the showboat. The showgirls on Billy's boat thought of it as romantic.

Cole was watching the crew of the *Storm Bird,* her lovely dark hair blowing against her face. As usual, every deckhand aboard the boat, to the last man, was on deck with a hat in hand, waving, whooping, and hollering, expressing their honest appreciation. Sunlight on the water made it look almost like butter on toast.

It was deVoss' first encounter with the show girls. "Hot damn!" he exclaimed, his thoughts and plans made obvious by his expression as he visually devoured the pretty girls on board Billy Bryant's brightly colored boat.

"Look at deVoss," Bess said to Cole, pointing. "He's a jackass on parade." The girls had prompted his meaningful, gap-toothed leer.

In reaction to the crew, the girls on the *Showboat,* having a flair for the fanciful and an equal urge for innocent teasing, got satisfaction in acting their part in this river drama. They laughed at the *Storm Bird* crew, frolicked, kicked up their heals, and showed a shapely leg. This prologue gave the crew a preview that perked up their desire to visit the Showboat next time they were in town. To the ladies aboard Billy's boat this was not a matter of guile, but one of sound advertising—free advertising along the river. This was one of many things to break the monotony.

"Old Billy is not only a grand showman, he is practical, a realist," Bess said, standing in the kitchen doorway.

The *Storm Bird* was only fifty feet from Billy's boat, and Chain was taking pictures of the flamboyant Billy and his girls. He would have been more satisfied if his pictures could have portrayed the heavy vibration of power in the thrust of the driving pistons of the giant paddlewheel, and the tons of water it stirred into motion. He believed that each of his photographs should tell a story pictorially. This was reality, dealing with the imagery of abstractions was meaningless. In regards to his capability in creative photography, it was as if some mysterious gene had given him a natural instinct for what was right. Photography contained all that was necessary to his salvation and he did not particularly care whether he made money from it or not. To him, photography was a refinement of reality, yet, something more valid than uncontrolled emotion.

Engineer Claude Schneider was laughing at Brant Mitchell as he stood on deck near the galley, a few paces from Cole. He was certain that the young river pilot was not waving and shouting out of respect for the Showboat captain, but that the pretty girls affected him this way.

Cole was subdued. She watched the laughing, waving showgirls and remained expressionless, her face frozen; all the expression in her eyes was fire. The stories of Brant's recklessness ashore seemed almost a revenge to hurt her. He was not, apparently, familiar with humility.

Cole stood silent and watchful as she leaned against the bulkhead, the light breeze pressing her plain dress against her. DeVoss did not fail to notice this. He was more interested in Cole than in the showgirls. Brant's laughter had drawn her attention and a hot wave swept over her. The expression on his face made her ache inside, but caused deVoss to smile widely, his eyes squinting in the sun.

As Bess studied the expression on Cole's face, it caused her to remember the words of Captain Mitchell when Cole had come aboard the boat. "Bess," he had said, "the girl comes to us from the County Welfare Agency and I'm placing her in your charge. The counselor at the agency said that it's important for you to know that her stepmother, prior to her death, suffered from a mental illness pertaining to depression, and it had a noticeable effect on Cole."

Brant Mitchell turned to Cole, looked into her eyes, and turned away. He had seen a deep shadow in them and preferred the sight of the laughing girls. She remained motionless, brooding, as though unable to escape a fear. At times her over-sensitivity increased her loneliness and irritated him.

When he heard old Billy toot, even the reserved Captain Mitchell found reason to come out of the pilothouse and be on the bridge to watch the showboat. He smiled and waved, and gave Captain Billy a grand salute on the steam whistle. No other boat on the river got this attention.

Cole glanced at Chain and wondered. Instinctively she knew that she could trust him. He was the only one of the deckhands with whom she could relax. Gossip had it among the crew that Chain had once been an actor on a showboat. No one was certain about him. Many stories were told. He permitted no questions about himself, but Cole noticed that he did not act like the rest of the crew as he photographed the Showboat and she moved to the deck railing where he was adjusting his camera. She appreciated his mature reserve.

A few minutes later the Showboat was out of sight, and Cole and Chain were watching their stern wheeler push through the heavy warmth of a late-afternoon haze along the deep beauty of the rolling hollows and hills. The boat was moving slowly, passing a small Kentucky farm with snake fencing. She knew that it represented a century of struggle. The fields were pocked with mole hills and a lone brindle cow stood by a five-barred gate, waiting to get into the barn to be milked. She could relate to their dread of a severe winter.

Chain sniffed the air. "Getting close to a mill town," he said.

A dog barked. "That sounds like my old dog, Jack," Cole said. "He was a brindled Plott Hound. My Daddy got him to keep the possums and raccoons out of the chicken yard and no one ever came on the property without Jack telling us we had a visitor." Whenever she heard a dog bark she thought of her dog. "You know, a dog can look at a person and sense whether they're good or evil." Chain nodded in agreement. With no brothers or sisters to keep her company, her dog was her playmate and when she did her homework her dog layed at her feet with his head on her shoe as a pillow. "He was the greatest friend I had," she said, turning to Chain, eyes wide. "Do you know what that means? The greatest friend?" He nodded, thinking of Bess.

In the late afternoon, half of the boat was in hot shade, the other half in glaring sunshine, the boat's shadow rippling in the warm water. Chain glanced at the shore. Soon it would be fall. The riverboat men, like farmers, measured time by the seasons. The landscape had altered radically, from rolling meadowland and farmland to steep hillside farms. Here, the silence had not been destroyed. The hills seemed high enough to imprison the wind. The greatness of the omnifarious trees was impressive to Cole; cool, sweeping spreads; scene after scene as they rounded bend after bend, seeing beauty after beauty. Such scenes were exhilarating.

"Why is it that when you study a giant tree it makes you feel so good?" she asked, changing the subject, enjoying the sight of a cluster of Kentucky coffee trees. The day's heat was building and there was little breeze. She could see a tree touching the clouds.

"I don't know," Chain answered, "but it sure does." One of the trees had been lightning-struck. He loved to watch Cole's changing expressions and was a man that never talked when he should be listening.

"And then again, it can make you feel sad," Cole said. Chain smiled. His smile was infectious.

"I know," he replied in a soft, southern drawl. There was nothing more to say. He was grateful for the opportunity to talk to her, to try to be of help to her.

"My father planted a peach tree the day I was born," she said, "and now it is huge. I miss our peach tree and the fall harvest. My favorite, though, has always been our magnolia tree in bloom." Chain nodded in encouragement. He enjoyed his rare few moments with her. His eyes were calm as he listened.

"I was born in October," she continued, thinking back as the deep quiet of a hot river day fell upon them, "and my foster father said, 'You're one of the favored people,' and October has been my favorite time of the year. I read that October is a passion, a dream, a vision. I wonder if that's true? My stepmother said it's the most beautiful month in the Ohio Valley." Chain smiled at her again. When thinking of her home, Cole's voice had become as soft as the summer day. 'The man month' she called it."

Large shoreline trees almost hid a small village they were passing. In the wooded banks Cole and Chain could hear the sound of songbirds, and occasionally catch a glimpse of unfrightened deer—their soft eyes sensitive and alert as they moved their long ears like radio antennas. They had come to the river at dusk to drink and were heavy with the dampness of the heady scent of musk. The timid fawns were nose-nudging the rumps of the does.

"Your folks live in the hills?" Chain asked, interested to know more about her. His father had migrated from the hills of Scotland at the turn of the century.

"No," she answered. "They're dead." She had remembered the few years with her parents all of her life, the picture as vivid as on the day the tragedy happened on that unforgettable day. "I'll never forget my father's pride in what he called his Commonwealth of Kentucky. He loved the meadowlands with all his heart. My father was from England and, like you, my mother carries the blood of the highland Scots," she continued with a soft smile. She carried a tucked away hurt that she had never been able to know them or her ancestry. Losing the material things was a temporary blow, but the loss of her loved ones was deep and lasting.

"My mother and father were killed in an automobile accident," she continued. "I was their only child." Her parents had immigrated from Scotland and she had no relatives in the United States. The Anglican Church had taken her in until a home could be found for her. She would never forget the last look she had of her parents.

"I was just old enough to remember the crushed bodies of my parents when they were carried into the house." It was a sight never to be forgotten. Another thing had remained vivid in her mind. The next day, a little boy from across the road found her father's spectacles and returned them to the neighbor with whom she was staying. She remembered staring at the spectacles without her father in them. "My mother was dead when they brought them into the house. I was holding my daddy's hand when he died. He knew I was there. He was trying to tell me something." She only had those last few moments with a life that was gone. All she had left were the death certificates.

Chain merely nodded in order to let her continue. He wanted to know all he could about her past.

"When you're seventeen and graduated and have no folks, you're on your own," Cole said in answer to his nod. "There is no county aid or state aid anymore." She had no money and no place to go. Her step-folks had been loving, but they had left no money. They had rented the farm on which they lived and worked it on shares. "One of my jobs was helping tend the kitchen garden. We had beautiful vegetables. I also helped care for our cow." She remembered how their cow had died. "Just laid down and died with a look in her eyes that no one could help her with." And she remembered how horrified she had been when their neighbor had to shoot his horse because he was too old to work. "Our neighbor didn't have the money to feed and doctor him properly, and he was suffering," she said, glancing at Chain. "That made me worried about my dog, Jack, but my stepfather told me: ' Don't worry about Jack. He more than earns his board and keep by keeping the varmints out of the chicken-house.'" Chain understood, realizing her need to talk and that her destiny would always lay along this river.

"After my stepfather died my stepmother became ill and I helped her as much as I could. What little money they had saved went to pay for doctors." She was remembering the time her stepmother emptied the piggy-bank to pay the insurance agent.

"Remember us always," her stepmother had said.

"I will never forget you," Cole answered. She could hear their voices.

She would never forget the bitter cold of that last winter. Just getting the ten cords of firewood in from the barn to heat the house that winter had been staggering. It had been so cold that her only joy was in the crystal world of Jack Frost on the window pane. Through her eyes Chain remembered such scenes.

"Then my stepmother died and I had to leave the farm," Cole continued. "I miss the gardening a lot." From her expression Chain sensed that she needed a garden to make her life complete. Flowers altered her; she blossomed.

"I miss the garden so much, but do you know what I miss terribly?" And she laughed a little embarrassed laugh, turning away from Chain. "I miss my dog, Jack, and I miss hearing the birds sing." To her, the simple things were the good things in life. "Jack went to church one Sunday," she said and laughed fully. The laugh was rich and spontaneous. It warmed Chain's heart to hear it. "He must have trailed us to church, and the service was almost half over when he arrived, but he strolled down the center aisle as sincere as the most devout communicant. Father Chuck was wonderful. He went right on with the service as though everything was normal, and it was, because Jack settled down quietly for the rest of the service." She shrugged. "I had no way of keeping him, or taking care of him when my folks died, so I had to give him to a farm neighbor. I raised him from a puppy and he was my best friend. He's in a good home, but I miss him terribly." She had had much experience with unhappiness and that all things change. So much stood out in the maze of her memory. "I remember the time my mother told me, 'When you look into the eyes of a dog you see true devotion,' and she was right, as usual."

Chain was well aware that it is not easy to shut the door on the past. Hardship and want had left their stamp on him. He nodded. "My parents told me that these mountains reminded them of the highlands of Scotland," he said, changing the subject, smiling. Cole smiled in return. She was fascinated when quietly, in an off-hand manner, he spoke of the many foreign places he had seen. He spoke as a dreamer with a restless heart, his life was a balance of memories and regrets.

The long, slow miles of their river progress were never boring to her. She loved the ever-changing view and the diversion. At one point the shore was flat and low, with farmland coming down to the river. She smiled to see a young couple, happy and laughing, in their canoe. Recent rains had broadened the river and increased the force of the flow. In the distance was a beautiful green hill that reminded her of the lush green hill behind their home. She smiled in memory as the movement of the boat stirred the clean mountain air in the valley of natural splendor. She could smell the warm wind off the river as she listened to the shimmering murmur of the water. The contours of the distant hills rolled like the flowing river, and in the bottoms were thickets of weeping willow.

Chapter Five

As Cole entered the engine room the coal heavers on the Storm Bird sweated, chief engineer Claude Schneider swore, and the bucket planks of the sternwheeler pushed, with dogged determination, the coal barges along the unhurried miles. Claude laughingly referred to the engine room as, "The old folks home," but Cole did not understand why as all of the firemen were young men. Each time she brought their coffee Claude delighted in telling her over and over the story of one of the old scows upon which he had worked. He loved to tell tall tales, and his stories of smugglers on the river years ago were better than a movie. Simmering in the engine room heat he mopped his face.

"I was just five minutes from coming on board when the boilers blew," he said dramatically, "destroying the engine room and most of the boat, killin' three men and injuring four." He rattled on a mile a minute. Then he would sing his favorite classic, "Take me out to the ball game, take me out with the crowd. Buy me some peanuts and crackerjacks, I don't care if I never get back. Root, root, root for the home team, if they lose it's a shame, for it's one, two, three strike him out at the old ball game." There was a touch of blarney in his voice. Cole's eyes widened with fear as she looked at the boilers. To her, the engine room was overpowering with heat and danger; to the crew, the engine room was the heart of the boat. Her eyes smarted from the coal smoke. The air seemed so heavy.

The coal heavers stared at the belching furnace and hissing boilers, watched the quivering needle on the gauge of the pressure valve, and looked at each other with boredom. The heat was intense. *But to Cole, Claude's hell-bent-for-leather stories were legendary. Some of his greatest stories were about his hound dogs. The deck crew laughingly joked about the sweating stokers, saying they smelled as sweet as a mountain goat. The stokers had spent so much time in an engine room that they no longer smelled the smoke and cinders. Claude shook with laughter as Cole returned to the deck. These were seasoned men who knew their work.*

It was a bright day of light wind and fresh air. The sun had made the water a pool of gold. As Captain Mitchell came on deck to relieve Brant in the pilothouse, he saw Cole talking to his son. He raised his eyebrows. *Time to put a stop to that,* he thought. Sun glared on the captain's face like fire. For weeks he had been aware of their closeness and had been watching, determining the extent of their relationship. Brant, sensing his father's suspicions, had been avoiding Cole for several days and the anxiety was shattering to her. She had not permitted him to her cabin since that one visit and he had been keeping out of her way on the boat. He did not want a showdown with his father. In desperation, she had sought him out.

From the intense expression on her face, it was evident to the captain that the conversation between Cole and his son was not casual, certainly not relaxed, unquestionably not that of officer to chambermaid. *Time for me to pull a tight rein on that young man,* he thought to himself, *or his mother will have me where the hair is short.* He was also watching the river traffic as his boat maneuvered in the mid-river channel. There was something certain about him, as if he did not doubt himself or his method of handling a situation. He glanced up at the flagstaff. He always flew the American flag aboard his boat. He proudly referred to it as "Old Glory in the wind." He had served in World War I.

Captain Mitchell was not a fancy man in dress or manner. He had a job to do and saw that the job was done simply, methodically, and without dramatics. He was a quiet man, and he had the capability of knowing and understanding his crew—especially his son. He was a mustang, having worked his way up from the deck. He was seasoned in knowledge and experience from years on the river in the various stages of advancement. This permitted him to seem relaxed without seeming ineffectual.

The morning sun passed behind a cloud, creating patterns of light and shadow and dissolving blends of glare and shade. The river was a wide, flat strip the color of silt. Again the bells in the engine room sounded as they slowed for the narrows. Captain Mitchell was watching a tanker that was moving past, his profile was sharp beneath the old peaked cap.

As the captain approached, Cole saw him, turned away from Brant, and came out of the pilothouse. Captain Mitchell noticed the startled look of apprehension, guilt, and fear. Her face had a look of shame, the same way that it shames a child to be stared at. She nodded to him and gave a half smile as she moved past. He watched her walking down the deck, then entered the wheelhouse, deciding not to comment until later. He would settle the matter before they reached home port in Cincinnati.

By noon the heat had clamped down on the Ohio Valley. The full force of the sun struck like a blow, its fierceness accentuated by the lack of a breeze.

It was the kind of day that saps the energy. The deckhands were moving slowly in the heat. The sun was blazing hot on their backs. Shark ambled down the deck, whistling. He was never in tune. Cole was listlessly watching an airplane. It was a novelty to her. She had not seen many airplanes. Then her attention was diverted to another activity. The boat was passing a government dredge boat, dredging the entry to a creek, and she watched them work until they were out of sight—anything to occupy her mind. *What is the captain telling Brant?* she wondered as she watched a flatboat entering a shallow tributary, noticing that a river mouth always widened where it flows into another river. She had heard that the Indians called this contributory, "The water of loneliness." She believed she was sailing those waters. The sun had cooked the mist on the river.

"You got that right, Glemp," Shark agreed, wiping sweat. "It's hotter than blue blazes." The sun was burning down on them like fire, the open deck seeming as hot as the engine room with the bulkheads and the deck radiating the heat. Tiny gnats flitted in the humid air.

Glemp pointed. "There's a cave back in under them rocks that I played in as a kid. We were pirates." Cole smiled, imagining Glemp shuffling his feet like a little schoolboy.

She was thankful the humid Ohio Valley hadn't reached one hundred degrees. As summer had advanced, she noticed that everything seemed to be seared. The heat seemed to be trapped by an inversion layer. The sluggish wind had the ripe smell of midsummer. It was almost a cider odor. The breeze brought with it the smell of hot land. Even the cattle in the river-bottom pastures were moving more slowly. The heat enveloped the valley—oppressive and enervating—making everyone testy. The fields and hills were gold, bronze, and copper under a cobalt sky and an occasional white cloud. The sun turned the leaves yellow green. Every detail of the landscape stood out as clear to her as her feelings; it reflected her feelings.

"There were boats on this river long before trains hauled freight!" Glemp shouted in an argument with deVoss. Pretending preoccupation with a mooring line, deVoss was watching Cole. When Brant walked past she watched him go into his cabin, her cheeks burning with a color not put there by the river sun, and deVoss observed it. She turned her attention to the deckhands who were making bets as to whether the Cincinnati Reds would win their ballgame that afternoon. A light breeze carried the scent of river water. They were passing a small, dilapidated stern-wheel steamer secured to moss covered pilings. deVoss called it a "rag-boat."

The river men were steeped in sun, tanned and burned, their skin leathery. The deckhand, Glemp, was stretched out on deck as contented as a hog in the sun. Down wind of the kitchen they could smell the fresh coffee. Engineer Claulde Schneider walked past. He was a man who liked to sing under his breath, and often wheezed as he walked, so it made an unusual combination of sounds. He was singing a tuneless mumble to the words, "'I'm a rambling wreck from Georgia Tech, and a hell of an engineer.'" The sky was so clear it seemed to have thickness. The sun glinting from the rugged stone bluffs had no mercy on them. Claude was wearing a hickory shirt and cord pants, reaching high on his shins, showing the tops of his Brogans. Cole smiled at his appearance. The crew was always plainly dressed, but clean. The captain would not tolerate a rag-tag crew.

"There's not a place on this boat where you won't sweat," Claude said to Cole, wiping his face, then taking off his shirt. "In a few hours we'll be at the locks at Gallipolis," he added, pointing up river. She nodded. The sun had made the deck so hot that Cole was sitting on an apple box in the shade of the bulkhead.

"When they dedicated that new dam there," Claude continued, "part of the festivities included a steamboat race and we entered the race in this old tub. And you know what? We won! You talk about stokers sweatin' and old Claude bellerin', I put that steam gauge up to where she nearly popped a boiler. Everyone was laughin' at the sight of our old steamboat churning past Gallipolis, but we were the ones that were laughin' when we crossed the finish line. She was the pride and boast of officers and men." Cole glanced at the pilothouse, proud to think of Brant navigating such a boat. *His profile is so handsome,* she thought. *Yet, a little arrogant, too,* she admitted. She was impressed when Captain Mitchell permitted Brant to navigate the locks. Before the days when dams and locks controlled the water level, boat progress was chancy because of sand bars and snags. She had been even more proud when their boat had set another record. They had taken twenty-eight loaded barges on pool water down the Kanawha River and the Ohio River to Cincinnati. "The largest tow in history," the newspaper article had read. She had the article in her scrapbook.

From the pilothouse Captain Mitchell called to Glemp to secure a barge he observed working loose. The sun, through the pilothouse window, glared on his face like a flame. With an expert eye, Glemp knew the distance between the boat and the barge timberhead, and with split second timing judged, aimed, and threw the flaccid coil of line. He handled a line like it was part of himself. It reached out into the air like a slithering snake unwinding for the strike. The large eye splice loop at the end of the line sailed through the air like a lariat and dropped deftly over the bollard. Glemp called for a mate to come ahead with the donkey winch and warp the barge into position. "It's hot as Hades, man!" he puffed, wiping sweat, watching a keelboat drift by.

The sweat glistened on the huge muscles of Glemp's sun-tanned skin as he worked, his powerful hands flaking down a line. He was chewing Juicy Fruit gum. "This is my favorite gum," he told Cole, and offered her some. He kicked at a hawser that lay in long bites along the port side of the deck, then grinned at her. He had an uncomplicated grin that was infectious. He was hot and getting hotter.

To Cole, watching this handling of lines was a marvel of men and motion. The brown of these men was deeper than her light tan. They were as brown as a hide from the tanners. They wore a hide that was of nature's tannery. It was a tanned hide from sun and wind, the cut of ice, and of blown snow and frosted air. For many, this boat was their only home. Cole turned her eyes and lowered her head when she noticed deVoss staring at her, sensing the evil intention. Looking down at the deck she saw his shadow. The shadow was misshapen and frightening. It was so long it touched her and made her shiver in the heat of the sun.

"Why don't you take off your shirt, too!" deVoss said to her. He was breathing heavily. Cole moved from his side of the deck to the other side. Some of the men laughed, embarrassed, as she walked away, trying not to notice the baiting. The blood was racing in her veins. A far better blood than deVoss knew as he stared at her in arrogance—half-hatred, half lust. Glemp stood with his arms dangling and rough hands half closed, embarrassed. "Cool it, deVoss," he said, "and quit parading around like a stuffed shirt!" Cole hurried on, turning her head in the other direction, ashamed to be included in deVoss' humor. She moved to where she saw Chain on the foredeck. Sun was staring him in the face.

"It would be best for you to leave that girl alone," Glemp told deVoss, though he knew that advice to deVoss was a waste of time. "You're an ornery cuss and you'd better take up on your tongue."

"Best for me, my twat," deVoss answered with a forced smirk, as he stared at Cole in the distance, his thoughts obvious. He was no fool, however, and knew when to back down. He knew how and when to play his cards. To tempt Glemp's sucker punch would be inviting the undertaker.

Glemp spat. "Okay, It's your funeral," he warned, then walked away. No matter what a shipmate did to help him deVoss was never able to say the simple words, "Thank you," or "I'm sorry."

Far to the right, on the Kentucky shore, Cole heard the whistle of a train making its way toward the mountain passes. The train had laid a layer of smoke through the valley.

The sound of a train had always been a thrill to her, usually a thrill that had been edged with an unreasoned sadness. To her the sound was poetic. When she heard a train she often thought of one of the ballads she sang, "Casey Jones." As she listened to the moan of the train she subconsciously moved closer to the railing. The mountains came into the valley in the shape of a bowl. The long, drawn-out whistle of the train drifted across the valley, touching her heart as it always did. Chain could sense her feelings. In the distance the sound was a moaning, almost as if it came from within her. She thought of the brief time she had with her real parents—how her father held her hand as they watched the train sweep past, waving with the other hand at the engineer of the Outward Bound as he waved back. She recalled the loving kindness of her foster parents.

"Someday, when we get a good cash crop, I'm going to buy you a train for us to play with," her stepfather had said, remembering a favorite toy—a windup train—that he had cherished because it had been given to him by his father. His stepfather had destroyed it on purpose and the beautiful toy piano that grandma had given his sister for Christmas to learn her scales. His stepfather had gotten rid of it on the sly, then tried to bully them into changing their last name from that of their father. For that reason he had sworn an oath that he would never change the name of his stepdaughter: Cole Hamilton.

Cole was remembering, also, the help of the kindly Anglican priest. He had come to get her at the train station when she came to the church, orphaned. *Yes,* she recalled, *trains had played an emotional part in my life.*

At times, as she watched, she could see the train winding through the hills. It looked like a long worm with one eye. She wondered if the people on the train would care about the problems of the people on the boat. As she stood there, her eyes traveled along the deck to the wheelhouse, then to the cabins. Chain knew that her thoughts were on Brant. He was angered by the talk among the crew, much of it filthy. They had not had a songfest for many nights. It was his belief that if Cole married Brant, the boy could eventually kill her love for him. "I wish there was a better answer," he said to himself.

Because of the look in her eyes, Chain asked: "Do you like that sound? The sound of a train?" Her black hair moved in the breeze. He was touched by her shyness. His question was intended to get her talking again.

"I sure do." Cole nodded. "It's sad for some reason, but I like it." She thought for a moment. "I've never taken a trip on a train, but I feel that the train has always been a part of us, sort of belonging to us like a beautiful day," and she pointed to the hills. "Those are the hills of my people over there." Just the sight of it, the tranquility, lifted her spirits. She turned slowly and looked carefully at him. "Do you understand the feeling?"

"I sure do," he replied, using her words, so happy that she was talking again. They were passing Greenup, Kentucky.

"Jesse Stuart lives and does his writing in those hills," she said. "I like that book of his called, *Beyond Dark Hills.* I can really understand that." An argument among the crew caused Cole to glance in their direction. Arguments made her uneasy.

During the course of docking, or other boat activities, the river men joked and made bets. A full round of cursing came from a deckhand who had missed his throw of the line, losing his bet and having to struggle with a tangled, wet line much to the delight of the men who had made their throw successfully and won the money.

Durand deVoss had just lost such a bet, and amid the jeers and glee of the men, his red-faced humiliation in front of Cole was acute. He was not a popular crew member and it was no secret to the crew that he cared for no man; He moved among them with the wariness of a coyote. He was incapable of being a friend or having a friend. He lacked the inner trait. Something was missing inside. He would not confide in anyone. He was like a lone dog, howling in the night. The crew was also uneasy concerning his unnatural attention to Cole.

In the network of their rivers deVoss did not like the Ohio River and Cincinnati. "German Town!" he scorned. "To a Creole," he added, looking at Glemp with assumed haughtiness, "all Americans are lower class! And down in New Orleans," he emphasized, "all Kaintucks are considered scum!" DeVoss did not like the Storm Bird. "A rotten garbage scow!" he called it. He claimed the boat to be ugly and repellent. "The French know how to build good ships," he stated. He only mentioned the aristocracy of his Creole ancestry to belittle others. No one knew much of his past. He considered his shipmates fools and held them in contempt, referring to them as "Shallow water sailors."

"Bull!" Glemp shouted in anger, "and I'd like to rub your nose in it! The Ohio's the riverboat-building capitol of our nation!" he bellowed. "When you sail the Ohio you're no back-water sailor! The Ohio's a thousand miles long and washes six states." Pointing to the river he said, "That water starts in Pennsylvania and feeds the mighty Miss. There are places on this river that are full four fathom," he bragged, "and the Ohio has as many islands as the Virgin. From where we ship you can go by water to any place in the world." DeVoss shrugged, but wisely remained silent. He always felt like an outsider and preferred it that way. Sweat darkened his shirt at the armpits.

Why deVoss sailed the Ohio River the crew did not know, could only guess, and did not care. DeVoss had never talked of his past and their interest in him was shallow. Gossip was that deVoss had killed a man in New Orleans, but this was said of every man who changed rivers and would not speak of his past. They would not be surprised if deVoss killed Brant because of Cole. Some bet that he would. Each man in the crew believed that there are those who had a reward on his head, yet there was not a "rat-catcher" on board.

DeVoss glared at Cole as if her presence had caused his shame. She turned and went to her cabin, her thoughts on the captain's son, remembering Brant's words: "I stood full watches and piloted the big sternwheelers when I wasn't tall enough to see over the brass and polished wood of the huge spoke helm. I had to stand on an apple box to see out of the pilothouse windows." He had spent many hours in the pilothouse, listening to adventure stories told in casual reference of the river, its people, and the great boats.

Captain Mitchell had said: "This river will flow through all eternity."

A few hours later the work caught up in the kitchen. Cole and Bess were standing at the boat rail, looking toward the shore. Warm sunshine shown on the tan river and the humid air was moved by a welcome breeze. The breeze was running ahead of the ripples on the water. The sky was so clear it made everything look bigger. Across the water the distant hills were sparkling with golden light and the valley was bathed in sunshine.

"Of all the watches," Cole was saying, "I like best the hour before dawn. It's like you're just about to open a door and look out on the whole world." Bess gave a little laugh.

They were at the Scioto River where it enters the Ohio at Portsmouth, flowing down from Chillicothe, Circleville and Columbus. Smoke was pouring from the industries of Portsmouth, turning their sky a different color than the farm sky, their sky hanging like a low ceiling. Cole and Bess heard the change of shift whistle at a mill or factory. During the depression the mills had been running a short week, most of the time only a single shift. A large billboard sign read, "Chew Mail pouch, Treat yourself to the best." The long sweep of a bend lay before them.

They rounded a bend and it gave them a commanding view of the terrain ahead. Around the bend the boat entered a wide, flat expanse, forming a small valley. It looked like a green valley imprisoned within a cup of hills. They were in under the lee of the northern bank of the bend and could feel the push of the current on the tow of barges. Cows were grazing in the lush pasture of a river-bottom flatland farm where the rail fences were carefully maintained.

As a short burst of steam broke from the pipe and a fluted whistle echoed across the river Bess pointed to a large white home with gray shutters and trim, crowning a crag bluff on the Ohio side of the river. Steam spurted from the pipe a second time as the whistle sounded. Each boat had its own sound. The noise was deafening. As they were passing the house Bess said, "That's where the Mitchell's live. That's their home, when they're home." Cole turned to look at the labyrinthine structure with particular interest as Bess watched her reaction closely. Hedges formed a beautiful green wall.

The stately house overlooking the river was on a bluff that formed a cuesta aflame with wild rhododendrons. The house was shaded by giant chestnut trees that were silhouetted against the skyline. Cole could see a row of tall Lombardy poplar trees leaning away from the wind, flittering in silver and acting as a wind-break. Tall, clipped hedges marked the estate boundaries, giving it privacy. Even at this distance she saw their hillside orchard heavy with fruit. A flock of starlings took off and filled a solitary tree in the distance. Brant's mother had dictated the layout of the formal garden, which stood on a promontory, jutting out above the river where conifers formed a shadowed line. The river looked butter-yellow in the sun.

The unusual sense of spaciousness of this house, with the rounded bay windows, impressed Cole. *This is where Brant was raised,* she thought, considering it natural for him to be raised in such elegance. Oh, how she longed to have a home of her own and children. It was an enormous one-hundred-year-old two-and-a-half story building with a beautiful fountain in the front yard. The house seemed too large now that Brant's mother lived in it with only his younger brother and sister. Because of that, Mrs. Mitchell felt it wise for an elderly aunt to move in to keep her company. Captain Mitchell and Brant were away most of the time. Cole leaned against the railing as she stared at the house, wondering about the history of such an estate that sat with particular grace on a sun-flooded rise.

The cupola of the Mitchell home, with its arched windows, the top border being of stained glass, rose above a slate roof. The gutters and downspouts were made of copper. The black iron weathervane was a prancing horse and the lightning rod stood tall as a spear. Cole wondered which room had been Brant's. She knew that he must have been a handsome child and longed to know everything about his childhood. She could sense the influence the chatelaine of this house would have on a son. There was a fancy railing that went around the widow's walk that looked out over the river and the valley. She counted the chimneys. Very few homes in her neighborhood, if any, had three chimneys—not even the banker's house.

"That was Mrs. Mitchell's grandfather's house," Bess said. "He had it built. It was erected before the Civil War." The historic structure was very imposing and situated on an impressive setting. The fine furnishings and hangings had been imported from England, France, Germany, and Italy. "It's been their family home for three generations," Bess added. Then she pointed. "Watch! Mrs. Mitchell will be up there on the lookout. She knows our schedule as well as we do and she waits for the whistle back around the bend. It is his big hello to her. Her people went from Shanty Irish to Lace *Curtain Irish." She handed the binoculars to Cole as she listened in silence, uneasy, wishing she would talk more of Brant and less of his mother.*

"Brant's mother didn't want him to go on the river," Bess continued. "She wanted her oldest son home with her, managing the estate. She thought it was his family duty. She's proud of the fact that she is often mistaken for his older sister, or so she imagines. I don't think she'll ever forgive Captain Mitchell completely for taking Brant on the river. She fought against it for a long time, then finally gave in, grudgingly. She wanted him to go to college. She believes that anyone without a degree from college is of the subset." Bess looked carefully at Cole. "She has his personal life well planned," she said suggestively, "and still has a strong influence over him. It's an affront to her when a child disobeys her wishes and tolerance isn't her strongest trait. If you stand up to Mrs. Mitchell, or don't go along with Mrs. Mitchell, you flat out don't go along. Don't ever get on the wrong side of Her Highness," Bess warned. "If he disobeys her she'll have him taken out of her will." No dances had been held at the big house since Brant left school and went on the river. Mrs. Mitchell loved her son fiercely as the son she demanded he be. "He's never known what it is to do without or be without," Bess added.

Cole stood in awe of the forcefulness of Mrs. Mitchell. She impressed Cole as the epitome of style and elegance. Cole remained thoughtful, silent. Each day brought new concerns. She did not know how to work through the situation. She could only hope.

"See, Mrs. Mitchell?" Bess said, pointing. "Beautiful, isn't she in those expensive clothes?" Bess had heard that when going out of an evening she wore dangerously tight dresses. "As soon as she hears the whistle she comes out on the porch to wave." Along the wide porch, where Mrs. Mitchell stood before a carved, stained-glass door, tall windows looked out on the river. From this promontory she could see far up and down the Ohio River. She knew the particular sound of her husband's boat's whistle. Studying her carefully Cole had the feeling that Mrs. Mitchell, a strikingly beautiful woman, was looking directly at her at the secret hope she carried within her, thinking that she had no right to such a hope. In that cold beauty she saw a startling resemblance to Brant. She was tall, Cole noticed, and held her head high, as if looking down on her. Her gracious manner seeming to float on the surface. She was a woman desperate to look young, but could not act young because it was not in her nature. Through his binoculars the Captain noticed that his wife had dyed her hair again, a glamorous auburn; It was the vainglory of an inner need.

"She's like the shallows," Bess said, "all surface and no depth. She's a know-it-all, domineering woman. All that put-on is only skin deep." *Sometimes the greatest distance is between the people who live together, she was thinking.*

Will I ever be permitted to enter that beautiful house? Cole wondered, feeling depressed. *Or, is it all an impossible dream? If only I could unlock that door and enter in. I'll cross that bridge when I come to it,* she thought, strengthening her resolve. To her the mansion-like house did not seem warm and inviting, and the handsome woman on the veranda seemed carved of marble. Yet, the mental telepathic message was so clear it shocked her.

Bess could see the struggle in Cole's face, the confusion. When the captain whistled good-bye to the Mitchell home the sound of the boat whistle seemed so invincible to her, so final; It was as final as the beautiful woman shutting the door of her grand home.

"What more can I do, Bess, than to offer my heart? I have so little else to give," Cole said, looking at Brant's mother and her estate with an expression of desperation, wishing she was more sophisticated.

Bess had become certain that Cole, by instinct, would never follow an empty dream. "You have the most precious gift in the world," she answered softly. "Love. You are worth ten of her," Bess said tenderly. "The person she thinks she is and the person she really is are two entirely different people," Bess said flatly and would say no more. Mrs. Mitchell seemed so unnatural to her, as if playing a part in a movie. She was a faithful wife who loved with determination, but little depth. It was as if it was her duty: "Ah, I must and therefore I can" attitude.

Soon the Mitchell home and family were out of sight and Cole, unnerved by the sight of Mrs. Mitchell, resumed her duty of cleaning cabins, unaware of the scrutiny of deVoss as she entered his cabin to clean it. Her only thoughts were on the Mitchell house and the regal beauty of Brant's mother. It was a world in which she hoped she would find a welcome home. "The walls of the Mitchell home are covered with family portraits," Bess had told her.

Brant Mitchell had been born and raised in the life of a well-established family and had spent every summer of his youth on his father's riverboat. When at home, he would stand on the bluff overlooking the river and dream of the day when he would be the captain of a big stern wheeler. School, to him, had been something that prepared and permitted him to think in terms of a riverboat career. At nineteen he carried a fully accredited and documented first pilot's license. He was not only the youngest pilot on the river, but Cole had been informed that he was destined to become the youngest riverboat captain to command a stern wheeler on the Ohio River. It was a river that had provided services and memories for generations of the Mitchell family.

Brant had the knowledge and experience that a captain is required to have. Since he was a boy his father nurtured this, training him in all things pertaining to skippering a riverboat. As a boat handler he was as calm, self-assured, and knowledgeable as most seasoned river captains.

"Born in you," his grandpa had told him. "It's genetic. Just as natural as a duck taking to water."

Cole believed Brant to be one of those rare people who are blessed with almost everything that is favorable in his work: pleasing and advantageous, quick of mind, resolute of spirit, and fast and accurate with decisions. The profession of the river had its demands and stamped this within him, and he had been encouraged and molded to strengthen this conviction. The river's voice was thought to be rich in a history that only those of its waters understood that its undertow could be deceptive.

In the wheelhouse, Chain was relieving Brant at the helm. There was no conversation between them, though a strong professional behavior existed between the two men, each careful to maintain it. The fire of the setting sun had glazed the pilothouse windows to the color of a red hot-poker. The river seemed to radiate the heat.

They were passing the packet boat, *Tom Green,* skippered by the twenty-three-year-old captain, Tom Green. Brant Mitchell honored the young skipper with a salute, which was returned. The *Tom Green* was in route to New Orleans and soon lost itself around a bend. Each boat was going its own way for its own reasons. Brant continued watching as the steamer disappeared, hoping that someday he would be like that respected, young captain—a dream of any young pilot.

A boy, fishing on a small dock, waved a salute.

Cole looked up to study Brant's proud and serious face. Her foster mother had said, "You will reach a fulfillment when you find the right person, that special one." *Will our love ever reach fruition?"* Cole wondered. *It will take a miracle.* Cole turned and saw deVoss watching her, leering. His moods came and went, changing like the weather, and whenever she passed him on the deck the meaning in his sidelong glances was frightening. Breathing heavily, she turned and walked down the deck, relieved to be out of his sight. The sunset was dimming, the sky was darkening, and the hills were becoming a blur, yet there was no touch of wind to lessen the humid heat.

Chapter Six

As Cole cleaned deVoss' cabin she noticed initials that had been carved into the woodwork decades ago and wondered if old Rip would remember who it was. *I'll ask the old timer,* she thought.

A few minutes later the door to deVoss' cabin closed with the faintest click. Cole looked up, startled, her face pale. DeVoss was leaning against the closed door, a sly look on his face. His quick, shrewd eyes were turning from side to side, seeing everything, boring through her. She stared at him as if transfixed by the expression. His face had gone scarlet from excitement. She looked at him with eyes going suddenly wide, trying not to show fear. She closed her eyes, but his face floated in her vision. Her heart pounded. The smell of deVoss and his cabin overpowered her. He smelled sour. A distant hum of voices was heard from the galley. She lifted her gaze to meet his, wary, her voice a whisper, her throat tightening in a knot. She sensed his intentions.

"What are you doing here?" Cole said with dry lips, her face white against the blackness of her hair. She stood frozen, staring at him, the hair crawling at the back of her neck. She wanted to shut her eyes and open them to find him gone. She wrinkled her nose. The cabin needed a thorough airing. Several silent seconds passed.

He was smiling a trained and unnatural smile of cunning, and his eyes burned as they bored into her. He could see that she was terrified and was excited by it.

"I got a right to be here," he said, watchful, hard, and bright. He licked his lips, looking her up and down. "This is my cabin. I'm not breaking any rules." He kept staring at her as if she was undressed, with the impulse of craving attainment before being caught. Cole was slow to grasp the meaning, then hurriedly put her hand to her breast to see if her blouse had become unbuttoned. He took a step toward her and reached out his hands. His closeness magnified her fright. She could smell his breath, see the craving in his eyes and on his face, smell his lust, and when he moved his hips she saw his desire. He had never learned the value and rewards of decent behavior. It was in his mind and in his blood. She knew that he would take what he wanted, muffling her cry with a hand and gambling on fear making her silent, or the noise of the boat covering her sound. She sensed he could kill. Her nerves twitched violently and she was unable to control them. She stiffened, powerless to move. She could have felt no more helpless had he tied her with a mooring line. She was in fear as to what extent he would go.

"I only do the cabins when the men have duty on deck and you know it," Cole said, attempting coolness, standing in the middle of the cabin and staring toward the closed door. Her eyes, darkened by fear, moved frantically in panic and disgust.

There was absolute silence. She did not even hear the sounds of the boat. The cabin walls seemed to be closing in on her. She wanted to reason with him, but had no words to use, knowing how useless any reasoning would be. Her pulse was pounding in her ears. She felt trapped.

"Those are the captain's orders," she managed to add in the hope of a warning. She could almost see his mind working, the meaning speaking louder than words and revealing the brutality of a man twisted inside.

His eyes were searching. His thinking was focused on one thought. His smile had disappeared.

Cole bit down on her lip to keep from giving in to fear. What was it about this man that cautioned her so?

"I came for my gloves," he answered smoothly, the skin on his face tight and flushed. He moved toward her another step. He was so filled with an excitement that he could discharge it only through touching her with his body against hers. His movement toward her was so quick that he bumped the chiffonier, sending a wine bottle to the deck.

Cole backed away, frantic for a way out. He thought she was helpless, but she was thinking as she spoke.

"I'll get out until you are back up on deck," she said, in frightened anger at something so terrifying, and tried to move around him. The back of her neck crawled. She was breathless and choked with loathing. There was no escape from this small cabin that was crowded with her fear and his desire. Fighting through a panic, her mind raced to plan a way of escape.

"What's the hurry?" he said softly, caressingly, touching her. "I don't have to rush back. They won't miss me. We could have a little fast fun and no one would be the wiser. You're good at having fun. I know. I've seen it," and he caught her with both hands. His pocked face was so close she could see the sweat running down his temple. The cabin was stifling hot. She felt her legs were numb, as if paralyzed, yet she leaped back as if he had struck her. Where he had touched her was unthinkable.

"What do you want?" she asked with her head averted, afraid to look at him, knowing. Her eyes moved nervously, searching for a way out. She wanted to escape the searching look, the reaching hands, the foul, excited breathing. Sickened, she stared at him in fear and disgust.

"I won't hurt you," he said. "I promise." His voice was tight with danger, his hands trembling with anticipation. Her quick breathing excited him. He was accustomed to getting what he wanted and had little regard for anything but his own desires. His eyes revealed what he was thinking. His emotions made him almost incoherent.

She continued to stare at him in horror.

"Why don't you be sensible," he said, his face twitching. He dreamed of her body. "I'll give you whatever you ask, whatever you want. I only want to be good to you. Just try to be reasonable," he whimpered, his eyes intent. "I have plenty of money." She said nothing, remembering the rumors that he used the riverboats to secretly smuggle and transport drugs. He always had more money than deckhand wages.

Reasonable! Sensible! Cole wanted to scream at him, to laugh insanely. Something was going to happen, she was certain of it. She must escape, or suffer the awful alternative.

"You know what I want," he said, and he stared at her in shame and hatred, unable to control it. Cole felt as if she had been stripped of all her clothes. She was sickened with loathing. Closing his eyes he imagined them in bed, his face changing with each thought. He did not want to stop staring at her, could not. His hand touched her body, caressing her. Beads of sweat were oozing from his forehead.

Cole's face had gone white and sick looking. She *was* sick. Backing away from him she said, "If you touch me again I'll go to the captain. I'll scream!" She did not remember having felt so frightened before, so helpless. It was unreal.

"Please." His voice changed. "I don't want trouble. I want you. I'll buy you anything you ask for. I'll pay you anything you want. Even more. I'll marry you," he said, hopeful. He was the first member of the crew to have guessed her intentions toward Brant. The false tone of his pleading sickened her. She heard the dangerous pulsation in it. "I had to take this chance," he added, almost to himself. He had not raised his voice. Then he went silent for a moment.

"I'm going to the captain," Cole repeated coldly. Looking straight into his burning eyes she willed her face to show no expression. Something throbbed in her deeply and heavily: the thought that her screams would be unheard above the heavy sound of the engines. Staring at him, face-to-face, she saw in his eyes the enormous hunger. It was a blend of lust and hate. He narrowed his eyes, knowing that she could see to the bottom of his soul. She stood very still, looking into his face, trying to control the situation, at a face implanted in her brain. She was reading his thoughts. She sensed that he hated to be looked at.

"I don't think you will," he said, suavely, his small body tense with desire. His face more cunning than an ordinary face. "I don't think you dare, all things considered. You have too much to lose, and you know it. If you do, and the captain gives me trouble, I'll tell him about you and Brant in your cabin that one day. I saw you." Bess had warned her that his tongue was more poisonous than a snake. He paused. "Get smart! He'll dump you as soon as he finds a new one. Wait and see," he sneered. Cole took in her breath and put her hand over her mouth. She felt like one condemned to death. His attitude changed from weaseling to anger.

"Let me love you or lose Brant," deVoss demanded. He felt the blood rushing to his face, pounding at his temples with enough power to explode in his head. The threat was his last hope before using force. His voice had become harsh.

Cole was stunned. A fear in her rose like a scream, but there was no sound. Every moment she expected him to lunge at her and drag her to his bed. His mind was racing. He reached for her again, pulling her to him, his hand touching her breast. His breath smelled like a sewer.

"No!" The cry came bursting from her. "I'd die first." Cole looked around at the wall behind her, wanting a door that was not there. Very carefully, she moved toward the door that led out onto the deck, but he stood between her and escape. His look was quick and crafty. He was watching her with a longing and need, yet he hated her because she scorned him, because of all the things he could not have, would never have, never having known the dream or the truth. His face turned dark and he swore vilely under his breath.

As her eyes shifted rapidly, in search of the best way to escape, Cole saw a deck knife on the table. *If I can get to that knife,* she thought, *I'll stab him. I have to get past him to get out of here,* she realized in a panic, *even if he kills me.* She did not care. She only wanted to be free of him and her courage seemed to grow.

DeVoss's glance followed hers and his hand shot out as she lunged for the knife. He caught her wrist in a strong grip and pulled her toward him, and she could feel the heat of his body. She was sick with fright, her face drained of blood. Cole stared at him and shivered, then she put out her hand as if to hold his body away from hers. She could feel a dodging motion between them. There was a pause in the tension, as if they held their breath, then the struggle continued. His grip tightened around her wrist, his other arm going around her waist. His eyes seemed locked to hers. She was struggling to think of what she must do. What could she do?

He pulled her up to him. His face was inches from hers. She was holding herself still, hoping that calmness would turn him. She knew that if he failed in gaining his desires he would be pitiless, that she could expect no mercy. Bess had warned her.

"I know what you want and why," he said, "but you ain't going to get Brant Mitchell, and you're dead wrong if you think you are. You're wasting your time with him and before he gets done playing with you you'll wish you were dead!" He fairly shouted the words. The tenor of his voice was frightening.

Then, an idea occurred to her.

As he spoke, Cole made a move to one side, as if to go around him. When he stepped in that direction she twisted out of his grip, quickly moved to the other side and past him before he could grasp her. She was out of the door and gone before he recovered.

When she was out on deck she leaned against the bulkhead, shaking and breathing deeply. Her only place to hide was in her cabin and she ran there, locking the door. *To what extreme would he go?* she wondered. That remained the haunting question. Should she go to the captain? It was deVoss' cabin, and her word against his. There was no proof.

"There'll be another time, honey, there always is," deVoss mumbled to himself, furious at his failure. The lifelong establishment of the character of a man remains unalterable. Somehow, in some way, he planned to make her pay for this humiliation. He knew that everyone on the boat sympathized with Cole. *Who cares,* he thought. *I'll have her out of here one way or the other. All I have to do is wait.* He believed he deserved the best of everything. That was his right. He slithered away, planning.

When Cole finally fell asleep it was to dream of a home for her and Brant, overlooking the river where she could wave at her husband's steamboat. Their home would be on the Kentucky side and in the still darkness of the cabin dream the only sound was that of the vibrating engine.

Chapter Seven

Toward the evening several days later Brant was standing at the rail, watching a small river town. He had made liberties there. The golden glow of the setting sun was fading behind the hills, darkening the valley and making the river a gray ribbon before them. The softened sunlight had lost its intense heat. Shadows had already formed in the coves and the cooler evening breeze was a relief. Claude was telling them of a crash he had been in a long time ago when their boat was forced into a concrete bridge piling. He was showing the long scar on his arm to prove it.

DeVoss came up to Brant, asking, "You ever gone ashore with Chain?" DeVoss did not trust any man. Like many dishonest men, he suspected everyone. He was checking to see if Brant would be ashore while he was on board with Cole. He planned to slip her off the boat and disappear at the first opportunity.

"Look at him," Claude whispered, nudging Shark and gesturing toward deVoss. "He's all dolled up in them brand, spanking-new Sunday-go-to-meetin' duds." They watched him with distrust, knowing.

"Yeah, but underneath them clodhoppers he has more toe-jam than a grape arbor," Shark added, his eyes bright with amusement.

Brant did not reply to deVoss immediately. The sun was scarcely shinning on the river and he saw that the deep purple shadows under the trees along the shore were turning to lavender, their leaves still warm under the shade. He had purposely remained silent.

They were preparing to lower the rowboat. Five of the off-duty crew members were going ashore for a few hours of fun, each one eager to be first in the boat. They exploded in relaxation, their philosophy basic: here today, enjoy today! DeVoss was mumbling the tuneless words, "Cigarettes, whiskey, and wild, wild women..." After liberty they would take a bus to the next up-river town and catch the boat.

They were thankful for the sun and the heat. Last winter's record snow and ice had made their work a nightmare.

Pointing at Shark, Glemp shouted, "He can't wait 'till he gets to a movie to see that there Greta Garbo."

"Forget the movies!" deVoss shouted. "Eat, drink and make Mary, for tomorrow ye may die! That's my motto!" he laughed. Hour after hour they had struggled against the river at a snail's pace and were looking for relaxation.

"You making liberty, Hank?" Brant asked, ignoring deVoss.

"No, I'm pulling the graveyard watch tonight so Glemp can go ashore," he answered with a grin.

"Your turn to enjoy the Big Smile," Brant said, joshing Glemp. They were approaching a bend in the river of Greenup, Kentucky.

"The what?" deVoss interrupted, confused, his eyes intent on Brant.

"We're coming into the Big Smile," Brant answered.

"Why do you call it that?" deVoss asked, scornfully.

"You're new on this river, deVoss," Brant said, cheerfully. Some boats had crew members from waterfronts all over the country. Some had traveled many of the long rivers. "This bend has been called The Smile by river men for over a hundred years because of the beautiful women there." He smiled. DeVoss smiled also, but with a different meaning. His hard, cold eyes were measuring him. This boat and this river were new to him and he did not like being considered second rate.

"I'll bet Chain could have all the women he wants," deVoss continued suggestively, hoping Brant would grasp the insinuation toward himself. "More than he can handle, probably. I've never made shore time with him, but I'd be willing to take his throwaways." His voice had a mocking tone. He had attached a mystic power to Chain's influence and effect on women, but kept the thought to himself, knowing that his stories were known to be false. Glemp had infuriated him by calling him a liar.

Brant continued to gaze at the shore in silence. He was uneasy about Chain and Cole, and her respect for him. DeVoss forced his attention away from the town by nudging him.

"You ever made shore time with Chain?" he repeated. The query was deliberately crisp with no friendliness in it. His eyes were restless and flitted from one face to another. His tone was sarcastic. His attitude irritated the crew more than his remarks.

"No," Brant answered reluctantly, having orders not to discuss these things with the crew, though he had seen the personnel file in his father's cabin and he feared that there could be trouble. He looked at deVoss carefully. He was no tenderfoot when it came to sizing up a man. DeVoss was outside the loop.

"That brown-nosed punk don't go ashore with no one!" deVoss stated, and spit. "That man's strictly a loner and I'm glad. He told me one time he don't have no friends and he don't want no friends. I can believe it! He don't buddy up with nobody." Rarely did deVoss enter a conversation that did not concern himself and women, discussing Chain was one of the few exceptions. He was afraid of Chain, but enjoyed goading Brant. He had made himself unliked, big time, never bothering to mend his fences.

"One more word out of him and I'm gonna kick butt," Shark growled, "hacked off and fur up. He's wired for sound!"

"Better not rile the Shark," Brant warned deVoss. "He has a short fuse." His father had ordered him to show patience with deVoss, but a crewman on the wrong boat was like someone living in the wrong house.

Brant did not like or trust deVoss. He was aware that when ashore, beneath the bright lights, the music, the card games, and the gaiety, there was something sullen and dangerous in this man—a sudden urge to violence, though his record did not show that he lived with a code of vengeance. This was a violence that had been passed from generation to generation. His father had warned him of deVoss, that in a pinch he might cut a man loose like a sail in a storm.

Because of the personal files, Captain Mitchell was also aware that Chain had the suspicious reserve of a man whom life had hurt. The captain had felt it expedient to brief his son as first officer. All Chain had known since he left home was conflict. Worn, lonely, and healing from wounds, he had spent the greater part of his life trying to put himself back together. For years he had lived with bitterness and disillusionment, and he had a stiff Scot's pride. He had seen and experienced much in thirty-five years. He had walked the most dangerous streets in the world. He had turned his back on all that, asking favors of no man. He was a man on his own, proven. All he wanted was to be left alone. The inner Chain and the outer Chain were two different people.

"As the resistentialist he has survived with obstinacy and courage," the captain had told his son. He liked Chain and respected him. "Men have a strong profile when they stand alone," Captain Mitchell had said, "and in Chain this is especially evident."

"He don't go to the places we go and have a lot of fun with us," deVoss went on, speaking to a noncommittal Brant Mitchell. Brant knew that Chain was suspicious of deVoss and his intentions, and never asked a favor of him nor associated with him. He would converse with Bess and Cole, but rarely with the crew—not even Brant. He shared only a few words with the captain. "...And I don't like his ugly mug," deVoss added harshly, "He makes me puke!" he said, and swore under his breath. He would rather spread hate than praise.

"You'd better clam up if you know what's good for you, deVoss!" Shark stated, "or you'll get the dirty end of the stick!"

"Somebody's gonna deck that creep one of these days," Glemp growled under his breath, nodding toward deVoss. The words were hard and even.

Brant continued to look at the shoreline, not answering and trying to ignore deVoss. He was trying to keep peace. He did not want Chain baited into trouble. He had a begrudging respect for the man. He knew that the personal file on Chain showed that Lionel Chaney had attended photography school for one year prior to enlistment in the armed services during World War I. He had been decorated first with an American division on the Picardy front near Mont Didier in an attack against Cantigny, again at Chateau Thierry on the Marne, and once again at Belleau Wood on the Merz-to-Paris road. He had learned how to survive. Brant had been impressed. What Brant did not know was that in France Chain had helped bury the only two friends he had. Captain Mitchell had told his son that Chain had been humbled by the accolades heaped upon him—a montage of action, ceremonies, and medals. The file revealed that Chain's father had been a minister in a small southern mountain town. Captain Mitchell admired Chain. Brant was uneasy in his presence.

"What's his last name?" deVoss asked Brant, nudging him into an answer. "Where did he get a name like "Chain," anyway?" His manner was as relentless as a hound on a track.

"I don't know," Brant answered. He would have liked to have moved away. Chain had volunteered to be one of the oarsmen rowing the liberty crew ashore, and the young deckhand, Hank, was to be at the other oar. Chain liked young Hank and, in Chain, Hank had found a hero. "Why don't you just cool it, deVoss," Brant added, coupled with a lantern-jawed expression.

"No one seems to know his first name," deVoss exclaimed, "and I've worked with the puke all summer. All I know is that he calls himself "Chain." Whether that's a first, last, middle, or nickname I don't know, and I'm not asking him. I don't care. The lousy creep was probably on a Georgia chain gang from his accent. I'll bet that's where he got that nickname." His laugh was cold and hard. He spoke in jerky sentences. His odd humor was wasted on Brant, though a few of the deckhands laughed. He shrugged.

"Did he ever say where he was born, or when?" deVoss continued in his oily voice. His twisted personality galled the crew.

"I've never checked his personal records that closely," Brant answered evasively, edging away and remembering his father's advice.

"I don't think he was born," deVoss laughed, as he scratched his behind. "He was hatched out on top of a fence post." He put his sweat-dirty face close to Brant's. "I don't make any shore-time with that mother. You need him around like you need toilet paper. I'd rather pick a scab than talk to that slime ball," he shouted, waving his arms. He often worked himself into an emotional frenzy. His eyes were restless and flitted from one face to another. The situation could become explosive, as it had in the past. His waspish tone irritated Brant and his temper was rising within him, but he remained under control because of his father's orders. He studied deVoss in silence, then looked away. DeVoss was unwanted and mistrusted. His blaze manner irritated the crew.

Brant finally spoke. "Relax, deVoss," he said. "You're getting carried away again." Brant was uneasy with the emotionalism and twisted humor of deVoss and his never-ending rigmarole, yet one of the new crew members laughed at deVoss' odd sense of humor because he did not know him, yet stood in awe of him. He feared him because of his past reputation and because of rumors he believed him to be a violent man.

"A man like Chain will kill you," deVoss said. Glemp and the deckhands were not enjoying the conversation.

"At least he stays to himself and doesn't bother anyone," Brant suggested, not admitting to himself that Chain's photographing Cole bothered him. He spoke with impatience.

DeVoss shook his head, ignoring the barb. "I don't want anything to do with him. Do you, Glemp? That mother's mean! He'll put your eyes out! There's nothing more dangerous in the world than a mean white man!" A few of the crew thought Chain's aloofness was arrogance, that his silence was superiority, not realizing that intelligence is not academic, but native. They were aware that he studied. They spoke freely of a man they had never understood and condemned a man they had never known. They gave him a wide birth because of their instincts in judging the danger in a man. "He thinks he knows it all, but he doesn't know jack!" deVoss shouted.

DeVoss often changed a subject because he was easily distracted by a single thought. "You know when you bring the mail back to the boat and you look at who's getting mail and who it's from?" he asked Brant, looking at Glemp and a deckhand for conformation. "Did you ever notice the mail Chain gets? Never ever saw a personal letter come to him" Brant was uneasy because of the strange notions that cropped up in deVoss' head, but it was difficult to stop his ranting. The pleasure of goading showed in his eyes and in the tone of his voice. He was rolling a smoke as he talked. His voice was scratchy from years of smoking, his face tense with envy. "Course, I don't get many," he said, lying, knowing he did not get any. "All he gets is letters from photo magazines." He tried to speak with a superior tone, his voice crisp.

Why does he bug everyone with all this stupid talk? Brant was thinking, rubbing his forehead. It rattled him. He was aware that Chain did not receive letters from home. Captain Mitchell had told his son that Chain had often wanted a leave to return home, but felt that he could not go home. Not yet.

"I heard that about five years ago Chain killed a man in a tavern fight and got away," deVoss continued. "Heard that he killed this man because his woman taunted him in an argument that the other man was a whole hell of a lot better hunk. You believe that?" And he emphasized the point about the woman and man together, insinuating that Chain had an interest in Cole.

"I don't believe that," Brant said noncommittally. Yet, the deck knife that deVoss carried in his belt made him uneasy.

"Well, I believe it," deVoss said. "If a man tells you he's going to kill you, you damned well better believe him!"

"Shut your mug, deVoss!" Glemp said. "You're getting tiresome." Glemp had been in many slam-bang, knock-down, and drag-out riverfront brawls, and had always walked away the winner. More than one man had been treated to his "Liverpool kiss." Glemp smiled. DeVoss didn't. He was wise enough to remain quiet.

Brant had been informed by his father that a few of the crew on some of the riverboats had spent time in jail for minor infractions of the law such as unpaid child support, drunkenness, alimony, dope, and fighting, but that none of the crew of their boat had a known prison record. The captain checked carefully when he signed a man on. He respected Chain as an individual, admired his behavior, and was well aware of his creativity in photography. He admired the man, respecting his ability. He was a loner, true, but that was his business and no one in the crew rubbed him the wrong way. There had been no problems. They stood in fear of what he would do to them if they crossed him respecting him as a man equal to the challenges of river life.

DeVoss was the only deckhand who resented the captain's approval of Chain's hobby of photography and was scornful when Brant used his father's words: "His pictures are creative and sensitive." DeVoss did not understand the intensity Chain felt toward his pictures. It had become a passion.

What also irritated deVoss was the limited storage space on Chain's side of the small cabin, which was filled with his photography equipment, developing materials, and books. Because of this, the other side of the cabin remained empty as there was not room for anyone to bunk with him.

"His cabin looks like a boar's nest and smells worse," deVoss complained. "And he wastes all his off-duty time readin' them books." He was wound up rubber-band tight. "He's a pile of crap!"

"You should talk," Glemp stated. "No one will bunk with you. They'd need a gas mask. Your cabin smells like an outhouse. I'll tell you another thing, deVoss. You'd sure as rain better trim your sails if you're steering a course across Chain's bow," he warned. "You'd even steal a man's good times if you could."

When talking to Chain about photography, Brant had been a patient listener, but had no understanding when Chain said, "I've been told that photography is not an art, that it is a plaything, an adult toy, and yet I've seen seventy-five-year-old pictures of the Civil War that were sublime, and will last forever in history."

Brant did understand, though, his father's words: "Traveling the sea, ships, and experience have given an expanse of time for an emergent photographer." Chain was the only man on board who had tasted salt spray. He had wandered more from restlessness than poverty.

"In England," Chain had told Brant, "during World War I, I saw photographs by Gibson that were taken in 1872. They were of the Earl of Arron, a paddle steamer, partially submerged after being grounded intentionally. The paddle steamer had struck a rock in St. Martin's Neck and was sinking. I've never forgotten the dramatics of that remarkable picture." Brant had been impressed.

Brant knew that it was useless to tell deVoss that often he and Cole saw Chain with a light meter and camera. They were aware that Chain did not show his pictures or discuss them with the exception of Cole. Brant had even been surprised and bewildered when Cole told him of the anguish Chain had felt at what he considered his lack of success, how raw he was inside, and the deep complexes it caused. He not only resented it, but was jealous of the praise Cole had given Chain.

"Chain believes that if a picture doesn't have feeling it should be destroyed," Cole said to an uninterested and annoyed Brant. "And he told me he has destroyed many. 'The ultimate in a picture,' he said, 'was the touch of emotion before the grip of thought.' Think of that. he told me, 'I think' that excellence in a photograph is something that, although seen every day, makes a person stop and think about it.' He is overly critical of his work, though. He is a perfectionist in dread of failure. Those were his words."

Brant made no response.

"Prison eyes," deVoss was saying. "I've never seen eyes like 'em." He swatted at a fly on his sweating forehead.

"Foxhole squint," Glemp corrected, sucking on his pipe.

Brant knew that Chain was not crafty, but it was true; The hard coldness of his eyes was terrible. He had never seen eyes like them, he had to agree. Nothing was surface, he learned. Chain was a man who saw to the bottom of the crock. Brant remembered the time Cole had corrected him.

"Outwardly he may have the appearance of hard handsomeness, but few realize his inner sensitivity," Cole had said. "Bess told me so and your father also knows." She was certain Brant had not thought about it, that it irritated him.

"I also heard that he killed an officer on the front lines during the war and spent time in a military prison," deVoss went on, stepping backward. He was so busy talking and not watching what he was doing that he stumbled over a coiled hawser.

"Here we go again," Brant interrupted, tiring of the talk about Chain and throwing up his hands. Starting rumors was a major source of entertainment, with each man trying to outdo the other, and none of the rumors were complimentary or pleasant. It was useless to argue with them.

"That's a bunch of B.S. and you know it!" Glemp shouted. "And I'm tired of listening to the S.O.B.!"

Seeing Cole's wide eyes, Shark nudged him, whispering, "You ain't supposed to talk like that in front of a lady! Captain's orders." There was consideration in his voice.

Glemp pretended indignation. "I ain't said nothin' bad. Where I came from B.S. means Blarney Stone, and S.O.B. means Son of Brotherhood." And he smiled at how cleverly he got out of that one. Brant raised his eyes to the sky at the cover-up.

"You're both wrong," Rusty stated. "That ain't it. I know." To him it was incontestable. "The real story is that when he went overseas he sent a lot of his money home to his wife. When he got back home he found out she was living with another man and spending Chain's money on him; his blood money, his allotment check—spending it on the slacker she was living with. Get the picture? Can you imagine anyone pulling a shot like that on a man like Chain? He come right out and asked her about it before he killed her. It was a hometown jury who knew Chain and the circumstances and they gave him a sentence in prison as a Liberian. he got out in three years. That's what actually happened. I know, it was in prison he kept studyin' that photography stuff."

There will be no denouncement to these false conjectures, Brant realized. Chain was the type of man who became a myth by the very men who envy him promoting the mythology.

"How would you know?" deVoss snarled with a twisted, leering smile. When he smiled it drew his lips tight across his teeth. No one had ever seen a natural smile on his face. It irritated deVoss that this apprentice seaman was trying to outdo the dramatics of his cock-and-bull stories. His expression was ugly.

"That's all right how I know," the deckhand said. "I know, that's all. Just don't worry about it!" DeVoss' face hardened.

"That's a crock!" he exclaimed, his visored cap tilted back on his head. He was staring at him, hard-eyed. He seemed always to have a chip on his shoulder and all he did was complain.

"I don't want to talk about it no more," the deckhand said. "I don't want him against me. I'm not askin' for it." And he refused to talk to them about it. Chain had been a professional boxer in his younger days and he was not a man they wanted to aggravate. Though a big man, he was unusually quick on his feet.

Brant shook his head and walked away. Seeing Cole and Bess in the kitchen doorway he wondered if they had heard any of the conversation. He also wondered if Cole had any unrealized feelings toward Chain. Dusk was falling over the valley and the crew had resorted to the never-ending pastime of telling folklore stories of riverboat heroes, a pastime that none could resist. Most of the stories were factually true, though once in a while enhanced with imagination. All of them were intriguing. One of the stories told of the ghost of a former crewman that walked the moonlit deck each year on the date of his heroic death. They also told every visitor their version of the story of the Iron Mountain, a riverboat with a crew and fifty-five passengers that had steamed around a bend in the Mississippi River then disappeared into oblivion, never to be heard of again. "Just flat out disappeared," Glemp said in awe. "Here one minute and gone the next. For them it was the end of the world. I've been ridin' this river since I was knee-high to a grasshopper and I ain't seen anything to equal it." Some river men believed that ghost ships still sailed the rivers. Their stories of riverboat gambling houses and card sharks with a gun in their belt were fascinating. Many other historic stories were hidden beneath the smooth surface of the river.

The boat was now passing Maysville, Kentucky, which always brought a reminder to Glemp. His stories had become legendary. "Aw, that's nothin'," Glemp said in answer to a tale told by Shark, the coal heaver. "I'm a direct descendant of the historic frontiersman Lewis Wetzel," he bragged. He had mentioned it at least fifty times and no one believed him. They hooted at the suggestion.

Clyde joined the act. "There's no end to his stories. He claims that one of his ancestors was on that flotilla when forty-two people were massacred by Simon Girty back just before the Revolutionary War. Next he'll be tellin' us he's related to George Washington. Claims he knows everything, even before it happens." There was a huge smile on his suntanned face. He enjoyed Glemp's embellished stories.

Shark rolled his eyes. "Oh, my achin' rump. Here we go again!" The crew was well aware that some of his stories were more imagination than reality, but he was their best entertainment.

Clyde shrugged his huge shoulders, laughing. "You're wasting your time on this boat, Glemp. With your gift of gab you should be a politician." He was notorious for his melodramatics.

"I'll admit that's pretty far back for you guys," Glemp conceded, making allowance for their ignorance of his family history. "That was back when Maysville was called 'Limestone.' Back when the Shawnee Indians called old Lewis Wetzel, 'Death Wind.'" He howled with laughter, slapping his leg. He never stopped talking.

"That figures," Clyde yelled. "Even if your story's only half true, old Wetzel must have smelled about the way you do." And he went into gales of laughter as he squatted on a coil of line. "It's in the genes. You inherited it." The drowsy afternoon had had a mellowing effect on the crew.

"He hasn't told a story straight in the last hundred years, and every story changes a half-dozen times from fore to aft," Shark added with a broad grin that showed his recent dental work.

"He's got enough gold in his mouth to buy Fort Knox," Glemp bellowed, pointing, and he winked at Hank. A smile broadened his round face. "Time for shore and a break in the routine!"

"You should talk," Shark replied glibly, slapping Glemp on the back. "Look at you. You haven't had a haircut in months and you only shave about every three or four days to make shore time and impress the girls. Your hair looks like a bird's nest." He glanced at the others. "He looks like a rag-picker." Glemp's worn jeans were hitched up with a scarred leather belt. Actually, the two were as close as bark on a tree and had been cronies since childhood. "And you've got the Irish gift of gab," he added with a laugh.

"Yeah, they're as close as an Irishman to his bottle," deVoss growled, glancing at Shark. There was no humor in the remark. He trusted no man and liked no man. It was obvious. He stopped jabbering long enough to light his roll-me-own.

Shark's face hardened. "How would you like to take a dip in the river?" he retorted, tight-lipped, taking a step toward deVoss. He emphasized his point one slow word at a time. "I'll dunk your snoot in the puke bucket!" He had never been reluctant in expressing himself. DeVoss' face turned bone white. It didn't take much to rile the Shark. "Do me a big favor, deVoss," the Irishman said with a smile. "Please give me an excuse to change the shape of your mug," and he emphasized the word "please." DeVoss said nothing, looking shaken by the cold, hard words.

"You'd better shape up or ship out," Glemp said. "The Shark's circling. He smells blood!"

"All the Shark has to do is roll up his sleeves and no man in his right mind will mess with him," old Rip said to Hank. "He's got a punch like Jack Dempsey." DeVoss was no fool, he would not bait the Shark. That would mean a trip to hell in a hand basket and he knew it. The Shark was well proven.

It was growing dark rapidly and the off-duty men were anxious to be ashore. "Knock off the bull!" Clyde yelled, chewing on his cold cigar. "It seems like a month of Sundays since I've been ashore. It's shore time!" He climbed into the rowboat. He was anxious to challenge the waterfront card-sharks.

"Hey, Glemp!" Shark shouted, "you still countin' your pennies?" Since the crash of twenty-nine Glemp did not trust the banks. He had lost all of his savings and from then on his mother kept his savings at home.

"Oh, I got a few pennies for a brew," he said, shaking the coins in his pocket and grinning. The night air was coming down from the hills and was soothing. Darkness was gathering on the river. Many riverboat gamblers were considered dangerous men. Shark stepped closer to Glemp and in a low voice said, "Don't be a hair-brained fool. If you're going to do any cards with deVoss keep a close eye on him. He's slick and will do you dirt. I know, I've been there. Boatin's a cover. He makes a lot more moola at cards and loves the reputation of being a hotshot." Glemp often went to the card rooms, but it was more a matter of excitement than habit and greed. Gambling on the riverboats in the old days was legendary and it was in the blood of many river men. DeVoss was shuffling a pack of cards in anticipation—an illusive will-o-the-wisp, one step ahead of the law.

"This boatin's a dog's life," Glemp complained, glancing at deVoss. "I feel like quitting and make a living in the card rooms. I'd be all dressed up in a suit and tie—a real gentleman." It seemed to him there was more money in the gambling houses than in the town bank. The gambling house stretch along the river was referred to as the "Barbary Coast."

"Yeah, sure," Shark replied, "you been saying that for the last ten years, but you're not that phony." He looked around. "And another thing," he added, "your sister made me promise to keep an eye on you. 'Stay away from them hookers.' She laid down the law full bore, and she wasn't joking. And another thing: Don't say I didn't warn you to stay out of O'Brien's," he whispered.

"I wouldn't be caught dead in that two-bit dump with Pig Eyes. He's poison, man." It was Shark who had given the nickname "Pig Eyes" to deVoss. "Oh, sure, I know shipmates are supposed to stick together," he laughed, "but that lousy booger is cunning. You have to watch out for a man like that. A coward is far more dangerous than a brave man," he emphasized.

DeVoss had never asked for their friendship and had offered none. Tragically, he had never had a true friend, man or woman. Because of the reputation as free spenders, some river men were treated with kid gloves in most of the saloons and card rooms. DeVoss loved the feel of cards almost as much as the feel of money and women, yet there was no indication of what was going on inside him.

Shark nudged Glemp. "Wise up, Buddy. He doesn't want your friendship, he wants your money. Men like him come a dime a dozen."

"I'm watching him," Glemp replied, ignoring the joke about the hookers. He hunched his big shoulders under his well-worn shirt as they exchanged an understanding glance. Some itinerant boatmen were known troublemakers in the riverfront towns and deVoss had proven himself less than a homeless cur, considering their indifference toward him a taunt.

"Be careful," Shark repeated. "Don't deal yourself a losing hand." Nothing travels faster than a bad reputation, and the crew was well-informed. Every time deVoss got into a card game with a fellow crewman he took a month's wages from him. "Compared to him you don't know diddly-squat. Every time he gets in a card game he's loaded for bear. He'll go after your money like a bee makin' honey."

This crew had an unusually fine harmony with only the one note of discord; deVoss. Their customary humor overcame this. Because of his kinky behavior deVoss acquired the nickname, "Kinky," and this infuriated him. "Blah, blah, blah. That's all we hear from the creep," Glemp said with a laugh. "In town he's smack dab in every brawl."

Old Rip nudged young Hank and spoke with admiration. "That Glemp is so cotton-pickin' tall he could walk from Ohio to Kentucky and never get his chin wet. Dad-blast his hide he's got shoulders on him as big as them hills." Old Rip did not make any shore time during a trip. He put in his duty time on the boat and then took his allotted number of days off to spend at home with his old dog and their memories.

Young Hank grinned, agreeing with Old Rip and saying, "But more importantly, Rip, his heart's just as big as he is." Young Hank was proud of his idol. Glemp's family history went back to a time when only a few pioneers and Indians inhabited the Ohio Valley.

"Yeah," Shark said, tongue in cheek, "but he never stops talkin'. He blabs like an auctioneer. His mouth's as big as the blowhole of a whale. And snore! Claims he can't sleep. Huh? We're the ones that can't sleep. He sleeps more than a bear in hibernation." It didn't take much to tickle his sense of humor.

Glemp's classic performance was of Shark after he had over-imbibed and was trying to appear sober. Yet, when in a tavern, the toast Glemp always gave was a hearty, "May you always sail the river, buddy." The underbelly of his friendship could never be questioned. "When I'm ashore in my four-by-four I put the peddle to the metal," he shouted, "but here on the boat it's never more than paddle to the puddle."

The sun was setting over the river as they rowed toward the shore and a few hours of their own. Old Rip always spoke of it as "the river of time"—a river that would wind and turn forever, having made the river men of Old Rip's youth become legends through stories. He was thinking of the many voices long gone silent. Some of the stories chronicled the idealism of the early settlers who pioneered the river valley before the days when railroads captured much of the riverboat work. He spoke of men who had made history. *Where has it all gone,* he wondered. *If this old river told all it knows, the books would fill a library.* He had ridden this river since he was a boy. Cole was entranced with the dramatics of his stories back to the days when there were only rafts, flatboats and pole boats on the rivers. They were stories of the valley lost in time and of people who had become legends. She considered him one of the most gifted storytellers. Time had washed the riverbanks with history. Old Rip had taken part in the Civil War when he was merely twelve years old. Pointing to the riverbank with pride he said, "That cowboy actor, Roy Rogers, was born and raised on a riverboat on this river." He smiled in thought of his movies. Much had changed on the river since the original charts had been sketched—too much. These were years gone and long forgotten, but not to Old Rip. He had learned to take things as they come and make the best of them.

Old Rip turned to young Hank. "Just think," he said, "pioneers were able to watch buffalo come down to this river and drink." He paused in thought. "We'll never see that. It's sure a different river." Modern boating techniques were going full-bore and it saddened him at times to think of the modern changes. "Life is a one-way ticket, boy. It's the river of no return."

Bess had been watching and listening. She understood that Old Rip dreamed of the days of long ago, and knew how those men contributed to the making of their country. He never complained, but was thankful for his part in early Ohio riverboat history. She knew that when his time came he would return home like an old elephant to die. She turned to Cole and said, "There's an old expression my grandpa used to say: 'He who lives the longest sees the most.'"

"Remember what I said," Shark was whispering as he nudged Glemp. "DeVoss rakes off so much dough at cards that he can afford to flush his wages down the crapper. He guards that deck of cards like a dog with a bone. I'll bet he has a bigger stash than the local bank. The minute you turn your eyes away from him he'll give you the shaft, big time. The law to him is just something to be broken." Then he laughed boisterously. "And I heard that his daughter's older than his wife. Figure that one out."

They lowered the rowboat into the water that had taken on a reddish hue in the setting sun. They rowed toward the shore and liberty!

Young Hank stood at the deck rail, watching them row toward the shore, his freckles alighted by the setting sun. Turning to Bess he said, "Gee! I wish I was old enough to go with them."

Bess gave a hearty laugh and nudged him, saying, "You stay away from them. They won't leave shore 'till they drink the house dry!"

When the crew returned from shore-time the familiar question came: "How'd you do in town, deVoss? Any goodies?"

The customary shouted report, "Perfect as usual," he bragged. There were whoops of laughter. "My fancy clothes and good looks always make a big impression on those girls and you damned well know it," he crowed.

"In town that joker has enough false charm to sell a block of ice to an Eskimo," the Shark growled.

Old Rip turned to Bess and quietly said, "It's not what's on the outside that counts. It's what's on the inside that's important." Bess nodded, knowing deVoss full well.

When deVoss looked around and saw that Bess had heard him, he gave her a contemptible look as though she had no right to eavesdrop on him. The look in her eyes told him more than words.

Old Rip mumbled, "Now there's one man I wouldn't mind the job of digging his grave. There's an old saying that only certain men are meant to ride the river and he sure as heck isn't one of them!"

Bess nodded. "He's sure different," she commented, "and there must be a reason." She was aware that he had received a letter from New Orleans and concluded that it must have been alarming because he was so touchy and jumpy.

Old Rip shook his head in agreement. Among the crew it was a break of professional etiquette to question a fellow crewman's integrity unless warranted and Old Rip had seen enough to have reason to agree with Bess.

"Do you think he'll stay long-term?" Old Rip asked.

Bess shook her head. "No way! He'll bail out as soon as the crew catches on to his slick card tricks."

Chapter Eight

That evening Chain stood on the deck and looked out over the river to the hills beyond, thinking back to another place, another time. There had been too many rivers in his life, an unwanted past behind him, and an unknown future ahead. A blue haze enveloped the distant trees, yet his face was illuminated by the sunset. It was a strong face, tender and sensitive at the moment. Mist was forming in a marshy inlet and the riverbank was etched in shadowy beauty. Chain considered the setting sun at evening the most creative part of the day. He was looking at a sight as beautiful as any he could hope to see. To him the river was more than a workhouse, it was enchanting and poetic—a place of magic. He saw beauty where other were blinded by the work. The Indians had referred to the Ohio as the "Beautiful River."

The sunset tinted the rolling hills, and the warm summer night came down from the ridges and lay on the river in a bluish haze. As Chain watched, the horizon was darkening at the edges and the trees looked deep blue. The hot summer eve had closed to dusk and low dark clouds were moving over the sky. The sweltering night was thickening. The setting sun cast a rose-colored glow on the water and the edge of the hills was disappearing with the soft glow of the setting sun. Daylight was fading, the shoreline disappearing in the shadows. As the setting sun began to fade, lights were appearing in the small towns and farms. The air was beginning to cool. A new moon was rising.

A narrow main deck ran down each side of the cabins and in the galley Chain could hear the laughter of some of the crew. He wished that Bess was there to talk to, to tell her how he felt about this landscape. There was a kinesthetic beauty about moving quietly along the river through the hills. The sound of running water was like distant music, becoming a stimulant as well as being therapeutic. Night was coming on.

He felt closest to Bess and believed that she would understand. Not merely be sympathetic and kind in his belief that a picture should go beyond its immediate likeness, but that it should be an essence beyond a mirror, that the decision of what would make a picture had to come from within himself, and that a good photograph must tell a story. He would never forget the meaningful words of his art teacher: "No one can take credit for creativity, it is a gift." It was Bess whom he enjoyed talking to the most, telling her he believed that each of his pictures should be an expression, and most of his photography not only had beauty, but also had power. He was a man who would not compromise with quality. He strove to create beyond the gift of his ability. His inner integrity to this was as hard as his physical being. His self-respect as a creator was involved. He fought against failure as a drowning man fights to survive. A contemplative man by nature, he studied each scene in depth and within him was a poetic tenderness hidden beneath the rugged brawn. Though a silent man, he was a man of commanding presence and a passion to create.

In photographing Cole, Chain had treated photography as an art form, realizing that her inner beauty equaled her exterior beauty. He wanted to photograph Brant and Cole because they were such a graphic contrast, but Brant would not pose. Chain believed he must make each picture revealing and with meaning. He could capture a riverbank shanty scene of squalor and defeat and make it shine with the force of the illumination from inner beauty. It was the mastery of creating the illusion of light where there was no light. He believed that for a picture to succeed it had to be inspired, that something of himself had to be in every picture. He still had the daguerreotype of his grandfather and the memory, and he cherished it above all of his pictures. He searched for infinity beyond a finite statement. His strongest attribute was that he could recognize what would make a master picture and he had the creative talent to capture it. He believed that even the simplest things were spiritual and could be captured, so he strove to keep fractional vision out of his work, and sought understanding as a whole. He knew that no man is more than what he has seen and experienced and accomplished, that none of us see ourselves as others see us.

He drew a long breath. He felt an overwhelming exhilaration each time he saw this part of the valley. Its changing beauty reminded him of the changing moods of Cole, who believed the camera revealed unknown secrets to the extent of art becoming spiritual. He sometimes had the feeling that he had lived on these rivers a hundred or two hundred years before, and he wondered if a man's heart and mind had room for one more sunset. Surely there could not be one more beautiful. He knew that without a picture, or a painting, this, too, would pass away, and things would never again be the same.

The light climbed out of the canyons, leaving evening, the distillate of the sunset beyond the fold of the hills. The twilight was moving rapidly into darkness, and the evening sky was lilac and gold with the dark silhouette of trees at the horizon. The sunset was inspiring, a beautiful photograph with a lovely girl the subject of his view. Chain moved his eyes. The shadow of the valley was heliotrope and soft, an evanescent beauty, and the river was drenched in silver moonlight, causing the distant hills to appear like ghosts. A warm, gentle night breeze blew over the darkened river, the leaves rustled, and the water lapped the shore. He was watching the lights trail up the hills behind Ashland. He was experimenting with night photography.

Chain often wondered about himself and he wondered about the persons in the houses along the river—houses that gave no more than a faint glow in the darkening of the quiet hills. He thought of how tenderly Cole would settle into one of those houses, hoping that Brant would rise to the occasion. He was a quiet man, expressing in words little of what he was thinking. Travel and adventure had been the integral part of his life.

There was not enough light for Chain to capture the shadows of night swooping down from the hills to run across the river and, as the twilight fell, the deck darkened about him and his camera. The evening was coming fast, the breeze was falling, and the night air was warming. The shadows lengthened out over the water, just ahead of the oncoming night. As the twilight lay over the east, the late light of summer evening came over the river. Then the light vanished and the hills were gone. Chain hoped that what he had photographed would approach what he had seen. He would show the picture to Bess as soon as he developed it in his cabin.

The quiet of night closed over the valley river. The stars danced in the wake of the boat and the moon cast a white brilliance on the water. Night had come and from the ridge of hills only darkness came down to the water, accompanied by a dot of light from an occasional farm house. Long after dark he could still see the last striations of the sunset beyond the western hills.

Chain looked across dark waters and into the lighted houses as if prying into the illumination of a heart and soul. Some alighted the quiet life of happiness, others the dim life of despair. He visualized them as a family: children, man, and woman, gathering at a table, each mind occupied with personal thoughts, such as his thoughts concerning himself and Bess. Now he was realizing that love is the most powerful force on earth.

The crew had finished supper and were waiting on deck for Cole to play her guitar and sing. They looked forward to the evening and her songs. Her purity of youth was so sincere it spilled over into the entire crew. Her laughter meant more to them than a raise in pay. "I sure cotton to these songfests," Shark said. "They're really a hoot." Along the deck Claude could be heard bellowing in the galley. He was telling Bess a story about his fighting cocks and she was not interested. She detested the thought. Hurt and irritation were apparent in Claude's voice. Old Rip waved to Cole as he ambled down the deck.

"You can hurt Claude's feelings quicker than any man in the world if you don't listen to his stories," Glemp said. Bess came out on deck, laughing at Claude's pouting face. She then looked toward Cole as she walked down the deck. A light wind flattened the clothes against her youthful body. From a distance deVoss also saw Cole coming toward them. Her face was bright with warmth and her steps were light as she approached. His body chemistry changed. Everything about her looked newer and fresher than the soft summer evening and his breath quickened. He had plans.

Cole smiled at the gathering and said, "Waiting long?" The men shook their heads no, in unison and embarrassment. They would have waited all night. A moon-ray of silver lighted her lovely face. *Never have I seen her look more beautiful,* Bess was thinking.

"Good," Cole said. When she spoke it was with the lilt of a Kentucky accent. She looked around to see who else was there. She was hoping to see Brant, but was comforted to find Chain and Bess there, waiting in the gathering shadows.

The main deck was dark aft, but on the bow of the cabin deck on each warm summer night when there was no rain, away from the splashing sound of the giant paddlewheel astern, the crew listened to the music of Cole Hamilton blend with the sound of the water against the hull of the boat. The night wind was warm, and Cole's blouse was open above her young breasts, her lovely throat bare. She did not wear or need a brassiere to enhance an inherited grace, her physical beauty matched that of her gifted voice. The soft breeze flattened the light dress against her body.

"Many of the hill people still call the guitar the 'lonesome voice,'" Cole said, and laughed. Her laughter was like a song on the night air. The crew was enthralled. "Join us, she coaxed. Occasionally she was able to entice Glemp into singing the beautiful classic, "Old Man River." His deep, rich voice was unforgettable. Young Hank stared in wonder at Cole's beauty and the effect of her voice. She had the gift of melting words and music into the heart. The tiny waves were slapping the hull with the rhythm of a heartbeat from the guitar. Her fingers were magic on the strings—the low, sweet sounds flowing as soft as the river. Cole turned her face and the moon gave it a sudden flash of beauty. It gave a silver cast to the corn fields along the nearby bank. She looked into the still night at the river sparkling with starlight. The stage was set. Had she ever seen anything so stunning as this scene of transcendent beauty? She thought not.

These musicals may not be a classical soiree, Bess thought, *but the spirit is sure there.* It was an intimate gathering to appreciate the simple music from the heart. The songs that were sung on a boat on a summer night told something of the persons involved. The simple songs of love were the only songs. The songs blended with the scattering of stars. It was an enchanting evening.

"It's a pure wonder how much beauty can come out of an old guitar and a small girl's voice," Bess said to Claude, remembering the night Cole was singing in the rain. He nodded appreciatively. Her fresh young beauty reminded him of his daughter. A neighbor lady had taught Cole how to play the guitar and tragedy had given her voice a sweet, hard edge—breathy and husky in the lower register. The songs she sang were given life by an inner radiance, a natural gift. Her voice was as sweet and true as a bird in song.

"Her songs are the best pick-me-up in the world," Claude answered, his voice a slow drawl. Bess joined in the laughter.

On these nights, as the men listened, Cole sang two songs that are meaningful to all Kentuckians: "My Old Kentucky Home," and "Sleep Kentucky Babe." Claude joked at the sentimentality, but he stayed and he listened and enjoyed them. She also sang many of the plain mountain ballads, those simple songs whose words and music told of the feelings of unostentatious people. There were certain feelings, Cole believed, that only a ballad could do justice. She believed that was why poetry was put to music. Each nuance of mood, of feeling, and of expression was as natural to her as the sound of wind, water and rain. Her voice was as inherent as birdsong. Her lithe, graceful figure moved with every slight rhythm. How lovely she was. The songs told of her inner feelings more than she realized. Only Chain grasped the potential of what he realized could happen.

The listeners were unaware of the gradual darkening of the river, burying the outline of the boat deeper and deeper into the shadows. They enjoyed hearing Cole play her style of a soft, sweet guitar, and sing favorites such as "The Red River Valley," "Cumberland Gap," "Beautiful Ohio," and especially, "Home Sweet Home," because that was the song that played in the music box her natural mother had given her. That, and "Keep The Home Fires Burning." She would never forget. On New Years Eve on the boat, she would sing the immortal, "Auld Lang Syne." Music was a part of her very being. Then she would sing one of her favorites, "Beautiful Dreamer Awake Unto Me," and especially the song loved by all river men, "Flow Gently Sweet Afton." Her voice seemed to linger in the soft evening air.

The Shark sat and listened, all smiles, hoping it would never end. Though he was a ragtime enthusiast he also loved the old sentimental songs. He had waited all day to hear her sing.

"That girl will sing in the rain," Old Rip Mac Donald said, shaking his head. "She can change a gloomy day to sunshine." The songs were a voice from her heart. She had a natural depth of understanding in her rendition and interpretation of "Sandy Grove" and "The Trail of the Lonesome Pine." Still, she was looking for Brant. Although Glemp scoffed and called the songs mush, he was invariably the last one to leave. And then her entire being changed when she sang, "The Old Refrain." Everyone on board stared off into space in silent thought as they listened to the tender, meaningful, unforgettable words:

"For it recalls to me a bygone day,
It takes me back again to meadows fair,
Where sunlight's golden rays
Beam everywhere.
My childhood joys again come back to me,
My mother's face in fancy, too, I see.
It was my mother taught me how to sing,
And to that memory my heart will cling.
I'm never sad and lone while on my way,
As long as I can sing "The Old Refrain"...

"That girl has a voice like an angel," Bess said to Old Rip, tears in her eyes. Old Rip smiled and nodded in agreement.

Cole sang touching songs of the river people and the hill people—her people. She sang of the legend of Casey Jones of Casey, Kentucky. She sang those dramatic words with deep feeling, "He was coming 'round the bend going ninety miles an hour when the whistle broke out into a scream. He was found in the wreck with his hand on the throttle and was scalded to death by the steam."

Many of Cole's songs told of tragic lives, toil, hate, love, heartache, and loneliness. Her loneliness that yearned for someone to love her. She played the tenderness of the minor keys with a special style, the soft, low notes like an inner cry. Some of her renditions were very soothing and the men remembered home and loved ones. The ballads had a stirring effect upon the men, yet there was one song she dare not sing aboard the steamer. "The Hatfields and McCoys, They Were Reckless Mountain Boys." One of the crew was a Hatfield.

Then Cole turned to Clyde with a huge smile and struck a chord. It didn't take any coaxing for Clyde to sing, "Sweetest little fellow, everybody knows, don't know what to call him but he's mighty like a rose. Looking at his mammy with eyes so shining blue makes you think that heaven is coming close to you." That boy was his pride and joy, cherished like a long-remembered melody. He treasured every call home.

"Clyde sings as good as Al Jolson," Shark shouted and meant it.

The boat was moving slowly up stream along a moon-drenched river. Cole knew that Brant was there before he appeared at the deck rail. All of her thoughts, hopes, and intentions were focused on one person. Just to be near him caused her pulse to rise. It was something beyond her control. She could not hide it anymore than she could hide her love of poetry and song. Even when she could not see him she could feel the mysterious power of his presence and felt a thrill of longing in her heart. His presence always came to her as surprising as joy. She must have known he was there because she was singing the most special song in her heart, the song she always sang only to him: "I'm Thinking Tonight of My Blue Eyes." It was his favorite song and she sang it; "I'm dreaming tonight of my blue eyes." Her soft eyes were dreamy with a faraway look. The moon glistened on the strings that her fingers plucked. Then came the touchingly beautiful words, "Come and sit by my side, little darlin', do not hasten to bid me adieu, Oh, remember the Red River Valley, and someone that loves you so true." The depth of meaning was in her face for anyone to see in the luminescent light. A wonderful excitement sounded in her voice. All this had changed her. She saw no one but Brant.

The inner communication in song is more meaningful than words, Bess was thinking, enjoying the warm breeze.

Although he did not know that Brant was watching her, Chain could hear the difference in Cole's singing and guessed that Brant had arrived. Brant was unable to detect the change of tone. The longing in her voice was haunting. At times she would glance at Brant and away, softly strumming an unsung melody. The effect was simple and beautiful. Chain had the feeling that the songs could have been sung for Bess and himself. He hoped that some day it would happen. A star lit the sky into a trailing light.

Chain saw Brant nod to Cole formally and an answer smiled in her eyes, the most silent of communication. Smiling, Cole lifted her face to greet his with another song. What songs the river sang. What beating heart trembled on those waters to one beloved by her above all others. The beauty of her voice came from the music in her heart. Did he notice that her lovely eyes were glowing like the stars? It seemed to Cole that all creation centered in this valley, the starlight and the moonlight giving the river valley a sense of timelessness and peace—continuity which spanned millennia. DeVoss stood watching Cole. To see so much happiness hurt. She was unable to hide her longing and her need.

Cole looked into the shadows at an embarrassed Brant. The night air was warm and scented with summer. All through the enchantment of this summer no one else existed. The whole valley and the night and her hopes seemed more beautiful than ever and infinitely more peaceful. Rapture had given her hopes complete freedom. This was the valley of a summer night when a girl told a boy in song that she loved him, of the yearning to hold him in her arms, hoping for his love in return. It went beyond the physical, it was a longing and a need to share, a need that would last forever. With all her heart she believed that their love went beyond a boat trip on the river, beyond a lifetime of union and family, that it was for all eternity. *Surely he must know,* she thought. Was she yearning for the unattainable or would it be the fulfillment of her dream?

Brant had seen her flush, nothing could have stilled her heart. A cheerful little cover-up laugh escaped her open lips. Then she said simply, "Do you have a special request, Brant?" She felt her face burning. Brant felt embarrassed at being singled out in front of the crew and walked away. The entire crew was rooting for them.

Sensing and seeing the tension of the situation, Glemp altered the mood by singing his favorite, "'In Dixieland where I was born early on a frosty morn look away, look away, look away, Dixieland.'" His sincere, husky drawl was perfect for the song and Cole entered in with her guitar, her soft blue eyes alight.

Far off a boat's whistle, born across the river by a soft warm breeze, joined the song. The lights made a flood of quivering reflections on the water. Cole was remembering tender moments throughout the summer, a scattering of thoughts all of Brant.

Chain had left to make his official tour of the boat as on-duty deck watch, but had returned to the gathering quietly. He did not smile or nod and made no sign of greeting, but his eyes seemed to extend to Cole his protection. She nodded and played a few chords of "Carolina Moon." Then he smiled in appreciation, thinking of Bess, and Cole knew that he was pleased. One of her novels would have described his features as brooding severity, but a slight smile erased it. The night had turned the shore to black and, like a volcano, the moon seemed to erupt out of the top of a mountain. A line of trees along the bank were ghostly in the moonlight.

There was no evidence that the music on this still, calm night was having an effect upon Chain, but upon him Cole left a lasting impression of beauty and purity. Her simple songs moved him. Other than working with his camera, these were the only peaceful and tender moments he had on the boat. He had not revealed his deeper feelings for Bess.

Cole had been impressed by the lack of arrogance in Chain and she had never known him to act as anything other than what she believed to be a gentleman. She admired and respected him as a mature man. She was impressed with his bearing, his profile, and used the novel-word, "noble," in her mind. And she liked his calmness. The comparison between Chain's natural dignity and deVoss' false grandiose air was laughable. He was the only man on board with whom she felt comfortable, with the exception of Old Rip. He spoke too little to be eloquent, yet he was a sentient man, and there was dignity and real meaning in the conversations she had had with him. Although, she had been shocked when he had said that the world was a scar and that each suffers what they must. She did not know that he had meant that for her as well as himself. She felt that he was a man who would be remembered with vividness for a lifetime.

Upon one occasion Chain had told Cole that when he was in Paris he had met Bill Brant and told her of the English photographer's words: "It is part of the photographer's job to see more intensely than most people do. He must have and keep in him something of the receptiveness of the child who looks at the world for the first time, or of the traveler who enters a foreign country." He did not tell her that he thought of her as that child.

When Chain looked at Cole it was as if he were reliving a memory, the scar over an unhealed wound. There was still the old ache and vacant feeling.

They were wounds a long time in healing. When he looked at such youthful beauty it made him sad. He looked at her with a preternatural knowing, as though he had been haunted by memories of another time, another face. He had more to forget than to look forward to, there was too much of his past he could never wholly escape. His eyes seemed to look far beyond a beautiful girl, playing a guitar on a riverboat. *She might have been someone else,* he thought, *if things had been different,* and he hoped that she would be more fortunate in her love. And again, all these years after that, he could not force away the bitterness of memory. It was not in him to forgive and forget. He would wait for the right moment and then perhaps all the past would disappear.

It may be that he was running from the shadow of a phantom. Or, it may not be. It could be that he was doing what he most wanted to do. Often the difference is no more than a delicate, perishable thread in the hands of a ghost. The moonlight, brighter then, fell full upon Cole's face. Her lovely dark hair was blowing in the soft wind. *She has the innocence and purity of a child,* he thought as he listened to a girl with smoky blue eyes singing the old songs. There were moments when he did not consider his life so far gone, but at the threshold of a new creation, a new beginning.

Durand deVoss ambled down the deck in the darkness and paused beneath an amber deck light. Cole saw him. She tensed, but kept playing and singing. She had the feeling that he was always out there in the darkness, waiting. Brant noticed the motion, followed her gaze, and looked into the eyes of deVoss. Only an acute ear would have caught the change in the music, but Chain did. A quick flash of anger showed for an instant in his eyes and then became hidden. He crushed anger inside of him and kept it there. Only his eyes, like a recording instrument, showed his emotions, and he covered this with his eyelids. His cold, slitted eyes knifed through deVoss and he moved on. Chain's own eyes lingered on Cole for a few seconds and then he was gone. DeVoss had ignored Brant completely. He was not afraid of Brant, but he feared Chain.

Now that deVoss was gone Cole was leaning against the rail, her head thrown back, enjoying the coolness of the light night breeze against her face. Her eyes were closed as if she was alone. Her hair was like the night, touched with spangled starry beams. She belonged to the night. Chain moved down the deck slowly, following deVoss. He could not tolerate the man being near Cole. He knew deVoss and sooner or later, if it had to be, would settle with him to protect Cole.

Looking at Cole, Old Rip nudged Bess, saying, "There's a flower called baby blue eyes, and her eyes look just like them."

As the music followed him down the deck, Chain was thinking of Cole and Brant. He knew there were those, who if they could not make a dream come true, lacked the strength to search for another dream. Dreams floated as illusively as bubbles on the river. He hoped otherwise for Cole. He had seen her tenderness envelope Brant and the boy was uncaring of it. Her love hovered over him like the sound of her music and the words of the songs. Chain thought that it could be a mistaken love, but hoped her wishes would come true.

Chain mistrusted beautiful women, but he considered Cole a beautiful girl. *How can a girl know reality,* he wondered. He studied her in a thoughtful way, remembering a great photographer's work. *She could be a portrait by Bernice Abbott,* he thought. Only a man...certain men...could understand the meaning in the loss of innocence in a woman. He had spoken to Cole about Bernice Abbott. "Her portrait of James Joyce will become a legend some day," he said. His portrait of Cole Hamilton, singing, had won an award and a cash prize. The portrait revealed that Cole's beauty came as much from purity within as from the beauty of her features. There was a natural grace in the way she moved.

His picture of Cole had been full of light, but not made up entirely of light and shadow. It spoke of a realization to come. He knew the importance of angle and depth. He was not an impressionist. Each picture brought forth his vision of the world and he was in constant pursuit of these visions. He liked subjects that had quality, strength, and true proportion, such as Cole—a searching. He was modest about his work, but he believed in it. Only when creating pictures did he feel alive. His portrait of Cole had been stunning, depicting that her love was not the shallow emotion of a girl, but the deep and true love of a woman. This work had stirred comment from critics in national magazines.

In the portrait of Cole was his thought that character could be shown through the face. Even character to be. "Of first importance," a critic had said, was his belief that he should know why a picture was being taken." To him, mere form in a picture was flat unless it had substance and knowledge. What one felt about what they saw was of the most importance, and he knew what he felt about his work. To create the illusion of third dimension was craftsmanship. That made photography exciting. He knew that he had grown with each picture. In her portrait he had struggled for the expression of grace, balance, and the fulfillment of a dream. The turmoil in his life had enabled him to see more of that which he sought: his pictures had body, content, and a philosophical essence.

With part of the prize money he had bought Cole an expensively bound special commemorative edition of Kentuckian Stephen Foster—one of her favorites. She had been thrilled, and had thanked him with an impromptu hug. It was the first such precious gift she had ever received other than from her parents and his first such personal recognition.

This night, Cole's thoughts could be heard in the music. She was singing of the tender, hopeful search of a young and lonesome heart, not fully knowing the answer. She could smile, she could sing, she could dream, but deep down inside was uncertainty. From a time when she was very young she had learned that things in life did not always turn out the way one hoped. Her eyes were alive, but did not reveal, yet the heart of the guitar and the throb of her voice were a message to Brant. She sang with the simple conviction that the value of a song rests in the words and that the music without the words would have little meaning. "Singing talk," she called it. She had never learned to sing the blues.

Cole was singing of her love for Brant. To her it was a commitment as deep as the beating of her body. She did not study the thought that his need of her seemed different than her need of him. These were the hours when she forgot time and place.

Every man on the boat thought she was as unforgettably beautiful as her voice. Except, it was not the same with Brant. Cole was often out of his mind. As soon as he left her he forgot her, but she was aware of his presence no matter where he was on the boat. He kept moving in her mind like a wave on the shore. In its search for love, her spirit followed his persistently. She was devastated by love. To her, love had no special hours, it was a forever and an always, creating music in the water of the river.

In Brant there was too much of the boy in one who wanted to be a man. He was not aware of what she could give him. He lacked the maturity to have this keenness of observation and he went away from her empty. Cole was profoundly confused at some of the beautiful things he considered trivial, not realizing that what to her was tenderness, joy, and love was to him a release from sensuality. She loved him though she was not able to understand him or why she loved him. She was not familiar with what Bess called "a man's drifting ways." The river valley was dark and cool with a starlit sky above the hills, and long afterward Brant was to remember these soft summer evenings with clarity.

Cole was obtuse in the ways of men and unaware of games with the heart. She lived in a fear-happiness, unaware of the nights she cried in her sleep, of a memory in her dream, of a disturbing search, and in her dreams she kept hearing his voice, feeling his body, and the touch of his lips in the warm darkness.

Bess and Old Rip had been watching from the kitchen doorway. "We hurt ourselves far more than others can hurt us," she said.

Old Rip nodded in agreement. "Love is a gamble," he said, thinking back," and I picked a winner."

"Some win and some lose," Bess answered, remembering. She was wondering how Brant could make it through a voyage, looking at a shining moon reflected on dark water, hearing the soft sound of the river against the sides of the boat, and listening to a beautiful Kentucky meadowland girl singing the loveliest of all love songs without falling in love with her—without living, feeling, and experiencing the grandeur of those dreams. "When you look into some people's eyes you are uncertain of the truth," she said, "but when you look into Cole's eyes you know the truth. She was made for moonlight." Bess believed that God marked each saddened day and rewarded every sorrowing tear. She believed that each generation had its differences as well as similarities.

"Brant Mitchell is a lucky young punk," deVoss declared. "He can't lose."

"Oh, yes he can," Glemp answered. "He can lose her." And that was all he would say to deVoss about it.

As Cole continued singing the moonlight accentuated the silver beauty of her face and Glemp watched deVoss, slithering down the deck to be closer to Cole.

Old Rip turned to Bess and raised his eyebrows.

Chapter Nine

The following week, after the singing, the off-duty crew had gone to their cabins for a few hours of sleep prior to their watch. Only Cole and Brant remained on the foredeck, looking toward the shore and watching the lights reflecting on the water. In a small riverfront town rows of lights dotted the straight lines of the main street and a cool breeze drifted down from the hills. The town was quiet on this balmy summer evening.

To Brant, in the mist, Cole's blue eyes seemed black, questioning, and disturbed. Against the slate shadows of the bulkhead her face was a blur of paleness, her eyes reflected the deck light. Above the subdued vibration of the engine and the distant splash of the paddlewheel, all else was silent. Her mind was filled with an uneasy stillness, there was a constant nagging at her heart. She stood in fear of rejection. The shadow of doubt had crossed her mind. If only those hills could wall them in so he could never get away from her. The river was dark, the water smooth.

Cole was leaning against the deck rail. She had fixed herself to look beautiful for him in her best attire. The boat, churning slowly up the river, had moved through a pocket of mist. Then it moved out into the moonlight, casting an ashy light upon the moonlit waters. It made the rippling river a lovely sheet of Damascene silver. The churned wake of the paddle wheel glistened white in the moonlight. They heard the puffing wheeze of the smokestacks as if the old boat was having trouble breathing. Brant loved the sound. A brilliant moon made the shadows deep.

"Do you believe in magic?" Cole asked, wishing that a magic formula would transform him into her husband.

Brant shrugged, wondering. She laid her hand on his arm.

"Do you believe there is magic in moonlight?" she questioned, "Or do you scoff at that as moonshine from the hills?"

"I know there's magic in the moonlight on your face," he answered. She was thrilled by that. His easy charm took her breath. *It's easy to please a girl,* he was thinking.

Cole had so much wanted to go to a fine restaurant and then to a movie with him as other couples did, but there had not been one such night to remember. The gleam from the moon put tiny points of light in her eyes as she watched the river and the sky and the stars. Her stepmother had told her that there is music among the stars. Cole said, "I'm convinced that on certain nights, under certain circumstances, starlight has the scent of a moonlit garden." Brant remained silent, looking at her as if he had never heard or thought of such a thing. Cole rubbed her hands on the smoothness of the railing. She glanced at her hand. She had no engagement ring. She had nothing but words, and wondered about the words. Leaning against the rail tiredly, almost slumping. Her mind was preoccupied with their problem. She was waiting for those special words. Brant's thoughts were with the sound of the boat. As she waited for his reply she was filled with a resentment and love, her moods swinging from high to low then back to high again. It was a mingling of joy and fear—a softened mood happy with hope, yet uneasy with doubt. At times he seemed such an enigma. She felt a young girl's welling of love and desperation.

"I've waited all day for this." Her voice was cool, soft, and low. Their moon shadows on the deck were touching. She looked up at the night sky, then at Brant. "The stars actually do sparkle," she said and smiled, swelling with hope. Her face colored with emotion.

Their secret meetings were becoming more rare now because of his avoiding her and her desire and need to be talked to was like a hunger. There were so many unanswered questions. It had become an obsession. She so much needed him to say something, the right thing, but there seemed a stubbornness about him. Cole's life could only go on where she was loved. She wanted to just have someone there, someone who mattered. She expressed the love and yearning to have someone to hold. The need was deep inside. She had always felt a loneliness but since her love for Brant, in his absence, her loneliness, became more acute. She had not yet learned to listen to a warning, as a bell in the fog. The warm summer nights diffused her security, as if in the darkness her fears went to sleep.

They moved from under the deck light into the shadows, sheltered from the night breeze in privacy. Brant touched her hand and the blood rushed through her heart as if being close to him meant she could keep him. *Now he will ask,* she thought. She became radiant again at the first touch of warmth. He had opened his arms to her and her yearning for him made her chest ache. He was anxious to get off the deck and to her cabin,.

Yet, she felt each of these secret meetings with terrible intensity. It was like a fragrance, the more deeply she breathed the more ethereal the scent. Brant's eagerness for her soothed her pride. She did not feel snubbed and cheapened. Then she was in his arms, looking up into his face, holding him like a child clutching a doll. Their kiss was long and hungry. In his arms she escaped the complexities and surmises of understanding. Though she could not see him in the darkness, she heard his breathing. Her passion surged. Since the death of her father, Brant was the most vital presence in her life. In him she had experienced rapture. She was so thankful to be able to see him, have him near, and talk to him. She wanted to be as close to him as possible.

When he released her she was silent, then her face glowed with thought. "After we're married I can continue to work while you study to take the exams," Cole said, very low. "That will make it possible for us to live together openly. I'll take such good care of you." She had asked for nothing more in life. He had not asked her for marriage, now she had asked him. Her voice was submissive in presenting her simple reasoning. She felt she could undergo anything for him and the practical naiveté of it escaped her. Was it possible to survive on dreams and a wish? Her naiveté was genuine and the lack of pseudo sophistication of many girls was obvious. In the shadows Brant did not see the gentleness of her face. She waited. She was riding a high wave of expectation. Grasping this thread of hope, she said, "If it means defying your mother and father, and going on another boat, I'll go with you," she said. "Or, I'll go back to school if that is what you want." She knew that he was impressed by girls who had gone to college. "Whatever you want me to do I'll do gladly. Wherever you go I will go with you." She waited for his answer.

He tossed a gum wrapper into the river and watched the dark roll of the water take it out of sight. He did not want to be mothered, or sistered, or wived, he wanted to be romanced.

Brant was listening more to the varied sounds of the boat. Every sound had a meaning. The river had a resonance of its own. The hour was late and there was little time left before he had to go on duty. Cole was looking at drifting reflections in the water.

"No need to go on another boat," he replied with a shrug, as if he understood all there was to know in the way of the world. "I won't need help. I know every step of the way I'm going. It's all planned out for me." The feeling that he had other obligations had taken precedence. He did not look into her face. He looked off into space when he talked. "Talk of marriage and going to my parents right now is a little too early in our planning." He glanced at her, then away. Young, self-absorbed, career-minded—he had a one-track goal.

When it mattered most to her he was not of help. Cole no longer felt necessary. She was certain that he was shying away from a confrontation with his father, and it all evolved from his career and family. So far, her efforts to bring about a meeting with his father had failed. Many thoughts occupied her mind and she spoke words for him that he had never spoken. He had never spoken of his mother, or of Cole visiting his home. An emptiness seeped into her. *Does his thoughtlessness mean he will not stay with me after that one night of our intimate relationship?* She wondered. She did not know. *Was that one loss of control a final mistake?* Her face chilled suddenly. He looked at her, not understanding that she was shy with a bewildered hurt and was ashamed of her proposal. He did not realize her gentleness.

That soft summer night had changed her untroubled girlhood. Not understanding, a flood of emotion filled the night like a physical storm. In the distance the vague and hoarse sounds of the river and distant land noises could be heard. Suddenly, a blast from a steamboat whistle shattered the night. Cole's thoughts of the future had drifted into timeless dreams and were shattered by the steamboat's sound of reality, destroying her cloud of illusion.

"I'll stay with you through thick and thin," she said, her hand on his face, determined that he understood her thinking. It was such a simple expression. "Do you know that I would work myself to death for you?" She stopped, studied his face again. Another rejection. To her, this feeling of being unnecessary was the most demoralizing feeling in the world. She felt he must be made to realize that marriage was inevitable. She wished she could think of better words—more polished, more intellectual. She wanted to use words to impress her thinking upon him. He scarcely heard the words above the sound of the boat and failed to see the love in her eyes or the softness in her yearning. She loved the sight and sound and touch of him—everything.

He remained silent, but moved restlessly, chewing gum. He wanted to go to her cabin, she wanted to talk, reason, and get answers. She was looking for assurances to make plans for their future.

Brant thought he heard someone and moved away nervously to search, but no one was there. They both feared deVoss and were on edge. He had not told her of deVoss at her cabin door the night before. Often, the only sound between them was a sigh or a whisper, neither made long speeches.

Cole was a listener and he needed a listener, but he was talkative only about his plans for a career on the river and not about them. He was nervous with her out on the open deck.

To ease the tension, Cole laid a hand on his arm. "When I was a child, I thought you could walk to the top of the highest hill and step from one star to the other," she said. "I climbed the green hill on the open slope in the sun. I didn't like the dark woodlot." She was remembering the unforgettable sound and feeling of thunder among the trees. She had grown up in fear of darkness, remembering the night her parents had been killed.

Then she was in his arms again, her breast rising and falling, his lips crushing hers. He tasted the sweetness of her mouth and smelled the perfume of her hair. A few light stars were watching overhead. To her it was as beautiful in moonlight as at dawn.

"The river is so beautiful and so mysterious at night," Cole said to him, backing away, looking at him with loving eyes. She reached for his hand. Like the hand of a child, she slipped her hand into his, forgetting the rebuff of her proposal a few minutes earlier. She spoke simply, unguarded.

"Yes," Brant answered, though he did not have her poetic nature. He smiled cheerily, relieved. He had become nervous concerning her more serious talk of marriage.

Just that touch of a smile warmed her heart and brightened her eyes with encouragement. It made her feel good about herself. She put her cheek to his. The deck light made them one amber shadow. He was shaking, anticipating. The blood coursing through his body added to the pumping of his chest. Holding her close had warmed him.

He's pleased, she thought, and remembered the other nights on deck that summer during which she thought of nothing but this soft, summer dream, as if it were the first summer for the entire world. It was the moment of stolen bliss that had built the castles in her mind: their marriage, their home, their family. She had just begun to live and wondered if anyone had ever loved like that before. She looked up at the sky with the stars shining down. Hers was a love, like fire, that consumed. She was an entirely different person, though she remained simple and sincere. She ran her hand through Brant's hair and wished her heart would not beat so violently. A gentle softness showed on her face in the moonlight as she inhaled the fresh breeze coming across the water. All of her strength and hope was restored. Images flowed into her mind.

"I love you, Brant," she whispered, holding him. "Wherever you need me that's where I'll always be." Her imagination created many visions. Her voice was soft with feeling, her emotions flowing like a river flood. Her heart was racing.

Brant remained silent, kissing her in place of words. He was lost in the thought of the moment. She did not need words and she knew he was troubled by some words. *Is it only his fear of being discovered, or is it something more?* she asked herself. Into her eyes and voice came all the open love, need, and hunger that was hurting her. It hammered at her heart and yet an air of simple dignity was in her. She would remain alone in her cabin until they were married.

"Happy?" he asked in a softened voice, drawing her to him again. He was avoiding her statement, motioning toward her cabin. Her head moved up and down at the question. She shut her eyes as if nodding in pain.

"Oh, yes," Cole said. The words were so soft he strained to hear them. "But I can't get the fear of deVoss out of my mind. You must do something about him," she added, searching the shadows with a genuine fear in her voice. "He scares the daylights out of me."

"I intend to," he answered. "He'll be put off the ship when we reach our home port of Cincinnati. His days of terrorizing you are over!"

A ring, a halo, looked like a collar of steam around the moon. The moon, traveling, appeared to advance on the mountains, flooding over her life. Old tales about a ring around the moon had always made her uneasy. She was glad to know that deVoss would be gone.

"I'm so thankful to have you near," she whispered. The expression of her feelings was in her eyes and the meaningful depth of her soft words.

He reached out to her and her face lifted to his in the moonlight. The dark gods of fear were made silver-bright by the hope of a hungry yearning. There was a long silence. They were often silent. There was as much silence as conversation. She spoke very quietly to him.

"You didn't answer my question of marriage," Cole finally said. Her voice had grown stronger and richer during the summer; It had deep tones for a girl and was intense with feeling. She felt her hopes lifting a little. There was sincere eagerness in her tone.

They were looking out across the river as she waited for his answer, searching the many-colored lights of the small river town, which flickered on the water like star formations. Watching the lights leaping through the summer darkness, there was the never-ending sensation of leaving the flow of lights of another small town on a dark river night. The lights quivered on the river like crumpled tinfoil and made the hills look magical. Some of the river towns seemed to grow as a river delta, a coral reef, or like Topsy. She did not know what to think of his silence and looked at him in question, not feeling as confident as she had sounded. *Are my expectations beyond hope?* she wondered.

Cole had a mystical affinity with the river and the valley that influenced her thinking. She felt as though she were clutching for someone who was not there. Abruptly she tried to stop that thought, make it stand still, and clear her mind. Brant was scowling into the dark night when he heard a soft voice say, "Remember our first night after the singing?" She asked the question in a caressing voice, almost in a whisper. Realizing that he was not going to answer her question of marriage, she wanted his carefree summer mood back. Those were the happy moments.

"Yes," he said, lightly, "I remember." She could not read the look in his eyes. The sound of her words faded in the night, lost in the overpowering sounds of the boat. Her love for him filled her soul, but to love him was not enough. She needed his love. She drew him to her and kissed him passionately, hoping the magic of the beautiful night would grant her wish.

Unbeknown to Cole and Brant a dark shadow was cast on the deck, watching and listening. The shadow slithered to Cole's cabin door, hoping to enter and be there when she returned to her cabin. It was locked. The shadow slowly moved on toward the pilothouse.

Suddenly the entire deck lightened about them as bright as day. They broke away from each other and flattened against the cabin wall. Laughter sounded from the foredeck.

"DeVoss! Turn that spotlight off!" the captain shouted from the pilothouse. "You're blinding my vision!"

"Sorry, Captain," deVoss called back from the bridge. "I was just checking some of the barge lines along the deck. I thought one had worked loose."

"I've got to get out of here!" Brant whispered, in shock.

"When will I get to talk to you again?" Cole asked, terrified, yet desperate. She was trying to compose herself. Her pulse was racing.

"Tomorrow night, if possible. Otherwise, the following night."

"Where?" She was willing to dare anything to be together.

"Here. Behind the lifeboat. But be careful!" And he was gone. They had parted without saying good-bye to each other. If only she had the gift of previsions of what was to be. If only she knew what lay beyond the horizon. And the *Storm Bird* moved on, leaving a purling wake in the mysterious water among the dark shadows. Cole stood in thought until her breathing slowed, then went to her cabin.

Chapter Ten

The following night Brant stepped out of his lighted cabin into the darkness of the main deck. His cabin had been hot and stuffy, now insects were buzzing in his face. He had told Cole at supper that he would meet her on deck the following night, giving himself more time to think and devise a plan to divert her continual talk of marriage, and speaking to his father. *It's way too soon for that,* he thought.

He stood at the deck rail in the dark, trying to clear his mind of the uneasiness of how to talk to Cole and reason with her. He was unsettled about his father, and tormented by the thought of what his mother would say and do if she were to find out. She had been the dominating force in his life through his childhood years when his father was away on the river. He was a young man of nineteen and could go out on his own, but he did not want to break with his family or the family tradition. He was watching the shore. The streets of the small riverfront town they were passing were empty. It was bedtime. The oppressive heat was now tempered by a slight breeze that carried a refreshing coolness after a hot day. The deck lights cast a dull glow on the water. The shoreline silhouette was clear in the moonlight. He was proud of his unusually keen night vision as he stared out into the soft radiance of the night. He stood a long time, staring into space, thinking. In looking toward the shore he saw only the darkness outlining the trees and felt the darkness of confusion.

It was a clear, bright starry night as the *Storm Bird* pushed up the Ohio River past timbered shores and meandering meadows toward the remote mountains and coal mines of Reed, West Virginia. A three-quarter moon was bright enough to ribbon the river. This part of the valley was a mystic union of hills and glens—a quiet, dreamlike place so lovely that even the crew watched it with feeling. Brant sniffed the scent of the highland air like a hound.

In the hills the river was especially appealing to Brant at night, though he did not like navigating "black water," as he called it. The river wrapped a personal closeness around the boat, giving him a deeper perception of things unseen, yet known, such as the heavy pulse of the giant steam engine, the powerful, driving stroke of the piston arms, and the splash of the huge paddle wheel. Every boat had its own voice. They were all familiar, comforting sounds. The sound of the water as it slapped against the sides of the boat was as meaningful to him as the soft sound of the wind through the rigging. Certain sounds were never tiring, their wild poetry was almost therapeutic. They were sounds that had become a comfortable part of his needs. Never to anyone on board would he admit that he had a book of poetry hidden in his cabin.

"Hank!" Brant called, as the young deckhand came down the deck. "Get Glemp up here to relieve you on deck-watch."

Hank grinned shyly. "You know what it is like to try to wake him up," he said jokingly. "You have to take a club to him."

Aslant the reflective waters came the dancing lights on a summer evening boat excursion. There came, also, the particular sound of the calliope. These were sounds retained in Brant's memory. To him there was no other sound like the calliope coming across the water at night on the soft summer air.

He remembered the many summer nights at home as a child, sitting on the porch with his mother, brother, and sister, listening to the sound of the calliope coming from the gay party boats steaming past their home on the bluff. How he longed to be part of that excitement and adventure. In later years he wanted to be part of the dancing and parties aboard the fun boats. He considered them the elite of the "palace" boats on the Ohio River: elegant, lacy boats with all their filigree work that had layers of decks topped with colorful awnings, such as the *Island Queen.*

A clutter of shore lights twinkled like stars in a clear sky. The boat was close enough to the shore for Brant to hear the wake roll the pebble and sticks along the riverbank, and people sounds coming over the water. The wake had set the shore awash and its water sounds disturbed the birds in the cattails of the backwater. He could hear a bawl-mouth hound in the distance. The trees floated in a ground mist, their leaves rustling in a slight night wind. His own thoughts were as restless: He wondered what to do about he and Cole. What could he do? To keep her, he would have to take a stand against everything established in his life, everything planned for him in the future. His father may give in to the idea, but his mother would never consent. If he followed Cole's advice and left the boat, he would lose the advantage of his father's help, and that of the company for which they worked. They had a brilliant career outlined for him. He was a young man with a goal.

He was aware, also, that his troubled spirits were having an effect upon his relationship with the crew, and this was not good. He knew that his father was aware of this and thought of it as unprofessional and unacceptable. What the crew would tolerate in behavior from a fellow deckhand they resented in an officer, especially the captain's son and they reacted accordingly. It had already had an ill effect upon their attitude toward him, their work, and the boat. The captain would not and could not tolerate it much longer, even in his son, and Brant knew this better than anyone on board.

He thought that he might be in love with Cole, but he had not given it serious thought. *After I get my master's license will be time enough to think of a wife and a home,* he thought. He believed that he probably should express this thought to Cole, but was afraid that it would inspire her to put too much pressure on not to wait, possibly go to his father.

He considered this summer night more miserable, hotter, more still, and with more mosquitoes than usual, all of which were determined to live on his blood and sweat. Everyone wanted something from him, it seemed. He did not like hot summer nights. He had been told that some backcountry people rubbed coal oil on themselves to keep the mosquitoes away, but he would rather face the mosquitoes. He tried to stay away from the deck lights where the bugs concentrated, hoping for a freshness from the slight river breeze, but it was blowing from the hills that had been bathed in the sun all day and it was as warm as shallow water.

As his jumbled mind tried to clear itself, he became aware of passing a small town that was fronted by the river, and bordered by the rising hills and heavy woodlands. He saw the entire town at a glance and knew the town by the design of lights: a small cluster of lights with blackness on all sides. The boat was not more than a stone's throw from the riverfront street and he heard the voices in the night as he formed a decision. In the distance could be heard the cry of a nighthawk.

In his mind he wrestled with the pros and cons of whether to take Cole and run, as she suggested, or to stay and get his master's license and a boat of his own. He decided to wait. If she would settle for a later decision, fine. If not he would be forced to tell her good-bye before they arrived at home port. Yet, unknowingly, she meant far more to him than he realized. Deep within himself he loved her.

From the town he heard a fiddler playing for a community hoedown, probably the only entertainment most of the people could afford. On shore time he had attended many such gatherings. Outsiders often thought of these people as entombed in remote canyons and some of the local people thought the same thing, including himself, until he participated.

Across the short expanse of water he heard the plaintive wail of a country ballad singer and other faint sounds of the small town. It stirred his blood. He wondered if he was too young to settle down. It was the sound of a musical story with the meaning of a man whose heart lay along the river. In the blackest of nights there was no mistaking the sound and meaning of a fiddle, guitar, and a five-stringed banjo. To him it was a good sound. It was the kind of night when it was good to hear a guitar, a fiddle, and singing. It sounded as if it came from men who worked on the water, loved, and had a family.

He heard the gay hubbub of the dancers and the caller as he chanted to the fun-loving couples. He tapped his foot as he looked out over the water, thinking maybe he should go to her and tell her of his decision. His thoughts were of Cole and himself in her cabin. He glanced at her cabin occasionally, still wondering if he should go to her. He stood in a position in line of sight of her cabin door, waiting for her to appear. But in the dark he could see only the vague outline of her cabin.

He turned his attention to the river and the tow, seemingly unaware of the music, dancing, and Cole's sleepless eyes. But he was listening to the fading music of the small town, and in the following silence he heard the far off voice of a hound bawling on his chain, impatient for the night hunt, and the answering challenge of the farm dog's bark. It sounded like his grandpa's dog, Battle.

Brant remembered his grandfather with a heroic feeling. The love of the river was ingrained in him. His grandfather had been in the Civil War. He had been younger than Brant then and worked on the riverboats. As a cabin-boy before the war, he had met Stephen Foster when he worked in the office of a steamboat agent in Cincinnati.

"That was before folks were singing his songs on the riverboats like Cole sings them now," he had told his grandson. Brant remembered other conversations:

"Many ghosts sail these rivers and on their courses much of the history of our country took place," he said. Brant's grandfather had worked the riverboats when Mark Twain was a pilot on the river, though they had never met. His people had been on the river a long time. Brant recalled the words of an American folk song that his grandfather sang:

"Boatman dance, boatman sing,
Boatman do most anything,
Dance, boatman, dance.
Dance all night till the broad daylight
Go home with the girls in the morning.
Hey, ho, boatman row,
Sailing down the river on the Ohio."

"The family tradition is in our blood," his grandpa had told him. "I've given you this gift of genes as it was given to me. We've inherited a natural feel for the helm." It was true. Brant's thinking, longing, and devotion to the river, boats, and his career had six generations to anchor it beyond release. By some it was considered unusual, abnormal, even unwholesome, but not to the Mitchells. This is what Cole had failed to realize. She was too unknowing to understand the Mitchells placed their profession above personal matters. They did this without knowing why or thinking of it. It was a life for which they lived.

Brant knew his grandpa with love, but he longed to have known his great grandfather, a legendary captain. He longed to have seen his face, to have known his voice, to have seen his smile, to have heard the words of his thinking about the river and the great boats, to have heard his good laughter, to have known his wisdom, and to have sensed, and to have realized that which was within his heart—the substance of his love. He was saddened in thoughtful longing to have known that which was long past. It caused him a deep, unnamable sadness. He had never heard his stories. And he always had the sense of the endlessness of the river...the river never resting, always changing, sometimes gliding, sometimes storming.

It was then that a movement caught his eye. It was someone lurking in the shadows near Cole's cabin. Brant ran toward him, but when he got there the man had disappeared. For the first time he feared for Cole's life.

A few hours later, when they made an unscheduled docking at Gray's Branch for emergency replacement parts, deVoss slipped ashore for several minutes.

The telephone call from the unknown crew member of the *Storm Bird* to Captain Mitchell's wife was brief.

"Mrs. Mitchell?"

"Yes."

"If you care about the future of your son, you'd better learn of what a scheming woman is doing to him aboard the boat. Don't be fooled by the talk of her English ancestry. It's a lie!"

Mrs. Mitchell's call to the coal storage yard at Coal Grove the following morning was equally as brief. "Please have Captain Mitchell call his wife at home as soon as he arrives!"

The telephone conversation between Captain Mitchell and his wife was not so brief. It involved her intention of traveling on the boat to Cincinnati on the return trip and having a talk with her husband and her son. Her parting words were brief. "It would behoove you to pay attention to what I have to say," then the conversation was charmingly ended with all the proper clichés.

The captain, equally as determined not to have a family scene aboard his boat said, "I'll call you again, my dear, when you've quieted down." Even though she laughed her social laugh, he knew that she was offended, deeply offended, and would become more determined as time went by. A hungering to maintain position, prestige, and prominence had molded an attitude within her, and the captain's long periods from home had not been conducive to an idyllic marriage. This was a fact that she was determined no one outside of the family would know.

Chapter Eleven

The following night, in the late hours of the mid-watch, it was cooler with the midnight air of the hills. Cole and Brant met. Stepping from the lighted deck they moved into the shadow of darkness behind the lifeboat. She could feel the cool evening breeze drifting across the river and hear the water lapping gently against the boat. With the soft sound of water and the beautiful cast of the moon, how could a night be more perfect? She liked the soft, reassuring sound of the water along the hull. It was soothing. It was a friendly sound. Only the boat running lights were glowing in the dark. It was a night to uplift the spirit. She took a deep breath, enjoying the purity of the night air. Stars were scattered around the moon, the water glistening in the moonlight.

"Cat got your tongue?" She asked lightly, breaking the awkward silence, trying to lighten a mood while putting on a brave face.

"No," Brant answered slowly. His tone made her uneasy, his brevity was cautious. He did not like her many simple expressions.

She looked bewildered. "Is that all there is to it? Just 'no'?" she asked, trying to lift his spirits to assure herself. But then, looking more closely, she saw more. A full moon was sending enough light for her to see the expression on his face. It was not a subtle change. His eyes mirrored his thinking. "What is it?" she asked softly. To her, even his sullen look was handsome. She could also see his impatience.

"Nothing," he said in a forced way. He thought that at times she sounded too dramatic, too poetic—an alarmist.

"Is it because of the night before last? Because we were almost caught? Do you think your father planned that searchlight warning?" she asked, troubled. She was forcing a lightness into her tone of voice.

He shook his head, his face tight. "No," he said, and she sensed a constraint between them. "That was deVoss's sense of humor." He was having difficulty finding the words.

"Something's wrong, Brant. More than almost being caught. What is it? Tell me!" Cole was forever edging forward, restless to know and understand. She was searching for coherence, unable to see the reality behind the illusion. She wanted a statement from him concerning their future. He resented the pressure. She studied his face by the glancing moonlight. Because she loved him she knew his moods and cared. In return he gave her a blank look and paused lamely as she stared at him. Everything had become so confused for him. He glanced nervously toward the pilothouse.

"No, not really," he said, finally. "Nothing's wrong, exactly. Why all the questions? You used to be full of fun and laughs. Now you're getting too serious." She detected the strain in his voice and interpreted his uneasy smile. The expression on her face had the troubled gravity of a child.

Cole felt the pulse twitch at her temple, her face close to his. "Everything you feel is on your face," she said, a touch of alarm in her voice. "Tell me, Brant, did deVoss see us in the searchlight the other night? Has your father said anything?" She cried in growing anxiety, fearing their separation, but knowing he should talk to his father. Actually, she wanted him to talk to his father. She could hear the tremor in her throat, her voice sounded strange to her. *This can't go on,* she thought. *Or am I imagining things?*

"Tell me what it is?" Cole cried. "Don't sit there like a bump on a log!" It was as if she were calling in a voice he could not hear. "I have a right to know." The doubt on her face deepened at his reticence. "Why won't you tell me?" She spoke softly, moving toward him. He could see the rise of her breast.

"No, my father hasn't said anything yet. If he had I would tell you." His words seemed toneless. "It's true de Voss tried to spotlight us, but I'm sure my father didn't see us. I think the crew knows, or some of them, anyway, but I'm not sure about my father. You never know about him. He always knows more than he lets on. Then it's too late." She turned to him more in fright than in surprise.

"Surely you don't think we can go on like this without being discovered," she said, her anxiety mounting.

"I don't think about it." Cole knew this was not true.

Things were not working out as he had planned. Brant was miserable. "Maybe he's guessed." He shrugged. He did not want to gain trouble with his father, nor did he want to lose Cole, and he did not know how to achieve both. He was guided by unstructured impulses. He made a desperate effort to recover lost ground with her. "Don't worry about the old man. I can get around him. Why are you so moody all the time lately?" he asked in vexation.

Cole placed her hand on his. How she longed to take him in her arms. Her smile was more of an effort to assure herself. Yet, there was something within him that whispered to her of hope.

"Because you're troubled," she said abruptly. "You're holding something back. You're different." She looked at him questioningly.

"I'm not different," he said. "Everything's the same between us. Unless you change it," he added.

Cole knew this was not so. She knew, also, that if she pressed him too much he would withdraw within himself and find an excuse to leave. It had happened. before. Young and self-centered, he was blinding himself to her feelings, and to his own.

"Well?" she asked. "Has your father said anything?"

"I told you no," he repeated, irritably, wanting to change the subject and not seeing the entreating in her soft eyes.

She wondered at his sulkiness. "Then you should go to your father and talk to him about us," she said. "Don't wait for him to come to you about it. It will be too late by then. Face him. Tell him we want to be married." In the darkness she could not see his reaction. "I don't like feeling guilty," Cole went on. "It isn't right. It's contrary to everything I believe in." Then she said more gently: "I'll go with you to your father if that will help." She was watching a piece of driftwood disappear into the darkness. For him she tried not to show too much distress.

Cole halted her next question, embarrassed, wondering why she was doing all the talking and all the planning for their future. She was asking all the questions and caring. She imagined conversations between them that had never been uttered, but until she got answers from him her plans for the future were meaningless. He did not say anything. No matter what she said to him it seemed to evaporate like a wave disappearing in the river. She became less timid, pausing. Then she said gently, "Brant, please talk to me. Please." There was no answer as he made the pretense of checking their location and lines on the barges.

"Let me help you, Brant," she said, then went on softly, intensely. "Let's help each other. Let's face your father together." She felt guilty in questioning his love. "I'll always be there beside you when you need me."

He did not recognize the mute appeal in her eyes, her voice, or on her grave face; Her pleading, awkward and strained, was not understood. He had not reached that level of introspection.

"The time isn't right to talk to my father." He was frightened and angry at what had become an awkward and uncomfortable situation. "Just be like you used to be and have fun."

"Fun!" She could not believe his use of the word fun.

"Sure! What's wrong with that?"

She gave him an exasperated glance, then softened. "How? How can I be like I was when things aren't like they were? You aren't like you were." Her lower lip was trembling. Everything in her mind seemed tangled. *Am I making a fool of myself?* she wondered.

"It's your imagination," he said, his words having a lifeless ring. Cole had not reached the conscience of his perception. Her will was not strong enough to carry him. He turned away when she stepped toward him, as if he must hide his eyes against such an ordinary truth. He had not answered her question. He had not grown to that reality. "Okay. Let's say we get married and I go on another boat like you suggested. What then? I have to start all over, that's what. I have a terrific career ahead of me here with my father and with my own boat with this company. To start all over without that kind of help, it would take a lifetime to catch up," he said, with the self-centered expression of youth. "That's not for me." His attitude was stifling her hopes.

Everything within her became alarmed at the tone of his voice. Something, somewhere in her mind, was bothering her. It was an inner shrinking. In reaching out to Brant she was trying to solve their problem. She loved to have him hold her in his arms, yet had known almost nothing about him, only that she loved him. Yet, she was sensitive to the constraint between them.

"Something is troubling you deeply, Brant," she said once more. "It's so obvious, and I have a right to know what it is. Be honest with me. It's reached a point where we have to settle our plans." She looked at him, almost challenging. "It isn't like you to be so uneasy and worried. Where is all the laughter and bright talk of our future?" Brant's silence and tempers she could cope with, but this sullen brooding made her apprehensive. Brant remained silent. There was something unnerving in his attitude.

"We can help each other," she continued. "Talking opens the heart. My mother always said that."

Brant let out his breath. He tried to smile, but the muscles of his face would not permit a smile. His eyes moved nervously. He was not a liar, but could be evasive.

"I keep telling you there's nothing wrong." Brant stammered as he spoke. "Quit pushing!" His voice sounded hoarse and awkward. "Why all the questions? Why all of the doubts all of a sudden? Don't worry so much!" His dodging of the issue frightened her.

The tone of his voice was like an alarm bell to her ears. She was bewildered by all the things unknown. It was her first uneasy realization of being pushed aside, unneeded, and she shivered in the chill of the shadowed breeze. *Am I just being childish and sentimental or do I simply not understand the intention of what he is saying,* she wondered. Bess had warned her that hope was a matter of feeling and that reality was a matter of fact. *Was this summer a reality or was it an illusion?* she wondered

"Worry?" Cole faltered. "It's more than worry." She made a small, helpless gesture with her hand.

Cole was staring beyond Brant, out and across the river, as if her world was being washed away. Like the petals of a bloom, her thoughts and emotions peeled back one after the other. Brant tried to soften at the expression on her face.

"Well, it's my life, too, remember?" Brant said evenly, though he looked at her uncertainly. He thought she was placing all the emphasis on what was best for her and failed to realize the depth and purity of her meaning.

Brant's vague answers were too evasive for Cole to fathom. Her inexperienced eye and ear had not conceived this skittishness previously. She had gone as far as her reasoning permitted, but she was now beginning to realize, vaguely, that something tragic was going to alter the thin, golden thread between pleasure and pain. It was her first realization of how their relationship had eroded and she was unable to mask her fears.

"I know," Cole answered carefully. Intuitively she drew back into herself. "This is our life, our plans." She could not admit to herself that Brant might be trying to get away from her. In love and terror she turned her face, trembling. "It's been our love this summer," she murmured in hope. They both had become uneasy with the word love, avoiding each other's eyes. It was as if she had backed off a long way to look at things through different eyes. She longed for words of warmth, as one dying from the cold, and was trying desperately to hide a fiercely hurt pride, hoping to draw strength from the lovely scene bathed in moonlight. She wondered at the beauty of the night when her own feelings were so disturbed. The moon had emerged from under a cloud and the river had turned to silver.

Just one brief moment? she thought. To her it had been like a lifetime of summers. *Was this summer but the duration of a dream?* Her need of love went beyond yearning, instinctively knowing that a woman should not live without love. "Those without love are lonely and lost," her foster mother had told her.

"I never said the word "love" to you all summer." He spoke before he had time to think of what he was saying, or how he was saying it. She had opened up the opportunity for him to tell her and he was relieved. He was uncertain of his feelings.

It could have been no more of a blow if he had struck her. It was like an electric shock. His denial exemplified the disgrace of deception. A terrible feeling came over her as if an iron fist had gripped her innards as a premonition of an anguish to come. She stopped suddenly, forcing back tears. "Then you don't love me?" The simple words were all she could say. His frown stopped her.

"I didn't say that." He tried to speak with indignation. He really did not know. She stood, not certain of thought or feeling. She could not express in words what she felt.

A guilty resentment was seeping into Brant as he saw Cole's eyes glisten with tears. "Now why are you crying?"

"Because what you said hurt." And she remembered Chain's words concerning a photograph: "There is a moment when you can see and feel the pain in a picture." She wondered if this summer was destined to be no more than a painful memory.

Brant was no more able to cope with guilt than he was with pain. He experienced life as a boy watching an airplane go by: excited, thrilled, and wondering.

"Everything's been perfect 'till now," he said, defensively, at the sight of her face. The palms of his hands felt moist. "Hasn't it?" She looked at him gravely.

"We have held each other lovingly," she reminded him and turned her head away, her hands gripping each other slowly. She felt sick and ashamed, yet glad, also. It had all changed overnight, but even this did not undermine her love. "You changed my life...." The night breeze that moved her hair brought a darkness of the heart, a heaviness of the soul, and a weight of sadness. She felt the opiate of warm summer nights on the river with the scent of the hills, the sophistry of starlight and moonbeams, and the sweet poison of warm breath. A suffusion of shame was spreading over her. *Am I begging for love? This would hurt more than his abandonment,* she thought. All at once a deep resentment rose up in her. She wondered why she could not continue to speak. *What is the meaning of our love to him?* she asked herself in place of words. Like a story, each night enveloped them in mystery.

Brant was incapable of reading her pain. The fire that consumed her had gone unnoticed. He had no real understanding of her tears. He turned to look out over the water to the little lights on shore. It was a reassuring sight.

"I thought we were just having fun," he said. His voice seemed strange to her, not the voice she had loved to hear all summer. It was as if he had consciously sought to hurt her when she needed tenderness. It was like a slap in the face.

They were silent for a moment, staring into the night. In the deep shadows he could see the whiteness of her face. Every time she thought he was responding, something washed it away. *If only I had the right words,* she thought.

Cole spoke finally, out of the stillness within herself. Her voice carried the same note of entreaty. "Oh, Brant," she said huskily, "you know better than that." It was the simple, deep-felt expression of an unconditional love.

Brant did not want to give up their relationship, yet he dreaded a showdown with his father, even though he sensed it was coming. They had stayed together in the open longer than they should have, and he was afraid they would be seen by deVoss. All these things tormented him.

"I'm not saying it's over," Brant went on, jamming his fists into his pockets. "I don't want that. Everything's the same." The frustration of his evasiveness was agonizing to her.

"Then, why are you acting like you are?" Cole said, wanting to believe him in a desperation of hope. "Why have you been avoiding me?" A cold light of reality was bringing doubt and apprehension to her. Realities were clashing with dreams.

"All I'm saying is that maybe we shouldn't see each other for a while until we can work something out," Brant said in a conciliatory tone, "just a little while," he added quickly. "Let things settle down a bit." His words seemed to come mechanically.

"The only way we can work something out is with your father," Cole insisted. "We have to face it." No answer came.

The moon was slowly sliding behind a mountain and it was too dark to see Brant's face clearly, but Cole could tell from his voice that he was frightened. He had misunderstood her hesitation. It had made him feel better about himself to think she was accepting the alternative. He did not answer. They were passing Muletail Flats, and she was thinking that Brant was as stubborn as a mule. She stared at the river for a long time, her thoughts on his talk with his father. She had no idea of the outcome; She could only hope.

"Why?" Cole asked, finally. That was all she could think of to say as she stared from dark and intense eyes. "Why would you say what you did if your father hadn't told you to?" In his silence she asked, "Do you have some other reason? Why should we stop seeing each other? Why can't we go to your father? Why can't we get married?" she persisted. She was fighting to keep her voice steady. She was fighting for the one thing that was her life. "This couldn't be your idea. I know! I've felt your joy." She looked at him with the eyes of a dog pleading not to be kicked; hoping. "Even a dog knows when it is loved and when it is not loved." One word from him and she would have been in his arms, every instant hoping to see the expression change on his face.

He flushed with guilt and did not answer her directly, afraid to tell her the truth: that they would have to wait. He was ashamed and stammered, "Well..." and his voice trailed away. She gave him time, then turned back to him.

"Why?" she asked again, sick at heart. He had no answer and gave no comforting.

"It's against the rules of the boat for one thing," he managed to say with attempted forcefulness. "I'm an officer." He thought that boat rules would be the answer to everything. She looked at him with enormous blue eyes. It was a look of complete amazement. His ambiguous words were bewildering. The meaning was unclear in view of what was happening.

Brant's words rolled over her in a crushing wave. "It was against the rules for you to come to my cabin, too, but you did," she said at length. Then she added, "I wasn't thinking of rules." He flinched as she clenched her hands, pausing, trembling, and half-shamed. "And it was against the rules for you to make love to me," she went on quietly and relentlessly. The color coming back to her skin. Her eyes were shut tight, as if holding a thought.

"When I told you not to worry about us I had a good reason," he said, relenting. "It'll be best for us to wait. You'll see. Let me handle my father. He's never turned me down on anything I've asked for or wanted yet."

Though an ideal and empathetic listener, Cole exclaimed, "That's what you've said all summer." And the tears came to her eyes as she realized that she could not wait.

"I tell you everything will be all right," he repeated, placating, and not wanting to draw attention to them by loud voices. He waited for her assurance and departure. He was desperate to avoid a scene and anxious to be gone. DeVoss would be prowling the deck soon. "Just trust me," he said. It was not convincing or reassuring to her.

Cole gave him a fleeting glance. To her he had a hard-to-fathom expression in his eyes. She frowned, her fine dark brows almost meeting above her nose. She was looking at him questioningly, watching him without knowing him. The deep stillness of the night made the giant engine seem to tremble. The deck light threw long diagonal shadows across the deck in abstract designs. The water sounded like a remembered song, a river that sang the song of eternity, and she could not understand the words and intentions of a young man. She wished only the best for him. She wanted only good for him—for them—but after hours of talk she still had no answers. She wondered if she had the courage to endure the days ahead. Slowly, she looked at him, then turned away.

"I hope you're right. I hope everything will be all right," she said, exhausted. "I will try to understand." She was brooding over a subject she did not want to bring herself to understand, of which he would not be thinking.

Cole had been living outside the hard core of actuality, but now she gave thought to others. She thought of other women in times past, such as her mother, her stepmother, and her step grandmother, who had stood with their man and had looked out over this ancient river, a flow of fate as constant as the flow of water to the sea. They had withstood the test. They had faced reality. She so wanted him to know who she really was deep inside.

The moonlight was growing dim. They had talked until drowsiness slowed their voices. Scalding tears were trickling down her pale young face and as she looked up into the dark sky her tears made the stars dance. A drifting cloud moved in front of the bright stars. It was as if there had been a cry of anguish, yet not a sound had been made. She was afraid to break the silence.

She hardly knew what to say. She thought she had said everything. "I must go now," she said steadily. "I have to be at work early or your father will be angry." Dawn would soon break. Brant was watching her shadow, cast by the deck-light, thankful for the hour.

"Yes," he agreed, trying to choose his words carefully. He glanced at his watch, her father's watch, relieved. "It'll be time for me to go on watch soon.

Chain will wonder about it if I'm late." He reached for her hand in a reconciliatory way, but she withdrew it.

"I want things to remain the same between us," he said. He believed his words, thinking her only worry was being put off the boat. They stood in silence.

And on that warm summer night she strained for a sound, or a touch, that did not come. She stood small and submissive, waiting. Like a star, the pain lighted her eyes. She smiled bitterly at his confusion, not knowing the extent. She remembered the loving words of her foster father: "No one ever really enters where they are not wanted." She was staring after him, her eyes filled with tears. All the music of her summer had died.

Cole heard his footsteps on the deck growing indistinct in the distance, like the fading of a kiss. "I want you to remember...." but he did not hear, and her words trailed off. It was as if her soul had walked away with him. She stood on the deck until the final echo of his footsteps had vanished and she suffered an emptiness such as she had never known. "One does not relinquish dreams easily," she had read, and realized its truth. She returned to her cabin. It was her burrow, her only escape from the many unanswered questions. It seemed there was always the darkness beyond the next bend, waiting; The long dark hours were crowded with the need of response.

The boat moved steadily on into the night.

Cole lay on her bunk bed all night long, sleepless, thinking, and struggling for reason. She heard only the lifeless pulse of the giant paddle wheel, feeling the heart that beats in the darkness. Her conversation with Brant kept her awake a good part of the night. She felt humiliated, but had no control over it. She had a key to her cabin, if only she had a key to open Brant's heart. The restless night was of half-hope and half-dreams, blanketed with fears and the constant beat of the tumult within her. If only the realities of day would blend with her nocturnal dreams, but dreaming and hoping was of little comfort. It all seemed so far beyond her experience and comprehension. Through the never-ending night she had gone over and over every prospect to the extent that she was capable. All of her thoughts, plans, and dreams seemed to amount to nothing, and she wondered if it would always be this way. All she could see was the darkness of her cabin; All she could feel was the darkness of her soul. She dreaded the dark, lonely night and the lingering memories. She covered her tear-stained face with the pillow to smother her sobs. In the lonely darkness of her cabin she fought to cling to hope. Something was speaking to her in the shadows like a rising wind or a flooding river: the river of no return. She knew the eternity between the darkness and the dawn. Only Bess knew the entire story of that night when Cole sobbed until dawn like a brokenhearted child groping in the dark. The deep, crying sobs were a reminder of her past. It broke Bess' heart to hear her crying.

Cole lay in blackness for hours with the sound of power on water and a sinking feeling within, trying to push the dark thoughts out of her mind.

Formerly, night had brought peace to her, but now, even the blackness of night could not hide her grief. Oh, how she longed for the comfort of her little room on the farm. She closed her eyes and tried to relax, but cried until her emotions were exhausted and her pillow was wet with tears. Through the long night her lonely cabin seemed as still as eternity, with Brant in her every prayer. She often thought of her school friends, sheltered in their homes with loving families. When she finally dozed into a fitful sleep it was filled with nightmares, her dreams creating a restless night of feminine emotions she could not dispel. She had had more than one dream torn apart in her young life.

Cole awoke in the morning as a woman, having made a decision.

Chapter Twelve

A few days later the *Storm Bird,* though pushing a tow of empty barges, was making slow headway up the Ohio River against a stubborn current. Street traffic in the greater cities moved at a high speed, but the riverboats crawled like snails. It was rapidly clouding over, the accumulation of a few thunderheads had been building imminently in the later afternoon, rolling across a fading sun and casting a dim hue on the flat roof of terracotta clouds and on the river. There had been no dawn that morning. The cloud shadows were moving across an uneasy sky that was overcast. A vast cloud formed many miles long, darkening the sky. Then the cloud stopped, as though resting on the hilltops. The cloud was so huge it covered the entire valley. A wind out of the north began to ruffle the river. There was the smell of rain in the damp air. The heat was oppressive. It was the well-known atmosphere of a storm before it broke. "The calm before the storm," they called it; clouds low and heavy with warning.

"Storm workin' up," Shark said, pushing a cowlick from his forehead. He was accustomed to the endless moods of the river.

"We need it," Glemp agreed. They had a seventh sense regarding inclement weather. "Summer's been as dry as a bone."

"Don't like it," Shark replied. The sky had become sullen with warning of a heavy rain. "That sun's sinking like a boat taking on water and we're headin' into the brunt of it."

Captain Mitchell shaded his eyes and looked at the jagged outline of the hills. There was a look to the sky that told of a weather change. His senses warned him of the coming storm. Low, gray clouds came scudding across the ridges and moved down the valley, forming the scowl of a storm. A hazy light filtered through the cloud cover. He was more than aware that the sharper and more defined the storm clouds, the more the wind and thunder and the lightning would verify it. On the river there was a constant change of scenery, a constant change of weather, a constant change of events, and a constant change of moods. Cole was standing at the railing, enjoying the wind brushing her hot face and ruffling her hair. It had been a slumberous day of warm sun that made her drowsy after having only a few hours of sleep. The heat waves made her uncertain of her vision. She felt smothered. *Maybe it's my imagination,* she thought. There had been a brooding quietness earlier in the day.

The sultry air was so heavy it was difficult for her to breathe. Later she noticed the cool smell of approaching moisture. It was a copper haze that seemed to vibrate, forming small mirages. Though the heat was still hovering over the water, she observed that the wind was blowing with an edge of warning in it, moving the broken wrack of dark clouds into a fading radiance, clouds that were humped like a camel's back. She stood in wonder. It was a scene of half-sunlight and half-storm. *It must be over ninety degrees in the shade, she was thinking, and this boat is hotter than the boiler room.* The heat had become oppressive.

When Glemp came running along the deck at a dogtrot Cole stopped him. "Do you think the captain will make me go below out of the storm?" she asked. "It's so stifling." She always asked Glemp about the weather. He had learned the signs of the weather as well as a meteorologist. He had a premonitory sense, having experienced all the dark power of many storms. The clouds were heavy with rain. The river was rapidly changing its mood.

Glemp laughed. "There's an old saying along the river: If you don't like the weather just wait five minutes and it will change.' Storm, fog, rain, snow, tropic heat, cold—we get it all."

"Some men have a more natural ability to read and predict weather," Cole said. "My stepfather was like that. He was a farmer." Severe storms frightened her. The air was sultry and heavy with heat.

"Don't you worry none. The old man can tell what to do by the smell of the air," Glemp stated proudly. River men were more than familiar with the results of dirty weather.

Glemp pointed to the dark clouds and said, "When the black burial skies come, you don't need no orders from the old man to batten down." It was the sky of storm to a seaman.

"Are you sure?" She asked. She could almost taste the wind.

"This old boat's weathered many a storm come hell or high water," he answered. The wind was rising strongly; The river was becoming more dangerous. The humidity was so intense that the night watch found it difficult to sleep during the day. A storm cloud crossing the sun delivered the message as a flight of ducks dipped and scurried in the wind gusts. The wind had a bite to it. Looking at a private dock they saw an old platform boat that was worth more as a collector's item than when it was built a half century ago.

To Cole the weather had become as uneasy as her thoughts. She was looking at a heavily clouded sky with only an occasional patch of blue, well-aware that Mother Nature's mood could change it in a hurry.

"Will it be a bad storm?" It was a sticky heat that made her ill. She struggled to keep panic out of her voice, yet Glemp saw terror in her eyes. She was afraid of electrical storms.

"Could get real bad on this river," Glemp shouted in the rising wind. She could feel the perspiration rolling down her neck. "It's a norther," he added. "The wide-open river gets the brunt of it."

The ominous cast of the storm-shadowed sky chronicled the advance of a river squall, one of the sudden Ohio Valley storms that often turned out to be the front-end of a terrible blow. Nature produced violence as well as beauty.

"It's not unnatural for a gale to blow in the Ohio Valley," Glemp shouted, "but winds hardly ever get to hurricane force." Her eyes opened wide. *Hurricane?* she thought.

Having been raised near the river, Cole realized that all rivers have their individual qualities and meaning to the lives involved. She never ceased to wonder at the force, the beauty, and the majesty of the river under all conditions. It was invigorating.

Glemp looked up. "It's blowin' hard enough to make the smoke go the wrong way," he said, pulling his hat down tight. The wind flattened the dress over Cole's youthful body.

"Hey, Glemp," deVoss yelled. "Who's rowing the off-duty crew to shore tonight?" And he laughed at his poor joke, staring at Cole.

"From the looks of this river, it don't look like nobody," Glemp said stonily, not appreciating the jest nor the look.

Cole watched the wind-rolled shadows scud across the water. The breeze strengthened and the river took on a light chop. The wind was high—a gusty and exhilarating storm signal—and the clouds moved like dirty, boiling water mixed with steam. "My mother used to say, 'The wind sees all and knows all. If only we knew the words of the wind,'" she said. The wind was running across the river, touching the trees on the shore and causing a whistling sound. She was excited, but a little frightened, also, as the wind brushed her face with a warning.

To Cole it was the dramatic sight of a wind-driven sunset that she could escape, but to the men of the riverboats a storm meant hard work, sopping clothes, and a mixed-up schedule. They were proven men at just another day of work. They earned their berth in the worst of economic times. She could feel the wind tangling her hair as it fluted in the rigging and whispered to the stacks.

"Dog days," Glemp said expectantly, as if to prophecy the storm. It was the instinctive presage of men who work with the worst of elements. He actually seemed to enjoy a storm.

Bess was standing in the kitchen doorway, studying the scene. *Strange how conditions can change some men to dark and stormy moods,* she thought; *those with a secret and damning personality. Some change in a storm, and we sure don't need any more problems than we already have.* She was thinking of Durand deVoss in regard to Cole. The clouds were stacking up, pushed by the wind.

Cole noticed that a surging updraft now sent the black clouds hurtling high over the hills and the darkness spread over the valley like dye, heralding a change in the direction of the storm wind. The wind blew her hair straight back as she watched birds on the wing to home and safety.

"These storms make days as dark as a root cellar," Glemp shouted to Cole, laughingly, "and we're headin' straight into the teeth of it!" The expression on her face made him protective. Glemp was so huge that he looked as if he would be comfortable in a gale aboard a buccaneer ship under a full spread with the decks awash. "This one will be a gully-washer!"

She could see that there was some light lower to the horizon, but the high point of the sky was as black as the coal they carried. The clouds were like a charcoal wall.

Glemp looked up at the sky. "It's turnin' black enough to make the chickens go to roost," he shouted. Cole looked up at him with some amusement, but it did not allay her fears.

"We're in for some thick weather all right," Shark agreed as he watched the trees on a wind-swept hill. "I can smell it in the wind. Another consarned storm is all we need." It had a look he did not like. Cloud shadows were playing on the water.

"This will be a real gully-washer," Glemp predicted.

"Do you think it will be a hurricane?" Cole asked.

"I sure hope not!" Glemp yelled. "If it gets that bad we'll be swimmin' for it." The wind had veered a little, increasing. The humidity had lessened and they could smell the freshness of the wind. Cole could see the wind whipping up the dust along the riverbank.

Chain appeared without comment. The approaching storm did not change his expression, though he was concerned about Cole on the open deck and had come to check on her under Bess' orders.

"It's sure fixin' to storm," Cole said to him, then realized it was a ridiculous statement, but she wanted to talk to him. She needed his support. Seeing that she was safe, he nodded and smiled in comfort to her, then moved on as the captain watched from the pilothouse. Chain had his camera under his arm. He had been hoping for this opportunity.

Chain was an entirely different man when searching for a subject for a picture. He was then a whole man. It was a gratification nothing else could approach. He could ignore everything else when he had his camera, even personal danger. It was not a matter of catching storm-raged hills and trees, rocks and water in space and light, there had to be a more profound feeling.

He studied a scene in every light, from every angle—spurred on by the electrifying drive of a storm. He realized one thing above all else: that it had to come from within himself. It was not like a prize to reach for; It had to come from within. It burned within him like a white-hot fire, like the acid etched plate of a photograph, like a poet's soul.

Just one big, pink cloud remained, he noticed, like a huge tuft of pink cotton candy. Everything else was black. What a picture! He had waited all year for this opportunity. Huge shadows were driven across the valley and overhead a squadron of birds drove ahead of the sudden, heavy squall of rain. At first it was just a whisper of rain, then a downpour. He was relieved that Cole was with Bess.

"Nothing like a storm to clear the skies and hills of wildlife," Chain said to Brant. "Every bird and animal has gone to cover." The sun was now like a hazy disk behind the clouds.

Captain Mitchell had noticed that the day made the men nearly prostrate with heat and sapped their energy, making them edgy. But now a storm wind was blowing from the north that took the heat out of the day. The air was saturated with electricity and the men alert and active. He gave orders to take up on all lines to keep the barges from yawing. The sky seemed to have lowered, almost within reach. There was a gray, cold, thin rain falling.

"When the heat lies this still on the river we can plan on a rough heading," Captain Mitchell had told Cole earlier as a warning. He wanted to prepare her for what could happen.

"And when the wet heat comes up this bad," Glemp said, "we figure the dog stars will come bright in the sky tonight unless the storm moves in to cover them It looks like they're going to be covered tonight!" He could read more from the sun, stars, and moon than he could out of a book.

Cole could feel that the wind was intensifying, making a moaning sound in the superstructure, and the sweep of it required the yacht clubs along the shore to fly small craft warnings. She felt the wind coming in gusts, lowering the clouds until they touched the hills. She could see the rain advancing down the river. The river was up, and she could see a small craft tossing and bucking along the shore. In the distance the people on board seemed no bigger than children. There were fewer pleasure boats moored at the yacht club due to the historic depression.

Then the storm hit. It was an unwanted turn of bad luck for the crew. The sound of the gale swelled with the rising of the wind. It swept down upon them as though in hate, scattering the clouds like a flock of sheep. "Hey!" Glemp exclaimed. "Them drops are bigger than buckshot. This is going to be a gully-washer!"

Cole was remembering the words of her stepmother when she was a child. She had said: Rain means that heaven is crying." As she watched the tow, rolling and pitching, she could hear the sound of one barge grinding against another in the choppy water. The waves were battering the barges as she experienced for the first time aboard a boat the furious winds of an Ohio River gale, the pressure placing an immense strain on the forward barges.

Engineer Claude Schneider took one last look at the weather, heard the roar of the wind, and said, "I'm headin' for the engine room! That wind's too sharp for my likin'. It's getting as cold up here as a well digger's ass!" When the foul weather came, Claude holed up below deck like a mole. He felt more comfortable in the bowels of the boat when the rain was pounding heavily on the deck and he would remain down into his den like a bear in hibernation. The lightning seemed to ignite the sky.

Cole could sense the heaviness of the sound and swell of the wind and rain before each new onslaught reached the boat. The wind sounds changing from high to low, became an endless moaning and had brought a nip to the air. She buttoned her jacket. She saw the wind-driven sheets of water moving across the choppy river before it reached them and sought courage from Bess when she heard the great rolling claps of thunder as the lightning cut the stormy skies. One flash of lightning created the strangest light she had ever seen. It seemed that the electricity in the air from the lightning made her hair stand on end. It was as if the air was splintered like a tree. The river vanished into the storm. To her the storm wind sent a message as bitter as gall. The wind-driven rain hit like pellets and brought tears to her eyes, yet she did not want to close the door and go inside even though the bulkheads were streaked with rain.

"If you think this is somethin' wait 'till you're on the river in a heavy snow storm!" Glemp shouted into the deafening cataclysm of sound. It was Cole's first encounter with the power and majesty of a river storm. Glemp laughed, saying, "That wind's whining like a spoiled kid," and waddled down the deck like an old turtle.

First the thunder grumbled, then the wind growled in answer, and the rain pelted like a slap. She could hear the clump of their hurrying feet as the crew ran the dangerously slippery deck. Even Old Rip was hobbling down the deck on bunions, holding on to the weather rail, his old, veined hand swinging at his side. The old-timer huffed and puffed like an old dog on a hot day. He had suffered a permanent injury, but would not give up his job. "I'm beginnin' to show the miles on the river," he panted. He had run the river so long he could have worked the boat blindfolded. This was all he had for which to live. He philosophized, "The years come and the years go. Somewhere in between is your life." It amused the crew. The stories he told were riveting. He'd had his fair share of wear and tear.

"The old coot's older than dirt and has a voice like a frog," Glemp said, smiling, "but he sure ain't no quitter. Everything he does is full steam ahead." Rip grinned. He was a man who worked, watched, and listened. Other than his well-loved stories he seldom spoke. He had never learned how to quit. The rain continued to sweep across the deck in torrents. Cole saw that the quiet, peaceful valley of yesterday was now in a rage as the thunder rolled savagely down the river. In the coming darkness of the storm, distance and time seemed to have no meaning to her. "Old Rip used to work the log rafts," Glemp continued, "but we ain't seen a tow of logs in a long time." He pointed. "Look at him, shufflin' down the deck like an old hound dog on the scent. He's sure put his shoulder to many a wheel." Old Rip was a man well proven and it infuriated Glemp when deVoss referred to him as a stumbling relic who was not worth his wages.

Shark was watching Old Rip, a huge smile on his face. "Here I am nigh a grandpa, and Old Rip still calls me, 'boy.'"

Soon Cole heard the far off thunder rolling faintly over the hills and watched the lightning-torn onyx clouds illuminate with light. The rumble of the thunder was very faint at first. It all seemed so different to her on the boat. The streaks of lightning revealed things she had never comprehended before. The wind picked up the scent of the river and drove it into their faces. Old Rip referred to it as, "Danger written in the wind." Rip's old pea jacket was shedding rain like a duck, his rain-matted hair partially covered by a worn cap. A huge black cloud spiraled upward like a column of smoke. DeVoss referred to Old Rip as a basket case.

"Hell, he must be close to a hundred," Shark stated in awe, and believed it. "He's been through the mill more than once."

"The river's raisin' its voice," Glemp said to Cole. Then she heard the explosion of the distant thunder moving closer and a crimson flare of lightning lit the sky, followed instantly by a deafening explosion of thunder, rolling to the south. The boat shuddered and so did Cole. The storm seemed shocking in its brutality. A strand of hair had blown onto her face.

"When I was a boy," Glemp said, trying to assure her, "they told me that the sound of thunder was God's voice coming out of the clouds." He grinned, but still believed it.

As Brant came out of the pilothouse he said, "This will be your first storm on the river, Cole. You'll enjoy it if it doesn't get too bad." Her first river storm was becoming an incredible sight, and she was thrilled that Brant shared it with her. She felt much safer.

"That rain's sure here full force," Glemp said with disgust, looking at the sky, "and there won't be a dry hand on deck!" Then he laughed, pointing. "With all the science in the world I'll bet no one has ever counted the number of raindrops."

Cole saw that the light was failing and through the sultry dusk rushing the clouds made the wind look black. Driven, the clouds were being packed into the east, the wind increased in velocity, and the waves grew in size. Glemp had told her of men who had been ground to death between the barges. "Sucked under!" he shouted. She shuddered again. The river was building from flow to force. Sometimes it spoke in the anger of flood, other times as gentle as sleep.

"It's blowin' hard enough to crack your cheeks!" Glemp yelled. Then the rain came. Torrentially, the wind raged. "We haven't had a storm this severe in a number of years," Glemp said.

Cole pulled her rain gear tightly about her as the wind became a song among the rigging. There was a smudge of windblown scupper dirt on her cheek. On shore the trees were leaning heavily in the driving storm wind. The rain had become a vertical flood. She could smell the odor of a rain-washed deck.

"I've never seen rain come down like this before," young Hank shouted, pulling his hat down and glancing at Cole. The shore and the hills had become invisible. The gray sheets of rain were not falling so much as being driven. It was a warm rain despite the wind. Cole was carrying a bucket, and the wind almost ripped it from her hand. Water was running down the deck like a sluiceway.

"The wind's blowin' better than fifty knots, I'll bet!" Glemp called to Cole, standing in the hatchway. "She's blowin' a gale now for sure. This will stop all traffic on the river. You'll see! the old man will put in if it gets much worse. But not 'till he has to. He's a stubborn old cod." Captain Mitchell was accustomed to the burden of command. He knew the docking regulations of every town on the Ohio River and its tributaries that lay within their destination. Cole's eyes were wide and staring. Glemp enjoyed his customary over-dramatization. To Cole the sound and the fury of the storm was terrifying. It was a cacophony of sound natural to the valley in a storm.

"We ain't had a storm like this in a month of Sundays," Glemp shouted, and Cole shivered a little in spite of the sullen heat.

"If you think this storm's bad you ought to sail the North Atlantic," Shark exclaimed as lightning flashed a jagged fork and thunder boomed. His clothes were darkened with rain.

The captain looked toward the head of the tow, then up into the sky. The rain was coming at a forty-five degree angle. The boat and tow was moving against the muddy waves of the current and into the rising storm. The boat was drenched in wind-driven rain. He saw that the wind had caused the waves to lash the forward barges, causing the pounding barges to growl a deep thunder of their own. The noisy water, rushing against the barges, provided a background of sound and the rushing river alongside them foamed in churning streams of tan-white river scud. Captain Mitchell was very familiar with the savage sound of water on the rampage. The water was brownish-white blended with shell-pearl gray. The wind and the rain had changed the smell of the river and the entire valley was roaring with sound.

Cole could feel the shudder of the forward barges as they jarred against the waves, grinding together. Dusk was coming on, making the work of the men more dangerous. She could see the running lights of boats along the shore that had put in out of the storm as the river became a fury. The beautiful Ohio had become big, brutal, noisy, and dirty. It was a revelation to her.

Cole was watching the boy on the dog-watch. It was a scary sight. The teenage apprentice deckhand, Hank, had just gone on duty as the dog-watch, wheeling the coal into the engine room to keep the boilers going, which drove the huge pistons that turned the giant paddle wheel. Young Hank felt so proud that Cole was watching him. He looked at Cole with reverence, but was too shy to speak to her. The captain needed power to counteract wind and waves. Every faction must run smoothly under these conditions. The captain could not cut his forward way too much or he would lose steerage and the storm wind could turn the barges broadside to the wind, current, and waves. The barges could fill with water and sink, or break loose and become a hazard to navigation. As usual Hank was working like a dray horse because of his admiration for Captain Mitchell. He was hooked on the prospect of a riverboat career.

"You're the best dog-watch we have." The captain had told young Hank once, and he had never forgotten it. He had ducked his head with embarrassment, accepting the praise. Hank was eighteen years old, just out of high school. His mother was a widow with five children and in need of his financial help. Captain Mitchell knew that young Hank would give his life for his mother.

"The kid's learnin' in the most demanding college in the world," Shark said, "the college of hard knocks." Hank blushed at the praise, making his freckles glow.

"That boy's taken to riverboatin' like a duck takes to water," Glemp agreed proudly, with his bandanna in hand, wiping sweat. "Young Hank will some day be a ship's captain, mark my words."

The dog-watch was a dangerous job during a storm. The man on dog-watch wheeled a barrow of coal up a plank from the coal-tender barge that was secured alongside the boat. The coal was wheeled into the boiler room.

Lightning flashed a bluish-yellow light over the men who were tightening the lines, and Cole was often jostled aside by men coming and going. She saw lightning split a tree on shore.

"I've often wondered if this is what Hell would be like," Glemp shouted with a grin. "If it is I don't figure on going there."

In the brief moment the lightning lasted, the men were caught in the tumultuous beauty of an instant picture. Then darkness thundered about them again. Cole wondered if Chain thought of the flash of lightning as making a picture such as the flash of a camera. Tree branches were bending in the high wind.

Brant was telling her that death awaited the man that slipped on the wet boards as he ran the tow. "He'd be ground to a pulp between the heaving barges," Brant said. The river men often went for weeks, sometimes months, without an unusual conflict with nature that would snuff out a life in seconds. But when it came they sensed it and knew how to handle it.

"Haul it!" Glemp yelled at a deckhand. "This ain't the W.P.A.! You ain't workin' for Franklin D.!"

The captain had given orders for the crew to take up on all the lines on the barges, but this did not keep them from tossing and grinding, though it secured them from going adrift. All lines cinched up and the barges were braced against the storm, though the water ripped at them. A barge adrift in a river storm was dangerous. Loose barges had been known to sink boats and take out bridges. The deckhands scurried fore and aft with a calm that made Cole proud to serve them. She marveled at the surety and expertise among such apparent confusion. She had not understood this efficiency until she saw it being done. It was their life. The old riverboat had weathered countless storms with such a crew and steadily moved on with main deck awash and thunder rolling down the river. Cole was standing in the galley doorway with Bess, watching.

The captain was looking the crew over for a volunteer. "Where's deVoss?" It was a familiar topic and far easier said than done.

"He'll either be in the galley swipin' grub or back aft in the head taking a dump," Shark answered. "He's the only guy I know who can eat a sandwich while sitting on the throne."

"He's conked out in the sack," Glemp corrected.

"Rip, go get him! I want the full crew here!" the captain ordered. "I want a volunteer to go forward and check the barges to see if the waves are coming over the top," came the wind-distorted words. Rip, thin as a matchstick, stumped away, following orders. He was happier than a corporate C.E.O. The years had taken a lot from his face and frame, but there remained strength of will beneath the surface.

I sure as Hades hope it ain't me, Glemp was thinking, saying nothing. *This is the worst storm this season.*

"Don't look at me!" deVoss yelled at Old Rip when awakened. "I ain't walkin' them barges in a freaken storm for no man if I can get out of it. I've run them barges enough in bad weather. Let somebody else slip and grind a leg off!" He had to shout at Old Rip to be heard above the wind and water. If a man was injured aboard the boat, there was no way to get him to medical attention until they arrived at the next town and he was taken ashore in the rowboat if there was no dock for the riverboat to nudge up to.

It was not in his nature to feel guilt-ridden, but deVoss would have liked to have volunteered, if only to gain the respect of the crew in accomplishing the challenge, but he did not. It would have been gratifying to him to have his status corroborated by the men. They were all well aware that death lay in the wash of the giant stern-wheel.

"Push your luck and you're a dead mackerel!" deVoss growled.

Chain had listened without comment. They had excluded him from their conversation, as usual. He realized that he did not have many friends on board the boat among the crew, except for young Hank. He did not seem happy about it or unhappy about it. He seemed to accept it as a natural way of the world for him. He was thankful he had Cole and Bess to talk to.

Any of the deckhands would have gone forward complainingly, under orders. All were capable, accustomed to hard work and responsibility, but had been on the riverboats too long to volunteer. All had been tested and not found wanting. They experienced one crisis after another without breaking. Some of the men did not have the imagination to be terrified. There was the customary undercurrent of curiosity as to who was going to have to go forward under orders and get soaked, maybe hurt. There was not an easy berth on the boat. There were no soft jobs for an adventurer. Between them was the strong bond of the river and also the fellowship of the boat. It was their calling and was deeply ingrained in their nature.

They were aware of the heavy rain, making it more dangerous. The boat was plowing straight into the wind and a torrent was pouring down on them. Visibility was so poor it was difficult to see the end of the tow. Then there was lightning, and the tear of the forked white fire made Cole and Bess flinch as they stood in the galley doorway. Lightning had been known to splinter a boat. Their eyes turned to the captain, unthinking of the customary loneliness of command. Captain Mitchell looked at Chain and Chain nodded. It was understood that Chain would go forward on the heaving barges.

"I'll go along with you, Chain," the young deckhand, Hank, said, his hair standing straight out. He idolized Chain.

"I appreciate your help," Chain said. "You come along with Glemp when he brings the tools." He smiled. "And bring Knobby Thorensen with you. He's a good boy who is trying to learn."

Chain started forward on the tow and before he had traveled the length of the first barge he was doused with spray. His was not a dumb courage in accepting the task, it was a disciplined courage. His instinct guided every step. He was measuring his strength and abilities against the requirement. Every job he did was with competence. In a glance the captain had asked for the best man available and Chain had reacted. Captain Mitchell knew that Chain had common sense—the common sense in a seaman that runs in a straight line back to the Vikings. The tension among the men eased.

"I asked Chain once, 'Ain't you afraid of gettin' killed?'" Glemp was speaking. "You know how he looks at you with that deadpan look, them eyes. All he said was, 'It might be an interesting experience.' He ain't normal."

"Hope he's going to be all right," Bess said, tense with concern. Cole was petrified with fear for his safety. The wind was increasing.

"If he can drink that rot-gut at O'Brien's bar, a little river water ain't goin' to hurt him none!" Glemp shouted above the wind. "There ain't no boatman who ever lived who knows all there is to know, but we give it all we got." And that was more than sufficient. "All life's a gamble," he added, "and I ain't never yet heard of a man that got out of this life alive."

The captain called to Brant in the wheelhouse to slacken the speed of the boat, but to maintain enough headway to keep the end of the barges maneuverable. His voice rose above the storm. Visibility had been greatly reduced and the river had changed from a lazy flow to a serious current. A heavy swathe of rain had dimmed the shore. Turning to Bess Glemp said, "What would be impossible for some is a piece of cake for Chain."

As he inched along, walking the wall of the barge, Chain saw a ferry boat passing in front of them. It had the right of way. The small ferry boat, making a run between Aberdeen, Ohio, and Maysville, Kentucky, was rolling heavily in the trough, smothered in spray. No one was on deck. *It will be their last trip before securing,* Chain thought. The wind had a wailing sound to it.

He moved on, lashed by the wind. He was bending his body against the rain, hunched up like a cold dog. His philosophy in meeting danger was a head-on approach. He was not a man to become overly excited.

From where Cole and Bess were standing, looking out of the kitchen window, the rain made him part of the river. His foul weather gear was wind-flattened against his body. To them he seemed indestructible. He was leaning forward into the wind and spread his arms for balance as he worked his way, step by careful step, along the narrow sidewall of the barge. On one small move the life of a man could be decided. Bess prayed that nothing would happen to him, unaware that she cared so much. The wind became so heavy at times that it seemed the boat was standing still in the sloping rain and spray that lashed Chain's face.

"A storm of this magnitude can be deadly," Bess said, nervously. Cole heard the rain drumming on the deck overhead and was thankful they were in the kitchen. The storm wore on.

When Chain was buffeted by an exceptional gust of wind he staggered, caught himself, balancing like a tightrope walker, and moved on. The two women took in their breath, staring. As he looked down he saw debris rushing past the barges. He could hear and feel the water sucking alongside the hull and knew how quickly a man would disappear, only to be brought up in shreds over the paddle wheel. As he walked he swayed and balanced with the heave of the barge and at every roll he placed a foot carefully on the dropping or rising barge. The sucking noise of the water between barges sounded like giant slops and slurps. Noticing that the wind had shifted a point, he counter-balanced accordingly. The rain was coming down in cataracts as he crept head down and hunkered over, thankful that it wasn't a winter rain that chilled to the bone. To Cole it seemed that each gust of wind became more furious. Every sense must be alert. A mistake could be fatal. She swallowed hard.

It seemed like an hour to Cole and Bess, watching nervously, but it was only a few minutes and Chain was at the head of the tow. It was getting so dark they could scarcely see the wind-whipped figure. He waved his arms to signal a message as the fury of the storm made it impossible to hear what he was shouting. It would all be hand and arm signals. Fortunately, they were steaming up river to load the barges, which were now riding light, and not deep in the water with a heavy load. Even so, in the pilothouse Brant was speaking to the captain. "He says the forward barges are taking on water." Chain was holding his hands out and about a foot apart. "Says there's a foot of water in them already." Chain circled his right hand like a pinwheel. "Says we need splashboards up there." A clenched fist in front of Chain's chest meant "right now!" The captain had been reading the signals also and shouted an order to the crew. He had a ringing voice that could be heard from stem to stern.

"Chain's smart," Rip stated. "He knows you can't fight a storm, you have to work with it." His old face was seamed with wrinkles. He had lived to bury a number of careless, reckless men.

Cole and Bess had not realized how much the forward barges were rising and falling until they saw Chain standing on them as a gauge. "Look!" Cole said, pointing. There was awe in her voice. Up and down he went, bending his knees as shock absorbers, his head ducked into the wind with his face turned away from the bone-chilling water that was pouring over him and into the barges. With so much water in the air it seemed a wonder to them that he could breathe. Even the bill on his hat could not keep the rain out of his eyes. Bess was praying for him. They watched, not saying anything. The flash of exploding light and roar of thunder dominated the valley.

They could not hear him, but they could hear the booming thunder, saw the lighting, and were listening to the increasing wind hurling down the river. The rushing of the swelling river sounded like a great pipe organ that rolled and echoed between the hills and had the distant, muffled rumble of a fire-damp explosion deep in the innards of a coal mine. Watching, both of the women drew in a long breath, but neither of them said a word nor would they leave their vigil.

As the lightning flooded the river, all they could see of Chain was a moving silhouette. To Chain the distant thunder sounded like the salvos of the great guns in France. "I wish I had my camera in place of these tools," he mumbled into the wind, staring into the stygian gloom. Raindrops were running down his face.

Chain signaled again for the splashboards to be brought forward immediately, irritated by the delay, and the captain gave orders to the crew to stop all other work and hurry the heavy planks forward. "Now!" he ordered Glemp.

"Get you ass in gear!" Glemp yelled to the deckhands. "Move! This ain't no invitation to no dance!"

Watching Chain, Cole and Bess were fascinated by his actions. To temper the wind and to shield himself as much as possible from the rain, especially the deluge of river water pouring over him, he knelt to become less of a target. Men who inhabit the river become attuned to the wind and water.

As Glemp started for the splashboards, Cole called to him with concern. "Is Chain going to be all right?" His situation looked hopeless to her in the growing darkness and she was frightened for him. Her hair was soaked with rain as much as his.

"Don't worry! He'll be all right," Glemp said as he moved past the kitchen. "Don't worry about him. Worry about me!"

Each of the men hauled a plank forward, their arms corded with muscles as they worked, their voices of complaint lost in the wind. The planks, acting as a sail, made the men look as if they were doing a balancing act on a tightrope. Experience had taught them to face the end of the plank into the wind and it acted more like a rudder. They were wishing that it was lighter so they could see what they were doing, but they doubted if there would be a morning's brightness unless the storm ceased.

"You get caught between them barges and you'll never need a doctor!" Glemp shouted into the wind. Bess shivered, stone cold. The boat pushed on through the dark storm and bucking river. The lights illuminated the lighted froth on the dark waves as the raging scud floated past them. The wind was singing over the water, pushing against the men as they inched forward. Cole was staring at the wonder and agony of nature. The wind had become louder and louder. It seemed to her it was screaming in her ears. The lights of the small farms along the shore seemed snuggled into the canyons to avoid the storm, their windows were the only beacon.

When the crew arrived at the end of the tow, Chain was waiting to secure the planks into the brackets, which would raise the bows of the leading barges by about three feet. The rain made a rattling sound on their rain gear. Brown water, topped by white scud foam, hissed between the barges and shot up like geysers into their faces. They had years of proven ability and no man could take that from them. They went at it hammer and tong.

Captain Mitchell continued to watch, deep in thought. Rivers have challenged man since the beginning of history. *This is where bravery grows, he thought. Nature has never been concerned with the longevity of man. Her schedule has been for him to live long enough to reproduce and anything beyond that is a plus for him. More than one man has disappeared off of river barges, their bodies to be found days, later hung up on a sand-bar or caught on a skag of debris.*

Each of the deckhands handed a plank to Chain in turn, to be secured by the brackets. Water was flooding over him as he worked in half-darkness as unerringly as a blind man's movements in his own home. He was shuddering from cold water; It took his breath. It was as if he were immersed in the river, struggling to surface and gasping for drafts of air. He was soaked to the hide. He stopped for a quick breather, then worked furiously again. Fatigue became a stimulant and the weather a compulsion. His arms bulged like swollen inner tubes as he handled the planks against the wind and the pressure of the river water coming over the bow of the barges hit him full force.

Chain peered out from under a sodden hat. "Okay, Glemp," he said, "I'm ready for the next one." And it was handed up to him. He did not shout, yet they understood him. The men, however, were shouting at each other to be heard above the noise of the wind and rain as they worked quickly and surely. Working together had bonded them to meet such emergencies.

"I'll tell you one thing for sure," Shark shouted into the wind, "bouncing around in these barges will knock the crud out of you!" Chain grinned, his face dripping water.

"We done got it whipped!" Glemp yelled. To see them working together as a smooth-operating machine would have seemed impossible. They were a good crew, whether they liked each other or not. They were time proven men who made river transportation the legend it was. As professionals, they worked like men driven by the basic desire for a dry galley, hot coffee, and rest. They were anxious to get out of the mess and into dry clothes. The telling of it and the bragging would be pleasant then, but now the wind and the water had become fierce. The men worked in perfect harmony, electrified by necessity. Each heavy storm was a challenge and the crew was equal to it. They were born to survive. Glemp had lost his hat in the wind. His hair was soaked. They had lived with the river and its storms for a lifetime.

"That's the last one," Chain said to Glemp, "thanks." He wiped a hand across his wet face. "Let's head back!" The jury rig would do the job and keep the waves from swamping the barges. Only men equal to the river remained permanently aboard.

From the kitchen, Cole and Bess had been watching with uneasiness. The wind was blowing the rain sideways, cascading it down the kitchen windows, and the glass was as sweat-wet inside as on the outside. To see better they pressed their foreheads against the windowpane. The rain made an exciting sighing sound, beating against the kitchen windows, and they could feel the vibration of it. Bess was watching with genuine concern for Chain.

"How's everything going up there?" Cole asked Old Rip.

"Hunky-dory," he replied with a smile. "Couldn't be done better than by that crew."

Soon all was secure and the danger over. Wet and haggard the crew headed for dry clothes and a hot meal. Bess was ready. A few minutes later Chain came into the galley like a cold, wet dog, seeking the fire. He stood in silence, breathing deeply. Cole smiled at him, putting a hand on his arm. She was thankful that he was safe. Her smile was like a smile coming out of sadness, he noticed. Brant was nowhere in sight. Then a bell rang, indicating that the pilothouse wanted coffee, and Cole rushed off to serve Brant. Before

Chain could speak, or even sit, Bess placed a mug of hot coffee on the table, thankful with relief.

"Here," she said gently and smiled. A warm feeling began to flow over her as she placed the cup in front of him. Plain of dress and manner, Bess had a beauty that radiated from within. "Drink this before you go to change into dry clothes," she said. "There's a little treat in it." She knew the fury that was often in him. She sensed, also, that he was tender as well as tough and she had a special feeling for him. In certain respects she knew more about him than he knew about himself. With the first swallow he felt the heat burning its way down his throat.

He nodded a thank you. She thought there might even be a slight smile in it. She looked younger and prettier than usual, he noticed.

Bess puckered up her face. "Where's the rest of the crew?" she asked. There was a smell of wet clothing in the kitchen. The wet clothes had a sour smell of river water and sweat.

"They're putting the tools away," he answered. "They'll be here soon—wet, hungry, and dead tired," he added. There had been no rest for any of them in over twenty-four hours. They were a natural part of the wind, rain, and thunder. A man did not last long on the riverboats if he could not weather a storm and the work that went along with it. Bess knew he was homeless and adrift, the same as herself. All three of them in the kitchen needed someone. He sat drinking his coffee, thinking of Bess, and letting some rest seep into him.

"Thanks for the coffee," he said as he rose to leave. He had been served coffee in Cole's flowered cup. His smile was all the thanks Bess needed. Their eyes met and lingered. She had an admiration for him that she found difficult to put into words and her eyes revealed it. *He's the kind of man who always knows what to do and never asks anyone to do it for him,* she was thinking.

It was growing dark and as Chain stepped out on the deck he noticed that the storm had caused some of the small riverfront towns to lose their power and the wind had wrecked havoc among some of the boats at the yacht club. Flooding creeks and streams were overflowing the lower fields. He was hoping the downpour did not last long enough to cause a major flood. He could still hear the wind howling through the stacks.

Turning to Old Rip, Cole said, "There certainly is a lot to deal with on the river, isn't there, Rip?"

Old Rip grinned. "We'd never make it without Bess' coffee," he answered. "When you ship with Bess you're livin' high on the hog." A warm smile lighted her lovely face.

For nearly twenty-four hours the storm had howled out of the north. Then, as quickly as it had come, the storm ended.

Chapter Thirteen

The rain had beaten down most of the night, but by the following morning, a clean, rain-washed summer had descended on the Ohio Valley—a valley so fertile it enriched all crops, drying out the flies as well as the landscape. Winter rains were cold, wet, and miserable, but summer rains were welcome and refreshing. The land had needed the rain. Dawn light was breaking in the east and a beautiful golden light shone between the fluffy white clouds. Looking at the rainbow, Cole made the wish that her dream of marriage to Brant would come true.

The apex of the storm had died and the wind was rapidly blowing itself away behind the hills, the air had a fresh smell. All smiles, Glemp was singing his favorite song, "It ain't gonna rain no more, no more, it ain't gonna rain no more. How in the heck can I wash my neck when it ain't gonna rain no more." Cole was watching a convoy of ducks swimming in line, two abreast, in the wind-rippled water of an inlet. The hills were covered with second growth spruce and pine, and along the water were the hardwoods: birch, beach, oak, and elm. Never had she seen a land so beautiful. The sun was well up and getting warmer. She saw Old Rip dozing in the sun.

Sunlight flooded her face as she squinted into the sunshine, her eyes watering. It was the summer heat of early morning that had not yet become sticky. She noticed that when the wind and rain stopped there was no sound of nature except the trickle of water running along the low bulwarks of the deck and through the scuppers. The hawser mooring lines were soaked, heavy with rain and scupper flow. It was a dead calm. It surprised her how strangely conscious she was of the silence after the storm, of her troubled mind concerning Brant, and the uneasiness within her. Her mood was so pensive and wistful. The rain-swollen river was running smoothly, glittering in the bright morning sun. The birds were singing on the riverbank. She loved the variety. Each day was different, a new world of change. There were always so many changes along the river; the sky, the clouds, the scene, and the weather. It was never boring. They were approaching a wide turn in the river with high, wooded bluffs on one bank and green-clad hills on the other. *All this and Brant,* she was thinking, hoping it would go on forever.

She saw the trees turn to gold and the shadows leave the valley, and wondered when the shadows would leave her mind. The visit of Brant's mother that Bess had told her about was coming. There had been a warning in Bess' voice.

The storm had cleared the sky and washed the hills glistening clean. Her eyes were dazzled by the glitter of the sun on the river, but it had not washed her mind free of the worry about her continuing problem or the doubt of Brant. It was a humid summer morning and she could hear the birds singing on the shore. To the outer world it was the sun-flooded splendor of a clear, storm-free morning, but not to her. She envied the carefree occupants in their pleasure boats. The dry fields of the meadowlands of Kentucky had been nourished by the downpour of warm rain and welcomed the rising temperature of the day. The glare and heat of the sun was almost overwhelming to Cole. The smell of fresh vegetation came down from ridge after ridge of timbered hills.

Durand deVoss was lounging against the deck rail, watching the pilothouse. He had a sour line on each side of his mouth. He was wondering when the latest plan to destroy the relationship of Cole and Brant would take effect. *He schemed if that doesn't work, I'll try other more drastic ways. If I can't have her, no one is to have her.* Old Rip stood, watching him and thinking back. He could remember back to a time when some of the steamboat companies on the Mississippi River hired a special officer to make certain their cargo got through safely.

DeVoss watched Brant relieve his father of his watch and waited for the captain to enter his cabin. He intended to have a talk with the captain as his next step, because of a storm that was working up inside of him, but as he started for the skipper's cabin he saw Cole and stopped to watch her. A stiff gust of wind off the river suddenly flattened her skirt against her legs and body. DeVoss ached with the empty, lonely feeling of wanting a woman and knowing he would have to buy one. It was the agony of woman dreams. He was a man possessed. *How would you like to pig-out with that?* he asked himself.

Cole was walking toward the pilothouse to talk to Brant when she saw deVoss, but it was too late to alter her plan. She bowed her head to avert his telling stare and hurried into the wheelhouse. Just the sight of Brant made her heart beat with hope. DeVoss followed her, his movements as slick as a fish.

As Cole entered, Brant spoke without a greeting. "You know better than to come in here visiting," he said. "Regulations. We have to be careful." He said it as if the words were meant for a convenience.

"I brought you some coffee," Cole said timidly.

"We have to be more practical," he added. At the sight of her face, he tried to soften the harshness of his words. He believed that she wanted a commitment too soon, infringing on his freedom and plans, and he rebelled. His look hurt as no words could have hurt her.

"It's just for a second," Cole answered hurriedly, nervousness making her bold. Her eyes flashed anger at the curt greeting, yet the shock had not sharpened her senses. She felt rejected. She had not talked to him in several days. His silence was more ominous than his words, like a shadow moving before the sun.

"There's something I must tell you," she added, nervous. "Something you may not know about." Though she was frightened, she spoke rapidly, with the temerity of desperation. "You must talk to your father! Talk to him now! A talk with him would be for the best. It's the right thing to do. It maybe the only answer before it's too late. We just can't go on like this!"

"I thought we settled all that the other night, about waiting. I've got enough on my mind." His eyes slid to one side. "I told you I was going to talk to him and I will," he relented. "When the right time comes." He stared ahead at the river.

"The time has come!" she almost shouted. "Your mother's making a visit to the boat to talk to you and your father about us!" Her throat was pulsing. "You know what will happen then."

"My mother!" he said, eyes widened, and she realized the genuine surprise and shock. He was not faking or stalling.

"Yes. That's why you have to go to your father about us now, before it is too late. Tell him everything. The truth. Today!" She was astonished at how startled he was at the mention of his mother and that he was not aware of his attitude. She felt hurt and betrayed. She was angry, also, though her heart was breaking for him, for them.

"Who told you my mother was coming aboard?" he asked, suspiciously, thinking she had been fooled.

"Bess," she answered, knowing that he would not question the source. Bess had been certain who had instigated the visit and wondered what the next move would be, though she said nothing of it to Cole. She was more concerned than she dare reveal. Her fear was for Cole's safety.

It was high noon on a sultry day as Brant wiped the sweat from his forehead with his sleeve. To break the monotony, several of the crew members were watching a canoe race close to the shore and were making bets.

"How different their thoughts were in moonlight," Bess said to Old Rip as they watched through the galley window. Old Rip nodded, understanding, knowing that Brant and Cole had a problem.

"I don't believe it," was all Brant could say, but there was no conviction in it. His thoughts whirled.

Cole squared her shoulders, saying, "If you don't go to your father then I'll talk to him!" She was determined to have a conclusion. She had to have one. Each desperate day was passing like the flowing river.

"Wait! Let me do it," Brant said hurriedly, recovering, and knowing that they would soon be in home port and find a solution. "I can handle it better with him." He was hoping to delay until they reached Cincinnati. He would have deVoss paid off, shipped out, settle with his mother and father, and still keep Cole. At that time he could reason with her of his decision concerning them, that they would have to wait until he had his Master's License. He remained silent for a moment, thinking.

"Okay," he said in response to her reaction. "I'll do what you want. I'll talk to my father right away. But it'll be best if we don't see each other for a while," he added.

"Don't you miss me?" she asked with an echo of conscience. "We haven't been able to talk in days." She needed him desperately. Especially since she was without family and friends. *Why is it that I can't make him understand?* she thought. She had reached a point of no confidence and wondered at what she considered his indifference.

"Miss you!" he exclaimed, louder than intended. The surprised note said more than a proclamation. "How can I miss you when you're here and we see each other every day?" And she realized that the question meant absolutely nothing. It seemed as if there was a vast distance growing between them. He took a sip from the mug of black coffee.

She said nothing, just stared at him, speechless.

The thought of his words made her stiffen. She had a feeling of complete emptiness: the feeling of being useless when she wanted so much to be useful. Even in the heat of the day she felt that she would never again be warm. She pressed her lips together tightly, nodded. She was determined not to break in front of him and left the wheelhouse.

Cole had gone to him to remove the dark clouds and color the sky bright with peace and joy, but as she stood on the deck, leaning against the rail and looking at the water, she felt a darkness surging in the back of her eyes. The knuckles of her hands grew white as she clenched her fists against the railing. She believed that it was what was in her heart that counted, but she did not know what was in his heart. Her love for him was so unreasonable that she would have jumped into the river if he had asked her to do so. She felt as if her very being had been looted and stripped bare, leaving the spirit to tremble at the words that battered an aching breast. Yet, she was uneasy because she felt this way.

Emptiness seeped into her and a terrible sense of doom possessed her. The image of his mother was smothering her. She was afraid that she would never be with him again after her visit. They had been together for the first and last summer. The feeling was a truth stronger than her thoughts. All was gone. She had served him. The knowledge flowed through her like the torrent of a flooding river.

Never will I wait at our home for his return, she thought. Her dream of a life with him was gone. She would no more see his bright eyes, no more see his boyish smile, hear his careless laugh, or feel the pressure of his lips. She would no more hear the urging whispers, no more feel the fire of his love, or be held in the firm strength of his arms. There would be no more secret meetings on deck. She would never have the hope to lie down with him, not even in the grave. She would no more dream of a home and children. There would be no more hopes as boundless as the horizon beyond the hills. The plans she had made that summer seemed foolish and childlike. The sound of the river said, "No more!" And the sound of the voice flowing over the water was that of Mrs. Mitchell. She felt as if she were being ripped apart like a boat on the rocks in a storm. She was too hurt even for tears.

Like a punished child she hastened to her cabin to bury her head in her pillow. She was unable to lock the cabin door.

From the galley doorway Bess and Old Rip had witnessed the conversation. "The Captain has a lot more on his mind than boatin,'" Old Rip said, running his fingers through his thinning hair. "I can read it in him. I can feel it." Bess nodded, saying nothing and looking out over the river toward the hills. She remembered and understood that particular pain in heartache. Old Rip puffed thoughtfully on his pipe, then said, "There's trouble brewin'. I can feel it in my old bones. Seems like things always get worse before they get better." He was remembering the flash flood that destroyed his family. That fateful event had changed his life forever.

Who can possibly know of all the heartache throughout all the ages, Bess was wondering as she watched Old Rip, remembering what the Captain had told her about young Rip returning to his boat years ago, broken-hearted. He had lost his wife and child. Her dying words to a friend had been, "Help Rip find someone that will love him and take care of him." He still had the note written by his little daughter, "I love you, Daddy."

"It sure don't look good for Cole's hopes and dreams," Old Rip said, pointing with his pipe. His voice cracked a little at times. "She's got her cap set for that kid and I can't help but wonder how it's all gonna turn out. Some win and some lose." Old Rip had eyes that had never grown old, but had become more wistful and philosophic, with a more serene depth of wisdom. They had not aged and wrinkled like his face.

Brant's out of good stock, Bess was thinking, *just has a parcel ·of growing up to do. He just hasn't yet come to any depth of feeling or meaning, but he will. Someday he'll recognize the tie that binds.* "Well, there's one thing for sure," Bess said. "In spite of all theories life remains our greatest teacher. Time will tell." Old Rip nodded in agreement.

"That girl has a sweet heart if I've ever seen one," Old Rip said, "and she's fallen for that boy hook, line, and sinker." He smiled knowingly. *Those two are right for each other,* he was thinking. Then his thoughts turned back in time; the unforgettable memory of a haunting beauty. *Where has it all gone? Time seems to melt away.*

"And I'm hoping with all my heart that Cole will become his once-in-a-lifetime love of which he is not yet aware," Bess said. Old Rip became silent for a moment, looking out over the river and squinting into the sun. The lines deepened around the corners of his eyes.

He smiled and quietly said, "The heart that truly loves never forgets." The years of loss and loneliness had taken their toll, but when he smiled all those years fell away. He paused, the expression on his face like none Bess had ever seen there before, then added, "I ain't been back to home in a coon's age...nothin' there to go home to no more." He had lost his wife and child in a house fire resulting in years of heartache and loneliness of having no one to have, to hold, and to love. Memory was magnified by love.

Bess paused, smiling as she studied Old Rip's face. "You don't talk a whole lot, do you, Rip?" she asked.

Old Rip grinned. "You learn far more by listening than you do by talkin'," he answered. "The best things in life are free."

In studying Old Rip's face and expression Bess thought, *How little we know of one another.* Then she paused, sensing, and turned. There he was. DeVoss was nonchalantly leaning against a stanchion.

"You manage to be everywhere, always listening, don't you?" Bess stated flatly. *He moves as stealthily as a boat rat,* she thought, remembering the time when Captain Marshall was shot and killed by a robber, never again to see his loving wife and family.

"I just happened to be passing by," deVoss answered with a leer and moved on.

Old Rip turned to Bess and said, "He's always creeping around like a dog with his tail between his legs. He flat ain't the kind of man you could ever cotton up to, is he? He's an odd-ball if I've ever seen one." Bess said nothing, thinking much. She was more than ever concerned about Cole.

Later, Cole came to Bess and said, "Will you please have someone fix the lock on my cabin door. Something or someone has made it so that I can't lock it." Her face was pale.

"You bet!" Bess answered, her expression of deep concern and knowing. "Right away." Cole's distress tore at her heart.

After Cole had returned to her cabin, Bess turned to Old Rip and said, "If ever a man deserved to be called kinky it's deVoss. He's too slick for his own good."

Old Rip nodded. "His kind is a long time in the making. I'll bet he's been that way from the get-go." Then he lowered his voice. "He trails women like a hound on a scent. It's talk among the crew that he's unhinged and capable of anything. Think I should tell the captain?"

"He knows," Bess replied, "and he's watching. Very carefully. I saw to that. Enough is enough! Anyway, as the captain said, 'We can't prove anything as yet, but by the time we reach home port in a few days deVoss will be history.' Wait and see. He's a man on borrowed time."

"I sure hope so," Old Rip growled. "Whatever bad happens on this boat he's always the fly in the ointment. I'd like to see a warrant on the bum!"

"Don't be surprised if you do!" Bess emphasized.

"He's a blood-sucker if I've ever seen one," Old Rip continued. "I've shipped this river for over half a century and I've never seen a hand the like of him. He's more like a weasel than a man. He's mean enough to bite the head off of a snake! But me and the boys will help in every way we can. You know that. Shark's watchin' him, too, just achin' for an opportunity, so we'll just let the chips fall where they may. One false move and he'll be goin' down the river on a log."

Bess was well aware that no signed statement or witnessed contract could have been more binding.

"He follows money and women closer than a bloodhound on the trail," Old Rip added, and his expression had more meaning than words.

"His blasé mouth is one thing, but the meaning in those terrible eyes is another," Bess added. "His being on board stirs the pot!"

Chapter Fourteen

As deVoss was taking his first steps toward the door of the captain's cabin, Glemp came out of the hatchway from the engine room and walked down the deck, humming. The tune was unrecognizable, the only words he seemed to know were, "Nelly, put your belly close to mine." DeVoss watched him until he was out of sight, then off he went, slipping along the deck like a beaten dog. He stopped when he reached the Captain's cabin, looking up and down the deck. When he thought no one was in sight he knocked quietly on the captain's door. The crew was well aware that he was a snitch. When he saw the door handle turn he erased the smile from his face and adopted the expression of a concerned and disturbed crew member. He became cleverly on guard in the event he was questioned about his past. His eyes remained restless and flitted from one object to another as he pushed his visored cap to the back of his head, ready to remove it when he entered the captain's cabin. He stood silhouetted in the false dawn.

Captain Mitchell opened the door, hesitated, then stepped aside and nodded for deVoss to enter. "Unusual for you to come to my cabin, Durand," he said, staring at him with an intense gaze. He never turned a man away from his door. Whether he liked the man or not did not show in his attitude, as long as the man did his job. DeVoss was a good seaman, competent in his duties, and the captain had long since learned to ignore personal quirks or idiosyncrasies, up to a point. Instinctively, he did not trust deVoss and gave him a searching look, studying him. There were no pleasantries.

Captain Mitchell had once been offered a small fortune to deliver an illegal product. He not only refused with a storm, but bodily threw the man off of his boat.

DeVoss stood in the doorway, calmly asserting the right of a seaman to see his captain. He stared at the captain with guarded eyes; mixed with respect was the expression of wariness and the knowledge that a riverboat captain had the power of a king. DeVoss lowered his voice, as if fearing to be overheard. "Sorry to bother you in your private quarters on your time off, Captain, but it's a personal matter." He stared intently at the captain as if he were nearsighted, his eyes slightly bulging. Captain Mitchell nodded, looking at him skeptically. Sun through the cabin window alighted his face.

"Let's hear it. That's what I'm here for," he said candidly. "You know my policy of hearing a man out." His voice was calm and assured, yet he sensed deVoss was thinking craftily before answer*ing. He was determined to put a quick end to it, his tone demanding as he sat stiffly at his antique desk of which he was so proud.*

DeVoss considered that the seldom heard term, "portly," would apply to Captain Mitchell. He was a man of generous girth, though he was a fairly tall and solid man—immensely broad, heavy through the shoulders and chest, and muscular. DeVoss liked this berth, and Mitchell was known as a safe captain with whom to ride the river. He would put up with anything to be near Cole, to have her, and he was attempting to establish himself.

DeVoss smiled a bit smugly, but would not look the captain in the eyes. When he smiled it drew his lips tight across his teeth. His eyes wandered around the cabin, shifting from the captain's face to the bulkheads, the portholes—always moving. The captain stood, waiting for an answer, his face grim.

"It's a matter that concerns your son and the cabin maid," he went on, careful of his tone of voice. DeVoss spoke as if he were on the verge of something profound. He leaned back against the closed cabin door. He seemed to be smiling, but was not. His attitude angered the captain. "You know what the boat rules are for the rest of the crew, Captain," he said with a tone of innocence. Captain Mitchell clenched his teeth. He was fully aware of deVoss' intentions toward Cole. He had been informed by Bess. *He's hell-bent for trouble,* he was thinking, not knowing the full extent to which deVoss intended to dig into things.

Captain Mitchell's bushy black eyebrows raised in temper and through controlled anger he spoke. "I know all the rules, deVoss. I made them." The thin line of his mouth clipped the words. There was a lift to his voice. "What about my son and the cabin maid?" he demanded icily, his brows drawn in. It made him furious. The direct question riled deVoss and he hesitated, planning how best to commit himself. He shrugged his shoulders, then turned to face the captain, his head cocked to one side.

"Captain, I say this because you once brought me before the mast on a charge of molesting Bess," he admitted with less confidence. "I had a choice of straightening up or shipping out. I shaped up. Now, fair is fair, and the shoe's on the other foot." He pointed a finger as he talked. He was settling a grudge against the captain and hoping that Cole would be put off the boat and he could go to her as a savior. He had planned carefully. The captain was studying him as he spoke.

Captain Mitchell stood in silence, thinking and watching him with a look of suspicion. DeVoss had a habit of sticking his face close to the face of the one to whom he was speaking. Captain Mitchell stepped back, trying to control his temper. "It ain't that I want to cause the boy any trouble," deVoss added with a false air. It was said with malicious satisfaction. "As a matter of fact, I like the boy," he lied. He had spoken in a silken tone and he flitted like a nervous bird, knowing that if he dared cross the captain he would rue the day. Captain Mitchell glared at him. He did not like being pushed or manipulated. His expression hardened, his words emphatic and his eyes accusing. He did not hesitate.

"Get on with your point, deVoss!" the captain demanded impatiently, well aware of the hate seeping through the false front. The captain's eyes were wary, searching; Trouble was brewing. "What about my son and the chamber maid?"' he repeated with controlled brusqueness, his tone sharp and hard. The tone demanded a straight answer.

There was a major diminishing in deVoss' assurance and his reply was slow to come. He had more sense than to buy that kind of trouble. "Sorry, Captain," he mumbled, straightening his thin shoulders with nervousness, unable to look the captain in the face. "I thought you didn't know about them," he pretended, though he was well aware that the captain did know. He pushed his thin hair across his forehead, which made him look like Hitler. The movement was as quick as a squirrel as he turned back to face the captain.

Captain Mitchell's face tightened angrily. "I'm well aware of what goes on my boat," he said with threatening authority, his voice cold, professional. The captain cut an imposing figure in stance and uniform, and deVoss was becoming more uneasy by the minute.

The captain waited as deVoss quailed before the sudden burst of temper. A thin line of perspiration formed on his upper lip, his face became sallow. "No offense, Captain." He smiled thinly, his face shrewd. "I only thought that since nothing was being done about it that you didn't know." His boney, axe-thin features showed emotional strain. He was well aware that if he got on the wrong side of Captain Mitchell he would be up a dry creek without a paddle and spoke in a smooth and conciliatory tone. He was happiest when spreading trouble.

Captain Mitchell's face became red and sweaty. He would not have believed deVoss had he not seen the same evidence with his own eyes. "I know." He clipped the words. "It will be handled in due time in the proper way." His warning had an edge to it as he glowered at the deckhand, detesting people who complicated their own lives as well as that of others. The force of the words startled deVoss.

DeVoss straightened up, pretending to be hurt, and started to speak. Then he hesitated, his eyes on the captain. "I don't think it will blow over," he added slowly. "Not for her, anyway. She don't intend for it to." His voice was sullen, a suppressed emotion on his face.

Captain Mitchell did not answer. He was in fear that he would strike the man. He would not discuss one crew member with another. Neither man moved or spoke. Captain Mitchell stood looking at deVoss, measuring him. Only the throbbing of the engine could be heard. *I'll do my duty and listen to your complaint,* the captain thought, *but when we reach home port you're long gone.* His temper was growing.

DeVoss looked at the captain's face and glanced away, silently planning. His eyes were as quick as a fierce dog. He did not want to look directly at the captain. He could not. He saw the fury.

"I've thought of talking to the boy," he said, finally, "but I think it would have more meaning if you did." His words were soft and oily as he attempted a warm and friendly smile that failed. He thought he was able to deceive the captain, but the real deVoss was revealed in his eyes. Then, looking at the captain, he began to sweat more heavily as he shifted from one foot to the other.

Captain Mitchell had trouble controlling his temper. His face hardened, his eyes narrowed, and his voice showed quiet fury. "You stay out of it, deVoss!" he snapped. "I'm aware of my responsibilities. I'll handle it, so mind your own business! I don't need your guidance!" It was a command. Their eyes locked with intensity.

"Just talking, Captain. No improper meaning intended," he said quickly, his eyes wide and frightened. "Just trying to be of help to your son. Such a fine boy." His voice had a whine to it. His face was empty of feeling. The captain remained silent, struggling. His distaste for deVoss was growing. His face contorted with disgust.

DeVoss lifted his eyes in pretended innocence, squinting at him, saying, "They meet in little hideaway places like the pull boat. I thought I was the only one that knew." Captain Mitchell looked long and hard at him, then cut him off, well knowing that gossip fed on exaggeration and that deVoss's intent was focused and energized.

"I'm aware of the details," Captain Mitchell stated, taking a step toward him. The words emphasized his irritation and intentions. *He's as mean as a wild boar,* he was thinking.

"Sorry, Captain," he said obsequiously, "I thought that with so many responsibilities it might have escaped your notice." He sat motionless in the chair, hands gripping his knees as he rattled on, and the captain interrupted with a dark and angry scowl on his face as he paced the length and breadth of the cabin back and forth. He stopped abruptly.

"There are no little hideaway places for anyone on a boat this size," he said, emphasizing each word. "And you are more than aware of that, aren't you?" His patience was near an end. The words were tight in his throat.

DeVoss thought he was prepared to stall for time to answer unforeseen question, but not to a command such as that. It irritated him that the captain so easily saw through his attempted facade. He raised his eyebrows in feigned innocence. "Except her cabin, Captain. Right? No one goes in there, not even you," he said with an attempt at conviction in his voice.

"I'm well aware of that," came the warning reply. "I don't have to be informed of my responsibilities by you." His words hit like a jackhammer. He was having trouble controlling himself. He had struck a man once and swore that he would never do so again. DeVoss leaned back in his chair with his arms folded. He was certain of achievement.

"You wouldn't think of checking in her cabin, would you, Captain?" deVoss said nervously, watching the captain closely, prepared for anything. Captain Mitchell glared in silence, about to dismiss deVoss. "You're too honest for that, Captain. We all know that." His words were as smooth as silk and were soft with false comradeship.

"There was only one occasion, deVoss," Captain Mitchell said, his voice so soft it was ominous. DeVoss was stunned by the captain's knowledge of the details concerning everyone on board. He had not expected him to be so perceptive.

Dropping the quick smile the deckhand hurried on as he saw the captain was about to put him out. "She's no good, Captain. You know that mostly the lower class trash do that chambermaid work and she's using the opportunity to trap the boy."

"Don't say anything about her, deVoss!" Captain Mitchell warned, his face turned cold. He was aware this was not true. "I don't discuss one crew member with another." He had reached the limit of his endurance. Anger had tightened his face.

DeVoss felt that he could ignore the order. "Of course not, Captain, but it's not your boy causing it," he assured him. "We all know that it's her! Such a fine boy with such a good future. It would be a crime to lose something like that. She's just trying to hook the boy and marry into a family far above her," he added with a false look of innocence on his face. His story had a rehearsed delivery. He was hoping for her ruin so that he could have her, and made every effort to maintain his composure.

"I have nothing but respect for that girl," Captain Mitchell interrupted. "She comes highly recommended by a very close friend of mine." The tone of the remark had taken the glove off the fist. "I won't tolerate remarks against her!" He was so angry he had trouble controlling his words. There was a look deep within Cole's eyes that had touched him inwardly. He sat in thought at his desk.

Captain Mitchell was concerned about Cole. His personnel files contained a note from the director of the county welfare bureau that she had suffered an emotional imbalance after she witnessed the mangled bodies of her natural parents when they had been killed. Some ten years later she suffered another emotional setback when her foster parents had died within a year of each other. The note stated that she had developed an abnormal fear of losing that which she loved, that her instability could reach a dangerous point. "She has an unnatural dependency upon affection, causing dark moods," the director wrote. "She searches for someone to love and believe in. It is of life-saving impor*tance to her." DeVoss remained silent, staring at the bulkhead of pictures.*

"I have nothing but respect and affection for that girl." Captain Mitchell repeated. He suspected that deVoss had a personal plan for the girl, and was using his son as a weapon. There was a long pause between the two men as he studied deVoss intently, thinking. *His work skills are excellent, far above average, no question about that, but....*

DeVoss looked away, then spoke in a careful tone, craftily aware that a captain was king. "Of course you have, Captain. I well understand. But more than one man has been fooled by a woman," he said, pouring oil on uneasy water with a false laugh. It was his planned method of diverting attention from himself, Cole, and his intentions.

When alone with the captain he tried to make his speech soft and eloquent. It was his impression of an officer's tone, used when one gentleman was speaking to another. He glanced at the captain's books. He had not read a book of quality since required reading in school. "We see the girl a lot more than you do, Captain, and in a different light; We know her better. She's one of us, you might say. We know her type for what she is, hungry to be part of a wealthy and important family. She comes from the lower element, Captain." His eyes were measuring the expression on the captain's face.

Captain Mitchell had an instinctive dislike for the man, and he was infuriated at the intrusion, meddling, and especially the demeaning of a girl he particularly liked, yet he intended to remain fair and give deVoss a full hearing, but no more. That hearing would soon be over. Inwardly, he was seething.

"I know that your wife is from a family of money and prestige," deVoss conceded softly. "I understand the boy will enjoy quite an inheritance. We hear these things." He saw the blood pulsing in the vein in the captain's temple and knew he had scored a direct hit. "This is what she is after." There was now silence in the cabin, tension in the air. DeVoss had been careful with his words.

Captain Mitchell scowled, knowing in certainty that this was farthest from her mind. He knew, also, that nothing was sacred aboard a riverboat. Rising from his chair he moved toward the cabin door to order deVoss out. He spoke forcefully.

"That is totally untrue and you know it," the captain said. The words came slowly. The quiet tone was a warning. The muscles in his jaw were set hard and tense. DeVoss hesitated, thinking. His face was aflame, but cleverness kept him silent. He sat very still.

Captain Mitchell's personal files denoted the small towns in which Cole had lived. They were not industrial towns, but farming communities, and the doctor, the banker, the lawyer, and a few merchants were the backbone of wealth in the area. The captain knew that she had no conception of real wealth and social status, and did not dwell on such thoughts. She had seen these things in Hollywood movies, he was certain, and read about them in books, but considered them dreams and fantasies. DeVoss decided to press on.

"She was nothing but a share-cropper's stepdaughter, Captain," deVoss continued carefully, bitter against Brant for having her love, "and now she's an orphan kid working on your boat. This is her first, best, and only opportunity to get something big and she's making the most of it. You should throw her off this boat," he suggested, hoping that he would soon get her through necessity, knowing the value of careful calculation.

The captain stood. "Thank you for coming, deVoss," he said in cold, quiet fury. "Thank you for your concern and the information," he added. "You may go now! You've had your say, I've listened, we've both done our duty as we see it, and that's an end to it!" He was a direct man when dealing with uncomplicated men. Angry and defeated, deVoss sat in silent hate. He hesitated, his face had a sour look, and he did not answer.

"Do we understand each other, deVoss?" The captain spoke in a voice that was toughened by years of wind and weather. His expression was grim and his eyes were as cold as ice as he pointed to the door.

DeVoss looked cunningly at the captain, then nodded in agreement. He was beginning to sweat, and a quick caution came into his eyes. Hate was the motivation that drove him. He hesitated again, turning his gaze to the pictures on the bulkhead. There was a long pause before he answered, his face vacant of expression as he stood. "Yes, sir," he said softly. He became subdued, not wanting to seem jubilant in the presence of the captain in such a mood. He had scored his point about Cole and the captain's son. Cole would be his.

Captain Mitchell went to the door, opened it, and turned to deVoss. He found it difficult to control his dislike for this man. He had become aware of deVoss' past and did not want trouble aboard his boat. "You've presented the issue and I'll take care of it," he said dryly, leaving it at that, and dismissed him without so much as a glance. He was a tired man. He was a resentful man, filled with anger, frustration, and not a little bit of sadness. He knew that it was useless to tell deVoss not to mention this topic and this conversation. He was aware that the entire crew knew as much or more than he and watched for the father and son struggle to come. He merely nodded as the seaman was leaving the cabin, and said, "Have Chain come to my cabin."

DeVoss was genuflecting with satisfaction in each step as he slithered out of the cabin, but tried to make his smile sympathetic. "You're a good captain, Mr. Mitchell," he mumbled. "A good captain, and a good father." He was relieved to get out of the captain's cabin, thinking he held the trump card. He breathed freely when he was out on deck. It had gone easier than he had expected it would. He had triumphed over the captain, and knew that he could not ignore it. He could not evade it. He knew him as a father and as a captain, and knew there would be a showdown between captain and mate, father and son. *Perhaps I haven't lost Cole yet,* he thought, as he moved softly down the deck in a mist rising from the river. He went directly to Chain's cabin to inform him of the captain's orders. He was as smooth and smiling as an innocent child. Yet, to keep the nervous tremor of his hands from being seen, he placed them in his pockets. He was uneasy and jumpy.

Captain Mitchell closed the door, walked slowly to his desk, and sat wearily; He sat as a man alone, silent, and thoughtful. He looked up at the picture of his grandfather on the cabin wall: Captain Zuenglias Vandeveer Mitchell. He wondered what that captain would have done. He knew he could no longer procrastinate, hoping for a more favorable turn of events; He had a decision as a captain and as a father.

A few minutes later Chain knocked on the cabin door. Captain Mitchell opened the door and Chain asked, "You sent for me, Captain?"

"Yes," he said. "Will you please relieve Brant on watch and tell him that I want to see him." Chain nodded and strode toward the pilothouse. Distasteful decisions were part of the loneliness of command. He hated to involve his boat in a scandal, but planned to contact the sheriff at the first opportunity and have deVoss investigated.

That boy's in for a hammering from the old man, Chain thought as he made his way toward the pilothouse.

Captain Mitchell slowly puffed on his pipe, tapped the ashes into the spittoon, placed the pipe in his pocket, and sat in silence, thinking.

Chapter Fifteen

The big shock came to Brant a few minutes later when Chain entered the pilothouse and said, "The Captain would like to see you in his cabin." His face showed no expression, his voice had no inflection. He had given the message and moved to take the wheel. He had not said, "Your father." He had said, "The Captain." He was formal with both the captain and his son. He wondered about the outcome of Mrs. Mitchell's intended visit. His deep concern was for Bess. If Cole was put off the boat, Bess would likely leave the boat and go with her. Bess could get a job any place, any day. He knew it would mean trouble for all concerned. Brant was aware that Chain would say no more.

"Thanks," Brant said. "I'll see what the old man wants," and he forced a smile, but the forced grin went cold on his face. He liked to use the term, "the old man" among the crew. It made him feel professional and impersonal. He was wet with sweat. It was a typical Ohio Valley summer day: heavy with humidity. The only clouds were to the east, and a light wind brought the scent of the river. A flight of pigeons was winging by, unaware of the growing problems below them. It was high noon, the sun straight overhead was reflecting off of the pilothouse windows.

Brant stood on the deck a few minutes, trying to think and to plan. He was not a schemer and he was struggling for a solution. He was nervous and frightened, and now felt that it was necessary to see Cole before talking with his father. He had often thought of this showdown with his father, but had kept pushing it out of his mind. He decided to wait on deck until he saw her come out of her cabin. He was afraid to go to her cabin. It was not that he felt he needed her support, rather that he did not want her to make mistakes unknowingly if his father was to put her on the carpet. She was intelligent, but not clever. Actually, she was too forthright, he realized, too truthful. They must work this out together, calmly. He regretted not having listened to her advice.

He glanced up as the clouds moved aside and the sun poured through. He noticed that the hills held the sunlight like a cup. August had deepened the summertime heat and odors. Ugly, blunt barges lined the shore. The weathered black barges had become a mud color. When heavily laydened, the barges sat deeply in the water, without much freeboard showing above the waterline. Along the yellow bank he watched a hungry mongrel slinking up, hoping for food. The clay along the riverbank was baked and cracked like old brick, and the sparse wildflowers had long since burned and withered on their stalks. It had grown hotter every day, the sky a glazed blue and the river flowed brightly. Brant scanned the deck and saw Old Rip, off duty, dozing in the sun unaware of the blistering heat of the afternoon.

Though deep in thought, Brant was listening to the boat. The paddle wheel moved in cadence with the staccato barking of the exhaust pipes. As he watched, spurts of steam shot from above the pilothouse and he heard the heavy voice of the whistle. It sounded like the scream of a rebel charge in the movies. The twin funnels were raising columns of sooty smoke. It was a sulphorous smoke, belching forth like black feathers against the blue gilt of the sky. Fancy crowns capped the smoke pipes and on the spreader bars joining them the huge letter "W," for Whitfield, was framed between the stacks.

He was becoming impatient and irritated that deVoss and Glemp should be watching when he wanted to speak to Cole. The entire crew was aware of his situation, and awaiting the father-and-son struggle concerning Cole.

"That won't last long," deVoss said to Glemp. "Everybody on board knows it." He had to look up at Glemp and the sun made him squint. "The old man will have him up before the mast soon." He gave a nasty grin in appreciation. "I don't know who tipped off the old man," he lied. He enjoyed seeing an officer having problems, especially the son of the captain, whom he believed had deliberately robbed him of Cole, and gloried in it. He had a deeply rooted mistrust and dislike for officers.

Glemp's jaw tightened and his eyes narrowed. "Stow it, deVoss! You ain't gonna bamboozle this crew," he growled, but would say no more. He knew the source of the information. He headed for the kitchen and a cup of coffee. Bess was standing in the doorway of the kitchen and he did not want her to think that he was in cahoots with deVoss. He liked Cole.

As Brant continued to wait for Cole, the sunset was **amber** along the hills and over the low, rolling hills was the farm country, golden yellow. The farmers were getting ready for next month's harvest. It had been a good year for crops. The valley hung in the last golden sunlight. The evening was sultry with the warm winds of summer.

As Cole came out of the kitchen onto the deck, Brant called to her. She was surprised that he contacted her on the open deck and wondered if he was still angry with her for coming to see him in the pilothouse. It was a question she had pondered a hundred times in the past week. Silent and intent, she looked at him; There was no expression on her face, she gave no recognition in a smile or a wave. The question she asked was a silent one. She noticed that his mouth looked thin, and that the corners of his lips twitched. There were no preliminaries. He was tense and harried, in speech. She smiled at him regardless, because she loved him. She had wanted to speak to him, just in case there would never be a chance again. He cleared his throat and said, "We're going to have to be more careful, get our stories together. My father sent word that he wants to have a talk with me." Their eyes met briefly. His turned away.

"It had to come, Brant. There's only one story," she said. "The truth. When does he want to talk to you?" she asked, trying to push aside her fears.

"Right now!" She stared at him, wide-eyed, her eyes the color of the sky.

The color left her face. This was the moment she dreaded, the moment she knew was necessary. "He knows?" She looked deeply into his eyes. He replied only with a vague nod and turned away, saying nothing.

"It would have been best for you to have talked to him before he found out the wrong way," Cole said. "That would have been the most fair to all of us. Are you sure he knows?" She tried to change the tremor in her voice to calmness and failed. They were both frightened for different reasons. Instead of answering he turned to the river.

"Do you want me to go with you?" she asked, simply and bravely. There was always hope.

"No," he answered. "He sent for me."

Her eyes caught the flame of the sun from the river and looked glazed. Her mouth became as dry as paper and she could not take her eyes from his face. Was she to be put off the boat? "He knows?" she repeated.

"What do you think?" He answered her question tersely. "I'm sure he knows. He wants to see me right now in his cabin! This is the scene I've been trying to avoid."

"Is that all he said?" She hardly whispered the words, her voice pitched in an unnatural key, wishing the confrontation had come long ago and was over with.

Nervous, he gave a quick little laugh. "He's not going to say anything until I get into his cabin. Chain gave me the orders." How she wished Brant had Chain's strength of will and character. Her thoughts dwelled on Chain for a moment.

Cole pushed the hair back from her face and said, "You'll be careful?"

"You bet!" he exclaimed, widening his eyes.

"What are you going to do?" she asked, her voice shaking a little.

"Nothing." His thoughts were as uncertain as the weather.

"Nothing?" she burst out, too loudly, causing deVoss to glance up. The word struck a chill into her, but she could not give up following her dream:

Echoes of the summer swam into her mind. She did not say anything more. She thought she should not. She did not know what to say. She did not have knowledge or experience to add to the conversation. Instead, she was remembering with vividness a hundred glowing recollections, using illusion as an anodyne, the haze between dream and reality. But she still hoped and a timid joy returned with it.

"Try. Please try," Cole said. "Now will be our only chance." Hers was a heart that would not fade.

"What can I actually do to change his mind?" he mumbled, letting his eyes drift out over the darkening river.

"Talk to him, Brant. Please. With all your heart really talk to him. Tell him everything and ask for his help." It was as if her happiness, too, was wandering in the dark. She had to know. There must be an ending to the horrible suspense. "What will you say to him?" she asked, and her head canted to one side with the question.

"I don't know." He shrugged in honesty, then cleared his throat and spoke in an automatic tone. "It depends on what he says. I haven't thought about it." He did not know exactly what he meant. "I haven't had time to figure it all out."

Though she loved him with all her heart she was not too timid or afraid to express herself. "You haven't thought about it?" she asked with increasing intensity, looking hard at him. "You've had all summer to think about it! You had to know it would come to this!" She could not understand his seemingly careless attitude toward their romance. To her, his apparent indifference was unbelievable.

He hung his head, his eyes shifted nervously. The cycle of his thoughtlessness was closing in on him. Cole kept very quiet for a while, waiting for his reply. "What are your actual plans for us?" she finally asked as she stood watching him, looking up into his blank face and hoping for words that would never come. "Brant, please answer. Tell me."

He turned with a guilty look. "Oh, I'll try to work something out with him," he said, avoiding her searching face. "It's just that my mind is going around in circles. I told you I'd try, and I will." To her the words seemed careless and said in an off-hand manner.

"There's only one way. The truth. All of it. Don't hide anything. Don't evade anything. If you love me, tell him you love me." She paused, her eyes searching his face in hope of a sign of inner feeling, then continued. "I've wanted you to do that all along."

He did not want to make the decision that would make him lose her. Yet, he did not want to take a stand against his father, his mother, and his future, which he knew this would entail. He was unable to come to terms with her desperation.

"There's nothing else I can do now," he said vaguely, without looking at her. "I could never get away with a lie. Not with him. He knows too much, or he wouldn't have called for me."

She knew she was hearing the truth from him.

The shadow of an impending separation had put an enormous weight on her. Everything now depended upon Brant. When Cole spoke it was with an effort, the words were forced. "You'll tell me everything?" she asked, trying to renew hope. He saw her tremble as they stood, face-to-face. He was uncomfortable at being questioned, in shock at the thought of facing his father with such an issue. Yet, he was in a hurry to get to the captain's cabin to get it over with.

"I guess I'll have to tell you everything," Brant agreed. He spoke with agitation, his words becoming almost indistinct. She turned her burning face away, not able to admit to herself that doubt was in her mind. She did not want to think of it, that something might have gone out of their relationship. She had no more idea of what was to come than what the weather was to be next week.

"Brant?" Cole said softly, and moved a step forward, stopping very close to him. She was trying to understand, to manage living with a happy unhappiness. "Brant?" she said again, trying to force him to look into her eyes.

"What is it?" He continued looking with downcast eyes, as though inspecting the deck.

"Will you try? With all your heart? You will try for us?" It was a groping for love and understanding.

"Yes," He nodded without looking at her, "I give you my word." Studying him, she shook her head slowly, wondering.

"You're afraid?" he asked.

"Yes," she said, fighting the sense of futility that hung over her.

"Of what?"

"Of you." She could not seem to break the tightness gathering within her.

"Me? Of what I'll do?"

"Of what you won't do."

A cloud moved before the sun, plunging the deck into shadow. Caught in its gloom, Cole shuddered. She reached out to touch him, but he was walking toward his father's cabin. In that moment she knew the most awful loneliness in her life. All the brightness of hope had gone out of her day. She was to look on the next few days as a period of numbness. She could find no way to make it bearable. Brant seemed to give her no sympathy, and she would not ask for any. From the pilothouse Chain observed her pain and wanted only to help her as a daughter, aware that a time of decision was close at hand.

She was unable to smile at the honest laughter of men in the galley.

Chapter Sixteen

Brant knocked on the door and entered the captain's cabin. He had delayed as long as he could. He had delayed for four months. His father had his back to the door, staring out over the water at the quiet river evening. The cabin was plain: an old roll-top desk, a filing cabinet, bunk-bed, and several chairs. His pipe rack was on the desk.

Brant closed the cabin door and stood leaning against it. He was uneasy, and his father was aware of this. He had the boyish feeling that it was as if he had come to discuss a bad report card with his father. There was a short, uncomfortable silence between them. Brant was not certain what to expect. Then the captain smiled and nodded to his son. He wanted them to exchange a genuine meeting. He had decided not to tell his son of his mother's telephone call. *No need to thicken the plot,* he said to himself. All he said was: "Your mother wanted to visit and have a talk with us, but I convinced her it was better settled between captain and mate." He pretended to be fingering papers on his desk.

Even in uniform the captain was not a handsome man. His son inherited his height, handsome mien and easy air from his mother.

"Sit down, Brant, sit down," the captain said, eyes warm with affection. "Make yourself comfortable." He wanted his son to be at ease as much as possible, but he remained standing. He had a reverse psychology, even with the crew: He wanted them to be seated and for himself to be standing. He liked to move about, planning his thoughts. He glanced at his cabin. It was a man's room: old, somewhat worn, comfortable, and very cherished. This boat was his pride.

Brant moved to a chair and sat down without speaking. His whole expression had become watchful. The old, leather cushioned chair felt comfortable. The captain watched his son shrewdly. His experience told him to be cautious. Brant remembered himself as a boy enjoying his father's visits home and yearning to have his father's arm around him.

Brant slouched in the marked old chair in which so many men had sat and stared at his father, waiting with an unnecessary twinge of fear stirring in his stomach. He wondered why. He had never feared his father. His eyes roamed the cabin.

The bulkheads were done in dark wood paneling, and one entire wall of the cabin was lined with books. That was a surprise to all visitors. The captain did not waste the weeks and years aboard his boat. He had time for his books and he used it. He had spent the greater part of his life on the river, reading and rereading. On the other wall was a fine, large painting of a fully rigged clipper ship. It was an old original oil painting. Captain Mitchell's grandfather had been a saltwater skipper. The gilded frame set off the fine-grained wood of the wall.

The captain's index finger pointed to the unseen hills and valleys. "Your ancestors pioneered this Ohio Valley territory and never moved farther west or south," he said inflexibly, not attempting to hide his pride or purpose. To Captain Mitchell, other than his family, there could never be anything so close to his heart as this river valley, which held an immeasurable gratification. He was deliberately impressing upon his son family responsibilities. He smiled in memory of things that mattered intensely.

He pointed to a photograph in a plain wood frame on the bulkhead. It was of a riverboat captain. "That is your grandfather," he said, not casually. He was watching his son closely. Brant had seen the photo a hundred times. He admired it. It had meaning to him that he was the grandson of such a man. "Have you forgotten? You should remember how much he wanted you to follow the family profession, as my grandfather encouraged me." He spoke quietly, but his words were heavy with meaning. The captain looked at his son with deep, contained affection in his eyes, the familiar esoteric of a family tradition. "You have the inherent love for the power and beauty of a work boat. It's in your genes. I am a very fortunate man. There are six generations on the wall, and I hope to see the seventh." Captain Mitchell and his historic riverboat were well proven and a natural collaboration. He turned to look at his son. "You carry the blood of everyone on this bulkhead. When I retire these pictures will go on the wall in the cabin of your boat. Maybe my picture will be there, too. I hope so." The wall held a history of men and riverboats that had created storied legends. "When you get old the most precious things you have are memories." He remembered his grandfather saying that. He placed his hand on his son's shoulder, trying to impress upon him the importance that a river, unlike a lake, has a direction and a purpose, knowing that his son had yet to learn the stress and the responsibility of a command that he considered an unequaled legacy.

There was a pause. "Gee, Dad," Brant said, running his fingers through his hair, "I am following the family profession. And I like it. I'm doing well at it, too. You said so." He spoke with genuine enthusiasm. He got his push and drive from his mother, giving him more nervous energy than his father. He was trying, as long as possible, to evade the issue he knew was coming. It was not a comfortable situation. He looked at his father then looked away.

The captain nodded in agreement. "I know," he said. "I'm glad." His eyes saw deep within his son. He was watching Brant with pride, yet with concern. His frown eased. "Nevertheless," he said, in thought, as he considered, "that is my side of the family, and your natural aptitude and love for it is the reason I'm saying it and the reason for this talk. You are destined for a position of responsibility, but your future depends upon the merit of your conduct." He felt a disagreeable conscience in this duty. "That's family ego, I know, but every family that has accomplished has it." He smiled slightly. "When your grandchildren die you are forgotten, because no one else remembers you." He pointed to the pictures on the wall. "Except for tradition. That will live as long as there is a Mitchell on the river. When a man gets older he wonders about being forgotten. I want you to stay on the river in our tradition." He walked slowly up and down the cabin in thought. The pictures had triggered many memories. Thoughts stirred his blood.

Brant turned to his father, the eyes of the two men met, lingered, and the boy turned away. He knew the look. He was waiting for his father to come to the point. A tenseness had settled in the cabin, one of waiting, maneuvering. Neither were practiced in the diplomacy of statesmanship. The captain put his hands in his pockets and paced back and forth. He decided to lay it on the line and let the chips fall where they may. In thought, neither spoke for a minute. Captain Mitchell paced back and forth, staring at the pictures on the bulkhead. He hesitated, knowing that some subjects are better untouched, some questions better left unanswered. He stood for a moment in thought, murmuring something inaudible. With his shoulders squared, his face seemed as hard as seasoned wood. Then suddenly his manner changed, his eyes became piercing. He turned, and said affably, "You're doing a man's work, Brant, and I'm not trying to hog-tie you, but I have responsibilities." He had the habit of striking at the heart of a problem. Brant was familiar with it and expected it. He was not a cold man. He had a considerable obligation and sought carefully for the right words.

"I've noticed you talking to the chambermaid more than a first officer is required," his father said, compressing his lips. His voice was derisively kind. He waited for an answer, but received none. "You have a mountain of studying to do," he added, pointing to the books on his desk. His words were measured.

Brant did not answer immediately, but continued to sit in silence, eyebrows raised in question, twisting nervously in his chair. He said nothing, knowing his father was right. The statement was causing him to think and consider. He sat eyeing his father, waiting.

The captain frowned. "True, you're the youngest copilot and first officer on the river," he continued, pressing the matter, "and it's also true you can and will be the youngest pilot and captain on the river, which is no easy title to claim, but you won't be anything at all if you get tangled up seriously with a girl at too young an age, and you're too young an age." The tone of voice revealed concern.

Brant looked up with a start. He felt a furious beating in his throat and his face grew red. He jumped up suddenly. "Listen, Dad!" he said, "Who said anything about getting serious yet?" His father was well aware of Cole's seriousness.

His father paused, then said, "Try to believe in my knowledge as to what is best aboard this boat. For all concerned," he added. "It would behoove you to listen to good advice," he emphasized. There was an edge to his voice. The captain stood, looking out of the window at the river and waiting for Brant to speak. He hoped it would be acceptable. He was actually appreciative of the silence, hoping that Brant was giving proper thought and consideration as to what would be proper and workable for both he and Cole.

As Brant continued to sit in silent thought the captain continued in a softer tone. "I'm not trying to pressure you into a hasty decision that would be disastrous, but we must arrive at a workable decision." He spoke quietly, but his words were heavy with meaning. He was watching his son closely.

Brant tried to interrupt, but his father raised his hand to stop him. "There is far more of importance in your life at this time than a summer romance that could become a problem." His statement caused them to sit in silence for a minute. Brant knew there was no point in trying to lie to his father. The truth was too obvious. The tension showed on his face.

Brant did not fear his father, their relationship had always been good and he did not shy from angering his father. But he did not want to form a breach with him; The bond was too deep. He was not quarrelsome by nature. He had more of his mother's aplomb. He understood his place and his career, had pride in it, and wanted it. He shrugged. "What harm can it do?" he asked, sincerely wondering. The hope for some small understanding about Cole and himself was starting to vanish. He swallowed, wondering with misery if his father could be swayed. From past experience and despite what he had told Cole he did not think so. His father sat, staring at him.

Captain Mitchell leaned forward, his face grave. "She's serious. Dead serious," he said frowning, desperate for his son to understand. "That's what harm it can do." *It is a youthful mistake that could seriously limit your future,* he thought. "And you could become serious, too," he added. "Or in trouble." And he hurriedly tried to push that thought out of his mind. "Have you given thought to any ramifications that could develop if the two of you become swept away?" he prodded.

Brant sat in thought for some time, staring at the beamed overhead, not knowing what to say and waiting for his father to continue. The cabin overhead was low, not the full height of a home ceiling. Actually, he was almost afraid to face the depth of his feelings and was well aware of the sweat soaking his armpits.

The captain turned to face his son. "Don't be a damned fool!" he said impatiently when his son did not answer his question. He became less of a father, and more of a force. "Use your head!" Brant looked up sharply at the words and the tone. It was unusual for his father to become so emotional. He had never been dramatic.

Captain Mitchell surveyed his son steadily. The moment was tense and his look was determined. He said, "I can tolerate your reputation as a 'pisscutter' in the river towns, that's normal for your age, under the circumstances, but it's my responsibility to be concerned about any serious errors in your judgment that could effect your career and our family, such as being forced to get married right now." There was a hesitant silence.

Brant had a habit of walking around a situation with his father, if possible. The two men studied one another. The captain was sensitive to the growing struggle. Brant looked at his father's demanding expression and thought for a while before he answered. He was staring at his father with respect yet with an expression of uncertainty. Neither father nor son had expressed the affection that lay closest to their hearts since Brant was a little boy. The captain was not a man who could put it into words, but it was there, proven.

"On the average, I haven't made any serious errors so far," Brant said honestly, hunching his shoulders, feeling more uneasy every minute.

The captain cast that aside with a quick movement of his hand and leaned forward, looking at his son, waiting for him to continue, then said, "I can't accept average from you, Brant. Average is merely a fulcrum between success and failure." Brant hesitated, thinking about that, his face revealing his inner thoughts.

Father and son exchanged a quick glance and the captain's eyebrows elevated, the seams of his face growing deeper. His eyes glittered compellingly as he took an impatient turn across the room. "Then you don't call being seen leaving the chambermaid's cabin, and what could happen, a serious error involving your career?" He scowled as he talked, dissatisfaction showing on his face as Brant shrugged his shoulders. "What do you call that?" His words were curt. He was tired. He would never tell his son that deVoss had made an issue of it, forcing a decision. He waited. Silence.

"You are an officer, second in command. It's your job not only to enforce regulations, but to obey them. Your behavior is destroying the ship's morale." A trickle of sweat rolled from his temple down his cheek like silver in the light of the cabin. He did not want to seem to be the judge with his son being a culprit, but this was the way it seemed; Cole was a threat to his wife's family plans for Brant. It was not a personal dislike; he liked Cole very much, actually, but a pretty girl at this point in his son's career could be dangerous and upset important plans for the future. He had been a mature man when he married and he wanted his son to be more mature, wise, and seasoned when he made such a decision. Father and son stared at each other in the silence, breathing heavily. Brant had thought that he would be accused of holding hands or of a stolen kiss, but his father's opening guns had been devastating. He had known that words would be spoken, but he had not realized how glaring they would become and believed his father meant well, but that his words were a little wide of the mark. Again, no answer. "Your mother believes that you are letting emotion govern your judgment."

The captain sat at his desk and preoccupied himself intentionally by turning dog-eared pages in the log. He was pausing to see if the message was taking root. Brant was a young man of imagination and individuality, like his father.

"I guess you never did any playing around when you were young," Brant said, trying to widen the subject. An obscure pride kept him from admitting to his father that he could be getting serious about Cole. More importantly, he did not want his mother to know. In the silence Brant thought that his father had not heard the imputation and his glance was apprehensive.

"Go on, I'm listening," the captain said, drumming his fingers on the desk. He rose to his feet.

"Well, you weren't perfect either, I'll bet," he dared an answer. He had heard stories. The captain's eyes, deep in thought, turned away.

Captain Mitchell looked beyond his son to the dark hills, remembering his youth and his wild escapades on the river. The nostalgic reminder struck deeply. He turned to his son, watching him narrowly. *He's a good boat handler,* he thought, *but it's going to take him longer to grow up in his personal life is all. He'll grow into a man as fine as Chain someday, I'm sure. He has to, with all that behind him,* and he glanced at the portraits on the cabin wall. *He's out of a good line of stock.*

His voice softened. "No man can guess what another man knows or has lived," the captain said, knowing that some things can not be communicated with understanding. He grunted in thought of his past. "A man doesn't become wise until he's impotent." He spoke more to himself than to his son. He continued pacing the cabin, walking on wood planking worn smooth by years of pacing. He had planned, as fathers before him had planned, in single-mindedness, but the dialogue was not the way he had rehearsed it in his mind. He glanced at his bookshelves and remembered the words of the great stern-wheel riverboat pilot, Mark Twain: "We are born alone and we die alone." He felt that alone at the moment. Brant followed his father's eyes to the bookshelves. He glanced at titles that would have astonished his teachers, then turned to the captain.

"Shouldn't a father think of what will make his son happy?" Brant asked, breaking the silence. He was thinking of his summer nights on deck with Cole and his promise to her, his promise to defend their relationship.

Captain Mitchell nodded grimly. "Yes, he should. And he does. But it will be a long time before you know what happiness is and that it isn't long-term or sound enough to be the most important thing in life. Too often the momentary search for happiness pushes aside life's true aim of responsibility. It might surprise you to know that happiness comes from achievement. I think you have it confused with bliss and the promise of living happily ever after." He was thinking that his son had not reached maturity of emotion.

Brant shook his head. "I haven't promised her anything," he said, interrupting his father's thought, not wanting a lecture again. "I was careful not to, but it gets boring without something to do on this boat other than boat handling."

"Good!" the captain said, hoping that he did not intend to make promises. He dropped into a chair to become more personal with his son as they talked. The captain listened as Brant talked.

Captain Mitchell was not upset with what Brant had done, he merely wanted an end to it. He let his son talk himself out—boy talk. There was not much conviction in it. Something about plans that Cole had made for the two of them. He was aware of the impulsive nature and impassioned state of mind of his son. He also knew that Brant did not know how cruelly he might hurt this lovely girl. Knowing this, he intended helping his son as long as it did not mean destroying another person. He relaxed in his chair and said again, "Good!" He stood up, then stretched as he walked about the room. He disliked sitting and he detested the role of pedagogue, knowing it was as thankless as dividing an estate. He walked slowly back to his son.

"She believes it will work if you will just give it a fair chance," Brant said suddenly, thinking again of the promise he had made to Cole.

The captain sat down again. Brant was looking down on a man that had always seemed such a giant.

"Chance?" The captain repeated Brant's word. "Success of anything isn't built on chance," he said heavily. "There's no place between us for theories of chance. This goes beyond what could be or what may be. It's the concrete things that will build your life, block-by-block," he added, his voice veering back to command.

Brant turned from his father and walked to the cabin window. He stood, looking out at the river. "You've made up your mind, haven't you?" he went on hopelessly, "And it's closed to anything I might say, isn't it?"

"I hope not. And I hope that yours is not. She's a lovely girl, I know." He spoke in a kindly tone and he looked away to save embarrassment. In truth, there was an unusual fondness between himself and Cole, a natural liking, making this more difficult. He actually wished it could have been otherwise. "But my first duty and concern is for what is best..."

"Best for who?" Brant interrupted. "That's what she keeps asking me."

"Best for both of you," the captain said. "I'm sure you don't believe that at the moment, but in time you'll understand why." Brant could hear the sincerity in his voice.

The captain stood up slowly, went to the window, and looked out over the river to the dark hills beyond. The deck light reflected from his glasses. He stood there a long time, staring into the night, as if admiring the lights on shore. Through the open window they heard Glemp shouting at deVoss on deck: "Up yours!" he yelled.

"I do my work," Brant said crisply. "I deserve some personal life."

The broad back of the captain looked indomitable as he stood and stared out at the river. He turned back slowly, stopped short in front of the chair, and looked down at Brant. The father knew his son; it could be likened to where the stream and the river meet. Captain Mitchell lowered his voice.

"You're neglecting your studies if not your work," the deep voice rumbled on. "That means your future. A little heartache won't make you happy, but it has a tendency to make one more successful," he stated succinctly as he watched the expression of guilt on his son's face, as if he had been caught in some wrongful act. Brant spun around.

"Good God, Dad!" Brant cried. "If that's all that's bothering you, forget it! I can pass that captain's exam with my eyes closed." His voice had risen several tones.

"I prefer for you to have your eyes wide open in all respects," the captain said in a dry tone and looked critically at his son. His clear gray eyes were troubled.

Brant could only stare at him. He realized that his father was looking older; It was rather a surprise to him. Both had been doing more thinking than talking. Aside from the river and boats there had never been a great deal of talk between them.

"What harm can our seeing each other do?" Brant heard himself ask, then watched his father raise his eyebrows. "That depends upon the consequences," his father said emphasizing the word consequences.

"Tell me!" Brant said, "What's so terrible about my seeing her?" He was watching his father's expression. He was making one last attempt for Cole and himself.

"Several reasons," the captain said. "One, I've mentioned: it's against boat regulations. That is serious because you are an officer. Second," and he hesitated in a search for words, "this is 1932." His voice was not loud so much as firm. "Times are hard, Brant. Tough. The worst depression our country has ever had. No money. No work. No food. No folks." He was remembering deVoss' remarks. "How do you know how she supported herself before I hired her as chambermaid? That's the question your mother will ask; family means."

"No!" Brant said staunchly. "That I know! Never! That I can tell you for sure." He would not desert Cole in this irrefutable matter. "She's not a hooker!"

His father looked at him closely, agreeing, but did not question him further. He had wanted to test the fiber of his son. It hurt Brant to think that she might have worked the streets, might have been bartered for money before she came to him. "The county welfare bureau took care of her," he said with certainty. "She told me so and I believe it!"

"Good." The captain was pleased and impressed with the reaction. "I'm glad to hear that. I also agree." He did not want to say anything unjust. Not only because of his son, but because of the girl. He had a deeper liking for her than he cared to admit. The innocence of her beauty was unmistakable.

"What's so terrible about her and I seeing each other?" Brant asked. "Suppose we even get married."

"I'm not a snob, Brant. I'm well aware that when they throw dirt on you it makes no difference what your job title is, the size of your bank account, or the price of your home, but I have a duty as a father first, and as a captain second." He knew that someone could be terribly hurt, and he regretted that it had to be done in such a way. He was honest enough to admit that it was a difficult choice. Brant listened in silence.

"I know what will work and what will not work under given circumstances and in regard to the set types of people involved," he said stiffly, but not unkindly. "And you have a right to know." Brant frowned, wondering. The captain had hoped he would not have to speak of it.

Durand deVoss knocked on the cabin door and at the captain's bidding, stuck his head in to ask, "Change of watch, captain. Do you want me to relieve Chain at the wheel for him to have supper?" He grinned, blinking at the light. He held his smile like a grudge. He could smell the unrest in the room. Their pain gave him pleasure. The round, brass ship's clock on the bulkhead struck the hour.

"No," the captain said in a steady voice. "Brant will be there soon."

When deVoss retreated, closing the cabin door, the captain tilted back his chair and studied his son. He wondered if his son was changing his position in regard to the chambermaid or wanted to save face with an attempt at defending her. He was not certain how strong his son's feelings were.

"Many issues are factored into a decision," he warned his son. "Growing up in a family doesn't automatically mean knowing that family in all aspects," he remarked suddenly. "That takes time and experience and years into adulthood. Sometimes never. I'll give you a little of both right now, but only as much as is necessary at this time, for this purpose. You're justified in knowing that much as you are the one that will have to make the decision. I can't make it for you. Won't make it for you. I don't intend to tie you here, but you should be aware of what you are giving up. Losing."

He did not want this to become a clash, but he owed his son this honesty. He cleared his throat. This wasn't easy. Then, almost harshly he said, "Regardless of your age, if you're man enough to be captain of a boat you're man enough to be aware of the things that could affect a decision. Had circumstances been different there are private family matters that I would not have talked to you about, but I don't have the right to tell you what I believe is best in the way of a decision and then deliberately withhold family matters from you. Some family matters, that is," he put in a little brusquely. His son sat without answering, not knowing what to say.

Brant looked out of the cabin window waiting for his father to speak, not looking at him. He did not want open conflict; He was not equal to it. He nodded to his father to continue.

Captain Mitchell did not want the full details of the affair to be known by his wife. He stood in dread of it. Her constant warnings were foremost in his mind, and he wanted no problem at home. Yet, his conscience bothered him concerning Cole.

"You're responsible for his actions away from home," his wife commanded each time they left the house. She constantly warned her husband to be on the alert for the lower-level, ambitious women who used their bodily charms to gain their wants and needs to elevate their position in life The "subset" she called them.

The captain withdrew his eyes slowly from his son's face, and went on quietly. "She's a lovely girl." He could take no pleasure in this. "I mean that sincerely. I wish I could say bring her into our family, welcome her, and love her. I think that much of her, but I know it wouldn't work." He waited to see what answer his son would make, then went on. "And why it wouldn't work," he finished.

There was no answer, merely a frown at the deck from a young man as yet too inexperienced to crystallize his innermost feelings. His father sensed his uncertainty.

"I may be wrong," the captain continued, "but I don't think I am. Even if I am wrong, at best it would be a very difficult situation for an unalterable reason. None of us are completely free to act as we choose. The complete freedom of will is a dream of the young." There was a sadness in his voice. Memories. He hesitated, his face drawn.

Captain Mitchell looked about the cabin slowly, at the pictures, at his books, and continued carefully, "It would be slow, long-term ruination for her as well as for you. You should know that your mother would never accept it." Brant's unusual attachment to his mother prompted him to remain silent. When there was no comment from Brant the captain went on, uncomfortable. His hands were fidgeting. "Would never permit it," he added. "You have known this all along, subconsciously, affecting your relationship with Cole." Brant's silent watching of his face was not helping the captain. "Think about it," he said. Brant had not thought of his mother openly, but she would always have a great influence on his inner thoughts. She had raised him all the years the captain had been away on the riverboat. "Your marriage will only be acceptable to her in the best of circumstances," he added. A lifetime on the riverboats had deprived him of daily contact with his family.

The captain glanced at the bulkhead, at the white hair and white beard of his father, and continued. "You look at these pictures, you feel the vibration of this boat, you smell the river, and you think in terms of my side of the family, but your future family will have to live with your mother's side of the family: the judge, the doctor, the councilman, and the school principal." He was adjusting his glasses, his hands not completely steady. He was trying to save his son a more devastating scene at home with his mother. The singularity of his attitude toward this did not trouble him. His career, his son's career, and his family he valued above all things.

"Your mother has never objected to my work or interfered with it in any way," he said lightly. "And, in fairness of compromise, I have learned not to interfere with her social command of our home, family, friends, and associates," he added.

"What does all that have to do with us here on the boat?" Brant asked. His tone had become brittle. "Mother doesn't run this boat!" With a somber expression, the captain sat.

"No," his father agreed. "Actually, I wasn't speaking of your life on the boat. I was speaking of your family life and your future family life. Your mother was raised and steeped in a social order in the town her grandparents pioneered. She is a very refined lady, but she would always be uncomfortable with anyone whose background is different than her own. I am home too seldom to attempt to change that, and the same will apply to you. I am not certain that it would be worth the effort in regard to that small town, nor do I feel it is my place to attempt to change her or the town." The captain had always been a practical man.

He meditated, deciding to wade in. "The main thing is religion. That's it, pure and simple," he said bluntly. "You should know that by now," he confided. "And a strong second is family standing. Those two things are something that can never be tampered with in a woman such as your mother. For whom, incidentally, I have a great love and respect. Your mother would be stunned if she were to be called a bigot or a snob."

Brant nodded, knowing. He had not developed a strength against the disfavor of his mother. "I know all that, but..."

"That's why I pointed it out," the captain interrupted, "because that's where your family will be raised. Otherwise you will split your life from our family and I don't think you are up to that, nor want that," he corrected himself. "You would regret it later. If you become serious with the chambermaid, your mother will point out that this girl is not familiar with your friends, socially, and you're well aware that through the years your mother has refused you permission to associate with girls that were of much better family standing than our chambermaid. She's from the other side of the river, so to speak. It will be emphasized in subtle ways that she does not have the proper school background."

As Brant started to interrupt he raised his hand. "She's not of our area it will be said, and she's not of our kind. And, most important, as you go through life with the women of our family, she's not of our faith. She would feel as an outcast. This would only be brought up as a last resort. These are things that are important for you to know in advance of decision making." He hesitated. "I believe you have an honest right to know that I changed my religion in order to be acceptable to your mother and her family." Brant listened, making no attempt to answer.

"Your mother's family has been the main support of their church for generations; They built it, everything from the altar guild to the church bazaar and dances. Your mother would never be rude, of course, she's too well bred for that, but her preferences would be made evident." He cringed at the thought.

Brant continued to listen without comment, staring past his father at the dark river and remembering comments and attitudes of his family in years past. The familiar logic made him sensitive to his youthful, unproven judgment. His lips twitched in frustration. There was a long silence.

"I'll ask just one more question, and that'll be an end to it," the captain said, his voice less crisp. "There's no reason you have to marry her, is there?" The thought seemed insupportable in view of what he was telling his son. "That would be entirely different as far as I am concerned," he continued. "I would not want you to steer away from such an obligation. I'm sure that I could persuade your mother to see reason in that event, but she would never forgive the girl."

"No! Of course not!" Brant said emphatically, honestly. "Nothing like that!" The captain knew he was telling the truth.

"Good," approved the captain. "The girl would be the most unhappy of all, brought into our family under these conditions."

Brant was only half listening. He was thinking, just realizing, that not once in their conversation had he or his father used the name, Cole. "I don't know," he said. "I hadn't given a thought as to how involved it could be. I never talked of marriage to her. I enjoyed our relationship, but I didn't tell her I loved her." The realization made him thoughtful.

"Good!" The captain smiled, relieved. "Then you haven't committed yourself. That's important. Now you aren't obligated." Though he was relieved, he was remembering the troubling words of caution of his friend, the director of the county welfare bureau: "The girl evidences an alarming irrationality of passion in her fear of losing a loved one. Also, and of great interest, I received a letter from Scotland, from a man named Hamilton, who has reason to believe that Cole's father was his young brother. Said he will have full details when he arrives here."

Brant was embarrassed for Cole and wished that his father had not spoken of such personal things as his mother's attitude toward Cole. It detracted from his idea of his family as being perfect. He remained silent and uncertain, staring out of the window at the river and the hills and thinking of what he had said and what he had not said. He knew that his father was correct, that Cole would never be accepted at home. He opened his mouth to speak then closed it.

"One more thing," his father said. "Very important. I wasn't going to tell you of this. I was keeping it as a surprise. T.J. Whitfied said that when you get your master's license you'll have a boat of your own. You're that good. He has confidence in your ability and sound judgment." This news was placing a last step of an almost insurmountable distance between his son and Cole. Brant was staring into space as if seeing his future career, then turned to look at his father in amazement and pride, his thoughts centered on this achievement. His own boat, he swelled with pride and relief at the thought. The guilt he had at first felt, the impatience at the lecturing, was fading away. The fingers to hold Cole were slipping from the edge of the cliff. It disturbed him, but how deeply he did not know at the moment. He had not solved these things within himself. His only reaction, outwardly, was a hunching of his shoulders. He wondered, though he was not certain, if he was relieved to be getting out of a problem situation. He would worry about facing Cole later. He had tried, he consoled himself. He could tell her, honestly, that he had tried. He had stood up to his father and had spoken of their marriage. He would tell Cole that the future could still hold something for them.

The captain realized that there was to be no confrontation. He saw that his son was relieved at what he considered a postponement. He was not happy, of course, but not devastated—merely uncertain.

"I understand your position," the captain continued. "Your..." and he searched for a non-inflammable word "...your fondness for the girl," he said softly. "The opportunity will arise later on when you are ready," he added brightly, relieved.

Brant realized suddenly that the decision had been made, though he was not certain who had made it. He was surprised. Though his confidence in himself had swelled at the prospect of being a captain of his own boat, he felt ashamed, in a way, for not taking a firm stand in relation to Cole. It had seemed such a magnificent thing, but he was too young to experience self-contempt; He was too young to have established past experience to guide his future and as of yet lacked strength in the conviction of his feeling and emotions. Captain Mitchell said nothing to his son and Brant could not look at his father, whose tired face showed a deep concern.

The captain sat, watching his son out of the corner of his eye, and protected his own private thoughts with a shell that was familiar to Brant. He was studying a boy who was a part of himself, true, but also a larger part of his young wife, upon whom he doted. Then, fleetingly, his face became sad and haggard with the thought of Cole. He changed the expression immediately, attempting to push old memories aside as he thought back through all the vanished years to a young love that should now have been everything in life to him other than a memory, sadly knowing that it would never come again. And always the heartache of guilt.

"Of equal importance," he continued, settling his glasses on his nose, "what you are doing isn't fair to Cole." He was aware of the depth of her feelings and the need she felt. He was afraid of those feelings. "That must be settled right away, to prolong it could be tragic. She's not trifling. She's a remarkably fine young woman who deserves much better treatment." He felt deeply about the effect on Cole, knowing that all are a prisoner of their emotions. "You can't play with a life." He had learned that.

Brant nodded in realization. His father was right and he knew it. Then, out of a heavy silence, a light voice asked, "Who's going to tell her? As Captain are you going to talk to her?"

"No, you are!" the captain answered. "As her friend you will explain to her. It would be inhuman for me to tell her." His words were almost synchro-meshed with the steady beat of the giant stern wheel pistons.

"When do I tell her?" asked the son, wondering how Cole would react to the suggestion of their waiting until some future date.

"The sooner the better," replied the father. "Waiting will only make it worse. That would be very unkind, and I have a deep concern for her as well as a responsibility." Then he spoke with profound emotion, making obvious his true feelings. "Tell her as gently and as kindly as you can. I charge you with that as a father and as a captain. She deserves a whole lot better than what we are doing to her." In truth, there was hidden fatherly approval of Cole.

The captain straightened, glancing at the clock and said, "We won't discuss this any further. Better relieve Chain," he ordered softly. A deep concern lined his face.

Brant nodded, hating the thought of facing Chain, knowing his feelings concerning Cole. He would tell Cole of the decision in honesty, that perhaps someday in the future they...but he let the thought fade, unsure of the words.

As he left the captain's cabin Brant saw his reflection in the window and turned from it. He shut the door quietly, stepping from the lighted cabin into the darkness of the deck, not seeing deVoss in the shadows. He stood for a moment with his back to the light and his face in the darkness.

When the door closed, the Captain stared at the chair in which his son had sat, and in his harassed eyes was now a deep compassion through the memories of a love of long ago. He seemed to have aged as he sat in the chair, deep in thought, and he looked very tired. "Who is to judge?" he murmured as he stared out at the river thinking of Cole and the depth of her love, knowing that all the power in the world could not stop this river or Cole's love. *It might be dammed up, but it could never be stopped,* he thought. Sunlight on the water reflected the exhaustion on his face. He had not been sleeping well.

Chapter Seventeen

As Brant was discussing her with his father, Cole stood silent at the hand-worn deck rail, looking out into the fading light of evening. She was staring off across the water to the blue-misted valley, waiting, as though moving into another world, away from the only world she had ever known. Day was done, the sun had set, and the evening shadows crept along the deck. Each turn of the boat made the shadows move. A fresh night wind was moving her hair. A deep purple was falling over the valley, night was coming suddenly as it does in the mountains. It was the ending of a beautiful day. The undisturbed beauty of the endless expanse of hills was soothing. It was twilight, when all the lights were low, and the darkening shadows mingled in the soft glow of the moon and clouds, creating a half-darkness that was almost like the dawn. In looking at the shore she had the strange feeling that the boat stood still and the land was moving. She watched a flight of birds going to roost and absorbed the beauty of her homeland as if it were food for the starving. She was thankful for the refreshing night breeze from the hills. It was a gentle wind that brought the scent of pines. To her the nights were the most beautiful on the river. They hid many of the uglier things in plain view in the glare of day. Often the faraway lights on the highest hills blended into the silhouette of the skyline and mingled with the stars. Beyond the trees the soft wind was moving the grass on a moonlit field. In the small town she could see a church spire and could hear the tolling of the church bell. It had a reassuring ring that gave her hope. Stretching beyond the shore lay the endless reaching of the hills, silent and sleeping, unconcerned about her future with Brant. The soft sound of water against the hull was like a whisper. The stars were dancing on the river. Her stepmother had told her that the stars were the eyes of heaven watching her. She was convinced that God had blessed these hills with a special enchantment and her heart swelled at the majesty of the stars. The scene was so beautiful that she breathed softly in order not to break its spell. The deck was half-light and half-shadow. The afternoon heat had faded. The river was a ribbon of silver beneath moon and stars.

To Cole, the unknown lights from the soft-voiced, unseen hills changed the countenance to the world. They were like the flickering flame of a candle kindled. Sometimes they were mistily emergent in the valley haze, and sometimes they were as bright as the valley haze and sometimes they were as bright as the hopes and dreams of the dwellers along the quiet river and dark hills. Sometimes they gleamed as lights. Sometimes they shown as stars. And sometimes they were both, often disappearing as the boat moved into a dark stillness of receding hills. *Will the conversation taking place between Captain Mitchell and his son cause me to recede into the darkness of these hills? She wondered. Is our love to vanish, gone with the flow of the river? Am I to believe that my life is one of misfortune and adverse circumstances beyond control, the poignant memories of beautiful hours but a dream?* The sunset had been unusual; not red, not gold. There were often thunder-showers, and there were days when she could not stand at the railing of the boat, but she did not miss the sun as much as she missed the night and the stars. No matter how busy she kept herself, and the Captain and Bess kept her busy, a crushing sadness would come upon her without warning.

From a long habit Cole looked for the first star of night. The Evening Star. It was her star. It was the biggest and the brightest of the stars and it had a special meaning for her. Though she had been only four years old when her parents were killed she remembered the occasion. They had died in an automobile accident. That is why she was looking for the first star of night, the Wishing Star. From the boat rail she watched for the Evening Star. It was a ritual that had started when she was a child, and sat on the back steps with neighborhood boys and girls to wait and watch for the first star of night. Her school book called it the "Woman Star." If she could find that star she would make her wish for the future of her and Brant. Hers was the soul of every love dreaming of that rapture hour. She thought of her mother and father, her stepmother and stepfather, and wondered if she would ever again be so loved. She had that unimaginable feeling that she had no home. It all seemed so long ago.

She remembered sitting on the back steps of her old farm house in the cool of a summer evening, hearing the thick, sweet song of the whip-poor-will, who wisely hid from the heat of day to enjoy the deserted meadows and creeks at night with the heavy scent of the lilac, awaiting the pale glint of the Evening Star. These were all the things she remembered so well.

She waited and watched for the Vesper Star, the Evening Star, the first star of night that permitted her a wish—any wish. Anything she wished would come true—almost. She had wished the same wish each night when the first star of evening came out to shine on upturned faces: she wished that her father and mother would come down from heaven and be with her once more. The wishful dreams were as numberless as the stars she watched, but the Evening Star did not give her the wish: a sound to a child, a parent's voice heard no more. She looked pale, exhausted from work and anxiety.

The hills had become dark and still, the stars brightening overhead. Cole stood at the boat railing until it became dark enough to see the fireflies and in the growing darkness the fireflies danced beneath the soft light of the new moon. They looked like swaying lanterns moving in the dark. They were nearer and brighter than the stars. Her mother had told her that the fireflies only shine when on the wing. It was true. She remembered the childhood ritual: whoever caught the first firefly was permitted a special bonus wish, but the magic glow of the little firefly had not given her this wish and she wondered if it would give her the wish of marriage with Brant.

"Don't hope for too much," Bess had warned her. "Try not to hurt yourself with reality." Bess wiped her forehead with her apron and added, "Try to make a beautiful early love a memory of joy." Cole thought this was said in irony, but it was not. Bess had talked to her almost as if she were thinking out loud, from experience long remembered. She was familiar with a cabin where broken dreams and memories lived.

"I would hate the bitterness of growing old without beautiful memories," Bess added, looking out over the river. "No one knows what another may have put away in a drawer or in the memory. Tender letters and words." She looked away from Cole's eyes. *So much changes as the heart grows older,* she thought.

Cole leaned on the stout rail of the old stern-wheel riverboat that warm summer night, waiting for Brant, and the outcome of his talk with his father. Far off she heard the faint tolling of a bell with its gift of strength and hope like the beating of a loving heart. Yet, not even this beauty could draw her away from troubled thoughts. Something was speaking to her in the soft air, in the far off sounds from the flowing river, in a message from the rolling hills. It was a lonely voice in the soft evening air, a thought in the wind. The same wind seemed so different at night. And in the distance there was the sound of a train. They were all the sounds of the river valley she had grown to love. Was there a hope of a brighter morning with a new beginning or, again, the eternal silence of the river? If only the river could talk. She was to know.

Cole was trembling as she looked out over the railing, tears gathering in her eyes. One glistened on her cheek. As she looked she saw an infinite number of stars in the sky and wondered if there was one upon which she could hang her hopes as a gift from heaven. They were as bright as Christmas candles.

A softness enveloped her as she looked into the depth of a clear, starlit heaven, thinking of the nights on the back steps of her home as a child when evening came with the sweet breath of the west wind as though it walked on whispered grasses, and dared to take the scent of flowers and offer it to one so yearning to search the shadowed corners of a life. Was the sound of the wind a mourning for those gone or of hope for things to come? Her wish was not for the past, but of the future. She would forever associate this river with Brant. In this pale light a tremulous heart stood at bay. And in the soft moon cast even still a star danced upon a moonlit hill, and a child who wished upon that star reached out and caught the gleam of light and held it in her hopeful hands. *Oh, to have such peace of mind and the warmth of love,* she thought. She had heard of those who could read a message in the stars, hear a message in the wind, and prayed she would be given this gift. She remembered the day the migrant fortune teller told her future: a beautiful and fulfilling love. Was there a vestige of hope? The waiting seemed eternal, as mysterious as the flight of a bird to an unknown destination. Cole simply could not take her mind off of young Brant Mitchell. Nights were the most pensive, there was nothing to keep her busy, nothing to replace the dreams and hopes for Brant. And the giant pistons pounded like the beating throb in her breast. It was her dream to always be a part of this valley. And always the soft murmur of the river. What was it trying to tell her. The *Storm Bird* churned on, creating a ripple of thoughts and emotions.

Through the galley window, Bess was watching deVoss amble down the deck. When he was certain no one was looking, he tried the doorknob to Cole's cabin. It was locked.

Later, in the cabin next to hers, Bess could hear Cole crying in the night.

Chapter Eighteen

The following day Chain found an opportunity to join Cole at the deck rail. As they traveled up river the hills became steeper. The boat was moving slowly up the beautiful green valley of the Kanawha River, winding its way through steep mountains and hillside farms where the mountain streams joyfully ran full speed to meet their big brother, Kanawha. The long grass was waving in a gentle wind with the high mountains looming in the background. It looked so much fresher and cooler up in the mountains. In places the river had become hidden in the hills. As the river narrowed it became swifter. The river was up from spring rains and their headway was a little slower. The banks were high bluffs fringed with laurel. To Cole, the mountain solitude was infectious, a lovely grandeur. She loved the touch of the mountain wind on her face. The trees along the bank were leaning into the sun. All the sounds and scents of mid-summer came to her. She was watching the sun reflect from the glistening dewdrops on a spider web, wishing she could read a message from it. The hills were especially beautiful in the morning sun, the canyons deep in shadow, the trees looming black against the hills. The weather was beautiful, but could change in a hurry in the rugged mountain country of classic grandeur.

As they watched the shore, never monotonous, Cole's somber mood was obvious to Chain in the few words she had spoken. She had not smiled in days. Seldom did she play the guitar and sing in the evening. He missed that, but did not wonder about it. He knew the anguish and desolation of a clouded mind. He was glad she was talking a little, especially of herself. *How often the young slow the aging of the mature,* he thought. *Yet, how rarely such diverging channels flow serenely.*

Chain had always wanted to learn more about Cole, but she had not said more than a yes or a no in days. She was turning her head constantly, as if looking for someone. She was restless, her eyes betraying the strain of sleepless nights. She no longer slept the quiet, peaceful sleep of a child. Her simple prayers of childhood were forgotten. To her it seemed that each day was agony, endless. Hour after hour the throb of the engine was like the throbbing of her headache from the intensity of the-heat—cleaning, cooking, doing dishes, trying to smile—all had taken a toll. As she attempted to converse a little, she was wondering if Chain knew the depth and truth of her yearning.

Who can tell a girl what life really is when she believes her heart has been broken? Chain was thinking: *The instant, emotional decision of youth, all reasoning swept aside. Or, how it can change in realization. Who can hold thoughts on the fingertips like Braille, and read to them their blind stumbling through life? That the years need not wash away this young love like the river erodes the bank. The dream is in the girl, the impulsive yearning of a lonely heart, and when the dream is gone something could leave with it that would make her life unendurable. She's making it impossible for her to accept less than what has been dreamed.* He was hoping Brant would come to a realization and believed he would, given time.

Then Cole saw Brant walking down the deck toward them. Her smile was hesitant as she watched him approach. She had the bitter pleasure of seeing him, but not being able to talk to him, to learn of his talk with his father. She would have been grateful for any sign of attention. Her eyes seemed larger, more open to hurt.

All week she had lived with the hope of meeting him, yet all day she had been filled with foreboding. He was avoiding her, every casual duty becoming important and time consuming. She had the feeling of being dispossessed. She could not rid herself of the intense feeling of dejection, her body quivering as reeds along the shore. She would hide in her cabin, seeking a peace she could not find. Her cabin was the only little corner on the boat where she could hide. Brant did not answer her smile with a smile. When he saw her he stopped, nodded, waved a short salute at Chain's greeting, turned, and walked toward the pilothouse. Chain was angered, and wondered when and how it was all going to end. He knew things could not go on as they were. Yet, there was nothing he could do

Cole's heart missed a beat in a cry of despair; It was the hurt of unexplained punishment to a child. Brant could not avoid her on so small a boat and when they saw each other it hurt her to see him go on his way like any other crew member, less than that. The other crew members would always wave and smile, or stop and talk. The snub was crushing.

Cole's smile vanished and the warmth in her face drained to pallor. She had been unable to rest and found it difficult to set herself to any humdrum task in the galley or her cabin; The dream of magic was fading. Chain watched her, not confused at Brant's abrupt change of direction. It was impossible for him not to be affected by the look on Cole's face. The truth of it was within her. Not since the death of her mother, father, and stepmother, and stepfather had she felt this way—this single mindedness—and not even then.

Now Cole believed that she was out of place in Brant's thoughts, that she was lost to him except when he wanted her or needed her. Without his attention her days had become meaningless. She felt as if something final had happened, but did not know for certain what it was, or why. Cole was desperate to talk to Brant in search of an understanding, an answer. *Why is sorrow so much a part of love?* she wondered in confusion, but was afraid to express the question to Chain, who wanted to shield her and help her. Instinct did not tell her what her mind could not know. She blocked it out.

Cole was sensitive and self-conscious, knowing the crew was watching the affair with interest and with crude humor, she suspected. She also knew that Chain was not a part of it. She had heard some of their comments and tried not to show the shame and pain in her heart. She glanced at Chain and away. Chain saw her face as she did not mean to be seen. He saw the lost hope in her eyes and it hurt him. From the kitchen doorway, Bess watched Cole with troubled thoughts. Cole turned from both of them, looking down the deck. Bess had talked to Chain concerning Cole and asked if he would be of help to her from a mature man's point of view. Cole had been touched by Chain's unexpected kindness. She looked up to see the sun disappearing, the landscape turning gray.

A few minutes later thick billows of fog became so dense that the boat could no longer navigate safely. The heavy mist was almost a light rain. The huge belly of fog was moving down the river. From the pilothouse Brant saw it coming. The fog moved in slowly like a tide, turning the trees into special shapes. The hollows seemed overflowing with mist. Brant could see the tiny particles of moisture actually hanging in the air and glistening in the suffusion of the yellow deck lights. The air seemed to have a heavy weight to it, the day going from sunshine to being dreary. There was an ominous stillness in the air as the boat moved slowly into the wet murk of the dense fog.

Brant rang the engine room to lessen forward way. From deep within the innards of the old stern-wheel riverboat the steam power plant rumbled heavily as the great piston arms reacted to the order. The firemen sweated, Claude spit and grumbled, and the dog-watch cursed. All moved with an instinctive ear to the bells and, as always, the pulsing echo of the exhaust stacks.

Cole was listening to the great, heavy beating sound of the engine. Her eyes looked straight before her at the approaching fog bank with a fixed stare. A little wind was running down the river, moving the fog. She stood silently and rigidly, staring into the darkening water. Her mind traveled back to an orphaned puppy her father found drowned in the pond by which the magnolia spread. He was so quiet and at peace. She thought of the story her mother had told of the neighbor's child who had quietly died while nursing at it's mother's breast. All of these were associated with other disturbing nights.

The fog formed an enveloping canopy of soft, amber mist over the boat deck, fading into a white shroud covering the river and opaque valley. In the mist the foliage was silvery. Cole thought of it as ghostly, as the night wind made the dampness cold and she shivered in the wet air.

It was her first experience in a blinding fog on water. At first the fog was low-lying and the tops of the ridges were visible to her. The cat birds were coming in, settling in for the night, but the noise of the boat caused the mallards and pintails to rise from the marshes of the backwater. She strained her eyes to see the shore. There was nothing but fog.

Fog was one of the few situations in which it was mandatory for the captain to take the wheel. When the fog had rolled in heavily in the deep cut of the Kanawha Valley, Brant had rung for the captain, knowing the intricacies and danger of fog navigation. On shore the trees were dimly seen through the thickening mist.

"Heavy fog rolling in," he said.

Captain Mitchell was a master navigator, aware of each riffle, sand bar, eddy of current, rapids, shallows and submerged rocks on all of the rivers he navigated. In a fog, however, he knew that he could not trust his senses to navigate safely. *We'd be better off if this fog transferred itself into rain,* he thought.

He had been resting in his quarters, trying to read. At the sound of the call he put on his cap and centered it, "Square with the world," as he always said, opened and closed his cabin door, made his way down the companionway unhurriedly, and mounted the ladder to the pilothouse.

When he entered the wheelhouse, he nodded to his son and looked through the pilothouse windows, studying the river and the fog. He asked the copilot his location, down to the exact rock, bar, deadhead, snag, and bank cover.

"Gruner's Bend," Brant said. "Under the big trees, along the stretch of briars, just before you get to Palmer Rock." The stretch was a death-trap. They were passing a river bend that required special attention. The locals called it, "Bottom Bustin' Bend." Through the years it had caused countless boats to wreck their bottom. The old boat moved on through the fog like a ghost.

On deck Old Rip turned to Cole and said, "There's nothin' better than ridin' the river with a good man." He hesitated. "Nor nothin' worse than ridin' the river with a twister," he added as he watched deVoss slither out of sight into his cabin.

"Tell Chain and the crew that we'll beach the tow!" The captain said to Brant. "I'll need a volunteer." Brant nodded and left the wheelhouse. The captain rang the engine room. The seasoned crew knew all the prominent landmarks and were more than capable. They had an uncanny sense of danger and what to do, and worked in complete harmony.

Wise not to gamble, Old Rip thought. *Better safe than sorry.* The fog had turned the valley to a misty light. The shore vegetation was heavy with dew. They moved on into the valley of shadow.

"One quarter speed," he called into the tube.

Claude answered the order with a grunt, pulled back on a polished lever, then yelled at the fireman, "Put some sweat in it, Shark! We ain't treadin' water, you know." The stoker's cheekbones glistened as though they were oiled. Trickles of water rolled down his body and made onyx-like beads of coal dust sweat that shimmered on his parchment-colored skin. He licked his lips and got a tongue full of coal dust sweat. He was heavily tattooed on his arms and chest. When the black iron doors to the steam boilers were open, fire, heat, and smoke belched from them with a roar. From continual stoking before the giant boilers, the skin of the coal-heaver had turned the color of sweat-stained leather.

Captain Mitchell saw that the fog had climbed the hills and the ridge tops were now hidden in the mass of gray moisture. The hulks of huge hardwood trees were ghosts in the mist. Everything on the shore was still.

Cole, who up to this point had been uneasy, now became alarmed. She had read stories of ghost ships that sailed into a fog never to be seen again. Her eyes widened, and she wondered if her hopes for herself and Brant would go on the rocks like a boat in the fog. She did not know what the captain's orders meant. "Beach the tow!" he had said, and for all she knew, this meant that he was going to run the boat aground on the rocks, splinter and sink the boat, and every person on the boat should try to make it to shore as best they could.

She looked about. To her surprise the others were as calm as usual. To them the captain's voice was a reassuring sound. She was leaning on the moistened deck rail, looking into the dark fog as it spread over the river.

Chain smiled at her reassuringly and she smiled in return. It was her first smile in days. It pleased him. He noticed that she was even more beautiful as the fog moved around her in the subdued light of the amber deck lights. He was pleased that she respected his ability.

"First the storm, and now the fog," deVoss grumbled. "I wonder if we'll ever make port and liberty!"

"We'll be there on schedule come hell or high water," Glemp answered in irritation.

Cole could not see the shore, and all she could hear was the sound of water lapping gently against the hull of the big riverboat. Far off she heard the muffled sound of a fog horn and the doleful sound of an answering boat.

Captain Mitchell was hearing much more. He heard, not only the sounds of his own craft and the horns of fog-hidden boats, but he heard the noises of the river over the shoals. He heard the disturbed night birds and the sound of the water on the shore. From these sounds he gauged his location and measured the distance. He was a man of sound judgment under moments of extreme pressure, a man strong enough to stand alone.

To Cole, the murky water of night had always disturbed an inner feeling of fear. It stirred unsettled thoughts of death and gloom, and wild thoughts of disappearing into the dark mirror of the unknown.

"Sound for the shore!" the captain called out.

Cole wondered why, when he could not see the end of the tow, Captain Mitchell asked the lookout on the forward barge to fling a chunk of coal over the unseen water.

Chain was now on the forward barge, his face looking into what could shatter him if there was a collision, To Cole, the figure at the end of the barge looked ghostly in the gray fog. She heard the whine of the coal as it whistled through the wet air, whirled by the stout arm of Chain. He knew where to place the shot and the captain heard it hit. Not water, but land! From that the captain made the final judgment of the distance to the rocky shore. He rang the engine room. Chain had complete confidence. Not a breath of wind was stirring to move the fog.

"One third speed astern," the calm voice of the captain called into the tube. Another grunt from Claude and the timbers of the huge paddle wheel of the stern-wheel riverboat were in motion; They grabbed and pushed tons of water as they backed down, churning the water to foam.

The captain's knowledge and experience enabled him, as calmly as he would turn over in bed, to maneuver the tow to the shore without a crash. He had judged by the feel of it, by instinct—never by luck. A bell in the engine room had signaled Claude to stop his forward way and a bell had told him when to come astern with the giant paddle wheel. A bell had told him, at the exact moment, to secure all power. The bells told the principle involved.

In the thickness of a blinding fog, in which the captain could not see the end of his tow and acted solely by the telling signs of water and shore, he had signaled the men with the mooring lines to secure the craft and, as astounding as it seemed to Cole, the men on the forward end of the tow stepped out into the heavy fog that was as black as night as calmly as if they were going down the steps of their own front porch. They jumped ashore into nothingness and landed lightly on solid ground, never doubting, and secured the tow to huge white oak trees along the shore. "Hard and fast it is!" a deck-hand sang out. Driftwood lined the bank. The current drew the lines taught. The engine ceased to throb, and all became quiet. Old Rip was there. No matter what the job he was always there to give a hand, his old frame amazingly strong.

"A man does what he has to do," he said, "and these men know their business."

Looking about in wonder, it gave Cole the feeling that the rest of the world had disappeared and they were completely alone, enveloped in a solid blanket of white. She was more thrilled than relieved, thinking of the unusual qualities of a man named Chain and the crew. They had saved their boat for the second time. The *Storm Bird* had a reputation that made her crew proud. The captain had no trouble getting deckhands, jobs were scarce and many were looking for a berth, but he was particular and demanding and had a first-class crew. Most in the crew were second and third generation riverboat men and it was evident in their work. They existed on strength of courage and will, as well as physical strength and knowledge. The spell of the river had a powerful drawing for men such as these. Their work was a challenge, placing them at the mercy of the elements, and the captain had well-earned the full respect of this crew.

"They're there when you need them," Bess said to Cole. "Those are real men." Cole looked deeply into the knowing eyes of Bess and believed her.

"Working the riverboats can often mean life or death," the captain had told his son. "A riverboat deckhand has to have common sense, good judgment, and sound thinking or he won't last long." In return his crew was well aware that their captain's decisions in fog, storm, or emergency were based on knowledge, experience, and sound judgment. He had their complete trust.

To Cole, the crew's few words back and forth in the handling of gear and equipment had sounded like a foreign language. Old Rip smiled at Bess and Cole with knowing confidence. He had sailed the river and coaxed a horse and buggy long before the advent of the automobile.

Cole was certain that the memory of the ghostly shapes of the crew struggling to obey the captain's orders to save the boat in this deadly fog would remain with her for the rest of her life. An unforgettable picture of sweaty men with calm eyes and a job well done.

Chapter Nineteen

At daybreak the following morning the *Storm Bird,* one of the legend boats to sail the Ohio River, arrived at the bay of Reed, West Virginia. The loading terminal was located where Campbell Creek, flowing southeast through the rocks and trees of mountain country, entered the Kanawha River. This was as remote as Cole had ever been in the mountains. To her it seemed cooler and cleaner. The fresh air of the hills drifted down like water and the streams flowed down the mountain in a series of cascades. The Indians referred to the high country streams as "the beginning of all waters." The breaking dawn brought a light to the east and the mountain peaks were like a line drawn in the sky. The first streaks of dawn were straying past the broken edges of the hills and sections of light and darkness blended in the mountains and canyons with the dawn sun moving across the fields, creating a halo of shadow and gold. The hills were abloom with wild flowers, the morning dew glistening in the sunrise. The huge bulk of the great Appalachian Range looking up loomed in all its sunlit grandeur. It was rough country, heavily timbered with many wild-flowing streams. The salmon were running. The call of the mountain streams was irresistible. It seemed to Cole to radiate a spiritual quality. Like a crown, the crest of a mountain rested upon a bank of golden-bright clouds and sunlight glistened on the distant peaks as they cut into the pale blue sky.

Cole believed that nothing could equal the splendor of the mountains. The view was breathtaking, magnificent from a distance. But when the black clouds moved across the peaks, and lightning scorched the vales, it was no place to be. The wooded slopes came down to the river at the small coal mining town. The village was so old it seemed a part of nature's setting. It seemed a wilderness of soft green trees. A gentle wind was stirring their leaves. The grass lay silver in the early morning dew. A warren of plain-frame, company-built houses ranged along the dirt streets near the river. The Kanawha River, at Reed, was narrow but navigable for stern-wheelers. Cole was watching a band of pigeons circling overhead. On the riverbank she saw a young boy fishing. It was a familiar scene to Chain, but new to Cole. He was at home in the hills of his West Virginia. Cole stood, leaning against the deck rail, breathing deeply of the clean mountain air. The green willows and cottonwoods were lush, with their feet in the water they loved. In the distance impressive spires stood sentinel. There was the scent of pine and cedar on the light breeze.

"Reed, West Virginia, is named after Reed Whitfield," Chain was saying to Cole, happy to have the opportunity of talking with her again and cheering her. "Reed is one of T.J. Whitfields' sons. He's superintendent at the mines." He smiled. "Two thirds of this state is sitting on coal, some of it low-sulphur coal."

Cole was standing at the deck railing beside Chain. She was thankful for the attention. She needed someone who cared. He was explaining, "Many of the larger riverboats, such as the Palace Boats, are side-wheelers, but the *Storm Bird,* our boat, is more like a tug, or a push boat, actually, and that's why she's a stern-wheeler. We can navigate the smaller and more shallow tributaries like the Licking, Kanawha, and the like. As they approached the dock, ripples from the boat washed the pier pilings, causing the air to have a light scent of river water.

The *Storm Bird* tied up to the moss-covered pilings of the buckled wharf where the riverboat had been urged up to its moorings and the lines made fast by the deckhands. The river current rippled against the hull of the boat, pulling the lines taught. Noisy tackle lowered the landing stage to the old dock, and Claude Schneider blew off steam from the boilers, which indicated the captain's need to remain birthed for several days. When moored, with the engine shut down and the crew ashore, the old boat was as quiet as a tomb and Cole could hear the muffled noise of the street.

At the loading dock Cole saw the mighty Iron Duke in action. It was a frothing, pugnacious little boat that charged like a lion at everything it did. The small tug was dwarfed by the big stern-wheel steamboat, with its long tow of empty barges. Chain was telling Cole how the Iron Duke got its name. "Unlike the larger wooden stern-wheel riverboats that arrive, load barges and depart, the Iron Duke is one of the first of all steel harbor tugs for mooring barges," he said, pointing along the wharf. The old dock was well worn from years of activity.

The Iron Duke was a wonder to watch as it churned the river water into a boiling froth and moved the heavy barges about the loading area to be taken in tow by the steamboats. Cole stood, staring in wonder at the amount of work the tug managed in so short a time. She laughed fully at its attitude at this great amount of work. It would charge up to a barge like a David tackling a Goliath, take it in tow, and deliver it to the string of barges being readied to go down river with the steamboats. Cole looked at Chain in wonder, then grinned.

Soon, the off-duty crew was heading for town and pleasure. From the kitchen, Cole saw Brant and Chain leave the boat. Chain was carrying his camera in a leather case. If she could not talk to Brant, she had hoped that Chain would escort her to town. As she waited at the landing stage to go ashore she watched the moving of the barges, the loading of coal, and heard the work talk of the men. When a boat was tethered to the dock the wharf bustled with activity. She turned from it and looked toward the mountains. Their mountains represented eternity to them. The sun, reflecting on the top of a hill, made it look as if it were wearing a crown. She had never escaped the magnetism of the hills. "Hill haunted," the locals called it. *Oh, to breathe the mountain air again,* she thought.

Among the faint sound of children's voices echoing across the water, Cole heard a small child crying for its mother and became alarmed. But then in the distance there was the sound of the unseen voice of the mother and she was satisfied. The fragrance of burning pine perfumed the air. It was her favorite time of the year.

"I hope we have time for a movie," Cole ventured.

"I haven't been to a movie for a month of Sundays," Bess answered. A naked little boy, about three or four years old, stared at her and the boat. A dog fight had broken out, which kicked up a fine-powdered dust, and the children broke it up with sticks; Half grown children, scantily clad, were calling out to each other with shrill voices, the little scamps bright with life. They were not frightened by the dog fight.

As the barges of the tow were being assembled and loaded for the return trip down river, Cole and Bess went ashore, walking to town to do their shopping at the company store. They had crossed the New York Central Railroad tracks at the train station near the Route 60 Bridge. On the way they saw Brant and Chain, and Cole hoped they would catch up with them. Chain was taking pictures of an old man and a child with a coal tipple in the distance. The child had come to walk home with her grandfather, who had the hoarse breathing and cough of miner's consumption. The old man was withered and colored like an October leaf and he walked with a miner's stoop. His face was pitted, the pores ingrained with coal dust. He was thin to a point of near emaciation, with stringy, old-man muscles, and he had the look of a man who rarely saw fresh air. Yet he was an old man with young eyes. Brant and Chain did not know, and Cole did not know, that the old man was dying of Black Lung. His granddaughter knew. A nondescript dog was at their heels.

Brant was waiting with obvious impatience, reading a huge sign atop a two-story red brick building. The sign read: "Red Top Beer...West Virginia's favorite." When Cole and Bess arrived, they smiled in greeting. When Chain had found a subject for which he was searching, he had gotten permission to take pictures, and when Cole and Bess saw him he was so engrossed in his work that he waved, but did not talk to them. Brant merely stared off into the distance, irritated at Chain for delaying their arrival. Cole was wearing a lovely new dress—blue, of course.

Chain seldom dwelled upon past pictures and less often thought of future ones. His satisfaction was in the pictures of the present. He was capturing the essence of a withered old man who stumbled along as though he had palsy—a pocked little man, lean as a greyhound. Cole was becoming more interested in his work with each new subject and conversation. Chain had been told that the old man's forebears had pioneered this area when the Cherokees and Shawnees were hunting these hills.

The old man's veins were almost black against his skin, his temples and cheeks sunken, and he ambled more than he walked. His large Adam's apple moved up and down when he spoke. His face had been seared and hollowed in the dark caverns of coal. One of his suspender buttons was missing. Brant saw nothing of interest in him at all. All this and more would show in Chain's pictures. He believed that the closer the subject the better the picture. He was certain a picture must bring forth light and meaning. Some of his portraits showed the pores of the skin and the hairs in a mole, featuring not only facial structure, but the spirit that made it shine.

"A camera is a piece of equipment that lies," he had heard it said. He had told Cole that he did not believe this. He often thought of his work as a search. He wanted each picture to be different. On one occasion he had asked for her opinion and she had been thrilled. He tried to portray the drama, tension, strain, conflict, and force that he saw in the face of the old man, but of more importance, to bring out the meaning of the picture: the deeper, inner beauty and meaning of the old coal miner. He sought to create movement and motion of life into a still. It was the artist's yearning for forcefulness. His portraits were so expressive that Cole expected them to speak. His concern was for the human emotion, for the philosophic meaning of life, and when his pictures produced an emotional impact he was satisfied. Cole continued to watch him as he worked with his camera, aware of how different he was from most other men. The sidewalks were almost empty.

The girl's hand was in her grandfather's, her face looking up into his, alight with love. It created a picture of a heart shining through blue eyes. She was a plain girl made beautiful through the glory and the pain in a child's love. Her grandfather was a victim of the dreaded Black Lung from all those years deep down in the bowels of the earth with a mule and a coal cart. Many of those mules had never seen the light of day.

Brant turned and walked impatiently toward town, thankful for the opportunity not to be cross-examined by Cole. Bess, Cole, and Old Rip continued their walk in silence. They could hear the bees singing in the wildflowers, and in the distance a cock crowing announced the hope of a new day. Crickets were chirping. They seemed so cheerful to Cole. Small, white clouds hung above the hills and the wind had died away. The huge blue sky spread like an ocean. Cole stared in wonder at the haunting beauty of these mountains as she listened to the birds singing cheerfully in a ripe apple orchard. Soft after a light rain the earth smelled rich, though the steep banks were slippery wet. The high mountain air was cool and sweet. The squirrels were busy in the trees in search of food. After being on the boat for days on end the soft scent and color of the garden flowers touched her deeply. She loved the soft, smiling blossoms of the brilliant bluebells. The locals had told her that there had been a plaque of butterflies that summer. She loved to watch their joy among the flowers. The beauty of their Appalachia was stunning. She could smell the pines. It smelled like home. A meadow lark was singing. She could never decide which of the songbirds she loved to hear the most. All was still except for the birds and a chattering squirrel that was scolding her. Only a small puff of wind moved among the variety of trees that covered the rolling hills, emphasizing the sights and sounds that only high-mountain country can create. Two trees were rubbing together in a gentle wind, creating a familiar sound. To Cole it was music. The sound and the scene were so beautiful it caught her heart. Smelling the freshness of the high, cool air, something stirred deep within her. *Is it the warning of a storm to come?* she wondered as she watched an old dog meandering down the dusty road and heard the hounds baying full cry up on the side of the mountain. Deep purple shadows were hiding in the canyons where white water washed the rocks.

Old Rip touched Cole's arm to get her attention. When she turned to him he said, "There's an old saying among mountain folk, 'Beware of the mountain when it weeps.'" Then, seeing her expression he said, "Do you know what I miss the most here on the boat?"

"No," she answered, shaking her head.

He pointed to the old dog meandering down the sunny side of the street. "His heart's over-stuffed with love." Cole was touched by the tenderness of his tone, his eyes as honest as a child's. They continued walking down the road past secluded, tree-sheltered houses and well-cared-for lawns, and she heard the wind chime in a cozy little cottage that had a window box of beautiful geraniums. Joyous little children were scampering everywhere and two proud little boys were riding broomsticks in the yard. It was a glorious morning with birdsongs, sunshine, and the scent of flowers. The sound of wind in pines reminded her of home, with the endless range of mountains dominating the view. The high peaks seemed to be standing guard over the deep valleys and all the wonder of the mountain wildlife. It was an unforgettable scene, with timber stretching as far as the eye could see. It seemed to Cole that nature favored certain areas, blessing them with a combination of artistic features. Some of the yards were a forest of flowers. She looked up at the blue sky, fluffy clouds, and brilliant sun remembering her stepmother's words: "The best cure for a problem is sunshine." She could smell the early morning scent of vegetation.

Old Rip chuckled, pointing to a boastful rooster. The proud cock was strutting in the yard, puffing out his feathered chest as a squirrel jumped from tree to tree, scolding him.

Cole continued to watch the old dog meandering down the road, thinking of her dog, Jack. "I wish we were allowed to have a dog on board," she said with longing.

Chapter Twenty

It had been difficult for Cole to place events in order after the last night on deck with Brant. To her, the layover was a sensation of endlessness and interminable waiting. During that time Brant had avoided her except for a nervous wave, an embarrassed hello he could not avoid, a casual comment on the weather, or the loading schedule, remembering the words of his father to be kind. She watched and waited anxiously for a chance to talk to him, causing her to feel an aching emptiness inside, a hunger for which there was no food. It seemed that each hope had become less hopeful. She was unable to dominate the agony. Each day made the problem more acute and it seemed to her that Brant had erased it from his mind. In the kitchen with Bess she tried to work herself into complete exhaustion in order to sleep. The days dragged on. In a few months it would be Christmas, her first Christmas away from home. She wondered if there would be the old joy and singing in her heart.

The return trip on the stern-wheeler down the Kanawha River was much faster than the slow fight against the upstream current, fog, and storm; Weather conditions were favorable. They were passing Charleston, West Virginia, the state capitol, and Chain was pointing out to Cole the stately old capitol building with the gold leaf dome. It was an imposing structure, overlooking the Kanawha River where it met the Ohio River. The locals referred to their state capitol as, "The land of rivers." The morning sun on the river was like a ribbon of molten gold. The hills and valleys were aglow where the mountains formed deep canyons.

Cole often waited on deck, pretending preoccupation, just to see Brant in the wheelhouse or on his way to his cabin. She had to talk to him. She was desperate. The waiting seemed unending. She wondered how much longer she could go on like this. Her desperation was *obvious to all.* Was she wanted, was she needed, could she stay on board? *In her eyes was a deep misery that she tried to wear with a smile in the presence of others, but failed. He had not told her the results of his conversation with his father.* In two days we will be in home port in Cincinnati, *she thought.* If Brant doesn't come to see me by tomorrow night, I'll go to his father and tell him the truth of our love. *The deceit was crushing her.*

Chain saw her often at the railing, watching the sunset or the shore, looking at the water, and understood the frailty of youth in despair. *She dwells more on her failures than her achievements,* he thought with regret. Bess had asked him to be of comfort to her knowing that the young are often victims of their emotions without realizing it, causing the want and need to create tragedy. *Not even a mighty river can wash away love,* he thought.

Cole was alone most of the time, and it had become obvious to the crew that Brant was avoiding her. DeVoss was pleased, gossiped, and attempted to make bets as to what would happen, but he was shunned by most of the crew. They liked Cole. The fact that *she no longer laughed or sang most affected them.*

Glemp made an attempt to lift her spirits with his ineffective humor. Steaming down the river, away from the mountains and toward home port, he referred to it as "Outward Bound." He nudged Cole as he pointed up the Ohio River toward Wheeling, West Virginia. "Do you know the greatest physical feat the world has ever known?" he asked. She shook her head, scarcely smiling. He pointed upstream. "Wheeling West Virginia on the Ohio!" And he laughed mightily. "Get it?" And he made the movement of a discus thrower. "Wheeling West Virginia on the Ohio," he repeated. Cole shook her head in amusement. Some of their deliveries took them as far up river as Wheeling and then on into Pennsylvania. She felt comfortable with Glemp, Old Rip and their stories.

Glemp chuckled. "I'll give you an easy one. How do you get a rat out of a lee scupper?" Again she shook her head, trying to appear interested. "You turn the boat around!" he exclaimed, nudging her again and went laughing down the deck.

Old Rip stood next to her, not knowing what to say to relieve the pain he sensed, realizing that the humiliation of it was far less painful than the aching of her heart. He shook his head sadly as he gazed out over the water. "Fishin' shore ain't what it used to be down here to the river," he managed to say in cover.

Cole spent most of her off-duty time in her cabin, trying to read. In her cabin she cried herself to sleep. Only Bess knew of the tears. Only now did the constant pulsing of the engine grate on her nerves. She went quickly to bed, but not quickly to sleep. The throbbing of the giant engine, the splash and slap of the water on the hull, and the unknown of the next day kept her awake. *Perhaps someone else will have his name,* she thought, and lowered her face in her hands. It was killing the joy and warmth of her, and the anxiety worked inside her like a boil. The brilliance of her own sunlight had been the momentum that had carried her through the dark days of uncertainty. She saw little of Bess, except when working together. Bess understood. Hard, cold experience had taught her that throughout all history no one on the face of the earth has understood all there to know about the human element.

When Captain Mitchell was alone with his son he said, "Have you told the cabinmaid about your decision?" And he emphasized the word, "your."

Brant looked away, out over the river to the hills, and tightened his jaw. He noticed that one hill formed a knob, semi-spherical—like the crown of a hat. He did not want to look into his father's eyes. He was still uncertain.

"No. Not yet," he admitted, giving a nervous laugh.

His father frowned. "You'd better tell her soon and the sooner the better. This isn't fair to her. I can see it on her face. Delay is compounding the problem. She is relating this to an absolute failure in life."

"I'll tell her tonight," Brant mumbled. "I didn't want to tell her while we were still docked up," was his only excuse. "It'll be better when we're moving toward home." He did not like being maneuvered into a corner. Something unrealized was holding him back.

"Home? What home? She has no home."

"Okay, I've got it planned for tonight. I didn't have time during the layover," Brant said in half irritation, trying to evade the issue.

"Good!" the captain answered. "And be sure to tell her in a nice way. Be gentle. I'm very fond of that girl."

The huge paddle wheel flushed and churned the brown river water, driving the heavy barges without resistance. Going home, the old riverboat appeared to adopt a new attitude toward its work and its lot in life. They had entered the Ohio River at Point Pleasant, West Virginia, and were heading down stream on the much wider river. The dusky hills were soft in the twilight, the distant blue mountains rolling like the sea. The ancient hills were steeped in mountain pastures. A cool breeze was blowing across the water.

The boat was passing a community that was no more than a cluster of weather-beaten cottages along the riverbank. They were less than cottages. The small, box-like shacks were lined up in a row like railroad cars. The warped, weathered wood of these riverfront shanties, squatting on the yellowish red-brown earth, had not seen paint in years. In the small, dirt backyards were unpainted privies. Nowhere in sight was a lawn or a flower garden. The wildflowers had blossomed and faded. Floods had washed the yellow banks away and caved in the hillsides. The slow, but determined, result of a river basin is the work of centuries.

Cole watched the gangling, sick-eyed riverfront children staring at her with shy eyes, some naked to the waist, their faces had the look of starvation. Some of the boys looked as if they had spent their time rolling in the dirt. "The dirty faces of the poor," she remembered it said. "Depression babies," they were called: "Kids of the no-work folks." It was 1935. Their origins were spurious. Some wore braided pigtails tied with string, others pushed unkempt hair out of their eyes; Most were thin as a wraith. The mild, small face of one boy was flecked with freckles, and so were his wiry hands and arms. The slim faces of the children seemed sad and lonely. There was not a fat child in the group, she noticed. Some were wading in the mud-brown water. The children used the riverfront as their playground, their shadows dancing on the water. She wondered if their lives would some day blossom into happiness. She hoped so. Such desolation in such a beautiful setting was unnerving. She would never forget the story told by Old Rip of a cabin locked in an unusually heavy winter snowstorm. Never in her life would she forget the heartbreaking story of the child and mother who had been found frozen to death after starvation. It was a warning lesson told for years.

Cole knew that their meager food was of brutal simplicity, that ten cents for a movie was for the wealthy children of the nearby town, and that the children she was watching tolerated hunger in fear of starvation. A rough-coated cur strayed at their heels and sniffed suspiciously at the boat. The children came from the sun-bleached shacks where years of neglect had made the hovels looking worn and weary, as if they were without a heart—the pullulation of want, need, and hope. *If Brant were to marry me our child would never have to grow up like this,* she said to herself. *No,* she answered, *our hopes and dreams would overcome everything.*

The fathers, grandfathers, and great-grandfathers of these children, Cole was certain, had lived with a beautiful river that also taught them of the unmerciful, instilling a stubborn and despairing fortitude with which she was familiar. *The most basic trait of the river people is that they endure,* she thought. If a softness and gentleness existed, it came mainly from the women. Its timing blossomed through a heritage of a blood pride, leaving the inborn patience of silent need, and the endless sighs and shrugs of a determined forbearance. She was now experiencing this determined forbearance.

Their lives were hard and bare with nothing in view but toil and abnegation. This Cole knew. "The lower class prejudices," she had heard it called. They lived in a want and need that had become a generic part of their lives. It was the endless and timeless search for peace on a river, along its earthen banks, no longer in the keeping of the great forests of their ancestors. She could see that there was no brightness in their lives. They had become a people of sad eyes and heart-rendering songs. They fought a bitter struggle for survival, aware that the next day could be as empty as the day before, and in Cole came a fear of what her songs might become. She was well aware that many nights these mothers sat in the darkness of depression to save money on the electric bill to buy food for the children, hopeful that each meal would be better than the last with their only thought on how to survive.

It seemed incongruous that the narrow bodies so wan and spent, so young and innocent, and so frail and beautiful should look and seem so worn and weary at the dawn of their wretchedness. In their night of silent, cold, and lonely stars, there was an abjectness of patient hopefulness. And Cole knew that to look under the crust of this poverty was to see a trembling heart. She knew such a heart. Chain was wishing she did not have to see such reminders.

Some came from farm homes lost, such as hers. They came to the river to work and eat, but there was no work in 1935 and they had little to eat, squatting amid frustration, and the impotence of a raging patience. Harried with ruined hope to survive, hovelled in the dingy shacks on the fringe of cities and towns, the women lived with the shadows of passive woman fear, fading hope, and a deep resentment in their surrender and travail. Rimming their struggling lives, the mountains reflected hard reality. *Will I someday have this same fear?* Cole wondered. *Never. I'll fight against it like these women.* She heard it in their speech, in the solidity and firmness of faces now drained and empty in the unsounded sighing of surrender from within, which had become slack through weariness. She remembered the tragic words of a neighbor lady whose husband was a drunken brute: "Sometimes life is worse than death." Cole looked up from the children on the riverbank to a mother shadowed in the doorway of a dingy cottage with a broken step and crumbling porch. There was no expression on the woman's face, no recognition in a smile or a wave. She wondered if someday she and her child would stand like that in such a doorway. Children know.

The children had come bashfully from their dwarfed shacks to watch the steamboat and the beautiful girl, contact with a different world was drawing them like a magnet. They were thin because of their indigent existence. In bare feet and ragged clothes they stared at her, furtively, with somber, silent eyes. They were lovely eyes that lacked life luster that a child deserved; Instead they were a tableau of withered faces. They were watching a big house cat on the bank, waiting patiently for the movement of a river rat. It's only meal. The riverbank looked filthy and abandoned. Then their deep, knowing eyes turned to watch the boat again from stoic, unsmiling faces of wishing, yearning, and the ugly torment of bewilderment, until the boat disappeared. They seemed forgotten, but they would go on in life. They would succeed and they would achieve.

Cole was holding her guitar. She was seldom without it in the evening by habit, though she did not play it. It had become an understanding friend. As she looked at the far away hills and listened to the steam whistle of the train fade into the distance. She seemed to hug up to the guitar, as if in some sad loneliness she had the need of this friend. Unknowingly, she pulled it close to her body and hunched her shoulders over it, almost as if she were holding a child to her breast. Chain had hoped to comfort her, as Bess had suggested, but there seemed little he could do.

He was aware that the train and the riverboat were, in a number of instances, the only contact that many Kentuckians had with the world outside their hills—a world that lay beyond the solid rise of their mountains and the forever flowing of their rivers. The haunting sound of a train, or of a riverboat, remained a poignant part of the country memory. The sound of the train whistle was an important part of their lives, just to know that their faithful contact with the world was there.

He recalled the picture he had taken at Black Mountain, in the Appalachian Plateau, of an old mountain woman and a loving, happy family. She had used canning paraffin wax to fill in for her missing front teeth. She was rocking serenely, and smiled as she listened and nodded, disclosing the gift of wisdom in age through a woman's words for a girl child, so she would know the endless gift of women is to share in the natural blending of the very young and the very old. Their timeless knowing that nothing belongs to one, instinctively knowing, sooner than man, that without love to share there is naught. "No feelin' in the world can equal that of a woman holdin' a baby agin' her breast," she told the girl. Then, turning to Chain, she said, "I ain't got nothin' to give 'em 'cept what I know. They's no such thing as time. I live in three generations and all those gone are still with me. I walked these dirt roads when they was nothin' but a cow path and my grandpa walked them when they was nothin' but a deer trail." The creaking of the old rocking chair was a comforting sound to her. Chain smiled with the warmth of understanding.

It's a rare person who can see, recognize, and accept the truth, Chain thought. *Possibly only a few of the very old that are close to the grave, or the very young that are pure at heart can see it.* How he wanted to express her words of wisdom to Cole, but was afraid to invade her privacy. The old woman's depth of love and understanding was beyond the material. *There is no greater gift,* he was thinking.

Was this to be the old woman's last year? Chain wondered. *Perhaps she knew, as she sat rocking and dozing like the end of summer.* He was recalling the words of a tourist: "That ignorant old woman must be touched in the head. She talks to the trees." Chain realized that the tourist would not understand about talking to trees that had known three generations of her kin. "And she smokes a corncob pipe. Repulsive!" A neighbor mountain lady had described the tourist as, "A well-dressed, prissy snoot with a good-sized beak to look down." The tourist did not realize that the tobacco crop was their only meager existence and it was a struggle to survive. It was thin mountain soil that was causing poor crops, and a drought had not helped. They did not have the money for expensive treats.

Their only news came by word of mouth.

Chain watched a girl child rush to her granny, throwing her arms around her and sobbing her name. He remembered his granny holding fast a warm little hand. To touch a child is to know the blessing of unison, to look into the eyes of love, and know the pure and innocent delight and need of a child. *There is no more beautiful sound in all the English language than to hear a child speak the meaningful word, "Granny,"* he thought. *Other things may change through the centuries, but the joy of a child will never change. Women, and only women, have the gift to produce children,* he thought. He sensed Cole's want of a child, as did Bess, and Bess had asked him to try to be of comfort to her.

"I wished they was somethin' here more purty for ye to photo," the old granny said to Chain. "All they is an old woman and some childern." Chain's answering smile was warm with meaning, knowing that there is a little bit of the child in everyone. The little girl child was singing happily as she played. Another child was holding her doll up to her as if it was a baby.

What is more beautiful than the fresh purity of a baby calling? he wondered, *It is wonderful to know the depth of beauty and love in watching a child grow, their faces bright with the wonder of believing and their eyes alive with the glory of hope. They glow in the sincere laughter of a child. Nothing could surpass this purity.* He believed there was a reason and meaning for this special privilege. He believed that a very special people walked the beautiful mountains with a very special feeling for their hills—a majestic setting that had been their home for generations. Their life, in an unsurpassed scene of grandeur, had attracted famed artists and writers. Tourists stood in awe at the power and beauty of these towering mountains. *If only Cole had such a granny,* he thought. *If only Brant would come to a realization and make a stand.*

Chain thought of these things. He wondered if these children, would some day, emanate city-ward from the hills and hollows of their river in the first inchoation of the inborn urge to wander. He wondered if they would evolve from the seed and soil to the lost and lonely highways of steel and concrete, mesmerized by the sheen of the plastic and metal of the fabricated masses, with closed eyes to shutter out a memory. He wondered if they would lock a heart from hearing the soundless noises of grieving care: the crying for the child hands of love, lost to the heritage of a quiet, patient people where dreams were the hopes of wisdom. He knew that many had grown old with their children becoming strangers to them.

Cole felt a deep pride when Chain told her of the photography work of Emma Jean Cunningham and the effect it had had upon him. She admired Chain's natural dignity.

"I know there is no single greatest photographer since the beginning of the art," he said, "but my work has been much influenced by Cunningham and other early photographers. I remember Cunningham's work from a time when I shipped out of Puget Sound. I saw the portrait of her husband and knew of their love. That is why I say never give up your dreams."

"I will never forget this moment," Cole said. "Thank you." It was an easing of pain through sympathy. He nodded.

"Nor will I," Chain answered softly, thinking of Bess.

There were beautiful sounds in a troubled land, also, and they inspired exquisite dreams in despairing hearts, which were released in songs and ballads. To some, perhaps, the indolence of such self-sufficient dreams is not always considered a virtue, yet Chain knew that it was imperative that many Kentucky hill people held it a dire necessity, as a basic food. He knew Cole's heart would always be along the river as devoutly as mountain people never forget their home.

They were passing, a wide green valley with a farm house here and there. Her entire life had been akin and attuned to nature. Her foster father had said: "Nature may be cruel, but never false."

As they passed on deck later that evening Brant said to Cole, "I need to see you tonight after the singing." His face was empty of expression. She could not read his thoughts and remained silent. At just the sight of him her heart swelled with emotion.

"I've got to talk to you," he whispered, looking about. He tried to make his face impersonal. She nodded. He did not wait for an answer, but moved on and just walked away. Her heart went with him.

Cole licked her lips. A horrible sickness gripped her. She would know, finally. There had been no respite from the suspense of waiting. Never had she known such a moment of loneliness and heartache. Her eyes became big and staring, she was incapable of more suffering. She was thankful there would finally be an understanding, but she felt her body chill at the thought of the outcome. She was not able to push beyond her mental horizon the things that would happen to her inevitably. There had been no sign of hope on his face. Her need was great, but the encouragement had been so very slight that her mind remained in doubt. He might be able to forget, but she could not. Her hopes were those of a child.

There had been a grim, hard look about his mouth that frightened her. *What had they said, he and his father?* She held herself erect, tense, so as not to give way to the deep cry within her. He had given no indication of the decision. And deVoss was on deck, watching. He seemed always to be watching her, as though something was crouching and unseen. Even when she could not see him she knew he was there. She sensed it. She was in dread that before long he would make another move as he had in his cabin and she feared that she would not be able to escape him.

Brant's cold tone had kept her at arms length and his look had gone to her heart more than any words he could have spoken. It was only after their last talk that she wondered if she and Brant would ever love as they had loved. This wondering had come to her, not in a moment, not in a day, but through the hardness of a soft summer—a season of broken words and dreams.

Why is he so cold and hard? she asked herself, when she so needed the touch of a loving hand and spirit. *Why couldn't he have at least smiled?* She glanced at deVoss, fearful. She dreaded the night and what was coming.

Meanwhile, Chain guided the boat serenely down the river, ever-watchful on deck as Bess was watchful from the galley, listening to a child crying in the dark and well knowing that the discovery of the truth can be devastating.

The setting sun, the evening wind, and the flowing river had failed to answer her cry of hope. The last pale glimmer of light had come from the dying sun as the evening shadows moved in over the valley. And there still remained the huffing and the puffing of the train as it struggled through the mountains. Cole likened her hopes to the lightning-blasted pine tree on the riverbank.

Chapter Twenty-One

The following day Cole was at the deck rail, waiting. From the vantage point of the upper deck she watched the fields, valleys, and farms. *Soon the leaves will be changing color,* she thought. The sun was setting over the western hills and the river had turned to a liquid shadow. The hills were growing darker. The sunset had lost its strength and the soft glow was fading. Darkness was not far off in the gentle river night. The evening was deepening into twilight. She looked at the sky. There were the stars to bring grace and hope to the human heart. Her stepmother called it: "The magic of silver light." Cole was not thinking of the beautiful stars, she was thinking of the conversation to come. She had an uneasy feeling about their planned meeting tonight. She could smell the coffee and hear Bess washing dishes. The shadows were lengthening and the quiet of night spread over the water.

"You've dared to drink the dew of stars," Bess had told her. Experience had not warned her of its poison. Once the stars had been happy. She wondered if it was the throbbing of the engine, the pounding of her heart, or the pulsing of hope within her that caused a beat of fear and an aching void. In the distance she could see the cattle coming down from the hills, coming home, and heard a calf bawling for its mother. A farm boy and his dog were with the cattle and several plow horses were trudging along behind. The setting sun was burnished gold.

When twilight settled over the river Cole saw the gentle colors of evening fill the river sky, accenting the soft lights of the houses. The river glistened with light reflections. The night songs of birds came softly from the hills and a brisk wind brought the scent of trees. She wondered if this was the wind of destiny of which she had read. A few pale stars remained. The river air was sweetened by the scent of foliage. In all there was beauty, except in her own mind. Even the shadowed hills seemed more solemn and foreboding. The mountain peaks were silver in the moonlight and were accompanied by the familiar, lonely sound of the wind through pines. *Is there a message in the wind,* she wondered. She stared at the beautiful moonlit hills in silence—thoughtful and sad. The waiting and hoping seemed like a lifetime. All efforts to keep herself busy and her mind free had failed. Her future seemed as impenetrable as the distant, shadowed hills. It was a calm night. The river was flat and black with silver streaks of moonlight.

In the gathering dusk Cole was filled with foreboding. A sick premonition was growing in her. A hundred times she had feared the conversation in which her love would struggle for its life. Though a warm night she was frightened and cold. She looked about. The sound of the water began to sound like the murmuring of grief. She wondered if she was looking for a miracle to make her marriage to Brant come true. Her simple state of unknowing had become devastating. She wondered if it was an omen. Then she thought she saw a shadow slithering along the deck, but it disappeared. There was always that terrifying shadow.

Brant did not appear on deck until after the singing. He had planned it that way. When he came up to Cole it was with an attempted smile. A chill ran down her back at the failure.

Each was waiting for the other to speak, afraid to break the silence in fear of words. They were listening to the sound of the river. The swelling in Cole's breast made it difficult for her to breathe. The blood was beating in her temples. She was outside of something beyond her understanding, a reality enclosed in a dream. *If only somehow we could work through it,* she thought.

Cole noticed that Brant's lips were dry, as he was aware of how quickly she was breathing. They stood at the rail, watching the lights along the shore. They were steaming past St. Paul, Kentucky. Minutes passed before either of them spoke. If he had noticed, he would have seen that she was speaking with her eyes.

It was as if Brant did not see her because he was occupied with his own thoughts. It was cooler and the stars were shining. The river was silver in the moonlight. She turned to him, pointing and staring in wonder at the beauty of golden stars on black velvet. Her smile was beautiful. She wondered if the stars were winking at her in knowing.

"Remember me?" she whispered, trying to sound light-hearted. As if it was the echo of dream's mist her voice came out of the darkness. She wanted to touch his face, stroke his hair, and feel the strength of his embrace. She was not aware of reality waiting behind the veil of dreams and he was unaware of her unaffected warmth.

"Nice night," Brant said at last. They had spoken at the same time. His voice was husky, his face a mixture of guilt and dread. He put his hands in his pockets, staring out over the river.

"Yes, beautiful," Cole agreed slowly, drawing a hurried breath. It was a whisper. To her, he had sounded so thin and distant. It seemed as if the river sand was washing away beneath her as she first sensed the ancient knowledge of desertion. She almost understood, almost, as she felt the panic swell.

Cole gave him a hesitant smile and, going to him, placed her hands on either side of his face. "Look at me," she said, turning his face to look into hers. His mind seemed vacant. She was seeking strength, yet was forced to give strength. *If he won't talk, I will,* she thought. *If he won't take the action, I will. I'll go to his father.* She was desperate not to back down. They stood in silence, staring at each other. He had never seen her look more beautiful.

She leaned toward him. "Say something, Brant!" she insisted, desperate for words unspoken. She could not still the pain of doubt that was climbing in her. For a long while they stood motionless and silent, staring out over the river at a town asleep.

Cole stood, looking at him. She was hopeful in waiting for him to answer. There was a continued silence. In spite of all warning she was not prepared. It was after dark and the lights of St. Paul were fading, that Brant told her. They were leaning against the railing with his back to it and her facing the hills. She tried to smile, but was too deeply effected. His answer seemed an age in coming.

"Say something!" she repeated, tensing. She was searching his face and waiting. There was a need in her eyes, a longing on her lips as she listened for those precious words. It was impossible for her to dispel the want, the need, and the longing. Hopes and dreams washed over her like a waterfall. She believed that without him she had nothing and the world was void. Her throat was suddenly dry; she swallowed. Yet her heart refused to give up. She could not believe that something so precious was beyond expectation.

Silence. The perfect, irresistible words did not come.

He paused a moment longer, struggling with decision and his manifest intention to be kind yet honest in his wordage. "There isn't much to say," was his short reply, his voice husky in his throat. Then, his tone changed, the hardness slipping from it. "I've been meaning to tell you of my talk with my father." Another pause. "We just can't go on like we were. We can't see each other except in the line of work." It was as simple as that. His voice sounded nervous. He did not know how to say it more gently.

Another silence. She looked as if she might cry.

Speechless, she stared at him, too deeply hurt for words. Her heart sank. There was a long pause when only the sounds of the boat and water broke the silence. His words were as shocking as if he had shouted. In a matter of seconds her spirits had gone from hoping to despair with his words hovering over her like a dark cloud. She stared at him as the night dissolved away from her. "Do you mean never?" she cried, and her breath caught in her throat. His brief statement had blasted her soul. It seemed that he was asking her to sacrifice the whole meaning of her life to set him free. The words, like the destruction of a belief, chilled her heart. He seemed unaware of the depth and substance of her feelings.

She paused, taking a deep breath and hoping her voice would not break. Her eyes were welling with tears. "Is that all you have to say?" she pleaded. The frightened tone did not soften him. In the moonlight his features were grave. Her face was soft and giving.

He paced back and forth as he spoke with his hands in his pockets. He was struggling to maintain a distant perspective. "That's all I can say for the present," he said to counter her question. *A man's career comes first,* he told himself defensively. *The personal life comes later. It is a necessary pattern.* He was enchanted with the prospect of his professional future as captain. She realized it was not a bluff and he wasn't teasing. She stood stock still, not knowing what to say, tears blurring her vision. *Will I be gone like a draft of this river wind?* She wondered.

The silence between them grew deeper. Cole was feeling as grim as a winter dawn. She shook her head. "It seems to me there's a great deal more to be said," she stated. Dread made her words edgy. The voice was not hers. "It seems to me," she continued, "that all the important things have been left unsaid. All the necessary action left undone." She was willing to believe anything but the truth in order to cover her pain.

He could feel her eyes upon him. He straightened and faced her. "I'm only doing what has to be done." He was breathing heavily. He saw the expression on her face change, as though she was drawn toward some outer distance. He could see the question quivering on her lips.

"Why have you been avoiding me, avoiding our situation, and avoiding an answer?" She spoke slowly, as if from a long distance away. She was in dread to the bottom of her soul. "Why?" she repeated. "Why couldn't we have talked this out? Gone to your father together?" A great helpless grief was rising in her. Another need, another love was lost. She was fighting it away and struggling for her future life. Her love had become an inseparable part of herself; He was all her hopes and needs. He failed to detect the loneliness and need in her voice. She felt empty. In those short seventeen years she had lost everything in life.

"I didn't think it was necessary. I took care of it." His look and tone told her he did not like the questioning and he was hoping she would make it easier for him. "I didn't think it would get this serious so soon," he added, thinking of his father's words. His voice sounded strange to her. It was not the boyish voice of those few summer months. Bess had warned her that hope could be cruel.

"What did you think?" She smiled crookedly. "You've never bothered to tell me." He knew that it was true.

"I thought we were just passing the time," he stammered, his thoughts and emotions in confusion. He was unable to relate the true meaning of love. "That is, I thought it wasn't going to be serious until later on. I thought that we would wait to make such a serious commitment," he hastened to add, stammering.

"You should know better than that," she exclaimed, not waiting for him to finish. Something caused him to regret the way he had said it. He remembered his father's remark about playing with a person's life. He wished he could escape the moment.

"I didn't realize you were taking it that seriously," he corrected evasively, wishing that the situation had not become so heavy at that time in his career. He only wanted to think of the future and what it held in store for him professionally. His cold words hit like a blow. "We can't get serious right now," he added.

Tears came to her eyes. Experience was telling her how ruthless the lessons of life could be, one after the other. She knew she would never be able to forget. Her voice broke for a moment.

"Oh, Brant," and anguish ripped her heart, "how can I tell you if you don't already know?" *If he only understood more,* she thought. She was consumed by a fire she was unable to quench. "I've tried to tell you." She sensed his withdrawal. She waited in hope of his reassurance, his understanding, for anything that would help. It seemed that she could not do anything right to get the so-needed response. She believed that he was her entire life and that she was fighting for the deepest meaning of her existence. Then the most important thought came to her again.

"Maybe we'd better start with the talk you had with your father. Maybe we can rebuild from there." She could hear her pulse beating in her ears. "Is that why you stayed away from me?" She spoke simply concerning the issue of the separation of their lives. There was a haunting softness in her eyes that he could not fail but see, a tenderness as soft as the twilight shine of the river. "Maybe," he said, jamming his hands into his pockets and shifting from one foot to the other. He resented her gentle stubbornness. "Maybe I was just trying to think of what was best for you long term," he said, trying to put confidence back into his voice and hoping he was right in his approach to the troubling situation. He was unaware of the inadequacy of his words.

For the first time she was realizing things she did not want to realize. He had made love to her, and yet had not seen her, heard her, or known her. "And I thought what we had was real," she murmured, staring at the deck and struggling to strengthen her resolve.

Then Brant looked at her and understood for the first time that she loved him—truly, really, and deeply loved him. He had not realized the depth of her feelings, having thought it a summer fling. He turned away. It frightened him to see the love shining through her eyes. He did not know what to say or how to act. He had had no experience of such a depth. For him there had been no dark years in which he needed help, there was only the thought and promise of his career. He did not say anything.

"Best for me?" she asked brokenly, echoing his words. The understandable world of her summer dreams was slipping away. "You were thinking of what was best for me?" she repeated. No pain she had ever experienced hurt like the agony of the heart.

Every nuance of their summer night meetings on deck was implanted in her memory in guilt. Her mind was flooded with those summer-night memories that called at the edge of a dream. To awaken from that dream was to die. Her love had grown to be the most important thing in her life. She had never felt so empty and sick. She had experienced many heart-breaking things in her young life, but none had torn as deeply as that presentiment of tragedy, that summer of wasted dreams.

"I'll tell you what is best for me," she said quietly. "For you to talk to me honestly. Tell me the things I must know. What you truly feel, what we are to do, and what your father said. First, just tell me what you and your father talked about."

Cole spoke in a voice of essential truth of which Brant was not aware. To her it was simple. It was love. To him it was the problem of convincing her to delay until another day. They may as well have been invisible to each other, so far apart were their thoughts. She needed him, but did he need her?

She reached out her hand to him, then drew it back. To hold his hand and talk to him now was not a pleasure, it was a necessity. He remained silent, thinking.

Brant's thoughts did not come with his feelings and his words did not flow heart to heart. His mind was too heavily occupied with other more demanding thoughts. He was the unrealized victim of self-centered youth. His mind had been made up and he could not permit himself to consider any other viewpoint. Cole had often seen that stubborn look.

"What is best for our love is what is best for me," Cole said simply. "Best for us." Her innocent face and wide-open eyes were turned to him, trying to make him understand, trying to make him focus on the immediate. Her words were carefully emphasized. She wondered if she was hoping for something she could never have. The moonlight enhanced the pallor of her face. All the natural sounds of the river seemed unreal.

The river had darkened then disappeared in the moon shadows. She was ashamed of her forwardness, yet unable to control it. Cole wondered if that was where romance ended but love continued in the shadows of a starlit night over a dark river in the valley of the hills in the illumination of a lost life. She had always loved the stars, but on this night they were so lonely and remote. The night exuded loneliness. Even the moon looked dead. She had always hoped that it would be her and Brant, and that was all, nothing else mattered. But her hopes and dreams were becoming more and more uncertain. Utterly at a loss for words she fell silent.

As they stood, looking over the railing, Cole saw a reflection in the water of a boy she did not know. She could see his image, but she could not read his thoughts and feelings. She looked at the reflection as though the river were drowning her hopes. There were two voices along a dark river, then the reflection disappeared into the flow along with the warmth of love she so desperately needed. She had always liked the night because it hid some of the realities of day, but the darkness of that night could not hide the hurt and fear. A drifting cloud had covered the three-quarter moon. Her entire world seemed to drift with that cloud.

In guilt, Brant could not look at her. He felt ashamed that he did not appear more manly and was not handling the problem with maturity and capability. He was pushing aside his father's kind words. It had seemed so simple when talking with his father, but now he was uncertain and said nothing.

"And I thought you needed me," Cole said, and heard her cry for help from within as he did not answer. Her tear-filled eyes met his. Innocence, purity, and truth were written on her young face. She looked deeply at him. He turned away.

"Well, what do you think is best for me?" she asked again. "You did not say." He glanced at her, then turned toward the river. It was a glance that whispered in Cole's mind, a song that raced in her blood. The summer of her life had been short, lost in the loveliness of the river and the mountains. It was the bitter briefness of a summer, of a life. Brant was unaware of the slow vanishing of a beautiful girl. He had not yet realized that in Cole's mind she believed that was the only thing on earth for which she had to live.

"If you won't tell me what was said between you and your father, and why, then I'll go right now to him and have him tell me." She was determined to make an effort. Brant had no choice but to tell her the bitter truth.

"Wait!" Brant cried, believing that she would. His father had told him to handle it. He thought of it as a test of strength and learning.

"Well?" Cole asked again. She did not hear her voice climb, quaver, then crack. Brant was breathing hard. He was tense with the feeling of desertion and trying to conduct himself professionally, in fear of being ineffectual, of not living up to his father's hopes. Cole put her hand on his arm. Her hand was shaking.

"Brant," she said, and that time her voice choked, "let's try to be gentle with one another." Her hand was trembling. "Do you remember the things you said this summer? The depth of meaning?"

"Maybe you misunderstood," he replied. He resented the soft reminder of the truth. "Maybe you read something into them that wasn't there," he added, not realizing the pain in a shattered dream.

"Is it possible that it meant so little to you that you can that easily forget it and push aside the depth of the effect?" She was unable to explain, and Brant unwilling to discern it for himself. He stood woodenly. He had not yet reached an age to look into his own soul. He was thinking only of his needs and wants. He merely shook his head, searching for an excuse to justify his procrastination.

"I'm trying to be friends," he said, "remain friends," he corrected, remembering his father's warning. "I am your friend and I'm trying to say nicely that we have to wait. No use acting like a martyr." She flushed. The thoughtless words cut into her like a knife. She did not cry, but the tears were within her.

"Friends?" she echoed in disbelief. "Would you betray a friend? Our love has become more than a friendship, and I'm certain that you know it and feel it. I'm going to tell your father that we pledged our future to be together. We did and you know it." She spoke quietly with the desperation of need. She could never force him to make a stand on solid ground. It angered and saddened her.

"It was a summer relationship intended to build toward something permanent later," he insisted. "You and I...." and his voice trailed off at the sight of her face. "Best to call a halt to it for the present," he said in a sudden, determined statement that he had practiced. She was silenced by the careless remark. The look of a frightened child was in her eyes.

Her summer was covered with a thin layer of cold words. She wondered if things could ever be quite the same. A piece of her life was gone. She wondered if it would ever again be whole. Yet there was always the trembling of hope. She had to hope because of the love within her. Her dreams were the narcotic nymph that dulled the pain. She did not want to become one of those women who believed love is dead and hope is useless. She had seen too much of it in this world of depression.

"Is that all you have to say?" She had never abased herself before, but it seemed as if she were begging.

As she thought over their relationship through postulated reasoning, she realized she had hidden from herself the truth she sensed would happen using the will not to believe. Being so deeply and completely in love she had not been honest with herself. "Then what we shared had such little meaning to you?" she asked again, unaware of her repetition. Ashen, her face was a study in agony. She wondered if she was to blame in some way, if she had unknowingly gone beyond reason. She was inexperienced in the complexities of human behavior.

A choking sob broke from her at his silence; Tears were running down her cheeks. He had yet to realize the depth of reward in the true love of a girl.

"It had a lot of meaning. I enjoyed it as much as you did," he answered. She looked at him in amazement. The seemingly casual remark hurt. Something was gone—vanished like a cloud-covered star. Each mile they traveled seemed to draw him farther away.

"Enjoyed it!" she echoed, as though she were talking to herself. The remark was so brief and so thoughtless that she had difficulty believing it. "This is the end? Is that why you talk about some distant future and will not go with me to your father now?" His eyes slid away from hers to gaze out over the river. He had never anticipated a scene like this.

There was nothing to comfort her. It was as though something was dying within her. In that instant she looked into his eyes and saw inside, and knew that he was not completely hers. Realizing his confusion, she wondered if he would ever be totally hers, and her eyes filled with tears.

He's right about one thing, she admitted to herself. Despite the sincerity of his emotions and all the words he had spoken this summer that were imprinted on my mind, the word "marriage" was not one of them. To her, love and marriage were the same—one word. She had fancied the word "marriage" was there. What had been said in the last few minutes had come as a stunning shock, tearing something inside of her.

Brant swallowed hard, trying to control himself and remembering his father's warning to be gentle, but he did not know what words to use or how to convey his confusion. As of yet he did not fully understand himself.

Cole remained silent, her eyes upon the water. As she stared she could feel the steady thumping of her heart.

"This is best for both of us at the present time," he tried to reason. "After all, you're still a girl. We have a lifetime ahead of us. Everything will work out fine." He thought these words of his father would sound mature—a winning answer—and put an end to it until later. "Maybe you took too much for granted at present," he added. She turned to stare at him.

The thoughtless remark staggered her; It was an amorphous and insidious abstraction and its malaise was enormous. Yet her love hung on, like a candle the wind could not blow out. She sensed something within him of which he was unaware. Her young life had been a continual fight against despair. She could not admit defeat because of the depth of love within her. Because of this she would have accepted him under any conditions.

"You didn't say I was just a girl a few months ago when you held me in your arms so lovingly," she said, trying to see his face in the dark. Her face had become the color of faded paper. Despair and hope were balancing like her childhood teeter-totter. He had never seen her so white, so quiet. Her hopes were turning to hurt as she struggled to hold back tears.

"You're only seventeen years old. Try to be reasonable." A tremor ran through her at the sound of him. He could see the pulse beating in her throat. All the pent-up things had burst within her. She stared at him blankly, her heart sinking.

"I was just seventeen years old those nights on deck," she reminded him. His eyes darted to her breast and then away. In shamed silence she waited for his reply. "Do you cherish anything in your heart?" she asked simply, stunned by his casual reasoning.

"All I know is what I'm doing is right for both of us," he answered, trying to protect his judgment. He was agreeing with his father's reasoning and the thoughts of his mother.

"You think that's right?" No answer. "Right for whom?" She knew that what had been between them could never be pushed aside so completely. Not then. She had felt the depth of his emotions. "Do you think your father will say that is right when I tell him everything?" He could not come with a reasonable denial. He was unable to answer.

"Right?" she repeated. "You are speaking of what is right?" Her state of mind was tense. It came to her that a life could be changed forever as the result of an impulse. A feeling of irreparable loss was sweeping over her like a flooding river. It was the inescapable shame and hurt of rejection. She could not believe what was happening. She had heard of women who had loved more than once, but was certain that could never happen to her. He had become her entire life. "I gave my all to you."

When he did not answer, she continued, "Then tell me, from your heart, what is truly right, and not what you think as right or have been told is right." He did not move. He tried to consider. His face was in turmoil. He was struggling. He was not certain of the right words, yet unable to push the question aside.

"Tell me!" she demanded. His hands were clenched on the deck rail. There was still no answer. "What am I to do? Get down on my knees and beg?" she cried. "Not even I can do that. Not even for you. I won't crawl to you, nor will I beg from your father when I go to him." He still said nothing, remembering what his father had said about getting command of his own boat when he got his captain's license. He did not answer for a few moments, but stood, staring at her. She saw the distance widening between them.

In indecision he was staring at a face—her face. Her sensitive features were pale and thin in the moonlight, almost pinched. He saw how changed she was; Her paleness and thinness astounded him.

Cole sensed his thoughts. She had wanted so much to look her best that night, but she realized how she must look to him.

"You must think more in terms of the future rather than insisting on right now," was all he could say. "The talk of us going to my father is useless. I've come to a decision to wait." Her face raised to his in an open bewilderment. She looked into a face that was unable to acknowledge the real root of their problem. She could scarcely believe what she was hearing.

"When I do go to your father I will ask him who made the decision, and under what circumstances. If all the truths were known then there may be a different decision." When he did not answer she knew that he was not saying what he had said for her, but for a career.

"Hoping?" She repeated his word. The word went through her mind numbly, her thoughts retreating into the deep vacuum of her mind. She was looking into darkness, listening to soft water along the flow of hills, and wondering about the vast and endless things of life she would never know, of the confusion of an unskilled heart. At seventeen she should have known more than she knew. It was as if when he talked it was not to her, and when she spoke she could not reach him. She did not know what words to use to save her life, yet hope remained in her heart.

"Yes, I hope," Cole said. She was fighting for the possession of her happiness, her life, the promise of their future life together, and any hope that would rise above the ruins of her existence: their child.

When he glanced at her he realized that she was not looking at him. She was staring into the black water. But the river could not wash away the dread. He saw the purity of her heart in her eyes. He wondered if he would ever again experience that again in all his life?

"And what do you hope?" she asked. The pain was intolerable. Pale and still, she saw him ripping the ties between them: There was to be no reason in what had happened. Word by word, he was destroying, piece-by-piece, the life within her. How easily the most precious things could be snatched away. Once the vessel vibrated until it shuddered. They did not notice.

"Why are you doing this?" Cole asked. "What is the real reason?" It was asked as simply as if the words could create an answer. "What could be important enough for you to do this? You have never given a reason. These were not your words and feelings throughout the summer during those nights on deck behind the lifeboat." Again there was no answer.

"When you talked to your father did you tell him that we love each other and that we hoped to marry? That we spoke of our plans for the future?" she asked, her breasts rising and falling. Her voice was soft and low.

His cheeks twitched and he looked away from her. "No, I didn't tell him that," he admitted in honesty, though not intending to hurt her more. "I didn't tell you all those words, either. I never mentioned the word marriage because I thought of that as coming later." His words had the tone of finality and no more conversation.

Cole's breath quickened. It was all so unexpected and blunt. "You looked into my face, you looked into my eyes, and you didn't know the love in my heart?" she asked. To hide her trembling hands she put them behind her, half afraid of his answer.

"No, I guess you didn't, really," she answered for him, as though she had become crippled spiritually with shame and rejection. "Not in those exact words." She clenched her eyes shut. "What did you tell your father?" she finally asked, feeling sick inside because she had allowed herself to be carried away by dreams.

"I told you I didn't say anything about marriage or love...." The word stopped him. He had broken out into a sweat.

"Love?" Cole repeated the word. "I see," she went on, her eyes fixed on the river. Her face had become the face of a woman. "What we felt was not love? Did not have the meaning of love?" She moved toward him slowly. Step, pausing, and a step—like a child not certain of the person she is approaching. She was to learn more. She was becoming aware of a new dimension, of a different image. It was a dimension greater than her grasp. She stood there, hoping and waiting for a sign, a word—anything to relieve the feeling of suffocation.

"You felt no love for me those nights on deck?" she demanded gravely. "You will stand before your father and I and tell him that?" She was struggling through the pain to reach some reality. "Oh, Brant," she said, searching for words, "I felt your heart beat upon my heart and you say there was no love?" It was a desperate reaching of her love for his love'; Nothing else mattered. Those were not the words she had planned to say. It seemed to her that what she had experienced could not be expressed in words. She loved him beyond all expression. It was so real to her that it caught in her voice. She had had so much to offer and now she had only the feeling of emptiness through renunciation.

"I don't know," he said in a husky voice. It was true. He did not understand all of his feelings for certain. He wiped his forehead. His shirt was wet. His body leaned heavily against the boat rail.

"You don't know?" Her voice was tired. She felt drained and weak. "You held me in your arms and spoke of love, and now you say you don't know?" The thoughtless remark was devastating.

Brant thought of himself as a decent and considerate young man. He had been told that he was. He had been raised that way. He had not planned this. To him it simply evolved. He had not intended to hurt her so. He had good looks and charm, which gave him the instinct for conquest, and his susceptibility to her had been tremendous, his feelings bewildering.

"What I meant was, I don't know how it's all going to come out in the long run," he said in confused retraction, and wondered, with a not inconsiderable despair, how he was going to manage a situation of which he had never dreamed, and of which he was finding himself incapable. All he wanted to do was to wait, to be certain. "But, I do know that you going to my father will not change anything," he managed to say, desperate for time and reason.

"I thought our relationship was for now," Cole said. "You make me feel that I was as unknowing as a child—eager, thoughtless." Her courage was weakening, she looked suddenly as lost as a child.

All the rapture of the summer was fading. Nothing Brant was saying could put it in clear perspective. To her, the summer seemed years ago, lost in a river of time, and none of it seemed real. It was like a vapor in her mind. There was nothing behind her, what could there be before her? The days of doubt were over. She did not have to tell herself it was so. The truth of it was within her. Her brief life had not known a happy beginning or a happy ending. There was only a warm, sweet breath of a brief summer in between. She had lived all of her life in one summer. It would be impossible to close away those summer nights and what they had meant because they would drift back through other nights.

"You can wait," Brant said lamely in desperation, not noticing the changing beauty of her face. He was saying things that made no sense to her under the circumstances. Her eyes became those of a lost and frightened child as she thought of their child she had dreamed of having. "Give it time," he added, seeing only the advantage of waiting for a promotion. She continued to stare at him, wondering how so much could have been squeezed into a few months of one summer.

Wait? Nothing can be accomplished by waiting, she thought. *What are we waiting for? We love each other. We said so.* Oh, how she longed for his arms about her. It was the touch that would heal.

"Yes," he said in a struggle for delay. "The decision must be yours, Cole. If you feel that you can't wait for me, then the decision is yours that it's best for us to forget it." It was as if she had been struck a physical blow. A stunned look crossed her face as she stared into a night as black as the bottom of a well.

"Can you forget?" she asked in disbelief. No answer. "Brant, can you forget the words whispered in my ear?" She spoke his name across the space she feared would divide them. Her fine eyebrows drew together. "Will you ever forget?" Brant swallowed and flushed. "And in a year or two, ten years, anyway, you won't even remember my name?" She waited for an answer. He did not have an answer. She seemed to be out of his thoughts and plans.

To Brant, only one positive decision emerged from his confusion. "Only you can make the decision to wait or not to wait," he said. "Try to understand. To wait is the answer. It won't do any good talking about it." He wanted to go to his cabin and go to bed. They were to be on duty in two hours.

"You have said that before, but you don't say why. Why can't we go to your father and tell him of our love?" Her voice, low and stricken, stopped. *Not once has Brant mentioned his mother,* Cole thought. "Why?" she repeated, fighting back tears, not wanting to mention his mother.

"Okay, I just told you why," he said in anger, forgetting his father's warning, not knowing or caring that anger destroys. "You say I never tell you anything? Well, I'm telling you again. We have to wait because it's best for both of us," he emphasized. She was fighting back tears, knowing they would not defeat him. Brant stared down at the single teardrop that had splashed on the deck. His words seemed unreal, like a voice in a strange dream.

"We have to be practical," he continued, breaking her silence and parroting words. He was pleased with the maturity of his sensible approach, hoping this was the answer to their problem. She was mystified by his withdrawal to that extent. He seemed to have moved completely away. Her mind filtered through all his excuses, one after the other.

Cole felt as helpless as a fish out of water, knowing that his simple reasoning was not the answer to their problem. She looked away, out over the river, to the shore. There were tears in her eyes. "Practical doesn't blend with love," she answered, staring out into the night. "It's just a nicer word for not caring."

"I keep telling you that it will work best by waiting," he insisted. "You'll see." He tried to use a confident tone. "We have plenty of time." His hope for their future was sincere. "I'll have a better position and better income by then."

Standing, watching, listening, it came to Cole that this was the second time he used the practical theory. She was obsessed with the thought that love, truth, and purity were inevitable things of the present, not some distant and questionable tomorrow. She was unable to correlate this with his version of practical reality, fearing that it had more to do with what Bess said of his mother.

Brant stood, watching Cole as she sought to understand all of the ramifications. She would never really be told everything, and he had nothing more to say. She had received no complete explanation.

"I can't believe that it was only a dream," she said aloud to herself. Brant was startled. "How can you live without a dream?" she asked, turning to him. "It's like living without hope." She recalled Bess saying: "In love, as in life, there can be no flower without the seed." There was no answer.

It was as if Cole was starting to retreat into darkness, waking from a dream to find that what she had thought of as the most precious thing in life was gone. There was no longer the fear of the subtleness of not knowing, but she tasted the bitter waters of lost hope. This knowledge seeped into her traumatized consciousness, splintering any dream of the last wild spasm of hope. It was as though she was in a world of living death when realization finally spoke to the deepest blood. She could not recall the origin of her fear. Her entire future seemed a vague uncertainty—the feeling of sinking in a river of darkness. She felt her relationship with him was only the whisper of memory.

It opened in Cole's mind like a stuck drawer, slowly being forced open. It was as if some black magic, a dream-veil, had been lifted, and she now saw into a new world beyond. "What is there in life without love?" she asked, almost to herself. Without him there seemed to be nothing but emptiness in her heart. Brant stood without words. *How do you rebuild a dream?* she wondered, studying him.

"You held me in your arms with that much feeling of emotion and it had no meaning? And now you speak of something possible in the future? A maybe, or a could be?" She could not go on. She simply could not believe this turning away of his mind. She was amazed at how quickly things seemed to change.

He swallowed dryly, but felt that he must be man enough to stand by the decision he had given his father. He cleared his throat. "In that I was wrong," he admitted, shaking his head, "but I'm trying to plan it out, work it out.

There's so much involved, like my future career and family matters, as well as our feelings."

She stared at him in search of the truth. "Just tell me one simple thing," she said. "Do you truly and sincerely love me as much as you said? Enough to marry me and not speak of that sometime in the unknown future?" She waited for his words, the words that would make her hopes and dreams come true, or words that would have no meaning but to cloud an issue. He had no words. "Tell me," she said in a low voice, her head turned away.

Bess had told her of her own devastation in regard to a promise of the future. Cole turned from Brant and looked into the dark water as if the river had drowned his reasoning and ability of explanation. Through the heavy yearning she was feeling the first hopeless warning of absolute defeat, which she had been resisting and pushing aside in hope. She felt the first deadly anguish of not healing, the first touch of nothingness toward which she was moving. It was that summit beyond pain.

"I was wrong," he said again. "I admit it."

"It isn't a matter of right or wrong," she said, her words barely audible. "It's a matter of inner feeling, of love and sincerity." All she wanted was to love him and take care of him for the rest of his life.

"I'm convinced that the right thing for both of us is to wait," he stated, tight-lipped, unable to voice the tender words of love and feeling he felt—the need for her.

To Cole, the sound of those cold, hard words made it seem that all hope had ended. The thought of having a family of her own to love and care for had been among her richest dreams. "You speak of right? Was it right to speak in terms of love last month, but it isn't right this month?" she asked. The question beyond her concept and ruinous in its implication. A chill of damp air made her shiver. Again there was his convenient silence. He had nothing more to say. She could hear the wind singing a sad song through the rigging.

"Please tell me. Do you love me at all?" she asked, simply, in a last desperate search for salvation from the seeming ruin of her hopes and dreams. The directness of the question several times repeated merely made Brant shake his head in irritation. "Forget about your father, forget about your mother, forget about this sometime in the future. Forget everything else. Just be honest enough to tell me one thing, truthfully, and don't evade—no double-talk. Do you have any love for me?" She spoke with the simple directness of a child. "Give me a simple yes or no," she cried in anguish and in fear of the answer. She saw the moonlight on his face, the terrible struggle in his eyes, and his inability to express his feelings and his uncertainty. She remained very quiet, waiting and hoping. She was terribly in love with him. She could not help herself, though her hopes and dreams were dieing. Silence.

Then, quietly, with humility she said, "I loved you always. From the first day I saw you." The words were almost to herself. There was no answer. "All I have left is my love for you," she added. "Do you truly understand what it means to be loved?" She was offering him her most precious gift: the innocent love of a pure heart. She stood before him, exhausted and weary, with a longing unhidden by the night. Never before had she experienced such hurt. Again silence spoke the bitter truth.

Brant did not see the pain in her hunched shoulders, the fear in her child-blue eyes, with nothing to wash clean the hurt and give new life. He failed to recognize the depth of purity and strength in her simplicity. He had never experienced the tragedy and need to go on that had been in her life. He was not certain what to say or how to say it. Because of his youth and inexperience he had no answer. She searched his eyes. Her feelings were laid bare.

"Never mind," she said in the silence. "You don't have to say it. I can see it. I can feel it. I didn't want to believe it when you told me your plans were in some distant future. I love you more than life," she said simply. "You were all I had for which to hope and live." It was a need that had eaten into her heart.

The saddest realization of all was that Brant could not help himself in order to help her. She was emotionally exhausted and physically drained. It came to her clearly and with such force. She knew, finally. Only for what he wanted and needed had he come to her. She believed there was nothing left in life for her. There was no need to go to his father now as a beggar. Her natural pride would not let her crawl. She would not use an advantage to force an unwanted union. She stared at a wave on the river: there one minute, gone the next. The pause, the silence, the waiting for an answer seemed like an eternity. Yet she listened for the words she believed she would never hear. It was her need and breath of life, a call beyond his control. She put her hand to her lips as she listened for the words, stunned. She was never again to hear his voice call her name. He would never again hold her lovingly to his body.

"Oh, God," she whispered, putting her hands to her temples, trembling. "I thought you knew, had to know. How could you not know? I told you." She had the feeling that her hopes had been pulled out by the roots. "Surely you knew how I loved you." She had no understanding of why she loved and why he seemed uncertain. He had no answer for her at the moment. He had never asked himself the worth of a human life, and she thought more in terms of the heart and soul than of the mind.

She watched his fingers open and close nervously. They were the fingers that had caressed her. A boy saw the moonlight reflecting on her face, but could not see the light go out of her soul. He was unaware that he had crushed her entire world.

"Serious?" She murmured one of his words helplessly. "When is love not serious? Look at my face and into my eyes and know. Look very closely." He did not reply and she would not use this to hold him if he did not love her. She believed the failure was hers.

He did not recognize the inward look of a woman's knowledge of the love within herself. He had not fully understood the glow on her face, the depth of meaning in her eyes. He did not realize she had given him all because she loved him. She was beginning to feel foolish, knowing how she must look to him. She felt so diminished somehow, stricken that their love should have ended that way. She had been warned that without marriage she would be branded as unwanted. She felt a foreboding wind flow across the dark river. The smile was gone from her face, the light from her eyes. "And now good-bye?" she asked. "Just like that?"

Something had snapped within her, severed neat and clean. The dream had ended, fracturing any last hope she had. All the beautiful memories were overshadowed by the cloud of reality. Like a wounded animal, she wanted to crawl into a hole and get away from the world. A deep silence had fallen between them. Their conversation had died. His denial was causing her to retreat into herself.

She stared out over the water, her thoughts in confusion. The deck light cast her shadow over the reflective water. It was the shadow of a girl who had been denied. She realized how much she had hurt herself, believing that she was scarred and changed forever. She felt as if she were drowning.

She had never said to him, or to herself, "I cannot live without you." She was not conscious that she had even thought it. On her heart was a scar that would never vanish. There was something very heavy inside her. For a large part of her being there was no hope of recovery. Her dream had been shattered as those dreams of her childhood. Something so cherished and needed was gone forever.

Finally, very quietly she said, "Your father will replace me. He will send me away, won't he?" She spoke with childlike simplicity. "I'll be walking the streets." Was her life to end as tragically as some of the novels she had read?

A look and a meaning, like an eternity of unspoken words, passed between them. She moved automatically. He reached for her. She twisted away from him. Her face was pale in the river moon, the pain visible in her darkened eyes. There was no one.

"Just two more days and I'll be gone. Conveniently." She stared at the lifeboat on the deck where they had spent those precious hours. She composed herself enough to continue when he was unable to answer, did not know how to answer. Her large eyes were staring into his. She had had only herself to give—the natural gift of comfort and love—hoping it was enough. She had given her warmth and meaning, blind to complexities, flooded in the wash of forgetfulness, and lost to the torment of the transgressor. She believed from a pure and sacred heart. Her dream had been shattered like crystal. She wondered if she would ever be able to forget him.

"I so wanted you to be happy," she said. She did not know that love is often not enough and that he was cheating himself of the most precious gift he would ever receive.

"Maybe tomorrow, when we've both calmed down and had time to think we can...." She held up her hand to stop him. His voice faded at her expression. He had never seen her face look like this.

"Brant," she said, and the name was only a whisper, "there will be no tomorrow for us. No waiting." The sound of her voice was as if all emotion had been drained from it. Her face looked lifeless. It seemed to her his words were engraved on her memory, that their summer had been transient and perishable. Their two worlds were beyond reconciliation. She could not go near him or touch him. She had made her decision. She wanted to say good-bye, to leave him.

Brant would always keep the memory of the lonely figure of Cole Hamilton, standing at the boat rail, looking into the dark water. He was to remember her expression all of his life.

"I've tried to explain it to you, Cole, just why we have to wait, but you don't seem to want to understand." He looked at his watch. It was the watch she had given him. He was amazed at the hour. It would soon be dawn.

To have such a deep need so casually pushed aside was devastating. "I only understand that you don't love me enough to stand by me," she said in a flat tone. "That you don't love me enough to stand up against your family to keep us together." She was wondering how one wipes out the ability of the mind to remember.

"You want your watch back?" he said bluntly, not intending to be crude, but it was what he thought of as right.

"Keep it in memory of me for your son," she said simply, thinking of a son he would have that would never be hers.

"What son?" he asked, looking at her without understanding. It was as if he had not been listening.

"You might give him my name. It's a boys name."

He knew no other way to resolve their differences at this hour of his going on duty than to walk away. "Good night, Cole," he said. "I'll talk to you tomorrow." He was desperate for sleep. His words struck her like a cold wave.

"Good night, Brant," she whispered. It was a good bye. Another great loss had happened in her life. Like a sick dog she wanted to be alone. "And Brant, I don't regret it." In her eyes he read the truth, that her dream had been ripped asunder. Her eyes were wet with tears.

Suddenly he swung around and was gone. He needed time for thought and decision. Stunned, she stared after him as he walked toward his cabin. As he walked away her heart went with him. It seemed that all life had gone out of her, with her hopes and dreams disappearing like a wave along the shore. She stretched out her arms to him but he was not there. He simply turned and walked away. She understood, yet the realization shocked her. The familiar unreality of her summer had suddenly vanished. With tears in her eyes she whispered, "All I had was hope."

Cole believed that she loved for the first and last time in her life. She was certain that it would never come again. She was sure that her heart never again would be so full. It was almost a physical anguish, like ripping open a stitched wound, a nightmare beyond belief. Her last vision of him was the back of his head held high in pride. He did not look back. Hers was a cry that he could not help but hear as he walked away. Wanting to run after him, she was unable to move and barely able to breathe. There was only an enormous silence as she brushed the tears out of her eyes.

"Brant...." He heard the cry as he closed the cabin door. "No pain is deeper than that of a hurting heart." Those had been the words of Bess. The door closed and he was gone. "Oh, Brant," she whispered. Her voice seemed to break. "What will you do with all the memories?" She spoke in a faraway voice. *Is memory no more than the flowing of a river* she wondered. *Can a man erase the tears of memory? Or, will they whisper to him on warm summer evenings?* "Good-bye, Brant," she whispered again, but there was no one to bid her farewell. With great reluctance she turned from the sound of the closing of his cabin door, her eyes agonized and empty.

He had moved away from her, disappearing into the night, and with him went something of her. The only sound was that of the gentle wind as it was blowing as though through a ruined shell. When he walked away she felt the pain of desertion and the overwhelming sense of complete helplessness. A feeling of emptiness floated within her like a spent wind. Something had fled as unrealized as an empty shadow, an unnatural dream. She did not hear her own whispered words, "Love you and forgive you." She felt sorrow but it was not in her nature to harbor bitterness, anger, and hate. She was in a confused state of mind. She had experienced a drifting from the understanding of reality. She heard the quiet sound of the closing of his cabin door, his hoping for a few minutes of sleep before going on watch. Her summer of quietness, ease, peace, and hope had become a living hell. Something had broken inside her. They had met through the mystery of chance. She had loved through the magnetism of chance. And now all was lost through the fate of chance. It was the wreckage of a dream with no star of hope to fulfill a child's longing. Her stepmother had told her: "Do not place your hopes and dreams on a falling star." The enormity of the realization stunned her. She wished that she had never been born, believing that she had lost everything.

Cole stayed on alone. All was still except the painful pulsing of the great engine of the boat, with its throb of death. There was not only the darkness of the night, but a deeper darkness of the soul. The emptiness of loss had drained her face.

Brant did not hear Cole weeping in the night, for she cried the lost cry of the abandoned. Lost in the river of darkness, there was no answer in the black moving water. In the pulsing ebb and flow there was the history of men—good, bad, and unknowing. To her the river seemed to flow on forever, her life so short. In the dark of night, as they passed town after town, it seemed that she did not belong anywhere. The night seemed as silent as a graveyard.

A drizzling mist blurred the outline of the shore and obliterated the hills and the sky. The night closed with rain. The wind had changed to the north during the night and rain fell heavily over the valley. The beauty of the night had disappeared. Cole did not attempt to fight the tears that flowed as she stared out over the water, as if looking into nothing. She stood, staring into the blackness. "Oh, Brant," she whispered, "will you ever know how much I love you?" She moved numbly to the deck rail, staring out into the night and believing she had nothing to look forward to, nothing to hope for; It was the fatal trauma of a destroyed dream. She was seeing herself in a most demeaning aspect: the reflection of uncertainty and timidity. Never before had she felt such emptiness. Never would she forget those tearful moments of contemplation. She stood alone, feeling the loneliness and pain of loss. Her hopes and dreams had dried up like a shallow stream in summer. In the silence there was only the beat of her heart. She placed her hands over her face to hide the tears, then kissed her hand as though it were his lips in farewell. The future stretched before her as a blinding fog; The past was a sea of failure. It seemed that hers was a life of heartache and she wondered if she was doomed to failure.

Before going to sleep, Brant climbed to the bridge and entered the pilothouse to tell his father of his conversation with Cole. The only light in the wheelhouse was the soft glow of the instrument panel. He stood in silent thought. His father had insisted that he report his conversation with Cole, but he was having trouble with the words.

"You told her?" the captain asked.

"Yes."

"How did she take it?"

"All right, I guess. She didn't seem happy about it." He felt guilt in having caused her unhappiness. His voice had become inaudible.

"No, I don't suppose she was. How could she be? She didn't have any reason to be happy about anything." He frowned, but said no more. A deep misgiving stirred within him. His guilt was equal to that of his son. Brant nodded, thankful the conversation had ended. He left the pilothouse to go to his cabin for much-needed sleep. One had to be awake and on the alert when skippering a riverboat. He wondered if he would be able to sleep.

In the wheelhouse, Captain Mitchell felt for the letter that was in his pocket. It was a letter he had received in their mail pickup that morning. The letter was from Windemere, England, written by a Mr. Reginald Hamilton. The letter had originally been addressed to the Anglican Church in the United States, then forwarded to the Welfare Department of Covington, Kentucky, who sent it on to Mr. T.J. Whitfield, and thus was in the pocket of Captain Mitchell. He planned on discussing the contents of the letter with Cole in the morning. He had already talked to Bess about a special celebration dinner for Cole that day. It was her eighteenth birthday.

Chapter Twenty-Two

After Brant had walked away Cole's eyes remained fixed on the river, her face working. There was a pain as sharp as a carving knife in her heart, a grief that burned in her breast like a torch. All hope had been hemorrhaged from her. For the first time in her life she was shaking. She stared into the river, into the shadows deep, as if looking for something she had lost. The river flowed on like a fading dream, like a vanishing hope. She was too hurt to share her feelings with Bess. Looking out over the water she wondered how many times the river had tasted the bitter waters of failure. The river repeated the story of the past. She heard Father Chuck's voice, from Genesis, "My punishment is greater than I can bear." She was alone, a forsaken child without a secret place to heal her wound, lost and to death induced. In the shock of loneliness, she knew that she had never had hope, except when she had deceived herself, and would never have that which had become the flesh and blood of her life. The dream would never come again. She truly believed that without Brant there would only be emptiness and loneliness. Her deepest sorrows were the inner yearning for the salvation of protective love, a yearning for redemption from her transgression, and an intense longing for oblivion. She had read novels about such heartache, but had never dreamed of living it. She felt a depth of feeling beyond words, a young love past all logic. The night had become as dark as her hopes. She could see no moon or stars that night upon which to fashion her dream. She stood silent, fighting hack the sobs. *Death?* There seemed no other way but to never see him again. She had nothing left to lose.

When the door of Brant's cabin closed, Cole looked after him with her heart in her eyes and cried, "Oh, Brant," in a voice that knew death. Each word was like a fragment torn from her heart. Everything was empty without him. The whole world was dead. She was like a wounded animal, hiding from the hunter. She was looking out over the water so that she would not have to watch him walk away from her and hear the sound of the door closing on her life. She believed nothing could stop the aching inside. There was nothing to hope for, not anymore. Out of the black night that surrounded her the river had a sound like tears. They were passing the bluff where Brant's home stood. She could hear the wind moaning in the rigging. She wondered if her life was to always be as cold as a winter wind." She had heard Glemp speak of the "Death Wind," and wondered if she was feeling that legendary sound of death, believing she had suffered a lifetime of hurt. "So that's the way things end," she whispered in a small, hurting voice. "Very simply. By merely walking away and closing a door." It was another bird that would never sing again. She would never feel his warmth again. She seemed lost in another world.

Cole stood for a long time, leaning against the railing and gazing blindly out into the blackness, her eyes on infinity. The river reflected the realization of a changing face. She could not weep. Her lips, cold and white, could not whisper a prayer. She was the cub that hears the hunter's shot and a loved one never returns. She wondered if she was already dead? She could only sigh and seek without an answer. She had no answer. She felt numb with the effort of struggling for answers. She wondered if there was a final answer or only a voice from question to question. She had not given time the opportunity to blunt the sharp edge of pain. A child who had known defeat so well did not have the strength for this final defeat. She was alone on a river that was losing itself in darkness, facing a situation for which she had no answer. She was afraid to think. In the still of the night she whispered, "Where do you go to heal a broken heart?" There was nothing to soften the parting. She would remember him all of her life.

When she spoke again her voice was the barest whisper, as if a murmuring from the shore. "Oh, God. Help me," she whispered. She could muster no force of life to heal the spiritual wound within her. She was too young to know that she could survive the anguish of betrayal. Chain's kind words to her had been forgotten, the advice from Bess unremembered. Shock had left her mind in disarray.

Suddenly she cried with intense emotion, "Oh, God, if earthly love hurts like this take love from me or take me from this love, for I do not want to live as I am now living." Her tears were as soft as summer rain and no one was there to take her in his arms and say, I am here, beloved." She needed a refuge, and all there was to believe in was the truth, and the hard truth was bitter. In the depth of her grief she had forgotten the smiling courage of the poor blind boy who sold newspapers on her hometown street. She looked up into the ubiquity of the heavens. All the world was empty, her courage played out, her spirit crushed. She was so young to have lost everything in life. She had been denied a last hope in the fight to keep her soul from going with the flow of the river.

If she could but extricate herself from the tie. It was as if only death could cut her life from her. Since loving him she could not exist alone. She had no one to turn to, no place to go. She thought of Longfellow's lines: "The sea is still and deep; all things within its bosom sleep." She was so weary, so sick at heart.

Her emotions did not permit her mind to rationalize that the human spirit could recover from such a mortal blow. Something was pulling at her like a tide, or an undercurrent, in the river. It sounded almost musical in its soothing flow. She stared into the dark water where the mind could be quiet. The starved and hungry heart's instinctive reaching for oblivion—a yearning for the waters of the River Leathe. She wanted a resting place where there would be no memory or desire. It would be the source of a new life. She would give her heart to her river. Her body was shaking. Immature, inexperienced, she was fighting to keep devastation from governing her intentions. All hope was lost that her feelings, too, would pass. She felt the depression of loneliness. She had lost him.

She took a step or two toward the river, then stopped. They were the last few paces of walking alone. Her body had a weightless sensation, like the effect of going under water. Then she leaned forward and her hair fell across her cheeks. Tributaries had drifted autumn's leaves into the current of the Ohio. She wondered if she wanted to save herself from falling into nothingness like the leaves. She looked up into the blackness of the heavens, her eyes searching, straining, and pleading for relief, answers. She wondered if it was possible for one to ever reach a stage where they could no longer be hurt. At the time it seemed to her that, drop by drop, her heart was bleeding to death. She wondered if she wanted to be part of this world. She would be part of another world: Heaven. In the darkness, tinted by moon and stars, she felt a strange peace that was as deep as the waters into which she was staring; it was the silence of eternity. It was a defining moment in her life; time suspended.

All was quiet. It was the fleshless, lifeless blood of a dying hope. In the misty haze she heard Father Chuck's voice again, reciting Psalm 119:19. She remembered the expression on his face, the look in his eyes, and the tone of his voice as he said, "I am a stranger on earth." Cole was alone, stricken by the loneliness of a love and pain. She was experiencing the helpless grief and despair of the lost, stunned that love should demand such a price and that it would never come again. She was never again to feel the strength of his arms, the touch of his lips, the beating of his heart against her own, or hear the sound of his voice. She had forgotten the kind and meaningful words of Bess: "While there is life there is hope." Turning, she stopped for one last look at Brant's cabin door: one last desperate hope. She needed the strength of a loving hand. The entire summer had been but a tiny burst of flame. He was her first and only love, and now her last. Never before had she felt this lost and empty, but she was determined to muster the strength of will to go on with her life. She wiped away the tears. In a strangely sad way there was almost a sense of relief. All was silent except for the sad song of the river.

Out of Cole's need love had risen like a giant, yet over the most silken of perfumed waters love often sails as a destroyer. The dark river without an ending, the waiting shadows, betrayals, death, and the water stilling the voice. Silently, swiftly, a shadow moved toward Cole. There was a splash, then all was silent except a cry in the dark. Finally there was only the breathing sound of the river: a river that had flowed since time immemorial. She had left her heart aboard the *Storm Bird.* The darkness of night covered her and a name disappeared in the waters of the forever-silent river. The lonely journey was over. The sorrow was to lift out of her heart, float up through the brown water, and vanish into the dank air like a black wing. The dark song of the timeless flowing of the river would carry her to the sea. It was a very brief history. A light breeze brought the scent of churned river water.

When Brant left Cole and returned to his cabin, he at first considered returning to her, feeling a deep uneasiness and an implacable guilt with nothing to quench it. He lay thinking of her.

Then, when he fell into a few minutes of troubled sleep, it was to dream a scene so vivid in condemnation that it was to remain in his mind for the rest of his life; He realized his failure to recognize the depth of truth. He heard that cry and felt the pain and heartache of realization and remorse that comes too late: the silent cry of the heart.

He dreamed that it was just past daybreak when they saw Cole. She was curled on a sandbar as though frozen in a tender embrace. She was on the upriver side of a bar on a river bend near a still-water inlet where centuries of small waves had washed the shore. In the dream he could smell the familiar fetid odor of the still, brackish backwater tainted by the chemicals of industry and the filth of man. The dream was so graphic that he awakened with a start, jumped out of his bunk, and dressed.

DeVoss had not been sleeping. He had been watching. He had seen Brant leave Cole and go to his cabin, and he had been waiting for her to return to her cabin. He intended to visit her, and this time he was determined not to fail. He would take her by force then jump ship. However, Cole did not leave the railing and go to her cabin as he had planned. The smoldering hatred of rebuff still burned within him and he could only be satisfied with revenge. She would pay.

Though predawn, Brant was walking the deck. He sensed trouble. He had come out of his dream, sitting bolt upright with a terrible fear for Cole's life. He was confused by the depth of his feelings. He saw deVoss's shadow move toward Cole at the railing, and feared his intentions. He was determined to prevent it. It was too late, he saw the push. Above the powerful pounding of the engine and the splash of the paddle wheel, only two men heard Cole's cry for help, though deVoss was not aware of the presence of Brant.

DeVoss was standing at the deck rail where Cole had stood, making no effort to plunge into the river to save her. "If I can't have you then no one can have you. It's sink or swim, baby," he sneered in his self-centered dementia of unhinged craving. In his twisted thinking she had asked for it. *If this is the way you want it,* he thought, *then you're no good to me and to hell with anyone else. After all,* he reasoned, *no one is even aware that you have gone overboard to your liquid grave.* He was not a man to forgive or forget.

Brant had different thoughts. His dream had made him more than aware of what had driven her to these extreme circumstances and his only thought was to save her, to give her a new life, a new hope, and a new love to replace abandonment with devotion. It was the strength of his inherent character.

As he raced to the boat rail he yelled to deVoss to save her. DeVoss, seeing the onrushing figure of Brant and hearing his yells, thought that he was being attacked for what he had done, and his face turned as white as a fish's belly. He crouched to face Brant. He had no choice. He lunged at Brant with fists flying, forgetting Cole and thinking only of self preservation. He was a dirty fighter.

As Brant rushed up to the boat rail to save Cole, deVoss drove a hard left hook into the Brant's stomach, then kicked him, knocking the wind out of him. He struck with a solid overhand right that put him on the deck and continued kicking him, his intent was to knock Brant unconscious and into the river. Brant had been taken totally by surprise. There had been no chance to elude deVoss.

"Don't blame me for pushing her overboard!" deVoss shouted. Brant had blamed no one. He believed the guilt was his.

Brant was soon on his feet, his actions purely reflex and instinctive. Being the younger man, and more powerful and athletic, he soon had deVoss on the defensive with a natural dislike for the man lending power and purpose to his blows. An experienced fighter on the school boxing team, Brant was deflecting a blow as he came in fast, swinging a deadly punch. He soon dropped deVoss to the deck with a series of lefts and rights. DeVoss lay momentarily stunned. He was sprawled on the deck, unconscious. He carried a deck knife on his belt, but had not been given time to use it. Brant removed the knife.

Brant had lost minutes of precious time. In an instant his jacket and shoes were off, and he was in the water, but he was now hundreds of yards downstream from where Cole had gone into the river. His only thought and purpose was to save her.

A few minutes later, bloody and beaten, deVoss crawled to his knees, staggered to his feet, and weaved his way to his cabin where he holed up for the night, hiding from everyone and everything that had happened that night. He did not intend for anyone to learn anything from him. *Let them both drown and good riddance,* he thought. His philosophy was a matter of dog eat dog, every man for himself, and the devil take the hindmost. He was driven by the demented and craven desire to destroy that which he could not have and the unbalanced irrationality of self-destruction.

"The next time we tie up I'm jumping ship," he mumbled with a curse.

Chapter Twenty-Three

At daybreak, on the morning of Brant's dream, Bess knocked on the captain's cabin door. Through the door she could hear him snoring. After her light tap on the cabin door the captain was fully awake. He slept with an inner touch of consciousness. He listened as he slept. He thought it was one of the crew signaling a change of watch.

"Come in!" he called. Bess opened the door and stuck her head in. The captain looked at her, waiting. He did not look startled, but he was concerned. It was the first time she had entered his cabin and she stood, staring at him. The early morning light coming through the cabin window brightened his features.

"Well?" he questioned. He looked so different to her. Then she understood why. His teeth were in a glass on the nightstand next to the bunk and he was not wearing his glasses. His glasses were also on the nightstand. He put his metal rimmed glasses on, but was too embarrassed to take his teeth out of the glass. The skin under his eyes was puffed with lack of sleep. He had a restless night. His thinning hair was mussed.

"He's too honest to comb the side hair over his bald head," Bess had once told Cole.

He raised himself on one elbow, his open pajama top showing the heavy mat of hair on his chest. She noticed that it was graying.

"What is it, Bess?" He frowned. Her face was stark. He had never seen her like this.

"I hate to awaken you, Captain. I know you just got off watch, but Cole is missing, " she said, overcome with emotion.

"Missing?" he asked, wide awake. "What do you mean, "missing?" You mean missing from work? Sick?"

"No, sir. I mean missing from the boat. Not here. I can't find her any place," she said nervously. "She didn't come in the kitchen this morning to help. When I checked her cabin to see if she was sick she wasn't there." She was forcing calmness.

The captain was aware that Bess was not a panicky woman. He had much respect for her, believing her stability came from deep within her country origin. She was a woman of immense common sense. He swung his feet out of the bunk and sat up, pulling a sheet over his pajama pants.

"How could she be missing?" The rhetorical question was more to himself than to Bess: an evasion. He was wide awake though he had just gone to bed a few hours before. "You'll have to leave now, Bess. I'll be dressed in a minute and be on deck. We'll stop the boat while we make a search."

Bess left the cabin. The captain got up and, before putting on his pants, called into the speaking tube to the pilothouse. "Brant?" His responsibilities persisted night and day, around the clock.

"No, sir," came back the immediate reply. "This is Chain. I've been waiting for Brant to relieve me."

"Ring the engine room for one-third astern to hold us steady into the current! I'll be in the wheelhouse in a minute!" The captain did not let any of his thoughts show in his voice. He would settle with his son later.

Chain did not ask why, he merely said, "Yes, sir!" The cold, blunt, captain-to-mate tone had startled him. He had never heard that quality in the captain's voice.

Below deck, in the sweltering engine room, chief engineer Claude Schneider answered the order from the pilothouse, pushed back his wilted hat, and wiped the sweat from his forehead with an oil rag as he reached for the brass lever. Simultaneously, the half-naked fireman shoveled furiously into the boiler.

Captain Mitchell entered the galley and looked at the assembled off-duty crew. The situation was momentous and required seasoned professionalism. "It has been reported that our chambermaid is missing," he said without prologue. He did not use her name. His voice was without expression, his face emotionless. His profile was sharp beneath the old peaked cap. "We'll make an immediate search. Claude, you and your men search every area below deck! Don't forget to check the fuel tender. She may have slipped and fallen into it. Brant!" He looked around. "Where's Brant? I'll assign two men to help him search out every corner topside, including the barges." He turned to the young deckhand, Hank. "Go find Brant and give him my orders. And bring deVoss back with you! Bess, could she have fainted in the ladies toilet? Nothing must be overlooked."

"No, sir. I checked." The captain had guessed where they might eventually be conducting the search. There was no conjecture after Brant reported to him at the change of watch the previous day that he was going to tell Cole of his decision to break it off with her. The thought of a possible emotional suicide alarmed him.

"Check every place again, Bess," he said, believing that it was now merely a formality. Bess nodded, keeping her eyes on the deck. The search throughout the boat became routine. How she spent the rest of that day she could never afterward say.

When the young deckhand, Hank, returned, he reported, "I can't find Brant anywhere on board, Captain. Nowhere!" DeVoss was with Hank.

Captain Mitchell glanced at deVoss and noticed that he had a bruised jaw, a cut lip, and a black eye. *Fighting again,* he thought. *With Brant? I'll handle deVoss after we find Cole and Brant. This is the last trip deVoss will make on my boat.*

"Any problems, deVoss?" the captain asked, studying him and waiting for an answer as deVoss merely stood there, staring at him. He coughed as though he had something in his throat.

"No, sir," he finally answered in a tight, controlled voice. "I just stumbled over a line and took myself a bad fall is all, and...." He stopped abruptly, reading what was in the captain's eyes as he walked away. The issue was beyond evasion and he knew it.

Bess turned to Old Rip, genuine concern on her face. "What do you think?" she asked in a voice that was not her own.

"Don't know for sure," he answered, "but we'll find out. We won't leave a single oar unturned."

"It won't take a Sherlock Holmes to figure this one out," Glemp muttered.

The false dawn came to bring day over the eastern hills. The sky was turning pale to the east, bringing another shade of blue to the morning. Captain Mitchell stood at the rail in thought, looking out over the disquiet drift of the river. He was aware that his boat would travel faster than an non-powered floating object. He made no comment, but calculated that she could not have been in the water more than a few hours and his delay in contacting the sheriff would take several hours. He believed that by then she could be down river of them. He felt certain of it. *That is, if she surfaces,* he thought. *The river doesn't always give up its dead.*

"Secure the boat at the next river town," Captain Mitchell ordered Chain. "The sheriff will have to be notified about the missing girl." *But where is Brant?* he wondered. The question troubled him deeply and he thought of deVoss' battered face. *Could Brant have run away with Cole?* No, he answered himself. *Or, in a fight with deVoss, could he have been clubbed and thrown overboard? Anything is possible with deVoss.*

"Yes, sir," Chain answered, breaking into the captain's thoughts, his only thoughts being for the welfare of Cole.

"We'll be in Carrs shortly," Captain Mitchell said. They had passed Vanceburg, Kentucky. "When we tie up, you go ashore and tell the authorities. The sheriff will come aboard to get the information and details."

Chain nodded in agreement, his expressionless face hid strong emotions. Captain Mitchell was hiding the deep concern for his son and Cole. The *Storm Bird* gently nudged the old wooden dock, the mooring lines secured. Bess could hear the water gurgling around the wooden pilings of the dock.

"Give the sheriff only the facts he has to know," the captain said as Chain was departing, "and he can get the rest of the information here on the boat. I'll do the talking to him." He knew that Chain would give no more information than was necessary. They had no proven facts, only guesses.

"Yes, sir," was Chain's only reply. The captain nodded. "We'll probably be standing by at Carrs a few hours at most," the captain continued, "and we can see if, when, and where the body may surface," he added, hating the crude words. "Attach as little publicity to this as possible," he warned. *But where and what about Brant?* he wondered. He turned away from Chain and looked out over the river. "Then, if she hasn't been found by the sheriff, we'll continue on down the river, slowly, and keep all hands on watch. I want to remain upriver of her during the hours of visibility." He did not have to tell any of the crew to be on the alert. No one slept for the next forty eight-hours.

"I understand," Chain answered. They could read each others mind.

Captain Mitchell was aware that summer river currents would be sluggish, the river narrower. He intended to delay long enough to make certain that he was upriver of that for which he searched. When he tied up at Carrs he had already sent Chain ashore to report to the sheriff that Cole Hamilton was missing from the boat.

Later, the sheriff's visit was brief, routine, and to the point.

"I'm Haggedorn," he said, and shook hands with the captain. "I understand there is a missing crew member," he said, studying the captain. The crew stood grim and silent. DeVoss, stunned with fear, slipped back into a shadow with sweat on his brow, a nervous hand pushing the black hair away from his eyes.

Death was not uncommon on the river. His files had numerous such cases. He would have been under far more pressure had it been the mayor's daughter. Glancing, he read something in Captain Mitchell's look and searched the face of deVoss. Later, in his report, he noted that the case needed further investigation.

"The drowning of an unknown here on the river doesn't ever make the major newspapers," he said, and Captain Mitchell was relieved. "She could have slipped and fallen in," he ventured, studying deVoss. "Wet and slippery last night."

The sheriff was a tall, lean, sway-backed man who looked as if he suffered from Marfan syndrome, and his stomach led the way when he walked. His eyelids were pinkish, probably from granulated eyelids, and his sandy hair hung dully over his slanting forehead. Glemp glanced at Hank, but kept a straight face.

Surprisingly to the crew, after Captain Mitchell had told him of Cole and Brant missing and that he had no information other than that, the sheriff asked only three questions as he studied the captain and crew. "In your opinion, Captain, could it have been murder?" He spoke with a drawl, squinting over thick-lensed glasses and rubbing the stubble on his square jaw.

"I have no way of knowing yet," the captain said, looking intently at deVoss. He planned to wait until the sheriff left, then after five minutes in his cabin with deVoss he would know what had happened and would act accordingly.

"Would she have swum ashore to run away for any reason? Fear, maybe?" The captain shook his head and hunched his shoulders in doubt. There was a pause.

"Mitchell," the sheriff continued, peering over the top of his glasses. "Is Brant Mitchell your son, captain?" he asked, recalling information of Brant's escapades with river town flirts and well knowing all the delights of youth in a port town.

"Yes, he is," the captain answered, also thinking of some of the reports concerning Brant's shore-time activities.

Haggedorn rubbed his pointed chin and shook his head up and down in thought, almost guessing what could have taken place. The depth of his knowledge and experience was apparent in his searching eyes. All he said was, "Hmmm." He pondered for a moment, then changed the subject. "No need to file a missing report just yet he said. "We'll fish the river and search the banks. Know every farmer on the river. We'll find them, captain, on the river or in a town. Then we'll know. I'll file the reports after we find them," and he emphasized the word them. "In the meantime, I'll keep you posted." Then he added an afterthought: "Could they have run away together? If so, is there a rowboat missing?"

"No," the captain answered. "Never. Brant wouldn't run away." Whatever else he might do, Captain Mitchell knew that his son would not run.

"Hmmm," the sheriff repeated. "Interesting. As I say, we'll know something before long." He spoke in short sentences. "I've seen your boat a thousand times, Captain. Glad to finally make your acquaintance. If I need you I know where to find you," he said, and he headed for the gangplank. He had a hunch that no one on the boat would tell him everything they knew, but he did not sense that they were hiding a criminal act. He had a direct quality in his voice and manner. It was slow—not unfriendly, but knowing. He was an older man who had seen much and could read a man to his very soul. He gained far more information through civility than through official demands and threats.

The sheriff studied deVoss with suspicion and saw evidence of a brawl as well as the attempt to cover fear that was beginning to show on his face. Lowering his eyes to the deck he saw the blood stains where Brant and deVoss had fought. Then, in looking at Old Rip, the aged deckhand deliberately switched his eyes to deVoss with a very slight nod and the sheriff understood, planning a thorough investigation into deVoss' past after he found Cole and Brant. Until he talked to them he had no legal case nor cause for arrest. Then, when searching the eyes of deVoss, he saw a look of stark panic, a face gone white with fear. His features and expression were a study. The old sheriff had many years in looking into the eyes and faces of those he studied, and the truth was too obvious to be overlooked. DeVoss looked away, saying nothing. His world was crumbling.

Bess and Old Rip stood on the deck, watching the sheriff amble up the wharf, thinking of Cole. "What I remember most are the women in my life," Old Rip said, staring at the white clouds in a blue sky. He had been raised in a single-parent house. "My mother, she's gone now. And my wife, she's gone, too. And my sister, gone. All gone." Step-by-step his life had fallen apart. He was silent in memory with a tender expression on his face. Then he said, "Few of us have expressed the depth of our feelings when we should have." Old Rip had lived within those memories that had followed him for a lifetime. "Next year I'll be sixty-five and forced to retire. Like an old elephant I'll be going home to die."

Bess nodded, understanding. She was aware that lives are never the same after heartache, and that people live as long as someone remembers them. "The same with Cole," she said. "She has no family ties, no one to care, no one to turn to, and no one to remember her; She is a child that has well-known loneliness, absence, and loss." *We all carry the scars of destiny,* she was thinking. She was aware, also, without a shadow of a doubt, that the captain and the sheriff would not rest until the matter was settled, and she was thankful.

Chapter Twenty-Four

When Cole was pushed into the cold water the shock was more than she could have imagined. In the intense emotional confusion of her thoughts she was uncertain whether she had slipped and fallen into the river or had been pushed. She was wondering what actually did happen. When she surfaced in the dark water she burst out into a new world with new thinking, new hope. It was a reentry into a different world than she had left a few seconds before. She had gone into the water a girl and had emerged a woman, strengthened, with all fear erased that she would cease to be. The river had nourished her strength like spring rain on a field of wheat. She had surfaced to a new condition; She had been liberated from a terrible conflict. The sound of the river was no longer a sobbing for oblivion, but an inspiration to live a new life. Those few seconds below water, unable to breathe and shocked by the cold, gave her the instant realization that she had to save her life, that she had much for which to live. It was a woman's thinking, which yesterday had been the thoughts of a child. It crowded all other thoughts out of her mind. A more mature mind that was no longer bewildered. She realized now that her life could only be what she made it. Everything was clear in that reflected world. Needing Brant had been the spring that drove her. The spring was broken, but she could go on alone if need be. Something had come to life in her in that underworld of water. It was a measuring of the distance between reality and unfound dreams, the substance of the thing felt. She felt a triumph and a determination to go forward with a new life. She had a new plan, a new sureness in herself, and a new dream.

Those few seconds of subterranean struggle made her crying over lost hopes for herself worthless. It was of scant importance compared to the struggle with the deepest truths of life, the things that had become doubtless.

She was ashamed of her weakness. The truth had come and she believed it had been worth the agony. All of her strength would go into saving herself and her new life to come. A new shape of beauty had removed the pall from her dark spirit. The realization had burst upon her as a summer wind through an open window. A fair swimmer, she was not in fear of drowning. She looked about as she was treading water and, in the distance, she saw lights on shore and started toward them. She had subconsciously turned homeward toward the Kentucky shore: her native soil. The brooding over past mistakes had vanished and was replaced by the realization of how precious life was. It seemed she had matured a lifetime in the span of one summer.

When Brant surfaced in the murky water, he took a bearing on his location. The boat was moving steadily down river; No one was aware that he and Cole were in the water except deVoss, and he was certain that deVoss would not sound an alarm. The lights on either shore showed that he was approximately in mid-channel. He knew Cole had to be upriver from him and that she would be struggling toward the shore if she was trying to save herself, and he was positive that she would be. He felt certain of her inner strength. He was also positive that she would head for the Kentucky side of the river: her side, where she belonged. He did not question this. With that in mind he set out at an angle that he was determined would bring him to within sight and sound of her struggle. He was a powerful swimmer and he was making steady progress against the slow summer current.

After swimming for a few minutes he stopped to listen. There was no sound of Cole, so he continued on, confident. His overhand strokes were shortening the distance. When he stopped again to listen he was positive that he heard a noise ahead of him, as though someone was struggling in the water, and he continued on. He was anxious but certain she was drifting toward him.

After a few more minutes of swimming he stopped for the third time. That time he recognized the splashing noise as someone swimming and he called out, "Cole!" The sound of his voice traveled along the still water of the dark river.

"Yes, here!" came the answer as though from one exhausted and gasping for air. It was the answer to her prayer and at the sound of his voice her heart swelled like a rolling wave.

Within seconds he was next to her and had a strong arm about her. It was a touch forever remembered. From the lights and sounds he guessed that they were only about a hundred yards from the Kentucky shore. He had never felt so exhilarated in all his life, never had so strong a purpose. He felt as though he could have swum the entire length of the Ohio River to save her.

"Hang on to me," he panted. "We'll make it." It was the happiest day of her life . She could hear the underlying relief in his voice. He had found her. Pure joy ran through every vein in her body.

"Oh, Brant," Cole exclaimed between breaths, as if reaching out in the darkness for the assurance of a hand. She no longer felt alone. She was clinging to him as he headed toward the shore. A night wind had chilled the air and she shivered, her teeth chattering. The sound of the water was as steady as the breeze from out of the hills. She had never given up hope.

"I'm not at all surprised that it's you," she gasped, her eyes shining in a different way. "When I came to the surface I somehow expected to see you there." It was a knowing separate from the magic way of chance. A great joy shown on her face. Her heart swelled.

"I'm just thankful that I saw you go in," he said with unmistakable meaning. He had miraculously come to her at that exact moment. "And how you went in," he added. "There will be a reckoning."

After some minutes of steady swimming, Brant and Cole reached the shore and he helped her onto the bank where they could sit and recover. A full moon was casting a yellow reflection on the water and the stars seemed almost touchable. The light breeze made the sharp shadows move like torchlight and the river glittered in the moonlight. He held her close, gently searching her face He was too deep in thought to speak.

"You risked your life for me," she said when she got her breath. There was a new sound to her voice and it thrilled him. She was still clinging to him with the feeling of warmth inside her heart. All the months of pain and unknowing flowed away with that deeply felt embrace. To touch him and have him hold her in his arms heightened in her the feeling that she had been brought out of a world of darkness. It was a feeling that was inexpressible in words. It was like coming home to the security of a loving family. Her face was aglow; Nothing could contain her joy. Her dream had come true at last, and in her face Brant saw such a true and tender feeling that he was silenced. It was the look of need, care, longing, and giving. He was thankful to hold her to him, to keep her warm. She could see and feel the difference, the change, and the depth of meaning in him. The look in her eyes would remain with him always. He realized and understood things so differently as he held her close to him with a truly deep and loving meaning. He held her as though he would never let her go. Repentance fueled his understanding of what he had almost lost. In looking at her all the intensity of his feelings rose within him. He was an entirely different person. His unrealized love had grown to the depth of reality. He had never seen her so at peace. She was happy with all her being and her eyes, quiet and proud, were shining with new life. She was more beautiful than ever. It was the most precious moment of her life.

"I didn't risk anything," he answered honestly, overwhelmed with feeling. "When I saw you pushed overboard I realized what it would mean to lose you. I knew I had everything to gain: love." It was the simple truth. He knew, for the first time, that he would give his life for her. The revelation and significance was stunning. He had been brought to maturity by a near tragedy. Never before had he thought and felt like that toward another person. He had become aware of the depth of the human heart. He knew that when she touched his life things would never be the same again. It was a response that came from deep within. He was happier than he had ever been.

Cole looked at him in adoration, humbled by his words. "Oh, Brant," she repeated, resting her hand on his shoulder and looking up into his face. Her eyes were as bright as the day. She beheld him as a dream blending into certainty. *Perhaps all this was foreordained,* she thought. "How could I have been so blind and unknowing?" She was shivering. To answer her, he held her to him gently, their voices at times becoming whispers in the dawn. Between them a mutual understanding grew that was spontaneous, warm, and instinctive. What a glorious feeling it was for them. He sat, looking at her in wonder, her eyes searching his face.

"When I saw you pushed over the railing I knew then how much I truly loved you," he said softly. "And I understood how much I needed you." What he had experienced had burned into his being. He was also remembering his father's meaningful words concerning Cole. The warm morning air gave a feeling of substance to his words. "I plan on taking good care of you for the rest of your life." There was something in his voice she had never heard before. It was true. She could tell by the way he looked at her. She had lived for this moment. It was the culmination of all her hopes and dreams.

"Don't ever let me go," she whispered. She looked up, trying to see his face. She was staring at him, studying him, and frowning a little, knowing that nothing was unsaid. Her soul was made up of faith, gentleness, and hope. She became aware of a quivering in her voice, but was unable to control it. Her eyes dwelled on his face thoughtfully. Without words there was a meaning in her eyes so touching that he remembered it always. It was a deeper joy that was more solemn in the heart. To her there could never be a joy beyond that of loving and being loved in return. She loved everything about him. She was astonished at how much their love had deepened. She felt like a different person. She gazed up into his face, then put her hand into his hand. Their eyes said it all.

"Don't ever let me go," she whispered again. Her eyes were gentle, inquiring, and honest. She spoke out of the great stillness of the dawn and, as she spoke, she crinkled up her eyes as if water was getting into them. The early morning sun was breaking with golden light. He kissed her tenderly and the touch of her lips warmed him.

"I won't," he answered gently. "I learned the true depth of my love for you just a few hours ago in a dream." He saw more clearly the hidden things of love. It was his first realization of true love. Concerning the issue of their lives, he spoke simply. "I want nothing more than for you to marry me." Though she did not speak, the light in her eyes was his reward. Her heart pumped wildly. To be in his arms and listen to his words was a dream come true. It would have been a bleak and hopeless world for her without him. In looking into his eyes and hearing the sincere tone of his voice, there was no question in her mind of the truth. He really meant it. She believed she had been blessed with a joy so rich it made her swell. She felt strength flowing back into her; she wanted that moment to go on forever.

Cole's spirits soared, flooded with the recognition of a first tender joy. It was a devotion inspired by reasoning. *Was it only yesterday that I was so foolish and unknowing?* she wondered at her naiveté, and shook her head. She felt she was a new person, a forgetting of yesterday to create a new tomorrow. The thought of such happiness seemed to belong to another lifetime. Everything about her looked newer and fresher. She thought and spoke with the honest instinct of the heart. They had found their peace. So much knowingly existed between them that there was no need for words. They had entered a new and beautiful world, losing sense of time and place.

A sensation of happiness spread over Cole's entire being. Her feelings like the rising of the sun. Because of her heart's hunger she was awakened to a new day. She sat quite still, leaning against Brant, and in the stillness was a joy. Then she shivered with an exquisite pleasure. From her, toward him, burned a golden light. In the early dawn, waves of bright sunlight ran through her soul and though her lips were parted she could hardly breathe. In the still air the sound of the water seemed like a cry of joy from her heart. An overwhelming peace was creeping over her. The day was golden, tranquil, and sweet scented. She sat in complete silence as she remembered the loving words of her foster mother: "The most precious gift you will ever have is a good husband and children," and her mind became a kaleidoscope of visions for herself and Brant, and their family. She thought of the glory of a new day, a new life. "This moment and this memory will last forever," she whispered. Her night had passed from darkness to silver to gold. "The patient pain of waiting," Bess had called it. She never wanted the moment to end.

In looking at her, Brant realized how much she had changed: the joy, the expression, the music in her laughter, and her altered mood. "When you're rested," he said, "we'll go to that farmhouse over there. I saw the lights when we came up on the bank." He was certain they would receive help from riverfront farmers.

Fewer lights were seen in many of the farm towns along the river. The towns were diminishing in population as the farms failed and the people moved to the cities, looking for work. Small farm towns had held out against drought, flood, and politicians, but not failure to sell crops in depressed times.

When they arrived at the farmhouse Brant knocked on the door. It was soon opened by an elderly man. His wife was standing behind him, curious about a knock that time of the morning.

"I'm sorry if we awakened you," Brant said, "but we had a mishap on the boat and got soaked in the river. Would you be kind enough to let us come in and dry off?"

"Of course," the farmer's wife said, opening the door wide. "Come in the kitchen, child, and dry off at the cook stove. I'll get a wrap for you 'till your clothes are dry." Turning to her husband, she said, "Henry, take the young man up to your room and loan him your housecoat or some clothes."

"Thank you so much for your help," Cole said with deep gratitude when she was seated in front of the stove. Because of limited space the kitchen was well organized. "You're very kind. I know how outlandish we must look." She held a mug of steaming coffee in both hands. Oh, how she longed to do the simple, everyday things in a home of her own. She had shed her heartache and pathos as though they had never been. Her life had completely changed.

"You're more than welcome, child," the farmer's wife said. "Just doin' what's right and what comes natural. I'm a good judge of people and you don't look like any problem to me. Hoover is our name. I'm Helen and my husband's Henry." Cole had the feeling that she was a woman who could have pioneered America. *Her hair is as silver as a trout in cold water, she thought.*

As they entered the kitchen, Henry was saying to Brant, "I was soon fixin' to get up anyway. Time to start milkin'." He was a man of barrel chest, broad shoulders, and long arms. His face was blotched with brown freckles from years in the sun.

"Do you folks have a telephone?" Brant asked.

"Land no," Helen answered. "Hope to get one soon, though. Soon as they string the wire out this way."

"I need to get in touch with the sheriff," Brant said. "I need to send a message to my boat." Cole noticed that Brant did not use his father's name and title as prestige. He had not mentioned his family.

"Right! Best thing, since you tellin' me about the girl fallin' overboard, and you jumpin' in after her," Henry agreed. "There will be a lot of worried people happy to hear you're all right. Sheriff Haggedorn would want to know about things, too." He turned to Cole. "Where you from, miss?"

"I'm from just out of Covington, across from Cincinnati."

"The sheriff will get you back there safe and sound." Henry nodded. "Don't you worry none. We don't have no phone, but I'm fixin' to go to town this mornin' come daylight, so I'll carry you in." Cole's eyes thanked him.

"Don't stay any longer than need be, Henry," Mrs. Hoover said calmly. 'You know the brindle's fixin' to calf. She'll need dosing. I can do that." Henry nodded his thanks.

"Much obliged to you," Brant said to them.

They waited in the pale, opaline sky of predawn for Henry to finish his chores. Then, when a ribbon of pink gold appeared above the eastern hills, Henry's old truck with the Oklahoma dump box moved slowly down the dirt road toward town. Henry was talking a mile a minute. It was a clear blue day and Henry delighted in referring to it as "sky-blue pink." He laughed a lot when he spoke. Brant turned to look at Cole. Her face was as bright as a summer day with the clouds on the move, never the same for a minute and so beautiful that it was unforgettable. Their future was as fresh and new as the sunrise.

On the way into town in the old Dodge truck, Brant had his arm around Cole and her face was radiant with happiness. There was something in her face more beautiful than ever, he noticed. She wondered if it was a terrible thing to be so happy. She could not still the beating of her heart and her eyes told him how much she cared and how much he meant to her. To have Brant was all she needed. To her, he was not a man like any other man. She drew in her breath slowly, feeling a curious, dreamlike feeling. In return, the expression on his face and in his eyes was more than his words could have said. He was unable to take his eyes off of her. He reached over and rested his hand on hers. It seemed that her life was just beginning. His closeness warmed her more than the sun.

"Just imagine, together forever," she said, unable to hide the anticipation of the day before her and all it involved.

Henry Hoover had been correct. Sheriff Haggedorn did return them to a neighbor's home near Covington. On their way to Covington the sheriff spoke casually of many things, then nonchalantly asked, "What's the real skinny on her goin' overboard, Brant? They don't seem to know what actually happened back on the boat, but you do."

Brant told him the simple truth the way he had seen it. "I can't prove it. It's just my word against his."

"Well," came the calm reply, "he's walkin' a mighty thin line, but don't you worry none, son. I'll settle his hash." The pieces of the puzzle were falling into place in his mind. "I'll get the real skinny on him from where he come from." The sheriff was as good as his word. At the next docking of the *Storm Bird* Sheriff Haggedorn informed Captain Mitchell of the safe return of his son and Cole, and all that had happened.

"A mighty fine young couple," were his words to Captain Mitchell. Those simple, heartfelt words were all the captain needed to hear. "Now, may I see Mr. deVoss," the sheriff added with a cold look in his eyes.

When Cole and Brant were married, Father Chuck conducted the simple Anglican wedding service at St. John's Church in Covington and spoke the words that warmed their world. Cole admired him as a man of faith and courage. It had been her wish that he perform the wedding ceremony, which was to her the most sacred of life's memories. She felt a need for her church. Of the crew of the *Storm Bird*, only Old Rip, Bess, and the young deckhand, Hank, attended. Softhearted Bess was pushing back tears. Chain and the rest of the crew were operating the boat. Bess was thinking of Chain. Father Chuck's helpful, loving wife was in attendance, helping as usual. As Best Man, young Hank proudly stood with Brant.

Bess lovingly stood with Cole as the bridesmaid and Old Rip gave the bride away with a proud smile. Cole, her dark hair framing her lovely face, was stunningly beautiful in the white wedding gown and veil of which she had dreamed. Bess had seen to that. To Cole, Bess had been an endless source of strength and warmth. Cole's dog, Jack, was thrilled to see her and sat patiently, all smiles, his eyes bright with love. It was the happiest he had been since she left home. The only thing in life he cared for was his family. Cole had the feeling she was home.

Captain and Mrs. Mitchell stood with Brant. Captain Mitchell was warm, smiling, happy, and thankful. Mrs. Mitchell was beautiful, yet more reserved. How stunning she looked in her dress of gold. Her ruby earrings glistened with the light through the stained-glass windows. She had greeted Father Chuck and his wife warmly, then said no more as she stood looking around, wondering about the strange man sitting in the back of the church, waiting. Later she offered her sincere congratulations to her son and his bride, and took Cole in her arms.

Later, Cole turned to Bess, taking both of her hands in hers. "I'll miss you, Bess," she said with a soft smile and the warmth of love. Bess's grip on her hands said more than words. Looking at the deep blue sky Cole believed that a little bit of Heaven had come to her that day. She could not remember a more wonderful feeling. A little stream ran murmuring along the hedgerow of the churchyard. A soft-blue Midwestern sky roofed the valley. The clouds over the hills were bright with light as the sun slanted over the ridges and lay golden on the river. Early fall leaves were drifting slowly to the ground. The sound of a stern-wheel riverboat whistle echoed in the distance. It was a sound that was overwhelmed by the-clamor of their hearts and the ringing of church bells. It was a warm afternoon of sun and showers, and the flowers drank the sun with rain as Brant drew Cole tenderly to him with the realization he had found the true meaning of all human need: the blessed affiliation of love, marriage, and family—of all life. She was someone to have forever, to care for, to hold, to appreciate, and to thank. It was a vow for all eternity. It was the joining of two lives, two hearts, two people, and two worlds. They kissed with a lingering softness. Bess and Hank were smiling happily. They would never forget that beautiful day in the warmth of the sun. Their hearts were swelling.

Prior to the ceremony Captain Mitchell had nodded to a man in recognition as he joined the wedding party. Mrs. Mitchell had been studying him closely. He was a handsome, middle-aged man wearing quality clothing and who carried himself in a dignified manner. He had been watching Cole intently throughout the ceremony. After the wedding he slowly approached Father Chuck and, in a quiet, cultured English accent said, "Father, my name is Hamilton. Reginald Hamilton. At your convenience I beg a few words in private with you, if you please. It concerns my niece," and he smiled tenderly at Cole. "It involves an inheritance." Captain Mitchell recalled the letter from Mr. Hamilton that was forwarded by the Anglican Church and was sincerely happy that Cole had found her roots.

Young Hank nudged Bess. "Look," he whispered, pointing at the elegant man, "all the way from England to help Cole. Think of that."

"It doesn't surprise me to see him here," Bess answered. "Blood's thicker than water. Captain Mitchell told me all about it." She was proudly wearing her Sunday best.

After the honeymoon the *Storm Bird* was steaming upstream toward the coal mines at Reed, West Virginia. ¯Brant Mitchell at the helm in the pilothouse, rightfully proud of his new responsibility. His bride was waiting for him in their new home, overlooking the river. The spacious brick house was set in the most beautiful scene possible, with rolling meadows behind and wooded hills in the distance. The beautiful Ohio flowed before them and colorful flowers grew beneath the blue sky and clean air. How she loved it. She was busy making it into a comfortable and loving home where they would face the world as a family. She had feelings of warmth and safety in being with her loved ones always. She was home. There was so much to do, so much to plan. Her stepmother had taught her to keep an immaculate house. She was especially looking forward to the holidays—their first Christmas together. The river, the valley, the hills, the meadows, the forests, and now her home, were an inseparable part of her life. It was the most beautiful season she had ever known. She could no more stop smiling than the birds could stop singing. She was once again as happy as a child at Christmas. Laughter had come back to her world with a glow of warmth like sunshine. Her husband, her home, and the hope for children, were everything she needed. Home and family were life's most precious gift. "Family," the word was soft and warm with meaning. Her dog, Jack, was with her—all smiles with his tail wagging ninety miles an hour. To her it was heaven on earth. Time was passing as if in a dream. Nothing could be more wonderful than a home that would whisper only loving words. The yearning to be at home had ended. Every day was a fresh start with new hope and meaning. Her thoughts were warm and embracing.

The steamboat whistled. Young at heart, Chain and Bess were together at the boat rail, his hand resting gently on hers. Bess had the one for whom she had been waiting many years. She knew he would never be happy unless he was where the wind rippled the water, that change was difficult. She could understand why a man would grow to love the life on the river and that time was slipping away. They were looking in another direction, upriver toward the light of the hills: the hills that meant so much. They were her hills of Kentucky and his hills of West Virginia. They stood in silence, looking at a river that was golden in the morning sun. In looking at the towering mountains there was a depth of feeling beyond expression that the need of the river valley would last forever.

Watching from a distance Glemp turned to Old Rip and said, "The finest thing in the world is a good woman. I know."

Old Rip nodded in agreement, then said, "The most precious gift a man can ever hope to have is a loving, caring, and faithful wife." All he had left was what he carried in his heart.

Durrand deVoss was no longer a member of the crew. He had officially disappeared in the custody of sheriff Haggedorn and the sheriff from New Orleans, who had a warrant for his arrest under charges of the killing of a dance-hall girl in New Orleans. The news media spoke of it as one of the most heinous crimes in years. The pointing finger of guilt had tracked him, port-to-port, from New Orleans on the Mississippi River to Cincinnati on the Ohio River. His past had finally caught up with him. His future was unquestionable. "No one escapes the handwriting on the wall," Old Rip said.

The river flowed on eternal—like time, like life, like a dream, and like the way of man it knew so well.